Dudley Bernard Egerton Pope was born in 1925 into an ancient Cornish seafaring family. He joined the Merchant Navy at the age of sixteen and spent much of his early life at sea. He was torpedoed during the Second World War and his resulting spinal injuries plagued him for the rest of his life. Towards the end of the war he turned to journalism becoming the Naval and Defence Correspondent for the London *Evening News*. Encouraged by Hornblower creator C S Forester, he began writing fiction using his own experiences in the Navy and his extensive historical research as a basis.

In 1965 he wrote *Ramage,* the first of his highly successful series of novels following the exploits of the heroic Lord Nicholas Ramage during the Napoleonic Wars. He continued to live aboard boats whenever possible and this was where he wrote the majority of his novels. Dudley Pope died in 1997 aged seventy-one.

D1343211

BY THE SAME AUTHOR
ALL PUBLISHED BY HOUSE OF STRATUS

FICTION

ADMIRAL

BUCCANEER

CONVOY

CORSAIR

DECOY

GALLEON

RAMAGE

RAMAGE AND THE DRUMBEAT

RAMAGE AND THE FREEBOOTERS

RAMAGE'S PRIZE

RAMAGE AND THE GUILLOTINE

RAMAGE'S DIAMOND

RAMAGE'S MUTINY

RAMAGE AND THE REBELS

THE RAMAGE TOUCH

RAMAGE'S SIGNAL

RAMAGE'S DEVIL

RAMAGE'S TRIAL

RAMAGE'S CHALLENGE

RAMAGE AT TRAFALGAR

RAMAGE AND THE DIDO

NON-FICTION

THE BIOGRAPHY OF SIR HENRY MORGAN 1635–1688

GOVERNOR RAMAGE RN

DUDLEY POPE

This edition published in 2001 by House of Stratus, an imprint of Stratus Books Ltd, Lisandra House, Fore Street, Looe, Cornwall, PL13 1AD, UK.

www.houseofstratus.com

Typeset, printed and bound by House of Stratus.

A catalogue record for this book is available from the British Library and the Library of Congress.

ISBN 1-84232-471-3

For Hal and Marjorie
who shared our Culebra days

CUBA

HISPANIOLA

JAMAICA

CARRIBBEAN SEA

THE WEST INDIES

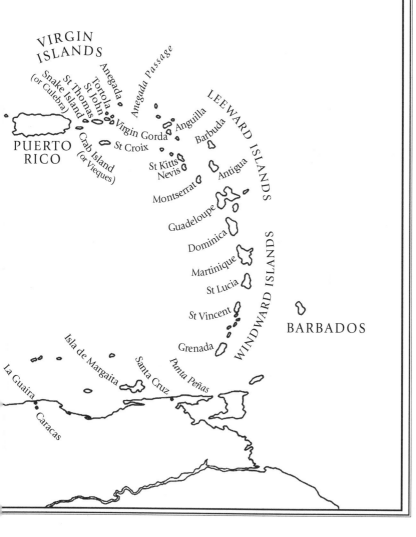

ATLANTIC OCEAN

VIRGIN ISLANDS

Anegada Passage

Anegada

Tortola
St John
St Thomas
Snake Island (or Culebra)

Virgin Gorda

Anguilla

LEEWARD ISLANDS

Barbuda

PUERTO RICO

Crab Island (or Vieques)

St Croix

St Kitts
Nevis

Antigua

Montserrat

Guadeloupe

Dominica

Martinique

WINDWARD ISLANDS

St Lucia

St Vincent

BARBADOS

Grenada

Isla de Margaita

Santa Cruz

Punta Peñas

La Guaira

Caracas

CHAPTER ONE

The captain's cabin on board the *Lion* was small, even for an old sixty-four-gun ship now rated too weak to stand in the line of battle. As he looked round, Ramage reckoned that at most it could comfortably seat a dozen officers for a convivial evening and still leave room for an agile steward to haul on a corkscrew and keep everyone's glass topped up. When, in their wisdom, the Lords Commissioners of the Admiralty suddenly decided that the *Lion* should carry Rear-Admiral Goddard across the Atlantic to take up his new appointment in Jamaica – and escort a convoy at the same time – they did not give a thought to the fact that her captain and officers would have to move over, like passengers in a crowded coach, to make room for the Admiral and his staff.

They certainly never visualized the ship lying at anchor under a scorching tropical sun in Carlisle Bay, Barbados, the cabin packed with forty-nine masters of merchantmen, the captains of six ships of war, and the Admiral. Her own commanding officer, presiding over them, looked like one of Mr Wesley's followers preaching in the crowded parlour of a fisherman's cottage.

In about a week's time, Ramage thought sourly, it'll dawn on Captain Croucher that he could have held this convoy conference up on deck under the big awning, or in any one of a dozen buildings on shore in Bridgetown; but among his

other shortcomings Captain Aloysius Croucher lacked
imagination – and was so thin there was probably not enough
meat on him to notice any difference between tropical heat
and arctic cold.

Ramage guessed that Captain Croucher's mind was fully
occupied with two considerations: relief at having brought the
convoy safely across the Atlantic to Barbados, and the need to
make sure that the masters of the merchant ships understood
that here fresh frigates took over as escorts for the last leg of
the voyage, westward across the Caribbean to Kingston,
Jamaica.

For a variety of reasons the next and shortest section of the
voyage was by far the most dangerous. It was obvious to
Ramage that, unlike Captain Croucher, the masters of the
merchantmen had only one idea in their minds: to stop him
talking so they could get out of this furnace-like cabin as
quickly as possible and cool off on deck, where a brisk Trade
wind breeze was blowing.

The canvas covering the planking underfoot was painted
chessboard fashion in black-and-white squares and the
masters, slumped in canvas-backed chairs from the officers'
cabins or hunched uncomfortably on narrow forms brought
up from the messdeck, reminded Ramage of a jumbled set of
pawns. The simile amused him because Captain Croucher
made a perfect bishop.

Croucher tugged at the lapels of his coat in an attempt to
make the shoulders sit squarely. Although the Captain's tailor
had obviously worked hard, all his artful skill with scissors
and thread could not disguise the fact that nature had sold
Croucher short: a bonus of half a hundredweight of flesh
would not have stopped him from looking like a skeleton
wrapped in parchment. No wonder the seamen, with their
unerring instinct for the apt and ambiguous nickname, called

him "The Rake". He was every man's idea of the prosecutor at an Inquisition trial. He had the features of a fanatic, and one could imagine him fervently condemning a heretic to hellfire and damnation amidst a welter of prayers and exhortations. Or perhaps he could even be the victim; a few hours' torture on the rack might leave a man as long and thin.

The bone of Croucher's brow protruded so much that the deep-set grey eyes looked like a lizard glaring out from under a ledge of rock. His hands and wrists were so skinny they would pass muster for lizard's claws. Was he married? What sort of woman could love a man like this? Even the thought was repellent.

If Croucher was the bishop on this bizarre chessboard, then Jebediah Arbuthnot Goddard, Rear-Admiral of the White, was the knight, Ramage mused. Being prevented by the rules from going in a straight line would not worry him: Goddard always chose the devious route instinctively and would find the knight's dog-leg move, two forward and one sideways, no hindrance.

Croucher's voice was as monotonous and unavoidable as the drip from a leaking deck in a seaway, but even more depressing. He was giving his instructions to the masters like a weary and disillusioned parson delivering a sermon written by his wife and castigating something he secretly liked. From time to time he glanced nervously at Goddard, who was sitting to one side, as plump as Croucher was thin: a pink frog squatting grossly at the edge of a pond. Perspiration trickling down the creases of his bulging neck was rapidly reducing the starched neatness of his lace stock to a necklet of overcooked lasagna. Goddard frequently mopped his face with a handkerchief which he occasionally tossed to a young and pimply lieutenant, who replaced it with a fresh one from a bag beneath his chair. Nor did the Admiral attempt to hide his boredom, yawning every few minutes and removing the diamond pin from his stock for inspection by the glare of the sea reflected through the stern lights.

The cabin was comfortably furnished. The fitted racks above the mahogany sideboard on the larboard side held silver-lidded claret jugs and several square-sided, cut-glass decanters. On the sideboard itself, out of place in such company, was a large silver tea urn. Heavy, dark-blue and gold brocade curtains hung down each side of the stern lights and the covers of four armchairs were of the same pattern. On the starboard side a large, highly polished mahogany wine cooler had a silver plaque on the side, and the rack above it held four rows of cut-glass tumblers, each sparkling as flashes of sunlight reflected up from the water through the stern lights. Other racks held an elaborate fighting sword, the leather scabbard inlaid with silver tracery and the basket handle of an unusual design. Below it was a dress sword with a black scabbard and sword knots of heavy bullion that would cost at least five hundred guineas from Mr Prater, the sword cutler in Charing Cross.

The whole cabin, formerly Croucher's and now Goddard's, showed that its present occupant was a man of wealth and, Ramage had to admit, of taste. The only hint that it was the cabin of a warship came from the heavy guns on each side, squatting like great bulldogs, the barrels and breeches gleaming black and the carriages painted dull yellow. The thick rope breeching and train tackles had been scrubbed and the blocks sanded and varnished until they gleamed.

The masters, oblivious to the Admiral's taste, were a motley group. Some had the weather-worn appearance and four-square stance of working seamen – obviously their ships were small, with crews to match, and they weren't above tailing on the end of a rope when needed. Others were well dressed; the masters of "established" ships trading regularly across the Atlantic and whose tailors had made them clothes of cooler, lightweight material.

The uniforms of the naval officers made no concession to the climate, and since they were visiting the flagship they were dressed in frock coats and white breeches, with swords. Each of the three frigate captains wore a plain gold epaulet on the right shoulder showing he had less than three years' seniority.

The two lieutenants were a complete contrast to each other. Lieutenant Henry Jenks, commanding the *Lark* lugger, was in his late twenties, sandy-haired and plump, with a cheerful face turned a deep red by the sun. A white band of skin across his brow just below the hairline showed he rarely went out in the sun without wearing his hat. Alone among the naval officers, his hat was of the old style, cocked on three sides, instead of the newly introduced hat cocked on only two.

Henry Jenks' jovial manner emphasized his stocky body, but Nicholas Ramage had the classic build that made his appearance deceptive. He did not seem particularly tall until he stood up and the width of his shoulders was not apparent until he was near a man of average build.

With a lean face and black, wavy hair, Ramage looked like an elegant young aristocrat. His eyes, brown and deep-set beneath bushy eyebrows, revealed an impetuous nature and a hot temper. The deep tan on his face showed that he had been serving in the Tropics for several months and was emphasized by two long scars above his right brow. One was white where the scar tissue defied the sun and the other pink, showing that the wound was more recent.

Jenks, able to watch him for the first time since they had served together four years earlier, noticed that he still had one distinctive mannerism: he blinked occasionally as though the light was too bright. He had also acquired another. When thinking hard, he rubbed the older of the two scars with the side of his right thumb.

As Croucher paused to shuffle through some papers, Goddard said suddenly, without turning his head from the inspection of the diamond pin, "I've no need to remind you people that the hurricane season is almost upon us."

He replaced the pin before adding in a patronizing tone that made several of the masters stiffen with annoyance: "The sooner we arrive in Jamaica the better."

Croucher waited in case Goddard had more to say. The Admiral replaced the pin and made a leisurely search of his pockets, bringing out a small and elegant fan and flipping it open to show finely carved blades of ebony and ivory. He waved it a few times, and then said with heavy sarcasm: "Punctuality pays, as the Royal Navy learned long ago. Most of you were a month late assembling for the convoy in England, and thanks to your habit of reducing sail at night, we're another three weeks late arriving here in Barbados. Now we all have to take unnecessary risks to get you safely to Kingston. So I'd – "

The angry interruption that Ramage had been expecting came from a master built like a barrel, whose tanned, deeply wrinkled face was flushing furiously. "We can't sail without freight," he growled. "If it arrives a month late at the London docks what d'you expect us to do – sail in ballast just so's you aren't late for some fancy gala ball in Jamaica? And if the Trades blow for weeks at two knots from the south-east instead of twenty from the nor'east, don't blame us – seems that even admirals can't conjure up wind for crossing the Atlantic. Not that sort, anyway."

Goddard flushed, snapped the fan shut and pulled out the diamond pin once more.

"Quite," Croucher interposed hastily to cover up the silence. "The Admiral was only stressing the need for not wasting time and – "

"Well, I'll stop wasting it now," the master announced, suddenly standing up. "All this useless jabbering's keeping me from getting m'rigging set to rights ready to weigh. An' I'll trouble you fine gentlemen to remember all our insurance rates doubled from the first o' the month, Hurricane season surcharge, in case you've forgotten why. Now, if you'll excuse me…"

With that he walked out of the cabin and several other masters murmured their agreement. Underwriters based their insurance premiums on past experience, which showed that the hurricane season began in July and increased to a peak in September. They demanded double premiums from ships still in the Caribbean in July, and most policies specified that they must sail by the first day of August. It was now the end of the first week in July, so Ramage could understand why the masters were getting jumpy: they would have to stay in Jamaica until November unless they arrived in Kingston within the next three weeks, discharged one cargo, loaded another and sailed again in convoy.

Ramage watched as Goddard replaced the pin with an angry gesture but snatched it out again quickly, having pricked his chest. Croucher was flustered and picked nervously at sheets of paper on the table in front of him. He glanced apprehensively at the Admiral, who had lapsed into a sulky silence, coughed to gain everyone's attention and said: "I'll just go over the Instructions – "

"No need; we all have copies," one of the masters called out.

"Nevertheless, gentlemen, I'm bound by Admiralty orders – "

"Ignore 'em," growled another master.

" – and so I must – "

Goddard interrupted sharply: "Whatever your premiums, your insurance policies are worthless unless you listen. You all know that."

The masters promptly began to show their impatience by scraping their chairs and rustling copies of the Instructions. Technically Goddard was right; the Instructions had to be read aloud. In practice no naval officer bothered – particularly in a tiny cabin when the temperature was well into the nineties.

"We can't take anything for granted," Croucher said pompously in the lull that followed Goddard's words. "Apart from the *Lion*, you have different ships escorting you from now on and conditions are very different. Your old Instructions differ in various details from these new ones I am about to go over – "

"They might differ, but we can still read."

Croucher glanced nervously at the master who had interrupted him and Ramage thought he sensed a slightly deferential attitude. The master was a tall man with a sun-tanned face. He was young and elegantly dressed, self-assured and had humorous eyes. A perfect subject for a portrait by the fashionable Lemuel Abbott, Ramage thought. He probably commanded one of the larger ships, but looked as though he was more used to luxurious London drawing-rooms and a life of leisure.

"They differ for particular reasons, Mr Yorke, which I'd like to specify," Croucher said lamely. "Hurricanes and calms in the lee of the islands, not to mention privateers and French galleys which can row out and board a becalmed ship – "

"What will you people be doing while all that's going on?" Yorke asked politely.

Goddard stood up and ostentatiously left the cabin, followed by his lieutenant, and tried but failed to ignore Yorke's cool and contemptuous stare. Hmm, thought Ramage, Mr Yorke must have a store of powerful influence hidden away to windward...

"Gentlemen," Croucher said pleadingly, "the sooner we finish our business the sooner we can leave this, ah, rather warm cabin – "

"Hurry up then – the hurricane season'll soon be over." This time the interruption came from a Scots captain.

Croucher held the printed Instructions as if they might be snatched from him. Perspiration poured from his brow and into his eyes, making them run, and Ramage began to feel sorry for him. He smoothed out the paper and said: "Gentlemen – *Signals and Instructions for Ships under Convoy...*"

He's the only man who can actually pronounce the capital letters, Ramage thought, and when several of the masters started coughing Croucher glanced up in embarrassment. It was quite unnecessary to read the title since everyone held copies.

"Well," he said, tapping the first page, "may I emphasize section four – *Ships of the convoy out of their stations are to take advantage of all opportunities, by making sail, tacking, wearing &c., to regain the same.* Gentlemen, I beg of you, keep your stations. Reducing sail at night is both useless and unnecessary here in the Caribbean, as several of you must know from past experience. We get a good breeze for a couple of hours either side of noon and the wind goes down with the sun. We should make sail rather than reduce it at nightfall."

Ramage nodded in agreement: dawn usually saw the captains of any of the King's ships escorting a convoy flinging their hats on deck in a rage. The light revealed the horizon littered with merchantmen, all jogging along at a knot or so under reefed topsails, many of them hull down astern. Nothing would get them together again under a decent spread of canvas before noon, and by six in the evening the reefing and furling would begin all over again. In the Tropics there were usually at least ten hours of darkness, whatever the season.

"And part five," continued Croucher, "where it says, *In the case of parting company, and being met with by an enemy...*you'll see it refers to page thirteen, and I've no need to remind you, gentlemen, that there it gives" – he turned to the page – "an extract from an Act of Parliament which says, *That if the captain of any merchant ship, under convoy, shall disobey signals or instructions, or any lawful commands of the commander of the convoy, without notice given or leave obtained...he shall be liable to be articled against in the High Court of Admiralty...and upon conviction thereof shall be fined at the discretion of the said court in any sum not exceeding...*"

Croucher's voice had become louder as he tried to drown the snores of a dozing master and finally he held up his hands in despair. "Perhaps one of you could...?"

"George!" the nearest master bawled, nudging the sleeping man. "This fellow wants to 'ear 'imself talkin', even if we don't."

The Master straightened up, rubbed his eyes, wiped his mouth with the back of his hand and growled, "Five hundred pounds or a year in jail, heard it all a'fore, scores o' times. And a hundred if he quits the convoy – it's all written here." He waved his copy. "Don't know why he's going on about it: must be trying to drum up business – he probably gets a percentage."

"Gentlemen!" exclaimed Croucher. "I have my duty to do, so please help me by being patient – "

10

"Yes, George," another master chided, "that was very unfair: it's the Admiral that gets the percentage."

"By another Act," Croucher said hurriedly, "as of course you are all aware, any master who shall *desert or wilfully separate or depart* from a convoy *without leave obtained* is liable to a penalty of one thousand pounds – "

"And fifteen hundred if he's carrying Naval stores," Yorke commented conversationally. "Curious how with a government cargo the penalty is always inversely proportional to the probable value."

"Be that as it may," Croucher said lamely, "I can only execute the laws – "

"And meanwhile the English language is executed – murdered, rather – by the constitutional lawyers who draft the wording of these laws."

"Please, Mr Yorke! Then we come to *Every such master is liable to a penalty of £100 who, being in danger of being boarded or taken possession of by the Enemy, shall not make signals by firing guns, or otherwise to convey information to the rest of the convoy, as well as to the ships of war under the protection of which he is sailing* – "

"They mean 'warn the rest of the convoy and escorts'."

"Of course they do!" Croucher exclaimed angrily.

"Then why not say it briefly and simply? Any fool can be verbose and obscure."

"Where was I? Oh yes – *he is sailing; and in case of being boarded or taken possession of, shall not destroy all instructions confided to him relating to the convoy.*"

He is reading now, thought Ramage, like a dog scurrying past his master, fearful of being kicked. Having got so far without interruptions Croucher rushed on.

"At the bottom of the page, *No lights are to be shewn on board any of the ships after ten o'clock at night* – "

11

"It gets dark by seven o'clock in these latitudes," Yorke commented.

"Quite so," Croucher said coldly, looking round accusingly at his clerk. "There should have been a note to that effect written in just below my signature. Would you remember that, gentlemen? Seven o'clock, not ten. And for the rest – *Great care is to be taken that no light be seen through the Cabin windows, as many mistakes may arise from them being taken for the commanding officer's lights or signals made.*"

"How true," Yorke said sadly with a shake of his head. "How very, very true."

Ramage put his handkerchief to his face to stifle a laugh but Croucher, oblivious to the irony, nodded in agreement.

"Well, gentlemen, the rest you know: page three – the signals are clear; page four – please watch for the section, *The ships astern to make more sail.* The signals you can make to the escorts are on page seven. Pages eight and nine – well, fog signals hardly apply. Night signals – yes, please use good lights, gentlemen; make sure your lamp trimmers are up to the mark. Finally, may I draw your attention to the memorandum on the back of the last page. *All masters of merchant vessels to supply themselves with a quantity of False Fires to –* "

The snoring again drowned his voice, and one of the masters shouted, "George, belay the snorin'."

" *– to give the Alarm on the approach of any Enemy's Cruizer in the Night; or in the day to make the usual signal for an enemy. On being chased or discovering a suspicious vessel –* "

"A '*suspicious* vessel'!" Yorke said. "How can a *vessel* be suspicious! Bows up and stern down, I suppose, sniffing the air like a gun dog."

" *– vessel, and in the event of their capture being inevitable, either by day or night, the master is to cause the jeers, ties and haul* *yards to be cut and unrove, and their vessels to be so disabled as to prevent their being immediately capable of making sail.* I think that just about covers everything," Croucher said, and flushed as Yorke said agreeably, "Oh indeed it does; both in the singular and the plural."

"Gentlemen, I think the Admiral…"

Croucher motioned to his clerk, who scurried out of the cabin. A minute or two later Goddard came back without looking at anyone, walked aft, stood against the bright glare of the stern lights and said: "Captain Croucher has told you that we risk meeting privateers and rowing galleys, as well as French and Spanish ships of war, all along our route to Jamaica. It is a grave risk, gentlemen, and I'd be failing in my duty if I didn't give you a further warning: there is a good reason for supposing the French will make a determined attempt to attack this particular convoy. That answers the question some of you may have been asking yourselves – why the *Lion*, a ship of the line, is part of your escort."

The masters glanced at each other, trying to guess which of them commanded the ship carrying a cargo so valuable to the enemy, and Ramage too watched closely – the Master with the valuable cargo would not be curious. They all looked round, obviously puzzled, except for Yorke. He was watching Goddard with the same amused tolerance as before. But if Yorke's ship was of particular interest to the French he would surely look concerned even if not puzzled. There's probably no such ship or cargo, Ramage decided; Goddard is trying to scare the masters into keeping their positions – and to be fair, he is justified in using any lies, threats or stratagems to ensure that.

"Unfortunately," Goddard continued, "I have to give you a further warning. The Admiralty intended that five frigates should be waiting for us here in Barbados." He gave an irritated sniff, hinting at his disapproval of what was to follow. "Regrettably the senior officer on this station has only three frigates available. But remember, the main purpose of the escort is to defend you against attack. In other words, I don't want to be forever sending the frigates off over the horizon to round up laggards.

"If you value your lives, stay with the convoy. That means keeping a sharp lookout and not reducing sail at night. Most of you already know that the wind drops away nearly every night, and anyway, losing a sail is of little consequence when the alternative is losing your ship to the French rascals who'll be lurking around like wolves."

He's scared, Ramage thought to himself. A regular convoy would count itself lucky to have a couple of frigates to carry it to Kingston. He has three frigates, the *Lion*, a brig and a lugger. But scared of what? Losing a ship from a convoy meant trouble for the commander of the escort if he was a junior captain. Trouble with the Admiralty and a sheaf of protests from owners and underwriters. But a rear-admiral with Goddard's patronage coming out as the new second-in-command to Sir Pilcher Skinner at Jamaica could lose a quarter of the convoy without too many eyebrows being raised. A valuable cargo would probably be money to pay the troops and buy stores, and the *Lion* would be carrying it. What could be frightening him?

The probable answer was that Jebediah Arbuthnot Goddard, Rear-Admiral of the White, could handle a squadron of the King's ships, where every captain obeyed his signals instantly, or answered for the consequences under the Articles of War, but the prospect of trying to deal with forty-nine aggressive individualists, each of whom had probably thumbed his nose a dozen times at a frigate captain who'd ranged up close and fired a shot across his bow to try to force him to set more sail, daunted him.

"Very well," Goddard said heavily, "you can rely on Captain Croucher to do everything in his power on your behalf, and the same goes for the commanding officers now joining us" – he gestured to them in turn – "Captain Edwards of the *Greyhound*, Captain James of the *Antelope*, Captain Raymond of the *Raisonnable* and Lieutenant Jenks of the *Lark* lugger."

Several of the masters looked across at Ramage, wondering what he was doing at the conference, and Yorke raised an eyebrow. Ramage had half-expected a sarcastic or ambiguous reference but the deliberate omission took him unawares and he glanced down, his face expressionless, just as Yorke stood up, stooping slightly because of the low headroom.

"Admiral Godson – I am sure I speak also for all my fellow shipmates in thanking you, in hoping we have a successful voyage to Jamaica, and in expressing our confidence in yourself and Captain Cruncher."

The masters grunted their assent as they began to leave the cabin, and those who noticed Yorke's deliberate mistakes over the names did not trouble to hide their grins.

Goddard flushed, but recovered in time to squeeze out a smile. "Thank you, Mr Yorke."

As Ramage stood up to leave he saw Croucher motioning the three frigate captains and Jenks to stay behind. As no signal was made to him he followed the masters out of the cabin. Had there been some change of plan? Was he not to join the convoy after all? That would be almost too much to hope for...

CHAPTER **TWO**

Ramage stood on the gangway abreast the mainmast. After an hour in the dim cabin he was almost blinded by the bright sun as he watched the masters waiting impatiently for their boats. Every few moments one would spot his and dodge out from under the tautly stretched awning to bellow an order to hurry up.

Whether smooth of manner or rough, the masters had something in common: each was a good seaman. He might be truculent when ordered about by an escort captain; he might furl or reef at night to avoid risking his owner's money on new sails; but he was every inch a seaman, whether commanding a large ship with a crew of thirty or a small schooner.

In peacetime the smaller ships would have been hard pressed to find enough cargo to trade from one port in the English Channel to another, and would sail without insurance because no underwriter would risk his money without prohibitive premiums. War had given these small, old vessels a new lease of life. The shortage of ships had driven up the freight rates so the owners could afford the insurance, and the peacetime race to be first at the market place with a cargo to get the highest prices, had been stopped by the convoy system. All the ships now arrived at the same time and the convoy's speed was that of its slowest vessel.

"Didn't you command the *Triton* brig?"

Ramage turned to find Yorke standing beside him.

"I still do."

"Where is she?"

Ramage pointed to where she was lying at anchor on the far side of the shallow bay.

"I've been hearing about you catching privateers off St Lucia and reading about you and Commodore Nelson at the battle off Cape St Vincent. I'd like to offer my congratulations."

"Thank you, Mr – should I adopt your style and say, 'Mr Yorkshire'?"

Yorke laughed. "I was rather pleased with that! Anyway," he said, putting out his hand, "Sidney Yorke, 'master under God' and owner of the *Topaz*."

"Owner?" Ramage exclaimed, as he shook hands, "Why, you're…" He hastily rephrased his remark, "You have a fine ship."

"And 'You're young to own and command her'?"

"Well, I didn't actually say it!"

"I inherited her. From what I hear, m'lud," Yorke said with a mock bow, "there are one or two senior officers not far from here who rated you young to catch privateers who'd escaped a couple of senior frigate captains – and would have rated you too young to trump the Spanish fleet at St Vincent."

Ramage grinned as he returned the bow, and Yorke suddenly waved. "There's my boat."

Although neither man was conscious of it, each shared a common inheritance, the sea. For Yorke it had taken the form of a ship; for Ramage it was a family tradition of service in the Royal Navy. The *Royal Kalendar*, in the section headed "House of Peers. Earls", devoted three heavily abbreviated lines to Ramage's father:

"Hen.VIII. 1540. Oct. 9. John Uglow Ramage, E. of Blazey,
V. Ramage, an admiral of the White. St Kew Hall, St Kew,
Cornwall."

A glance at the preceding names, for the earldoms were listed
in date order, showed the earldom was the third oldest in the
country, having been created by Henry VIII more than two
hundred and fifty years earlier, while the viscountcy – which
the eldest son was allowed to use – was even older. The index
several pages earlier gave the motto, family name and heir:

"Blazey, E.1540. *Nec dextrorsum nec sinistrorsum*. Neither to
the right nor left. Ramage, V. Ramage."

Although the facts were brief enough, a keen student of
history could hazard a reasonably accurate guess at what else
might have been said. The Ramages were a family that
supported Henry VIII at the dissolution of the monasteries
and, in return, received the title and grants of former church
lands. They were staunch Royalists a century later and, along
with many other Cornish landowners, had much of their
property confiscated by Cromwell's Roundheads after bitter
fighting. They lived to see the new King give it away to his
favourites after the Restoration.

But no student or reference book could even hint at why
the present heir to the earldom, Lieutenant Nicholas Ramage,
did not use his title; nor how it was that he spoke fluent
Italian (with an uncanny ability to mimic the colourful
Neapolitan accent, Italy's equivalent of Cockney), Spanish
and French. His skill in Italian came from a childhood spent
in Tuscany, since his parents had close links with Italy. His
knowledge of French and Spanish, he was always quick to

admit, was entirely due to his mother, a very determined woman who chose strict tutors.

From the day he first went to sea Ramage, on his father's advice, had not used his title: the old Admiral knew only too well the problems that a young midshipman might face if some well-meaning hostess gave him precedence over his captain at the dinner table because of his title.

As Yorke's boat came alongside the *Lion*, the young shipowner said with sudden seriousness, "Well, good luck; might be wiser to keep a sharp lookout over your shoulder than over the bulwark. I wish you were coming to Jamaica with us."

"I am."

Yorke spun round. "Oh! So I guessed right...Well, you're young to have fallen foul of an admiral who forgets his name contains four more letters after the first three!"

"It's a long story," Ramage said wryly.

"Let's hope it has a happy ending. Be pleased – as my Lords Commissioners of the Admiralty say – to keep an eye on the *Topaz* then! Incidentally, she's a legacy from my grandfather; made me serve an apprenticeship, then left me his fleet. Six ships, all named after gemstones. Dine with me?"

"Why – yes, I'd like to."

"One o'clock? You'll find I'm carrying an interesting cargo. I'd like to hear a bit of that 'long story' if you – "

"Mr Ramage, sir – "

A plump, red-faced midshipman was standing waiting.

"Captain Croucher's compliments, sir. Would you report to him in the cabin."

Although a dozen thoughts were going through his mind as he nodded, Ramage remembered to warn Yorke that he might be a few minutes late. Walking aft, he saw the frigate captains leaving the cabin, followed by Jenks. The moment Jenks spotted Ramage he deliberately slowed down to let the captains get well ahead of him. The two of them had served together as midshipmen and later as lieutenants in the same ship and as he passed he whispered, "Watch your luff – I'm sure they're brewing up something..."

The Marine sentry saluted as Ramage knocked on the door and was told to enter. Croucher sat at the same table by the stern lights and facing the door, but Ramage sensed rather than saw that someone was sitting at the forward end of the cabin.

"Ah, Ramage, here are your orders."

Ramage took the rectangular packet with a red seal on one side.

"And the new convoy list. Forty-nine ships, seven columns of seven ships. You have the latest edition of the Signal Book, of course?"

"Yes, sir."

"There's a copy of the Admiral's additional signals in with your orders. Sign this."

As Ramage reached for the quill and inkwell he saw that the slip of paper was a straightforward receipt for the orders and convoy list.

"And Ramage," Croucher said, his voice hardening and his hands clenching like claws, "at your trial last year you escaped punishment on a technicality..."

Ramage stiffened and looked directly at him, and Croucher's cold, grey eyes looked down at the table.

"Punishment for what, sir?"

"You know very well what I mean."

"Punishment presupposes guilt, sir. Of what was I found guilty?"

He spoke quietly, but every nerve in his body was alert: he felt lightly balanced on the balls of his feet, poised and on guard, ready to fence with a master swordsman.

From behind he heard Goddard's oily voice. "At the moment you are guilty of anything I choose to say."

Ramage realized he was right: the cabin was a trap. With only Croucher and Goddard present – a captain high on the post list and a senior rear-admiral – either could accuse him of anything, with the other as an unimpeachable witness. Mutinous behaviour, treasonable talk, even attempted murder – what reasonable men would believe Ramage's word against theirs?

Slowly, despite the heat of the cabin, he felt his whole body chill and every hair rise up spikily, like an angry cat's fur, his skin tightening in nature's response to danger. The ticking of a clock grew louder and more precise, the slapping of wavelets under the counter more distinct; overhead seamen's feet were padding on the deck. The colours of Croucher's uniform – and everything else in the cabin – were now brighter and sharper; the cut glass reflected tiny rainbows on the bulkheads. He knew that in a few moments he'd be gripped by a rage which slowed down time, speeded his reactions, doubled his strength and left him without humility or humanity. Such rage gripped him rarely – only twice before in his life – and it frightened him.

The Ramage family had never harmed Goddard. If the Ramages vanished off the face of the earth, Goddard would not gain a penny in cash or an inch of promotion; nothing except the congratulations of sycophants like Croucher who followed him for the rewards they got from his patronage. It was a senseless vendetta he waged.

Suddenly Ramage remembered his reactions at the trumped-up trial Goddard had staged in the Mediterranean.

At first he'd been shocked and overwhelmed, then he'd become too disgusted by their malicious cruelty and veniality to bother to fight back. Then he'd realized that his inaction was playing their game: by simply answering questions and not attacking he was letting them beat him.

Ramage had been in Barbados by chance when the convoy arrived but his presence in the *Lion*'s cabin was a new opportunity for Goddard to attack him. He was collecting the evidence for another carefully rigged trial when the convoy reached Jamaica.

Ramage didn't have to watch his words, since they could swear he had said or done anything they liked. So be it! In battle, doing the unexpected can be as effective as doubling the size of your fleet. He turned suddenly to face Goddard.

"With respect, sir, what do you want to charge me with?"

He spoke quietly and slowly, but each word was hard and unambiguous. He added: "Wouldn't you prefer to hurry it up and have me charged and tried before the convoy sails?"

Goddard's jaw dropped. Now for the second broadside, Ramage thought, and this will show whether that gross clown in admiral's uniform really is a coward.

"Wounding a superior officer, perhaps? That'd bring in mutiny, and Captain Croucher could swear to 'treasonable utterances' as well. But for a wounding charge I'd have to supply some tangible evidence…"

He was careful not to move his hand towards his sword.

Goddard stood up suddenly and warily, his eyes on Ramage. The young lieutenant's face was taut; the two scars over the right eyebrow were pale against the tanned skin and the deep-set brown eyes watched unblinking. Goddard realized he was fearless but tense, like an animal waiting to pounce, yet in complete control of himself.

Ramage's eyes challenged but his hand hadn't gone to his sword; there was nothing that could condemn him under the Articles of War. Goddard knew that he had gone too far: the young beggar was just calm and contemptuous, not cringing, and he could almost hear the metallic hiss of the sword leaving the scabbard. This wasn't his way of carrying on vendettas. He had been scores of miles away when the trial he had ordered was actually held in the Mediterranean. He liked things to be neat and tidy. Documents to be read, orderly numbered exhibits for the prosecution, and the evidence carefully arranged so that Lieutenant Lord Ramage would be found guilty on a capital charge.

Let's frighten him, Croucher had said; if he's frightened he's much more likely to make mistakes. All Croucher's advice had achieved was to frighten Goddard himself and get Ramage into a fighting mood. Goddard felt chilled, though his clothes were soaked with perspiration.

What now? Goddard needed time, and he also needed to reassure this young puppy; lull his fears and hopefully leave him complacent, so that when the blow *did* strike...

But Croucher was not a coward and he had already sensed his Admiral's fear: like Ramage he had seen Goddard's eyes glancing from side to side and noticed the sudden leap from the chair at Ramage's reference to "tangible evidence".

Croucher said, "No doubt you'll soon provide any evidence required, Ramage."

His voice carried little conviction but he had to support his Admiral. If Goddard continued to rise up the flag list, Croucher's fortunes rose also. If Goddard fell from favour, Croucher was doomed to spend the rest of his life unemployed, on half pay. Captain Aloysius Croucher, like any other officer sharing Goddard's favours, was a party to the vendetta against the Ramage family whether he liked it or not.

Ramage waited for Goddard to regain his voice, if not his poise.

"It's nine hundred miles to Jamaica, Ramage; I can only hope you carry out your duties satisfactorily for the whole of the voyage." The voice became more confident, as if he had remembered something else. "At Jamaica you will still be under my orders of course – Sir Pilcher, you know…"

Ramage knew only too well. The Commander-in-Chief, Vice-Admiral Sir Pilcher Skinner, was a weak, fussy and cautious man who had spent a long career successfully dodging responsibility. He played the game of favourites so flagrantly that it had become a scandal even in an age when patronage was no crime. Many a good captain tried to avoid serving under him.

Goddard had been Sir Pilcher's flag captain several years ago, and Sir Pilcher had pushed him, so that when Goddard reached flag rank, Sir Pilcher had another young rear-admiral indebted to him – a young rear-admiral who, thanks to a wise marriage, had influence at Court. Goddard was said to be one of the few men who could get any sense out of the old King during his occasional bouts of insanity.

Now Goddard was on his way to join Sir Pilcher as his second-in-command. I'm caught right in the middle, Ramage thought ruefully. Well, there's one consolation – Sir Pilcher can only bring Goddard authority; he hasn't any brains or boldness to contribute.

Ramage relaxed as he stood between the two men. The cabin was hot again and the sun bright in the stern lights. There was nothing to fear for the moment – thanks to his unexpected counter-attack whatever Goddard and Croucher had planned for today was cancelled. But another plan would follow; something calculated to bring indignity and shame on the real target of the vendetta, John Uglow Ramage, 10th Earl of Blazey, Admiral of the White, his father and the scapegoat so many years ago for a government's inefficiency and stupidity, and eventually the victim of its viciousness.

A sharp knock at the door made the three men jump, and at Croucher's call the Marine sentry said: "Mr Yorke to see you, sir."

Ramage turned in time to catch a slight questioning lift of the Admiral's eyebrows and an anxious pursing of the Captain's thin lips. Both were wary of Yorke – and perhaps a little afraid? Surely that was too absurd…

"Tell him to come in," Croucher called.

Yorke walked in and nodded affably to Croucher before he saw Goddard.

"Ah, Admiral! Forgive me for interrupting you."

"Not a bit, Mr Yorke, not a bit; you're always a welcome visitor."

Only one thing brought that ingratiating note into Goddard's voice: talking to someone with power and influence.

"I was looking for Mr Ramage. He was kind enough to accept my invitation to dine on board the *Topaz*, and as he hadn't joined me at the gangway I thought he might have mistaken the day."

"Mr Ramage is a fortunate young man," Goddard said heartily. "Ramage – I hope you haven't let such an invitation slip your memory?"

"No, sir, I was going over as soon as you had finished – er, giving me my instructions."

"Very well – now, let's see: you've signed the receipt for your orders? Ah yes, Mr Croucher has it. Well, I think that's all. Keep a sharp lookout on your side of the convoy, whip in the stragglers – the usual sort of thing, and you know it all anyway!"

Ramage had to admit that Goddard carried it off very well, even down to voicing a hope that Yorke and his passengers would find time to dine on board the flagship when they reached Kingston – a hope Yorke acknowledged with a perfunctory nod.

CHAPTER THREE

The black-hulled *Topaz* had a corn-yellow sheerstrake – to match her name, Ramage guessed – and was well equipped. There was plenty of new rope (the golden brown of manilla, the strongest and most expensive of all), the decks were scrubbed and the brasswork polished man-o'-war fashion. Large awnings rigged out with tight lacing were cleverly designed to give the maximum shade, folding chairs had their padded blue canvas seats and backs neatly fringed and tasselled, and the ship's company was working hard and was obviously cheerful. She looked like a newly launched "John Company" ship – usually only the Honourable East India Company could afford to keep their vessels so spotless.

Yorke had not spoken since leaving Croucher's cabin; he merely nodded when Ramage said he wanted to give a message to his coxswain waiting in one of the *Triton*'s boats. Now, as Ramage stood on board by the mainmast and looked round the *Topaz*, Yorke suddenly grinned and asked: "Does she pass muster?"

"If she was a King's ship, I'd say yes; but since I haven't seen the rest of the Yorke fleet I'll reserve judgment."

"You won't be disappointed; they're all like the *Topaz* – identical, in fact. Masts, yards and sails are interchangeable, Navy fashion. With everything standardized for all six ships I save enormously on refits and routine maintenance. The only difference between the ships is the sheerstrake: each has her sheerstrake painted the colour of the stone for which she's named. Drives the painters mad, matching up. Everything else is the best I can get, including the ship's company. I pay them more than anyone else."

"But money doesn't always get good men," Ramage said dryly. "It often attracts the bad ones!"

"True, but I pick them carefully and my scale of wages works differently. When I get a good seaman I pay him well enough to stay with me. If some other ship offers him a berth as a petty officer, he's usually a lot better off staying with me as an able seaman."

"So you have bosuns serving as seamen – and masters serving as bosuns, presumably?"

"Damn nearly," Yorke said, laughing at Ramage's dig. "Do you know the current hull insurance rates, hurricane surcharge apart?"

"No – five per cent?"

"Anything from six to ten per cent. I pay four."

"An uncle who's an underwriter?" Ramage teased.

"I wish I had. No, when underwriters see my ships they know their only risks – apart from the perils of war – are extremes: perhaps an early hurricane, a month of fog in the Chops of the Channel and so forth: not rotten masts going by the board when rotten cordage gives way, or sinking when butts of hull planks spring…"

"So by spending a pound more on rigging you can insure a hundred pounds' worth of hull for a premium of four pounds instead of six to ten."

"Exactly! And get the best freights: I let the others carry the bulky and dirty stuff. With a war on there's always plenty of freight valuable enough for shippers to pay extra to get safe delivery."

"I'm beginning to think you're a good businessman as well."

Yorke laughed. "A pretty compliment – I think. 'As well' as what?"

"As well as a good seaman."

"That's the finest compliment you can pay me."

Ramage shrugged his shoulders. "Very few shipowners are both! I've an idea more ships sink through perils caused by penny-pinching owners than through what the underwriters call 'the perils of the sea'."

Yorke nodded. Unfortunately Ramage was right – Yorke knew only too well that a penny-pinching shipowner employed a poorly paid master who in turn had to be penny-pinching, and was not above taking the opportunity to cheat his master and his men by way of revenge. Behind every master stood a dozen more, unemployed and eager to take his place. To keep his job, the master had to see that every old and tired rope was turned end for end to double its proper life-span, that ripped sails were repaired until there were often more patches than original cloth, and that his ship sailed with half the number of seamen needed to handle her properly. The owner, safe in his country house, knew that if there were not enough men to weigh the anchor in some distant port the Navy would send over men to help, if only to make sure the convoy sailed on time; and if the ship sprang a leak, the Navy's carpenters would set to work to keep her afloat. The convoy system had many advantages and many shipowners thought of it as getting some return on the taxes they had to pay.

"Come and inspect the cargo," he said to Ramage, who nodded politely but then exclaimed: "But they're *all* brass!"

"Every single one," Yorke said, as Ramage looked along the line of guns, and then at the small swivels mounted every few feet along the top of the bulwarks. "I had them recast a year or so ago. They were seventy years old, if a day."

"Any problems at the foundry?"

"No, they just add a little more tin – which is damnably expensive – because apparently it gets lost over the years and weakens the metal. But brass guns are an economy in the end – no rust, no constant chipping and lacquering."

"And you have good gunners?"

"No – hopeless!"

"But why?" Ramage asked in surprise. "What's the point of brass guns if...?"

"My gunners are hopeless, my seamen are landsmen, my petty officers are nincompoops...Until I know whether you're going to press any of them!"

"Then you can sleep in peace. I'm short but I haven't pressed a man out of this convoy."

"You must be one of the few King's ships that hasn't."

"I know, but I prefer quality to quantity."

"I wish some of your fellow captains felt the same way."

"Perhaps they do."

"True – but can they create quality?"

Ramage avoided answering – this was tender ground. He didn't intend telling the master of a merchantman of his contempt for the lack of leadership shown by some of his brother officers, however hospitable Yorke might be.

"Come along," Yorke said, "you must inspect the cargo."

Noticing Ramage's lack of enthusiasm and tendency to dawdle as he inspected the ship he added, "The female section of it are probably eaten up with impatience, and they won't be very flattered to find you were more interested in brass guns."

"Female section?" Ramage exclaimed. "Women? Hey, you showed me a false manifest! Since when have ladies rated as cargo?"

"Well, these do!"

Ramage was completely unprepared for the four people waiting in the airy saloon of the *Topaz*. He had expected a portly planter and his wife, a colonel or two and perhaps a general and his strident spouse, all with complexions matching the highly polished mahogany panelling and figures in keeping with the well-padded chairs and settees.

With easy grace Yorke bowed to the two men and two women.

"May I present Lord Ramage?"

Ramage had time only to glance at the men and notice that one of the women was young before Yorke completed the introductions: "M'sieur and Madame St Brieuc, their daughter Madame de Dinan, and M'sieur St Cast."

"We are honoured," St Brieuc said as they shook hands and Ramage kissed the ladies' hands. "Surely you are the young man who captured the privateers near here? Mr Yorke has been telling us about it."

As he spoke, in almost perfect English with an accent that only hinted at his French nationality, Ramage tried to think why the names had a curious – even spurious – ring about them.

Yorke answered St Brieuc's question. "The very man."

To Ramage he said gaily, "You might as well know you're going to have to sing for your supper!"

"Sing for your supper?"

The daughter looked puzzled as she repeated the words to herself, lowering the fan which had been hiding most of her face since her eyes had first met Ramage's a few moments earlier.

Her voice was little more than a deep murmur with a heavy French accent; to Ramage it seemed he sensed her words

31

rather than heard them; an intimate voice that brought a tightening in his thighs.

He was brought back to the reality of the saloon by Yorke. "An expression, ma'am – it means…"

"That instead of paying for my dinner with money, I perform some service instead," Ramage completed the sentence, embarrassed that his brief reverie might have been noticed. "Entertain you with a song, for instance."

"Or stand on his head, or juggle with a dozen wine glasses," Yorke added.

Ramage saw the joking had misfired because the girl was now looking embarrassed and said: "The juggling – I do not understand why…"

"My dear," her father said, "Mr Yorke was simply telling his lordship that we hope he'll tell us of his adventures. A warning, as it were!"

Madame de Dinan had large brown eyes set in a small oval face. She was about five feet tall, and her almost classic French beauty was saved from the coldness of statuesque perfection by the warm brown eyes and the wide, sensual mouth. She's married, Ramage thought sadly; all that store of love and passion reserved for someone else…

Suddenly he remembered that St Cast and St Brieuc were tiny fishing villages tucked behind the rocks and reefs of the Breton coast, not far from St Malo and south of the Channel Islands. They were only a few miles from each other and he could picture that section of the chart, with Dinan a few miles inland. So these people were probably travelling under assumed names, which was hardly surprising since they were obviously Royalist refugees.

St Cast spoke for the first time. A large, florid man with white hair and heavy features which could be friendly or haughty with little change of expression, he had an unexpectedly high-pitched voice, but he enunciated every word precisely, not through pedantry but as though accustomed to giving instructions.

"Are you coming to Jamaica with us?"

When Ramage said he was, Yorke took the opportunity of asking: "What *was* all that nonsense with the Admiral?"

"I don't think I'm one of his favourites."

"I'd guessed that much. Hope I did the right thing, dragging you from the cabin like that."

"Not only was it the right thing to do, but you timed it perfectly!"

"They looked like two cats deprived of their mouse," Yorke said. "A fat cat, a thin cat and a choice mouse."

Ramage laughed and then, before he could stop himself, commented bitterly, "But only a temporary deprivation."

Yorke turned to his guests and said, with what Ramage thought was unnecessary gaiety, "While I was on board the flagship I saw that the Lieutenant was also out of favour with Admiral Goddard. I'm not betraying naval secrets because about fifty other masters noticed the same thing!"

While Ramage puzzled over the "also", St Brieuc – a small man with the profile of a thinner Julius Caesar – was inspecting his nails. "A temporary affair, I trust," he said politely. "A temporary fall from grace...perhaps a passing cloud?"

Ramage saw that everyone was curious. Well, there was no need to keep secret something of which the whole Navy was aware.

"No, hardly a passing cloud; it's as permanent as – as the *Minquiers*."

St Cast's heavy features froze. He glanced at St Brieuc, as if asking a question, and received an almost imperceptible nod in reply.

"I see you have guessed that we are travelling incognito. I – "

Ramage flushed and held up his hand. "M'sieur – the allusion was quite accidental. Your names – the villages are familiar because I've served in a ship based on the Channel Islands. They must have been in the back of my mind when I tried to think of some – some symbol of permanence, like the *Minquiers* shoal."

"No harm is done," St Cast assured him. "We simply – "

Again Ramage held up his hand to silence him, embarrassed but assured.

"If you are travelling incognito I am sure there's a good reason, and in wartime the less one knows the less one can be forced to reveal if captured…"

The girl shuddered and her mother reached out to touch her arm with a reassuring gesture. Ramage and Yorke tactfully glanced away but St Brieuc, standing more erect, said with quiet pride: "Maxine has reason to know what you mean: the men of the Revolutionary Tribunal tortured her for three days to force her to reveal where in Brittany we were hiding."

Ramage said quickly, "Your presence here proves that they failed."

"Yes," her father said simply, "but she'll carry the scars of their handiwork to her grave."

The girl suddenly glanced up with a smile, snapped her fan shut and, pointing it at Ramage, said gaily, "You have to sing for your supper!"

Grasping the chance to brighten the atmosphere, Ramage gave a sweeping bow. "Madame has only to name the song, and you'll hear singing that will make a frog envious!"

"The song of the *Triton*."

"I think, indeed I hope," her father said slowly, "that that song is long and fascinating, and best sung later at dinner. For the moment I wonder – if I'm not being indiscreet, and Mr Yorke will warn me if I am – if we might hear something of your fall from Admiral Goddard's grace: I – we, rather – have a particular reason for being curious."

"You certainly have!" Yorke exclaimed. "May I explain to the Lieutenant?"

St Brieuc smiled and nodded.

"My passengers – a clumsy word for such company – originally began their voyage from Portsmouth to Jamaica on board the *Lion*, with Admiral Goddard as their host," Yorke told Ramage. "They count themselves fortunate that the *Lion* and the convoy had to call at Cork to collect the Irish and Scottish ships, because it gave them an opportunity to leave the *Lion*…"

"A horrible man!" the daughter said with a shudder, and Ramage felt she had as much contempt as dislike for Goddard.

"He is not a gentleman," St Cast said, his jowls quivering. "Despite – "

St Brieuc interrupted so smoothly that it took Ramage a few seconds to realize that the Frenchman was unsure what St Cast was going to say, and for reasons difficult yet to understand, St Brieuc was the one who made the decisions.

"Because of the Admiral's – ah, activities – I had no difficulty in persuading him that despite the Admiralty's orders making us his guests, we would prefer to travel in another ship."

Tactfully put, Ramage acknowledged, and I'd back my guess as to what happened with guineas: the gallant Admiral made advances to Madame de Dinan…and in all fairness I can't blame him.

"I was able to offer them the hospitality of the *Topaz*," Yorke said, and Ramage guessed that the original passengers had been given suitable compensation to postpone their voyage or travel in another ship.

These people must be influential enough for Goddard to be worried because they were not travelling in the *Lion*. The Admiralty would want explanations. *That* accounted for Goddard's anxiety about the convoy: these people were the "important cargo" and that explained why Yorke hadn't bothered to look round at the rest of the masters...

But who were they and why were they going to Jamaica? St Cast seemed to be an aide or major-domo of some description; the small and birdlike St Brieuc was the man that mattered. But where was his daughter's husband? Already Ramage disliked him because no one could deserve such a wife, and he was jealous – of a husband he had never seen of a woman he had met for the first time ten minutes before. It's been an unusual sort of morning, he thought sourly to himself.

"My own story goes back a little further," Ramage said, "but it's a boring one of jealousy, vindictiveness and obsession."

"We have some experience of all that...It's almost a relief to know we're not alone in our misery," St Brieuc said quietly.

"Please," the girl pleaded, "tell us, if you can."

"Say the word and we drop the subject," Yorke said, "but..."

Ramage laughed and reassured them, but they saw he was rubbing the older of the two scars above his right eyebrow. Yorke remembered seeing him do the same thing at the convoy conference when Goddard ignored him and introduced the other officers. It was obviously a habit when he was tense or concentrating. Yorke watched him snatch his hand away when he saw they had noticed.

"The story starts with my father. He's an Admiral, but not serving now."

"Not an old man, though, surely?" St Cast asked.

"No – simply out of favour."

St Brieuc snorted with contempt. "Politics, always politics!"

Ramage nodded. "Politics, yes; but in a roundabout way because he isn't attached to any particular party. He was regarded as one of the most brilliant admirals of his day, but he had – and still has – many faults. He is impatient, he doesn't suffer fools gladly and he is a very decisive sort of man. He hates indecisive people."

"Hardly faults!" St Cast protested, almost to himself.

"No, but he also had strong and very advanced views on new tactics and signalling which would have revolutionized sea warfare – "

"No wonder he was unpopular," Yorke said wryly. "Pity all those other admirals. After spending a lifetime learning and practising the old-style tactics, along comes a bright new admiral wanting to change everything. You can't teach an old dog new tricks – and the old dogs know it!"

"There is something in that," Ramage admitted, "but then politics came into it."

"Ah," said St Brieuc, as if Ramage's story had reached a point he could fully understand.

"No, not what you think, M'sieur; just the opposite. My family are Cornish, but we have kept out of politics since Cromwell's time, or since the Restoration, anyway. We learned then not to put our trust in princes."

"The Cornish – they are like we Bretons," said the daughter, missing the significance of Ramage's last remark.

"Yes – even the place names are similar."

"We keep interrupting," St Brieuc said. "Do please continue."

"Halfway through the last war, word reached England that a French fleet had sailed from Brest for an attack on the West

Indies. The government had been warned months earlier that it was being prepared, but did nothing about it."

"I remember," St Brieuc murmured.

"The Admiralty could scrape up only a small squadron but they put my father in command and rushed it to sea. Even before sailing my father knew that, outnumbered three to one, his only chance of avoiding a disastrous defeat was to use new tactics."

"To achieve surprise," St Brieuc murmured, "not to use some routine tactic the French admiral would know and be able to counter."

"Exactly," Ramage said, "but it failed."

Both Yorke and the girl said, "Why?"

Ramage shrugged his shoulders. "The manoeuvre was revolutionary, and halfway through it the wind dropped, so only a third of his ships got into action."

"I begin to remember," Yorke said. "I was only a boy. The Earl of Blazey must be your father?" Ramage nodded, and Yorke continued, as if talking to himself. "Didn't lose any ships, by a miracle, but naturally the French escaped. Great row in Parliament...The government shaky...Admiral blamed and court-martialled...The government saved...The row split the Navy...Something to do with the Fighting Instructions, wasn't it?"

Ramage nodded. "Your memory is good. The two main factors were the old story of sending too few ships too late, and the Fighting Instructions."

"Fighting Instructions?" repeated St Cast. "Are they what they sound like? Orders about how to fight a particular battle?"

"Not quite; not a particular battle, but a set of rules for fighting all battles."

"Like the rules of chess?" asked St Brieuc.

Ramage thought for a moment and then nodded. "Almost, but they don't set down the actual moves each individual ship – or chessman – can make: instead they give the admiral the sequence of moves *all* the pieces must make together in various circumstances."

"Do you mean, keeping to the chess analogy," Yorke asked, "they set down the moves for the *whole* game? Once the admiral chooses a particular sequence, he's committed to make every successive move?"

"Yes. Of course they give you various alternative sequences, allowing for differences in the wind, the relative positions of your ships and the enemy's, and so on."

"But," protested Yorke, as if certain he had misunderstood Ramage, "it leaves the admiral no initiative! If the orchestra plays this tune, you dance these steps; if that tune, then those steps."

"Exactly," Ramage said.

"But surely there are dozens – if not scores and hundreds – of situations an admiral might meet. Surely they're not all covered?"

"There are scores of situations, but the manoeuvres listed have to be used to cover them," Ramage said in a deliberately neutral voice.

"So what happens…"

"If you're my father, you ignore them, decide on your own tactics, trust to the limited vocabulary of the Signal Book, and attack…"

"And if the wind drops, my lord?" St Brieuc asked quietly.

"If the wind drops and the government needs a scapegoat to save its own skin…"

St Brieuc nodded, deep in thought. "Yes, I can see…In politics it is simple: proving the admiral guilty automatically proves the government innocent. The mob are too stupid to realize that finding an admiral guilty of disobeying the Fighting Instructions – however outdated and absurd they are – doesn't make a government innocent of stupidity, neglect and acting too late…Pamphleteers, rumours, lies and accusations circulated as gossip…The methods don't change with the centuries or the countries."

"The vendetta with this Admiral Goddard," St Cast asked – a wealth of meaning in the way he said "this" – "how did that begin?"

"My father's trial split the Navy. Most of the old admirals – those supporting the government – were against him, while the young officers were on his side because they wanted to change the old tactics."

"But the vendetta?"

"It's complicated! The officers forming the court-martial…well, they were senior, and they knew the government could fall…"

"If they found him not guilty," Yorke commented, "they could say goodbye to further promotion."

Again Ramage shrugged. It was true; it was obvious; men as sophisticated as these three needed nothing spelled out.

"He was found guilty and dismissed the Service. The young officers protested, petitioned the King, fought the verdict – or, rather, the significance of the verdict – in Parliament, but to no purpose. There were five admirals and one captain forming the court. The captain was comparatively young but he had plenty of 'interest' – patronage in other words. His wife is a distant relative of the King…

"For reasons no one has ever understood," Ramage continued, "long after the trial was over, long after the government was saved and new elections had put them back in power and when the affair of Admiral the Earl of Blazey was a matter of history, this captain continued to attack my family in every way he could."

"And his name," Yorke said, "is Goddard."

St Cast's fingers tapped the arm of his chair. "Motives... surely he must have reasons...why?"

St Brieuc glanced up. "*Pourquoi?* I will tell you. First, he did what he thought would gain him favour. Afterwards it became a habit and later an obsession...Such men always become obsessed by something: religion, gambling, the mathematics of chance...It gives them a purpose in life – something they previously lacked. In politics, certain insignificant cretins spend their lives constantly attacking a great man. When he falls – as he will, though not because of their efforts – they hope to reap a harvest. Do you agree?"

Ramage nodded slowly. "M'sieur...I'd never thought of it as a habit or an obsession, but I think you are right."

St Brieuc also nodded, but Ramage had the feeling he had merely read his thoughts because he continued: "A vendetta is never more than a habit. Its victims, whichever side they're on, inherit it like an estate. The Montagues and the Capulets. Each family had an entailed legacy – a hatred for the other. Hatred or obsession is the easiest emotion to sustain because it feeds its own flames."

"Is it against your brothers, too?" asked Maxine.

"I am the only child."

"Against you alone, then."

"Against my father, through me."

"Have *you* no patrons?" her father asked.

"No, but a commodore – "

"A *commodore!*" exclaimed Yorke. "Why, you need at least a vice-admiral."

"As many as possible," Ramage said dryly, "but anyway, this commodore helps bring my story up to date."

"Ah, I can guess," Yorke exclaimed. "I take back what I said about commodores if this one's called Nelson."

"He is, but this was before the battle of Cape St Vincent."

"Come on," Yorke said impatiently, "the plot thickens!"

"In the Mediterranean," Ramage began, wondering quite where it had all started, conscious that he was being indiscreet, but feeling a great relief as he talked, "I was under Sir John Jervis' orders – he became the Earl of St Vincent after the battle," he explained to the Frenchmen. "One or two things went wrong. I was court-martialled – on Admiral Goddard's orders."

"For what?" St Brieuc asked, his interest overcoming his tact.

"Cowardice," Ramage said in a flat voice.

"Were you a coward?" the girl asked, equally flatly.

"No."

"Then how could Admiral Goddard...?"

"Another man did behave as a coward. He had to save his pride. Accusing me instead was a good solution as far as he and the Admiral were concerned. At the trial his cousin unexpectedly gave evidence against him and I was acquitted."

"Against him? He must have been an honest man to go against family ties," said St Cast.

"A woman, actually."

"Oh *non!*" the girl exclaimed. "Papa! It was Gianna, Papa, I remember the story now."

A dozen emotions chased across St Brieue's face before he thought of looking at Ramage for confirmation.

"My lord," he said quietly, "was it the Marchesa di Volterra?"

Ramage nodded.

"Permit me the honour," said St Brieuc, holding out his hand. As they shook he explained, "We are old friends of her family."

"So are we," Ramage said, "in fact she is staying with my parents in England at this moment."

Maxine was watching him closely; Ramage felt she was undressing him. "So," she said, "you saved her from Buonaparte…from under the hooves of the French horses."

"To coin an old phrase," Yorke said, "this really is a small world. We know the story of the Marchesa's rescue, my lord, but I don't think any of us understand why Admiral Goddard…?"

"He ordered the trial and sailed from Bastia, leaving Captain Croucher to be president of the court – "

"This *same* Croucher?"

"The same! In the middle of the trial, Commodore Nelson arrived and the trial had to stop because he ordered all the ships to sail."

"Could they not start it again?" asked St Cast.

"Fortunately no; legally the court was dispersed. And the Commodore reported the true facts to Sir John Jervis – I'd been under his orders – and the whole thing was dropped."

"The Commodore ordering the ships to sail," commented St Brieuc, "this was…"

"Simply a coincidence."

"Ah, but he found out about the trial…?"

Ramage nodded.

"Justice sometimes waves in your direction, my lord. From what I hear, Commodore Nelson will be a powerful man one of these days…The battle of Cape St Vincent…"

"Where Ramage turned the trick by preventing the Spanish from escaping. You must have been mad to think of throwing them into confusion by making their leading ship collide with your little cutter. But it worked, because Nelson and the rest of the fleet were able to catch up!" Yorke interjected, adding cheerfully: "Ah well, as far as Goddard is concerned, *Proprium humani ingenii est odisse quem laeseris.*"

St Brieuc nodded, looking at Ramage, and his daughter asked: "Translate please, Papa – my Latin…"

As he searched for words, Yorke said: " 'It's human nature to hate someone you have hurt.' Virgil, was it not?"

Again St Brieuc nodded. "The men tried and wronged the father; now they attack the son. But – *Audentis Fortunas iuvat!*"

" 'Fortune is ally to the brave' – let's hope so, eh?" Yorke said.

Ramage laughed. "More Virgil?"

"Yes," said St Brieuc. "But come, Mr Yorke. If his lordship is to sing for his supper, I think you ought to give him at least a hint that you do have supper to offer him! What about the champagne?"

CHAPTER **FOUR**

Ramage was hot when he sat down at the desk in his tiny cabin on board the *Triton* later that day. He was pleasantly drowsy from the champagne Yorke had produced and pleasantly bloated from a superb meal cooked by the French chef in the St Brieuc entourage.

The perspiration soaking his clothes and trickling down his face was not entirely due to the sun heating his box of a cabin. Warmth came in waves, as if a furnace door was opened, when he thought about the past couple of hours on board the *Topaz*. He was flushed with embarrassment for his behaviour.

My only excuse, he thought to himself, is that it's been months since I talked to intelligent and sophisticated people. And they are the first people outside the Service or the family with whom I've ever discussed the Goddard business. And, dammit, I feel all the better for it. Indiscreet I may have been, and Goddard and his cronies would call it disloyal, but somehow the idea of Goddard setting a trap for me doesn't seem so frightening now and I don't feel so damned lonely. There's nothing Yorke or the Frenchman can do; there's nothing anyone can do, short of wafting Goddard off to the Indian Ocean. He and Croucher have a free hand but maybe I can survive by staying wide awake...

On board the *Topaz*, because of an encouraging word from St Brieuc, a puzzled lift of Maxine's eyebrows, a polite question from St Cast and a blunt question from Yorke, I talked and talked. I told them about the rescue of Gianna, the trial at Bastia, losing the *Kathleen* cutter, the battle of Cape St Vincent and capturing the St Lucia privateers. I also amused them with tales about Goddard and Croucher…

Come to think of it, he mused, I don't feel as embarrassed as I should. In fact I feel curiously free: the sensation of being trapped, so strong at the conference and almost crushing later at that bizarre interview with Goddard, has gone completely. I have got my confidence back and feel positively jaunty. Somehow they all seemed to understand much more than I'd expected, and Maxine seemed to grasp how lonely it was being on a distant station at the mercy of a vindictive admiral…

Ramage shook his head; Maxine with her exciting body and delicious accent wasn't a convoy plan, and he had a convoy plan to draw up. He put the instructions and orders to one side, with the list of the forty-nine merchantmen on top, cleaned the point of his pen, unscrewed the cap of the inkwell and then scratched his chin with the feather of the quill.

The convoy comprised forty-nine ships; they were to sail in seven columns of seven. He smoothed out a clean sheet of paper and drew seven evenly spaced dots in a line across the top. These were the ships leading the seven columns. Beneath each dot he added six more, one below the other, until he had drawn a square full of dots, seven along each edge – and seven horizontally, vertically and diagonally. A pity seven's not my lucky number, he thought inconsequentially. Six letters in Maxine's name and in his surname. Fascinating – and probably forty-nine dots make a magic square, and if you keep on making the knight's move starting from one particular dot, the track you make spells out your sweetheart's name.

Not many captains bother to draw convoy plans; but not many captains have an admiral watching every move for a mistake and probably working out ambiguous orders and complicated manoeuvres to make sure a mistake occurs. Having a clear plan showing every ship in the convoy by name and pendant number was good insurance. A sudden order from the flagship would not mean rushing to look up written lists and wasting time.

Most shipowners had no imagination, to judge by the names on the list. They seemed to favour the husband-and-wife tombstone names. The *William and Grace*, the *Benjamin and Mary*...Might be worth suggesting that Yorke use *Samson and Delilah*.

Dip and scratch, dip and scratch...The names of the seven leading ships were in place. The champagne was no help; nor was Maxine's face smiling up from the paper. In the tropical heat and the privacy of the *Topaz*'s saloon she'd worn a dress of thin lacy white silk. The new French fashion had its advantages: without corsets you could at least see a woman's natural shape, and the clinging silk had cupped Maxine's breasts as if...he jabbed the pen in the ink and looked at the next name on the list of ships.

The present system of numbering for small convoys had been invented by his father, he remembered sourly. The left-hand column was led by No. 11, with 12, 13 and 14 and so on following astern, while the second column was led by 21, the third by 31 and so on right across to 71, which led the seventh column, and down to 77, which was the seventh (and last) ship in the seventh column. The advantage of the system was the ease of finding a ship: number 45 was the fifth in the fourth column; 72 was the second in the seventh column.

Round the box of ships were the escorts. No point in marking in their positions since the Admiral hadn't given any indication of what he intended and they would probably change frequently, governed by the direction of the wind. Obviously Goddard would keep the frigates up to windward, ready to run down and drive off enemy ships or investigate strange sail. He expected to see Goddard's flagship in the middle of the convoy, but no number was allocated to the *Lion*. Apparently she'd stayed outside the convoy all the way from England, instead of being in the middle as a focal point. Was Goddard afraid of the indignity of having his flagship rammed by a merchantman in the middle of the night? It was a reasonable fear.

Yorke must be regarded as a steady captain: the *Topaz* was No. 71, leading the seventh column. On a voyage like this, where the wind would probably be from the east or north-east – providing the Trades stayed constant – the seventh column would also be the one to windward. This meant the *Topaz* would be the pivot, and providing she and the ships in her column kept their positions, there was a good chance the rest of the convoy would too. As the Marines and soldiers termed it, the *Topaz* would be the right marker; the ships leading the other columns would keep in position on her larboard side, each two cables' distance – four hundred yards – apart; each ship would be a cable astern of her next ahead – in theory, anyway.

In practice, Ramage thought savagely, the frigates and the *Triton* and *Lark* will be dashing back and forth like snapping sheepdogs trying to keep the flock together. The merchantmen would scatter, not giving a damn for orders, and apparently oblivious that the convoy's safety lay in concentrating, so that the escorts could protect them from enemy ships lurking on the edge of the horizon, just far enough away to be safe from the guarding shepherds, just close enough to dash in and carry off a sheep that strayed in the night…

It's bad enough for any man-o'-war's captain to have to escort a convoy, Ramage thought, but when people like Goddard and Croucher are in charge it savours of the "cruel and unnatural punishments" forbidden by the *Regulations and Instructions*…

He filled in the other names on his plan. They were an odd collection; proof, if any was needed, that Britain was short of ships and shipowners were sending anything that would float to sea. Some of the ships would stay in Jamaica for the hurricane season, so the convoy's arrival at Kingston would be the signal for ships of war to lower their boats and send lieutenants and boarding parties off to the merchantmen to press as many seamen as possible.

The masters would let their best men row for the shore, to hide until it was time to sail or until the ships of war left them in peace again. There was little chance of the men deserting – the masters ensured their return by keeping most of the pay due to them. Still, for the seamen, hanging around the quayside was to risk being picked up by a roving press-gang or falling into the hands of a crimp who sold his victims to the highest bidder – a master short of men, a Navy captain desperate enough to buy men out of his own pocket rather than risk sailing dangerously short-handed.

A clattering of feet on the ladder outside the cabin was followed by the Marine sentry stamping to attention and calling, "Mr Southwick, sir!"

At Ramage's hail, the *Triton*'s Master came into the cabin, his mop of white hair plastered down with perspiration, his forehead marked with a band where his hat had been pressing the skin.

"Boat just left the flagship and coming our way, sir."

"Who's in it?"

"A lieutenant, sir. Thought I'd better warn you."

Ramage glanced up. Gossip must travel fast – the old Master was obviously worried on his behalf.

"There's no need to worry until you see our pendant and the signal for a captain!"

"Aye aye, sir. It's just that with those two…"

"No disrespect to the flag, Mr Southwick." The mock severity brought a grin from Southwick.

"I'm not being disrespectful, sir," the old man said with a sudden burst of anger, "just mutinous, seditious, treasonable, and anything else that's forbidden by the Articles of War."

Ramage felt a great affection for Southwick. The Master had the chubby, pink, almost cherubic face of an amiable country parson – and the build of one. Once stocky, he was now verging on portly. His hair, grey and white, long and usually sticking out like a windblown halo, would have looked well on a bishop. But Southwick's looks were deceptive. Apart from being an extremely competent seaman and a good navigator, he was a born fighter: the prospect of battle transformed the benevolent vicar into a malevolent butcher.

Southwick was as old as Ramage's father. For many men in late middle age, taking orders from a lieutenant just past his twenty-first birthday was hard to accept. They had to accept it, of course, because it was part of the system, backed by tradition and the Articles of War. On board a merchantman the master was the captain; in a ship of war the master was simply the sailing master, the man responsible, under the captain's orders, for the sailing of the ship. Masters held their jobs by virtue of a warrant; they did not even have the commission granted the lowliest lieutenant a day past being a midshipman or master's mate.

Ramage's relationship with Southwick was unusual. In many ships with young captains, an elderly master just did his job: no omissions, no errors and no helping hand. If the captain made a mistake, the master pointed it out later but rarely in time for it to be avoided.

Southwick understood – without ever having experienced it – that commanding and making decisions was a lonely occupation, and he made allowances. He treated all the seamen impartially as well-meaning but oft-erring scallywags; schoolboys to be taught patiently what they didn't know and forever watched because of their capacity for mischief.

Southwick looked at the convoy plan.

"Forty-nine ships and quite an escort," he growled, as though suspicious.

"It's a big convoy. The Admiral expected more frigates."

"No admiral ever had enough frigates. Still, it's a biggish convoy for inside the Caribbean," Southwick admitted grudgingly, "but small for the Atlantic. All for Jamaica?"

"No – four for Martinique, and three for Antigua. These," Ramage said, pointing to the last ship in each column.

"Surely we're not having to make a great dog-leg northward just for the Antigua ships?"

"Apparently so," Ramage said, sharing Southwick's annoyance, since it meant the convoy had to cover two sides of a triangle.

"Aye – and any north in the wind and these mules will scatter to leeward and end up beached on the Spanish Main."

That was only too true. The course for Antigua was northwest; the Trades blew between south-east and north-east, and the Atlantic pouring into the Caribbean caused a strong current between each of the islands.

Ramage laughed at Southwick's indignation, but the Master protested, "That's no exaggeration, sir; have you seen 'em?

Why, there's only one ship with decent rigging, and that's the *Topaz*: the rest have rotten rigging, rotten masts and spars – and a bunch of coasting mates commanding 'em."

"And all on a 'share the profits' basis, no doubt, so they're making as much as admirals," Ramage teased.

"Don't let's talk of it, sir," Southwick said crossly. "It's hard enough keeping my temper with them now when they're at anchor: just think of 'em shortening sail and dropping back every night...If I think – "

The Marine sentry's call interrupted him.

"It'll be that lieutenant from the flagship," Ramage said. "Send him in."

With the receipt signed and the lieutenant gone to call on the other escorts, Ramage slit open the sealed packet. It was innocent enough after all, a plan giving the positions for the escorts, and informing all captains that an extra ship would be joining the convoy, and her number would be 78. Ramage glanced again at the name, *Peacock*, and put her on the convoy plan, the eighth ship in the seventh column.

Where had she come from? Could be a runner, one of the fast and lightly armed ships that usually sailed from England without a convoy, hoping speed would save her from capture. Good profits – at high risks – for such shipowners: arriving weeks ahead of convoys meant merchants could always get very high scarcity prices for the freights.

He was impatient for the convoy to weigh; even more impatient for it to arrive. Kingston meant an unpleasant voyage over and the possibility that he'd avoided any of Goddard's tricks.

Reaching up to the rack over his head he pulled down a small-scale chart of the Caribbean and unrolled it. His eyes followed the islands. At the bottom right-hand corner was

Barbados, where they were at the moment; and to the westward, in a line running upwards, to the north, the chain of the Windward Islands – Grenada, then St Vincent, St Lucia and Martinique – merging into the Leewards – Dominica, Guadeloupe, Antigua and several small islands at the top right-hand corner. How the islands had changed in the last few years – only Guadeloupe was still held by the French...

Then, going left across the top of the chart, Virgin Gorda, Tortola, St John and St Thomas – the Virgin Islands; then the Spanish islands of Puerto Rico, Hispaniola – part of which was French – and Cuba. Just below the gap between Hispaniola and Cuba lay Jamaica. He walked the dividers over the chart, measuring the distances against the latitude scale: 260 miles from Barbados up to Antigua, then just 900 westward to Kingston.

With the hurricane season just beginning the refuges were few enough. English Harbour, in Antigua, had a tiny and mosquito-ridden dockyard for the King's ships to refit themselves, but was otherwise of no importance to man or beast. Bereft of drinking water and as barren as a mule, it was cordially disliked by everyone. An almost enclosed bay at St John in the Virgin Islands; a similar one at Snake Island – Spanish owned and named Culebra by them – between St Thomas and Puerto Rico; a couple on the south side of Puerto Rico, which the Spaniards would stop anyone else from using; and precious little else.

All of which meant that if a hurricane hit them with the usual few hours' warning, only three or four ships were likely to survive. The flagship, the *Topaz*, probably the frigates and, less likely, the *Triton* and the *Lark* lugger. He was being pessimistic but much would depend on Goddard. Would he disperse the convoy in time to avoid them having a barrier of islands in their way as they ran before the winds? Sea room, plenty of sea room – that would be their only hope. In a hurricane the wind eventually goes right round the compass. It was a comfort that Maxine was in the best ship, anyway.

He was just rolling up the chart when Southwick came down again. He came into the cabin and simply raised an eyebrow.

"Escorts' positions – and an extra ship joining the convoy," Ramage explained.

"Oh – I thought they were up to something."

"Not yet!"

"Extra ship? Where's she come from?"

"I don't know. Late arrival?"

"No," Southwick said. "They didn't lose anyone on the way out. Maybe a runner."

"I was thinking that."

"But why join the convoy now? His only chance of a profit is to get to Kingston afore the convoy and beat 'em to the market."

Ramage shrugged his shoulders. "She's joined us, and one more to chase up won't make any difference."

CHAPTER FIVE

Almost the last of the sixty-one names written in the *Triton*'s current muster book, now locked in Ramage's desk, was Thomas Jackson, and the details entered in the various columns beside it recorded all that the Navy Board, Sick and Hurt Board, Admiralty and various other branches of the Navy would ever need to know about him. In the column headed *Where and whether or not prest* was written "vol.", showing that he had volunteered instead of being one of a press-gang's haul.

In the next column, under *Place and country where born*, the neat copperplate handwriting recorded "Charleston, South Carolina" for Jackson. Compared with most entries in muster books, this was a wealth of detail, and showed that both the clerk making the original entry and the person it referred to could write and spell. A newcomer from a foreign town that was difficult to spell usually had only his country noted down. Various other columns yielded the information that Thomas Jackson, forty-one years old, was the captain's coxswain and had been serving since the beginning of the war.

Like any government form, the muster book failed to indicate that Thomas Jackson was a human being. It did not show, for instance, why a thin-faced, sandy-haired and wiry American was voluntarily serving in the Royal Navy, nor reveal that for the past couple of years he had rarely been more than a few yards from Lieutenant Ramage and had shared in all his adventures, narrow escapes and triumphs. Nor did it give a hint of the curious bond that existed between the two men as a result of those shared experiences.

Standing beside Jackson on the fo'c'sle just after dawn as the convoy sailed from Barbados was another seaman who had had a share in many, although not all, of Ramage's exploits. Will Stafford, born twenty-seven years earlier in Bridewell Lane, in the city of London, was a true cockney, with the perky humour that traditionally went with the accent. Stocky with curly brown hair, a round and open face, and a confident, jaunty manner, he had a habit of rubbing a thumb and forefinger together, like a tailor feeling cloth.

An observant person might well have been curious about Stafford's hands: although the skin was tough and coarsened by handling ropes, scrubbing decks, polishing brightwork with brickdust and a dozen other tasks, they were delicately shaped, and he was very proud of the fact that before he was pressed into the Navy they had been deliberately kept soft. His original trade was locksmith but he was not afraid to admit that he had not always worked in daylight, nor invariably at the request of the owner of the lock. Working at night was more risky but a lot more profitable.

"Nah," Stafford said, waving a hand at the merchantmen, "never did like all this work wiv a fleet."

"Hardly a fleet!"

"Well, there's an admiral, ain't there? Anyway, I didn't mean it literalilly." He paused a moment, cocking his head to one side, then corrected himself. "I mean literalally."

"If your tongue was a key, you'd never get a door open."

"Not a lock yet made…" Stafford said airily. "What I'm tryin' ter say, Jacko, is that I like it better when we're on our

56

own. None of these admirals waving flags so's we run rahnd like kids at a Michaelmas fair."

"Count yourself lucky you're not like me and responsible for reading the blasted signals," Jackson said.

"Can't read nor write proper. Keeps me off jobs like that."

"You really can't read?" Jackson did not hide his disbelief.

"Well, I can akshly, but I don't let on."

"Why not?"

"Where I was born, mate, it don't always pay ter let on. 'Ere, Jacko, ever bin ter Jamaica afore?"

"Ain't it near where you comes from?"

"Yes – as near as Gibraltar from where you come from."

Stafford sniffed. "Hm. Ever thought of going back? Ter Charleystown, I mean. After all, yer got a Protection; they'd 'ave ter let yer go. Or y'could run."

"Nothing in Charleston for me."

"Wot, no family?"

"No."

"Only us lot, eh?" Stafford commented. "Mr Ramage an' Mr Southwick, an' me an' Rosey...?"

Jackson nodded, and the moment Stafford realized the American was serious he said quietly: " 'Ere, Jacko, I was only jokin' about runnin'; never could see you desertin'. But yer mean it, about no family an' no friends?"

"Yes. The ship's my home. Gives me a big family, too," Jackson added dryly.

"Cor, well, s'funny you should say that, Jacko; that's 'ow I feel. In uvver ships I've always looked rahnd fer a chansk ter run. Now it'd be like leavin' 'ome."

"Ever thought why?"

"Well, got a good bunch o' messmates, fer once."

"Wrong," Jackson said. "Half wrong, anyway. You've got a good bunch o' messmates because Mr Ramage picked 'em. Trained 'em, anyway."

"I know that!" Stafford said scornfully. "That's wot I meant. It always depends on the capting whether or not a ship's 'appy. Speshly a small ship."

Jackson ran his hand through his hair, which was beginning to recede.

"Better stop that; you'll be bald soon enough," Stafford warned amiably.

Jackson laughed, and suddenly Stafford asked suspiciously: " 'Ere, wotcher keep lookin' at that ship for? Any women on deck?"

The American, watching the *Peacock*, said: "That's the one that's just joined the convoy. Her sails have got an odd cut – just look at the roach. And she's floating so high: can't be above half laden."

"Where'd she come from? 'Ere, you sure there ain't any women?"

"Yes. From the Atlantic, as far as I could see."

"Might be a light cargo. Bulky and light. Clorth, silk, that sort o' thing."

"Maybe she's a runner. But her sheer – and that forefoot. There's something – "

"Flagship," Stafford interrupted.

Jackson snatched up the telescope, looked at the flags flying from the *Lion*, glanced at his list, and called: "Captain, sir! Flagship to convoy: *To bear away, and sail before the wind.*"

Ramage said, "Very well; repeat it."

Southwick walked over to him.

" 'Bout time," he grumbled. "Thinks he's manoeuvring a squadron off Spithead. He'll never see this bunch of mules in such good order again."

Ramage grinned and pulled his hat forward. "If he does, he'd soon be ordering us to send over carpenter's mates to repair the damage after they ran aboard each other!"

"Captain, sir," Jackson called. "Flagship to convoy, *For all ships to come under my stern.*"

"Repeat it."

The escorts simply repeated the Admiral's orders, hoisting the same signal so every ship in the convoy could see it.

"Follow father," Southwick grunted. "But let's hope he knows where he's going."

Once the convoy got out of the lee of Barbados it was much cooler on board the *Triton*: the damp, cloying atmosphere of Carlisle Bay was left behind as they sailed into the brisk freshness of the Trade winds.

The sea was now a deep blue and frequent shoals of flying fish emerged like silver darts, dropping back into the water after a brief flight a few inches above the waves. Out of the wind, the sun was scorching; the decks were still uncomfortably hot – no one stood still unless he had to – and the pitch between the seams was as soft as when the caulker first poured it. But in the wind seamen moved without bothering to seek out the shade and went less frequently to get a mug of water at the scuttlebutt. The burly and red-faced Marine sentry guarding the water supply looked less wilted, although he was careful to hold his cutlass out of the sun. The heat could make metal unbearably hot to touch in less than a quarter of an hour.

"Getting away from the land is like a shower of rain on a flower garden," Southwick commented to Ramage.

"The flowers don't look so wilted!" Ramage said, gesturing towards the seamen.

"Aye, sir, the breeze freshens them up."

"No weeds, either!"

"No, we can be thankful for that," the Master said, mopping his face with a large handkerchief. "Six months and not a flogging…never heard of longer."

During the next hour, in obedience to a stream of signal flags hoisted from the *Lion*, the escorts tacked and wore, cajoling and threatening the merchantmen until they were in their proper positions. Eventually the *Antelope* frigate was right ahead of the convoy, followed by the *Lion* which in turn was ahead of the leading ship in the centre column. The *Lark* lugger was astern with the *Raisonnable* frigate to leeward over on the larboard quarter and the *Greyhound* frigate to starboard, up to windward.

Ramage took the *Triton* to the position Admiral Goddard had assigned him on the windward side of the convoy, abreast the *Topaz* and ahead of the *Greyhound*.

"A pretty picture," Southwick growled, waving at the convoy. "I'd like to think these mules were secretly plotting to drive the Admiral mad," he continued maliciously, careful the seamen could not hear him. "The masters know that if they get into exactly the right position for an hour or two it'll show the Admiral they can do it, and he'll go berserk when they start spreading themselves across the ocean…"

Ramage laughed. For the moment the convoy was in perfect formation, the symmetry spoiled only by the extra ship, the eighth and last in the *Topaz*'s column. Southwick saw him looking at her.

"Something about that ship, sir," he commented, pointing at the *Peacock*. "That hull wasn't built in England, nor those sails cut by Englishmen."

"Scotsmen, maybe; perhaps she's a Clyde ship!"

The Master took off his hat and scratched his head. "No, I – "

"I know what you mean, but she is probably a prize bought by someone or other. And in ballast – a runner come over to find a cargo. She looks odd with all that freeboard. You're used to seeing ships fully laden – aye, fully laden and a few tons more!"

After looking at her again through his telescope, Southwick said, "That's it; she was a prize. French built, or I'm a Dutchman."

The merchantmen and escorts were reaching to the north-west with a comfortable quartering wind and pitching only slightly.

"With a steady breeze like this, let's hope some of the mules are having another look at their standing and running rigging," Southwick said sourly.

"You're an optimist: they've already sailed four thousand miles from England with it; they're just hoping it'll last another few hundred until they get into Kingston."

As if aware that with the routine of watches this would be one of the few opportunities for chatting with his captain, Southwick said, "I still don't see why the *Lion* is out there ahead of the convoy, sir. Her place is to windward; she ought to be out beyond the *Greyhound*," he added, nodding towards the frigate astern of the *Triton*.

"I think it's the Admiral's idea, not Croucher's," Ramage said, since the Master was echoing the question that occurred to him the moment he received his latest orders. "Croucher's an odd fellow but he knows his job."

"Odd!" Southwick snorted. "After that courtmartial you call him odd? Well, the Admiral has weakened himself by a ship o' the line by sitting out there to leeward. The *Lion* can't do a thing unless we meet an enemy dead ahead: she'll never be able to beat up to windward to get at a privateer unless there's a gale o' wind blowing. We ought to be ready for light airs, not a gale o' wind. Up to windward, that's where the Admiral ought to be with that haystack, so he can run down to anything. Hmmp – hey! Watch your luff!" he suddenly bellowed at the quartermaster, who gestured to the men at the wheel.

Within an hour Barbados was already so far astern that the curvature of the earth dropped the beaches on the west coast below the horizon, hiding the band of almost luminous pale green sea that marked the shallows and reefs stretching out from the shore. The palm trees had long since merged into strips of dark green, and from this distance it was clear that the land was losing its parched brown appearance as the thirsty dry earth soaked up the first heavy rains heralding the approach of the rainy season. Rainy season, Ramage thought to himself; a nice euphemism for the hurricane season.

For anyone brought up in the uncertain and unpredictable weather of European waters, the comparative predictability of the Caribbean – outside of the hurricane season – was almost unsettling, Ramage realized. It was so predictable that it made a man apprehensive; it was like worrying when too many things went right.

At this end of the Caribbean the wind always blew between north-east and south-east; wind from any other direction – apart from the land and sea breeze – usually meant the weather was about to change for the worse. And even then the change was predictable – the wind south or south-west, bringing rain and stronger, gusty winds.

Almost always the wind dropped in the evening and stayed light or calm throughout a starlit night. About nine o'clock next morning a breeze would start ruffling the water and steadily increasing until it was a fresh breeze by nine or ten o'clock. It was the best time of the day in the Caribbean – the sun bright and warm but not yet scorching, the wind cool and not yet strong, and the sea flat. It was the time the Caribbean seemed the finest sea in the world for ships and seamen. By ten-thirty it would usually be a strong breeze, except in the hurricane season, and the seas would begin to build up, short seas which sent the spray flying in sparkling showers from the bow of the ship beating to windward.

Small clouds would start appearing from nowhere, small balls of fluffed white cotton which soon formed into regular lines running east and west, the bottom of each cloud flattening and the top forming a weird shape. Some looked like the marble effigies of ancient knights and their wives recumbent atop their tombs; others were turtles, alligators and mythical beasts. Often they looked like the profiles of politicians lying flat on their backs, glassy-eyed and copied straight from one of Gillray's more outrageous cartoons.

By noon most well-found ships would be carrying all plain sail and making their maximum speed, while one of the King's ships in a hurry would cheerfully hoist out studding sails. Then by four o'clock the wind would start to falter and by five o'clock would be light and fitful while the clouds began shrinking and vanishing in the reverse order of the strange way they appeared. Soon after six o'clock the sun would set in an almost cloudless sky and darkness would fall with a startling suddenness, and another tropical day would be over.

Although the ritual never ceased to fascinate Ramage, who loved the Tropics and hated the chill, northern latitudes, there were exceptions to the weather pattern: the Trade winds often fell away in the hurricane season – unless there was a hurricane actually nearby – and close to the big islands like Puerto Rico, Hispaniola and Cuba, the offshore breeze of the night and onshore breeze of the day were more pronounced.

Ramage found himself brooding that it was late in the season to be fooling around with a clutch of merchantmen. He looked eastward to the broad Atlantic, which stretched three thousand miles to the coast of Africa, a great sea desert all the way. Somewhere out there – although how, where and why no man knew – the hurricanes were born. Between July and October the people living in the Caribbean waited in fear for the winds which tore down houses, sank ships and brought torrential rains that washed land into the rivers and the sea. Hurricanes could even conjure up tidal waves: in 1722 the port of Port Royal that had survived the great earthquakes of 1692 had been largely destroyed by one.

Traditionally the only early warning a hurricane gave was swell waves, which could be felt for days before it arrived, and long periods of calm. These calm periods often prevented ships from getting to shelter in time. But not all swell waves or periods of calm presaged a hurricane; probably not one in fifty. Hurricanes were so unusual and unpredictable that apart from avoiding voyages in the hurricane season one could only wait and hope.

At the convoy conference, no one had tried to gloss over the fact that the convoy was well over a month behindhand and that they were crossing the Caribbean dangerously late in the season. If anyone had wanted to make light of it, every master knew that the underwriters were already charging all those merchantmen double premium for being at sea in the Caribbean in July, and that in a couple of weeks' time all policies would be cancelled. The underwriters made good livings because of their skill in basing their premiums and wording their policies on their past experience.

Ramage felt it verged on melodrama to be so gloomy when the sun was bright and the sea such a sparkling blue, the wind steady and the sky clear. Yet the very clearness of the sky could indicate a change, since the clouds should have started forming by now.

As if reading his thoughts, Southwick said, "Swell's more noticeable now we're out of the lee of the island."

Ramage nodded. "I've noted it in the log. About three feet high."

"Probably nothing to worry about. Not for a few days, anyway."

Ramage was fascinated by the swell waves. The short seas knocked up by the wind were streaming in from the eastward, and would disappear as the breeze died in the evening. The swell waves were much lower and less frequent and were coming in from the south-east so that their crests moved diagonally under the others, making a herringbone pattern.

Ramage could not resist the temptation to ask Southwick: "There's no rigging that should be changed, is there?"

"No, sir; everything at all doubtful was replaced the minute I clapped eyes on the first of the swell in Carlisle Bay. While you were on board the *Topaz*," he added, and Ramage knew the old man intended only to indicate the precise time, not make an oblique criticism of his captain's absence from the ship.

The sun was behind a small cloud but still above the western horizon, deep red, its rays already a peacock's tail of alternate stripes of orange, yellow and blue. In an hour it would be dark and the wind was becoming fitful as the clouds began dissolving.

Already the convoy was beginning to straggle. The seven leading ships were in position, and so were the next one or two in each column; but after that no telescope was needed to see men out on the yards of many ships, reefing topsails and furling topgallants.

"Look at the mules!" Southwick fumed. "They'd be slow enough if they were setting stunsails; but they're actually *furling* their t'gallants..."

Ramage shrugged his shoulders, and imagined daybreak next morning when he would stand at the main shrouds and stare at the convoy with a telescope, counting the number of ships as soon as it was light enough to discern them, and then search the horizon astern for the missing ones.

Suddenly Jackson called: "Captain, sir, the flagship's signalling: our pendant, *To pass within hail.*"

"Very well, acknowledge."

The response was mechanical, Ramage realized, but his reaction was not, and he glanced across at Southwick and told him to carry on. As the Master began bellowing the orders which sent the men running to the braces to haul round the yards and to the sheets to trim the sails as the *Triton's* wheel was put over, and the brig turned on to a course which would take her diagonally across the corner of the convoy, Ramage tried to guess the orders waiting for him on board the *Lion*.

Routine, or something to catch him out? Since they'd be shouted to him as the *Triton* came close alongside, there'd probably be only a few seconds for him to react: a few seconds in which to haul in what had been shouted and give the requisite orders to Southwick. But, Ramage told himself, there's one sure way of making a mess of it, and that's to start fretting...

It was curious that the Admiral had left him alone since the convoy sailed. Perhaps he was going to send him beating all the way back to Barbados on some footling errand, with orders to rejoin the convoy by noon tomorrow. A small and unimportant task to make sure Ramage had no sleep.

Glancing at the flagship way over on the larboard bow as he went down to his cabin to rinse his face – the scorching, bright sun of the afternoon had left him sticky and slightly dazed – he knew he must beware of getting obsessed with the idea that Goddard was persecuting him. He was, but it didn't do any good to think about it; on the contrary...

He clattered down the companionway, acknowledged the Marine sentry's salute and went into his cabin, ducking his head under the low beams. It was dark down here, and everywhere he saw red orbs – the result of staring at the sun as he paused for a moment before coming below. He squeezed his eyes shut a few times and the orbs vanished. He took the deep metal jug from the rack, pulled out the wooden bung and poured water into the equally battered metal hand-basin. One thing about the Caribbean, the torrential rain so frequent in late-afternoon thunderstorms, often without a lot of wind, meant that they could catch rainwater and not worry about spray making it brackish.

As Southwick brought the *Triton* round to larboard Ramage felt her motion change; the combined roll and pitch on her original course, with the wind on the quarter, changed to sluggish pitching as she ran almost dead before the wind to pass across the corner of the convoy. He reached for a towel, wiped his face briskly, crammed on his hat again and ducked out of the cabin.

He paused at the top of the companionway and looked astern: the swell waves were longer than he'd thought as they ran up under the wind waves. He counted to himself and saw that the interval between the crests was still the same. It must be an optical illusion; just a trick of the light that made them look longer and larger. Probably because the sun dropping had lengthened the shadows. And he was getting jumpy, too...

In a few minutes the *Triton* would be passing across the *Topaz*'s bow. Would Maxine be on deck? He walked aft to join

Southwick, and took his telescope from the rack by the binnacle box.

The *Topaz* was a smart ship and Yorke a lucky man to own five more like her. Lucky and obviously shrewd, and one of the few men he knew that deserved the legacy he'd received from his grandfather. A group of people...he put the telescope to his eye. Yes – there was Maxine, looking through a telescope held by Yorke. Her mother and father were laughing and St Cast was struggling with another telescope. Ramage waved and she waved back – and from Yorke's gesture and her wriggling he guessed she had accidentally moved the telescope and they could not train it back on the *Triton's* quarterdeck.

The brig was moving fast now as she headed for a point just ahead of the *Lion*: a point chosen by Southwick as being the place where the two ships, travelling on different courses and at different speeds, would converge after covering the minimum distance. In a few minutes Ramage could distinguish the *Lion's* rigging as made up of individual ropes, so she was a mile away. He took the convoy plan from his pocket, unfolded the page and glanced through the names to refresh his memory. Looking up again, he could recognize men on the *Lion's* decks – a third of a mile to go. Now he could pick out the gilding on her name carved across her transom. And the inside of the transom, behind the stern lights which now reflected the evening light like dulled mirrors, the cabin in which the convoy conference had been held, and where Goddard and Croucher had clumsily revealed that they were watching – and waiting.

The *Lion* was pitching too, in response to this low swell; pitching more than Ramage expected. It was emphasized by her slow speed – she was already down to double-reefed topsails so that she did not outsail the convoy.

Ramage knew – for he was clasping and unclasping his hands like a nervous curate – that it was as much as he could do to leave the conn with Southwick. The old Master was more than competent to take the *Triton* close alongside the flagship; it was simply jumpiness on Ramage's part; as though everything would go wrong if he was not doing something active. Then he remembered a comment of his father's – true leadership is being able to sit at the back, watch everything, give the minimum of orders and yet remain in complete control.

"To windward, sir?"

Officially, Southwick was asking his captain a question. In fact he was making a statement. And as he spoke, Southwick knew the answer was equally predictable.

"Yes, to windward, Mr Southwick; we don't want to have her blanketing us."

She was big: Ramage could see that the *Triton*'s deck was just about level with the *Lion*'s lowest row of gun ports. And as she pitched she showed the overlapping plates of copper sheathing below the waterline; sheathing foul with barnacles and weed. She had obviously been drydocked before leaving England, and Ramage knew that the two days spent at anchor in Barbados – plus a few days in Cork while collecting the rest of the convoy – were the only times the ship had been at rest since then. It was a miracle how the weed and goose barnacles managed to get a grasp and flourish. He was so absorbed in the eternal problem of keeping a ship's bottom clean that he only half heard Southwick's shouted orders to bear up and bring the *Triton* round a point to starboard to run close alongside the flagship.

"Man the weather braces…Another pull on the sheets there!…Tally that aft, men, and step lively!"

A brief order to the quartermaster and an injunction to "Watch your luff, now!" then Southwick's stream of orders stopped as quickly as they started, and the *Triton* was thirty yards to windward of the *Lion* and a ship's length astern of her. She would pass clear of the great yards which towered over the *Lion* and extended out several feet beyond her sides, and yet close enough for Goddard to shout without effort.

Speaking trumpet! Ramage turned to call to Jackson and found the American standing just behind him, the speaking trumpet ready in his outstretched hand. Ramage took it, stepped over to the larboard side and jumped up onto the breech of the aftermost twelve-pounder carronade. He turned the trumpet in his hand: he would first be putting the mouthpiece to his ear so that it served as an ear trumpet.

The *Triton* was overhauling the flagship fast and as he glanced forward, checking on the trim of the sails, Ramage saw that every man on deck was standing precisely at his post. Those that could had edged over slightly to larboard, as if to hear what was shouted from the flagship and be ready to anticipate any manoeuvres and orders. The sails overhead were trimmed perfectly and drawing.

As Southwick bellowed out an order to clew up the maintopsail, reducing the *Triton*'s speed to that of the *Lion*'s – and so judging it that by the time it was done and the brig began slowing down, she would be abreast of the flagship – Ramage could hear an occasional deep thump high above him as the *Lion*'s sails lost the wind when she pitched, and then filled again suddenly. And the creaking of the gudgeons and pintles of her rudder as the *Triton* swept past her transom, and the sloshing of water curling along her sides and round her quarters.

Then Goddard was staring down at him, a gargoyle on the edge of a church roof, and Croucher had appeared beside him at the break in the *Lion*'s gangway. As Croucher lifted a speaking trumpet to his mouth, Ramage held his to his ear. Croucher's was highly polished. When he put it down his fingers would smell brassy, Ramage thought inconsequentially.

"Make a complete sweep southabout round the convoy and stop any ship reducing sail unnecessarily – even if it means getting inside the convoy. Then resume your position."

Reverse speaking trumpet; jam to the lips. "Aye aye, sir."

That's all. Down from the carronade, wave to Southwick indicating he was taking the conn, speaking trumpet to lips again, clew up the foretopsail, the ship slowing down, and the *Lion* drawing ahead again, Goddard watching because he probably expected the *Triton* to clap on sail and try to cut across the *Lion*'s bow.

Bowsprit and jibboom now clear of the *Lion*'s stern; let fall the main and foretopsails; down with the helm as we brace round on the larboard tack.

Everything drawing nicely, the convoy coming down to him as he beat across its front, and the sun sinking fast – it always seems to speed up when there's plenty to be done before darkness.

Southwick sidled over and said quietly, careful none of the men heard him, "Wasn't as bad as I'd expected, sir."

"No, just routine. Worrying, isn't it! And the order was passed quickly."

The last sentence was tactfully acknowledging that Croucher could have kept the *Triton* close by for twenty minutes or more, delaying passing orders on various pretexts. In that way he could force Ramage to juggle with the helm and sails to stay in position and avoid a collision. He could see himself eventually making a mistake which would result in the *Triton*'s jibboom poking through one of the stern lights in the captain's cabin – now of course occupied by the Admiral.

"We won't get far round afore it's dark," Southwick grumbled. "Weaving our way through the columns just to crack a whip across the backs of these mules – so help me, one o' them is bound to hit us, or mistake us for a privateer in the darkness and sheer off and collide with someone else."

Ramage laughed at the dejection in the Master's voice. "Well, tell the carpenter's mate to stand by with a boat's crew; we might need him to patch up one of your mules."

Ramage walked to the binnacle and bent over the compass bowl. Then he glanced at the leading ship in the first column. They'd pass well clear of her. Then he looked along the columns of ships as the *Triton* reached fast across the front of the convoy.

"We'll get all the first column into position, Mr Southwick. Maybe the rest will take the hint."

"A hint's a shot fired across their bow," Southwick said miserably.

CHAPTER SIX

It was dark before the merchantmen were finally cajoled, bluffed and threatened into position. The *Lark* and the two frigates had helped by chasing up the ones at the rear, a task they had taken on themselves without orders from the *Lion*, who could not see them. Ramage had the feeling the frigates helped because they thought the signal must have been made to them as well and they'd missed seeing it.

As they finally passed the last ships in the northernmost column, led by the *Topaz*, Southwick took off his hat and ran a hand through his flowing white hair.

"It's not quite what their lordships have in mind," he said admiringly, "but it's the best way of getting mules back into position I've seen."

"It could be expensive on jibbooms," Ramage said.

"Worth it, though. Still, we mustn't do it too often, or else the element of surprise will be lost."

Ramage felt embarrassed at Southwick's praise; he'd done the right thing for completely the wrong reason. Exasperated by one particularly stubborn captain who flatly refused to shake out reefs or stop his men furling topsails, though the ships astern of him were having to bear away to pass because he was down to little more than the steerage way he intended to maintain all night, Ramage had finally lost his temper. He too had ordered his men to clew up sails until the *Triton*, which had been almost alongside the merchantman – with Ramage standing on the quarterdeck, speaking trumpet in his hand, throat sore from shouting at the Master, almost trembling with rage and frustration – began dropping back.

Eventually the merchantman had drawn ahead, and Ramage had conned the brig into a position directly astern of her. Then he had given the order to let fall the maintopsail, and the *Triton* had begun to pick up speed again. Gradually the distance between the merchantman's transom and the *Triton*'s jibboom end narrowed: fifty yards, thirty, twenty-five and twenty.

Jackson had been sent out on the bowsprit and passed the word back through a chain of seamen how many feet were left – Ramage did not want any shouting. The gunner's mate was ordered to fire one of the forward guns with a blank charge in it, and then Ramage had looked up at the clewed-up foretopsail, crossed his fingers and given the orders to let fall and sheet it home.

He could see the merchantman clearly, and knew her captain could see the *Triton* – and the foretopsail, now beginning to belly out as the men tallied aft the sheets. And because the merchantman's taffrail was a good deal lower than the outer end of the brig's jibboom, he knew the warship would give the impression of being much bigger than she was, an impression that she was towering over the merchantman.

And with Southwick thoroughly enjoying himself and standing by the men at the wheel, an eye on the compass and on the luffs of the sail, and looking as if he was standing on tiptoe to make sure he did not miss a word of any order Ramage might give, Ramage watched the black shape ahead and listened to the message relayed back from Jackson.

"Forty feet, sir, Jackson says, and dead ahead."

"Very well. Watch your luff, Mr Southwick."

"Jackson says thirty feet, and four feet to larboard of the middle of his taffrail."

"Very well." Nice of Jackson to be so precise.

Southwick said nervously: "That spare jibboom of ours ain't much of a spar, sir."

"Too late to worry now. Maybe you won't need it."

"Didn't really mean it like that, sir."

"Twenty feet, sir, and right on course, so Jackson says."

"Very well."

And Ramage hoped the *Triton* would not suddenly pitch in a particularly heavy sea and catch the merchantman's mizzen boom with her jibboom end.

The seaman muttered a stifled oath of surprise.

"Fifteen feet, Jackson says, sir! An' he's out on the end of the boom and says should he drop on board o' 'er and deliver a message."

"Tell him not to be impatient," Ramage snapped.

Jackson would know it was a joke but the rest of the crew wouldn't; it wouldn't do any harm to let them think their captain was a cool chap. Southwick nearly spoiled it by laughing.

Suddenly there was a bellowing from ahead. Ramage turned sideways, jamming the speaking trumpet to his ear. It was the merchantman's captain shouting plaintively.

"Are you trying to ram me?"

Ramage grabbed the seaman's arm. "Quick – get forward: Jackson's to tell – no, belay that."

Ramage couldn't resist it and didn't want to spoil the joke. Telling Southwick to take the conn, he ran forward, speaking trumpet in hand, until he was standing by the forebitts.

As he lifted the speaking trumpet to his lips he was appalled at the sight of the merchantman: in the darkness her transom seemed like the side of a house. But even before he could speak he heard an agitated hail.

"*Triton! Triton!* Watch out, you crazy fool! You'll be aboard us in a moment!"

"What ship's that?" Ramage asked, keeping his voice to a conversational tone.

"The *William and Mary*. Bear up for pity's sake, you'll sweep us clean in a moment."

"The *William and Mary*, you say? By jove, it can't be; her position's five cables or more ahead of where you are!"

"We're the *William and Mary*, for God's sake, let fall the foretopsail – no, not you sir, I mean – *No!* Let fall the maintopsail as well – *Let fall*, you bloody ape! Not you sir! My mate," the agitated voice tried to explain. "My mate seems to be paralysed – get for'ard, y'gibbering psalm-singer! Oh, not you, sir! The Devil's got into everything! Let fall! Let fall or we'll be skewered. Sheet home! Get them drawing, y'fool!"

A seaman tapped Ramage's arm respectfully: he had been whispering for several seconds without his captain hearing him.

"Jackson says 'Minus two feet', sir. I think he mean's he's hanging over her taffrail."

"He does, eh?" Ramage said shortly. "Very well."

There was a bang from ahead as the merchantman's foretopsail flopped down like a great blind and suddenly filled, and almost at once the merchantman began to increase speed. The maintopsail followed, and Ramage could see the gap between the ships opening up. When there was a good twenty yards between them, he called forward into the darkness.

"All right, Jackson; you can come home now."

Ramage walked back to the quarterdeck and a moment later Jackson joined him, proffering a bundle which Ramage took, saying: "Most unexpected, Jackson, and thank you. What is it?"

"A souvenir, sir, that ship's ensign. They didn't lower it at sunset and it kept flapping in my face, so I cut the halyard."

Southwick, who had heard the exchange, commented dryly: "Better stow it somewhere safe, sir; any trouble tomorrow night and we can use it as an excuse for another visit: send Jackson on board to return it with a rude message."

There were low cloud banks on the western horizon as they sailed along the northern edge of the convoy, heading back to the *Triton*'s original position. The ships ahead were no longer silhouetted against the stars.

"It's like playing chess in the dark," Southwick grumbled as he took another bearing of the lights being shown by the *Lion*. "Wish the Admiral's lamp trimmers were up to the mark."

As the *Triton* passed the last ship in the windward column led by the *Topaz*, Ramage automatically began counting and inspecting them with his night glass which, with its inverted image, showed them as if they were sailing upside down.

Soon the count of ships they had passed reached eight, and they were abreast their original position; back where they should be in the convoy screen. The lights on the flagship seemed brighter against the darker western horizon and were just forward of the larboard beam.

Ramage swung the glass the length of the column before going below, leaving the conn to Southwick, and unconcernedly counted the ships again. Seven?

Puzzled, he began again at the head of the column and counted carefully. Still only seven. Since the *Peacock* had joined the convoy that column should have held eight. And anyway he had counted eight as the *Triton* sailed past to get back into position. It must be the angle…He counted a third time but there were still only seven.

He called to Southwick, who picked up the other night glass.

"I can make out only seven, sir. That's odd – we passed eight just now because I counted 'em. That's the *Topaz* just abaft the beam – yes, I can see right across the front of the convoy: the leading ships of all the columns are just open now. Aye, and that's the *Topaz* there, all right. But why only seven?"

Ramage rubbed the scar over his brow and leaned against the breech of the nearest carronade. This was absurd; there must be a logical explanation.

"We passed eight – you're sure of that?"

"Counted 'em off on my fingers."

"I counted them too, and had a good look at each one as we went by. But now I can see only seven with the glass. So one has vanished."

"But it can't just vanish!" exclaimed Southwick. "Not in a matter of minutes!"

"It can't," Ramage said dryly, "but it has. Check with the lookouts: one of them may have kept a tally."

Muttering to himself, the Master began walking down the larboard side, pausing beside each of the three lookouts.

A ship missing…it was absurd. The *Lark* had been out there since long before darkness fell and she would not have missed a laggard. He swung the glass up to windward – yes, the *Greyhound* was in position. It didn't really matter all that much if a ship was missing – there would be plenty more out of position by dawn – it was just absurd that they'd sailed past eight ships in a column and a few minutes later he could only see seven. In that few minutes no ship afloat could have sailed out of sight…

"Eight, sir," Southwick said. "All three of the lookouts on the larboard side confirm eight, and the starboard for'ard lookout, too. He could see quite well. Apparently he was helping the man on the larboard side."

"Eight – and yet one has vanished like a puff of smoke. Pass the word for my coxswain."

Three minutes later Jackson was standing in front of him.

"Believe in ghosts, Jackson?"

"Not when I'm sober, sir."

Ramage laughed, knowing that Jackson rarely drank.

"Very well then, take the night glass and get up the mast There should be eight ships in the nearest column – "

"But there are, sir, beggin' your pardon: I counted them as we passed."

"So did I and so did Mr Southwick and the lookouts. Now get up the mast and count again."

"How many d'you expect me to see, sir?" Jackson asked warily.

"You count 'em and report."

Jackson took the glass and ran to the main shrouds; a moment later Ramage saw him jump lightly into the ratlines and disappear upwards into the darkness.

Every bloody thing seems to be disappearing upwards into the darkness, Ramage grumbled to himself and almost giggled as he pictured Admiral Goddard reading: "Sir, I have the honour to report that on the night of July 17th one of the merchantmen in the seventh column of the convoy under your command disappeared upwards into the darkness..." It'd make a change from sinking and disappearing downward, anyway.

"Deck there! Eight ships, but..."

"Belay it!" Ramage interrupted. "Come down and report – unless there's any reason why you've got to stay up there."

"None, sir; coming down."

Ramage muttered to Southwick: "No need for everyone in the ship…"

"Quite, sir. But the scuttlebutt…"

Southwick was right. The day that the ships of a fleet could pass messages to each other as quickly as gossip passed round a vessel, an admiral's task would be easy.

Jackson was standing there and as he went to speak Southwick suddenly snapped at the men at the wheel and the quartermaster near them: "Watch your luff, blast you!"

There wasn't an ear in the ship that wasn't trying to listen to Jackson's report.

"Eight ships, sir; but from on deck it must look like seven."

"Explain, Jackson; explain for people with little intelligence, like Mr Southwick and myself."

Ramage regretted the sarcasm as soon as he'd spoken; Jackson had a difficult report to make.

"Sorry, sir, I was going to. From aloft I can see that the seventh and eighth ships are alongside each other. That's the one that joined us last, the *Peacock*, and her next ahead."

"How do you know it's the eighth ship?"

"I can make out the seventh ship in each of the next two columns. This column's the only one with an eighth ship. Seems to me she's got out of position and gone aboard her next ahead, sir."

"Are they still under way or dropping back?"

"Under way, sir: the seventh one is in position."

"No lights showing from the seventh ship? No sign of distress?"

"Nothing, sir. Everything looks normal – except they're alongside each other!"

"Very well; get aloft again and give a hail when you sight anything more. Particularly if they drop astern."

Again Jackson disappeared quickly and quietly.

"Mightn't have actually been in collision, sir," Southwick said doubtfully. "Their yards would lock...At that distance and from this angle...might just *look* as though one's aboard the other."

"That's why I sent Jackson up again with the glass," Ramage said pointedly.

"I know, sir." Southwick was reproachful. "I was just trying to understand why two ships running aboard each other don't do something about it. Flash lanterns, fire a gun, light a false fire...Not reasonable for them to carry on on the same course with sails set, as though nothing had happened."

"Never trust mules..."

"Quite, sir," Southwick said. "And never assume any of the other escorts will spot something."

Southwick was right: the *Greyhound* or the *Lark*, both of which were much closer, should have spotted something amiss. Still, both were used to convoy work and wearily resigned to half the convoy dropping astern in the darkness...

"Deck there!"

"Captain here."

"Last ship's dropped back now, sir. Both of 'em in their rightful positions again, and both under reefed topsails."

"Very well, down from aloft."

"Just mules," Southwick said sourly. "The *Peacock*'s mate dozed off, I expect. I'll bet he's getting a brisk rub from her captain."

Ramage paced back and forth along the starboard side of the quarterdeck for ten minutes, trying to decide why such a tiny episode seemed important. Was he getting things out of proportion? He would have asked Southwick if he could only think of a way of phrasing the question.

"I'm going below: you have the night orders."

"Aye aye, sir."

Down in his cabin Ramage bent over his desk, trying to write up his journal by the dim light of the lanthorn. Little of the guttering candle's light penetrated the horn shield, but anything stronger would show through the skylight. He began writing a three-line record of the day's events, occasionally referring to the Master's rough log.

He had relieved Southwick, stood an uneventful night watch and slept again before he was woken with hot coffee before dawn next morning. As the steward began methodically setting out washing and shaving gear round the washbasin, Ramage discovered that by some magic process he had reached a decision while he slept. He would report the *Peacock* episode to the Admiral in writing, and risk being sneered at as an alarmist. It *was* just a tiny episode and probably either or both captains had a perfectly satisfactory explanation. But the *Triton* could not go back and find out without orders from the Admiral, and no such orders could be given until the Admiral received a report.

As soon as he'd drunk his coffee, washed and shaved and dressed, Ramage picked up his hat and telescope and went up on deck for the dawn ritual of general quarters. In time of war every one of the King's ships at sea met the new day with her men at the guns ready for action. No one knew what daylight would bring – a clear horizon, or an enemy ship, or even a squadron – lurking a mile or so to windward. Even as he reached the top of the companionway the bosun's mates were running through the ship, calling men to quarters.

Southwick was on watch, having just relieved Appleby, the young master's mate, and greeted Ramage cheerfully. For Southwick every dawn had the attraction of a bottle of rum for an alcoholic. Ramage almost shuddered; he needed at least an hour after quitting his cot before he felt cheerful.

"No more nonsense over there," Southwick said, gesturing towards the tail of the convoy. "Have you decided whether...?"

"Yes," Ramage said shortly, "I shall."

"I'm glad, sir, but it's going to be hard to put in writing what's really just a – a sort of feeling, like a twinge in your back when you know it's going to rain."

Men were gliding to the guns. Thanks to many hours of training and constant exercises there was no shouting and no fuss; a landsman would have no idea that the movement of those shadowy figures now meant the *Triton* could open fire within a few seconds.

It was chilly on deck now but within an hour or two of the sun rising the wooden planks would be uncomfortably hot to stand on and the air warm to breathe. Now there was a delicious chill and more than a hint of dampness which brought out the smell of things, whether stinking or mildewy clothes, the sickly-sweet of the bilges or the clean tang of fresh, hot coffee.

As the black of night turned to grey, Ramage could distinguish the binnacle box, quite apart from the faint light inside illuminating the compass. In a few minutes, he'd be able to identify the two men at the wheel and the quartermaster standing near them. He could see the outline of the capstan just forward of the companionway and the gilding on the top of it would be noticeable soon. The mainmast seemed curiously big in the half light.

It would soon be time to order the lookouts aloft. It was a thankless job – yet one Ramage had always enjoyed in his midshipman days. In the Tropics it was hot up the mast and in a cold climate there was precious little shelter, but you were alone and you could see all that went on: the ships on the horizon and everything that happened on deck. And it was exciting, after days and weeks at sea, to spot another sail, or land, and to be the first to hail the deck and report it.

Suddenly Southwick was bellowing, "Lookouts away aloft!" and Ramage realized that he had been staring into space, oblivious of where he was. By the time he pulled himself back to the present, the lookouts were reporting.

"Deck there – horizon clear except for the convoy."

"Search to the north-east again," Southwick shouted.

"Horizon to the nor'east clear, sir."

That covered the arc for which the *Triton* was responsible. Ramage thought for a moment and remembered that Jackson would be on watch now: it was easier to send him than give instructions to the lookouts.

"Send Jackson aloft with a glass, Mr Southwick. See what he makes of those two mules now."

Two minutes later Jackson hailed the deck.

"Both ships look normal. No damage showing. The whole tail of the convoy has straggled. Several ships on the horizon from the middle of the convoy. The *Lark*'s out there chasing 'em up."

Southwick looked questioningly at Ramage, who shook his head: there was nothing more for Jackson to do so Southwick ordered him down and, at a further word from Ramage, gave the orders that set the men securing the carronades. Dawn had not revealed any enemies, and down below the cook was rattling his coppers and lighting the galley fire – a new day had begun.

Sitting at his tiny desk as soon as it was light enough to see, Ramage drafted his report to the Admiral. His pen spattered ink as he crossed out words and phrases and wrote in new ones. Finally, with the page looking like a schoolboy's exercise book, he took a fresh sheet of paper and wrote the corrected draft so that he could read it through without pausing to decipher his own handwriting.

It still read oddly, but he decided that this was because the subject was odd rather than because of his wording. He folded the paper, took the stub of candle from the lanthorn, heated some wax, then pressed his seal into the red blob. He blew out the candle, pushed it back into the holder in the lanthorn and called on his steward to serve him breakfast.

Late that afternoon Ramage sat in his cabin with Southwick and the ship's surgeon, Bowen. All three were drinking the fresh lemonade which Ramage's steward made from a stock of lemons and limes which he kept to himself.

Southwick sipped his drink and said amiably to the doctor: "How long is it now?"

The doctor frowned as he thought. "Five months or more."

"Do you ever feel you want a glass of rum?" Ramage asked.

Bowen shook his head. "Not spirits, nor wine. It's curious – I never even think about them now. It's not that the idea nauseates me, or that I'm fighting myself not to have them: I'm just not interested."

"You're lucky," Southwick said bluntly. "When I think of all those games of chess…"

He sounded so mournful that both Ramage and Bowen burst out laughing.

"It improved *your* game, anyway!" Bowen said. "You're a passable player, now."

"Southwick regarded the chess as the hardest part of your cure," Ramage said.

"It was – for him," Bowen said. "And a miracle for me. My wife will know by now," he said with obvious pride. "I wrote to her from Barbados."

Ramage nodded because there was nothing to say. When he had first joined the ship, Bowen, who had once been one of the finest surgeons in London, was a besotted wreck, unfit to practise medicine and unable to open his eyes in the morning without a stiff drink. Ramage could hardly believe that the cure had worked. It had been hard for him and Southwick – and in the later stages had involved playing interminable games of chess with Bowen to take his mind off drink – but it had been unbelievably hard for Bowen. Ramage could still remember watching him in the grip of *delirium tremens*, screaming as imaginary monsters swooped down to attack him.

"You'll soon be reopening your surgery in Wimpole Street," Ramage said. "Do you look forward to London again?"

Bowen shook his head. "No. I want to see my wife again, of course, but I'd like to serve with you for as long as…"

"But in London you were…" Ramage broke off, unsure if he understood the look in Bowen's eyes.

"In London, sir," Bowen said softly, "I spent most of my time treating imaginary ailments with useless nostrums. My patients were rich and I presented them with large bills. They judged the success of the cure by the size of the bill. There's more to the practice of medicine than that."

"But you could be a rich man," protested Southwick.

"I could, I was and I probably still am. My wife is not without means, anyway."

"Well then!" Southwick said lamely.

"Well then yourself," Bowen said affably. "Tell me, Southwick, does it give you any satisfaction navigating this ship safely from one side of the Atlantic to the other?"

"Well, the Captain…" Southwick said, embarrassed at the question.

"Don't be so modest," Ramage said. "Answer the doctor's question!"

"Well, yes, it's bound to."

"Why are you such a special man, then?" Bowen asked, still grinning.

When Southwick shook his head, puzzled at the question, Bowen said: "You get satisfaction when the *Triton* arrives safely in port. I get satisfaction when the *Triton* arrives with all her crew fit. Not one name on the sick list!"

Ramage stared at Bowen.

"Surely you can't be interested in all the costive problems, venereal disease, cuts, blisters and abrasions of more than fifty seamen?"

Bowen shook his head but said simply: "Not as such. But a true answer to your question would be that I find the most worthwhile thing I've ever done in my life is to make sure that more than fifty shipmates on board the *Triton*, from the captain to the boy drummer, remain fit. I believe in preventing disease: that's the best way of curing it. My pleasure comes in writing in my journal, day after day, 'No cases reported.' "

Southwick nodded appreciatively, and Ramage said simply, "Thank you."

"It's nothing," Bowen said with a wry grin. "The two of you have saved me from a fate worse than Wimpole Street."

"We'll probably end up the chess champions of the Navy," Ramage said. "We must start a tournament."

"We're a set of pawns at the moment," Southwick said with sudden bitterness.

Bowen glanced at Ramage. "Might we ask how things went on board the flagship, sir...?"

"A certain amount of cynical indifference."

"I can imagine," Bowen said sympathetically.

Ramage doubted if he could. After being given permission to pass within hail, Ramage had taken the *Triton* over to a position just to windward of the *Lion*. Very grudgingly Captain Croucher had agreed to heave-to long enough for a boat from the *Triton* to get alongside and Appleby, the Master's mate, had delivered the letter and returned to the *Triton*.

Half an hour later when the *Triton* was back on station, the flagship had signalled for the *Greyhound* to see if the *Peacock* or her next ahead required assistance.

It seemed a stupid order, but for the life of him Ramage could not be quite sure why he thought so or why he was so angry. If either ship had wanted assistance she would have made the signal long since, so Goddard was simply covering himself. Lieutenant Ramage reported possible trouble, the captains of both ships reported that they were quite all right. If he had been the convoy commander he would have sent an officer on board each ship to find out what had happened. But, to be fair to Croucher and Goddard, their only information about the incident came from an officer they distrusted.

"We don't have to fret about it," Bowen said in an even voice, tactfully offering advice to someone who was half his age but still his captain. "Tell me, sir, do we call in at Antigua?"

Ramage shook his head. "I doubt it; probably won't even sight it. I expect the Admiral will detach the Antigua ships and order one of the frigates to see them in the last forty or fifty miles."

"Pity," Bowen said, "I was looking forward to seeing the island."

"You're not missing anything," Southwick said. "It's dull and dry and English Harbour is airless – and bad holding ground."

"And Jamaica?"

Southwick shrugged his shoulders. "They can't be compared. Jamaica's a big island and Kingston a big city. Many parts of Jamaica are very beautiful – the Blue Mountains, for instance. But all these islands keep you doctors and the undertakers busy."

Ramage took out his watch. This was the accepted signal that their afternoon's relaxation was over. The cabin was growing dark as Bowen stood up and asked: "The swell is increasing, I notice. Is this a bad sign?"

Ramage nodded. "I'm afraid so, at this time of year."

"Does it definitely mean we'll get a hurricane?"

"No, by no means! It might mean that there's one out there in the Atlantic, but there's no telling if it'll come our way. They're like thunderstorms – impossible to guess which direction they'll take."

"Well, it'll be an interesting experience," Bowen said.

"I'll remind you of that remark if we run into it," Southwick growled. "It blows so hard you won't know whether you're a pawn or a bishop."

"Heaven forbid a bishop," Bowen said.

CHAPTER SEVEN

By nightfall the convoy, having gone through the chain of islands, was some twenty miles west of Dominica and steering north-north-west to pass the butterfly-shaped island of Guadeloupe, the only land in the area still held by the French. By passing far enough to the westward to be out of sight from the mountains, Ramage guessed, Goddard was hoping the convoy would not be spotted.

Ramage shrugged: whatever the French might do he was now more concerned about the swell. He had just noted in the log that the waves were about five feet high. The wind was still light – too light.

"Something's killed the Trade winds," Southwick commented.

"Stunned them, anyway," Ramage said wryly.

"Still, I suppose we shouldn't complain; the mules have behaved themselves today."

Ramage nodded. "They haven't had much choice, with the *Lark* chasing them up."

"I think the word's been passed along about the way we chase up, too."

"Yes – I was thinking about that merchantman when we went alongside the *Lion* this morning. Must have been like having a ship of the line coming up astern of us."

"I hope so," Southwick said fervently, "I'm in favour of anything that keeps these mules in position." He glanced round at the gathering darkness. "General quarters, sir?"

Ramage nodded, and glanced to the eastward where a thin layer of cloud on the horizon showed Dominica. "We'll leave the guns loaded and run out tonight."

He wasn't quite sure why he had decided that, but he picked up the telescope and looked round the convoy as Southwick bellowed the order that sent the *Triton's* crew running to their stations for battle. As he focused on the *Greyhound* he saw her guns run out and nodded approvingly: it was well done; the guns might all have been on one huge carriage. The same orders were being given in all the ships of the escort and he imagined that, as the world turned and dusk moved across the oceans, all the King's ships at sea sent their men to quarters and, as the world continued turning and brought the dawn, the men were roused out again to greet it.

He held the glass steady as he looked at the *Peacock*. A couple of men were at the wheel with another figure near them – probably the captain or a mate. Two men on the fo'c'sle, perhaps having a quiet smoke, since merchantmen did not have the strict rules laid down in warships. The ship ahead of the *Peacock* had the same number of men on deck. Everything looked normal on board both ships. He still wanted to know what the devil had been going on last night, but thanks to the Admiral's absurd signal to the *Greyhound* no one had yet asked either ship a direct question.

Yorke was at the taffrail of the *Topaz*: by now Ramage could recognize his stance. St Brieuc was with him and for a moment Ramage was envious of the young shipowner: he would have interesting company all the way to Jamaica. Southwick and Bowen and Appleby were good men, but their conversational range was limited. Yorke had Maxine's company too. As Ramage watched the men running out the guns and reporting as they did so, he tried to console himself with the thought that Yorke did not have a Gianna waiting for him in England…He went below.

It was dark when he got back on deck and the lookouts had been brought down from aloft. There were now six of them stationed round the ship: one on either bow, at the main chains both sides, and on each quarter.

The sky was clear and starlit except for a big bank of cloud to the south-west. It was hard for Ramage to pick out the ships on the far side of the convoy since they were against the cloud bank, instead of against the stars. The *Lion* stood out clearly, quite apart from her lights, and so did the *Topaz*. The *Greyhound*, too, and what was probably the *Lark*. Ramage moved the night glass slightly, hoping to make sure, and saw a movement.

The glass was swinging, and he had to move it back slowly to spot what had attracted him. It was the *Peacock*, the last ship in that column. He looked more carefully and, as he watched, there was another movement – the fore course was let fall, the canvas of the big sail came tumbling lazily down in the light wind. He could see it gradually taking up a billowing shape as the seamen braced the yard round and hauled home the sheets. Her main course was already set – that must have been what had first caught his eye. The *Peacock* was already turning slightly towards him, to starboard and out of the convoy.

"Mr Southwick, get your glass on the *Peacock*. Quartermaster – pass the word for my coxswain!"

"My oath!" exclaimed Southwick. "What's she up to now?"

Jackson reported and was told to get aloft with a night glass.

"Report anything unusual. Watch that last ship, the *Peacock*. She's leaving the line with her courses set. And see if the *Lark* lugger and the *Greyhound* spot her."

Ramage could see the *Greyhound* and she seemed to be continuing on the same course. Her masts were in line, she had reefed topsails and no other sails were being let fall. Apparently she hadn't noticed anything suspicious. But the cloud to the south-west now covered more of the sky and from the *Greyhound*'s position the *Peacock*'s silhouette probably blended in with the blackness.

"Could be in trouble, sir," Southwick said in a voice flat enough to show he had little enthusiasm for the idea. "Might be hauling her wind to close with the *Greyhound*. Sprung a leak…needs a surgeon…hard to say."

Jackson was hailing from aloft: "She hauled out of the line to windward, but now she's back on the convoy course and maybe fifty yards to windward. They'll never notice anything from the *Greyhound*," he added.

"No, the angle's wrong," Southwick muttered. "The lark might notice."

"I doubt it," Ramage said. "She's pretty far over."

Jackson called: "She's overhauling her next ahead. Both courses and topsails set. I think she's shaking out the reefs in her topsails."

"Not leaking," Southwick said. "Not on that course. So help me, why is it always us?"

Ramage was thinking the same thing. The *Greyhound*, whose captain was not out of favour with Admiral Goddard, and who was a post captain already on his way up the list, could afford to make a mistake. The *Greyhound* was nearer the *Peacock*, too. Why had the responsibility fallen on the *Triton*?

"Shall I turn up the hands?" Southwick asked.

"Yes, but quietly: don't let the bosun's mates pipe it, and no shouting. Noise carries on a night like this."

"Aye, we don't want to look foolish."

"Or warn anyone," Ramage said grimly.

"Deck there." Jackson called. "She's abreast her next ahead."

"With all that canvas set she'll come through like a surfboat," Southwick grumbled.

She's coming to the head of the convoy – that is obviously her intention, Ramage thought to himself, because she's set a lot more canvas and she's hauled clear of the line.

"Maybe she's leaving," Southwick said. "Decided to sail independently. She was a runner anyway, before she joined."

"I don't think so," Ramage said. "She's for Jamaica. If she was leaving the convoy why not reduce sail for a few minutes, let the convoy draw ahead and then bear away to the westward? Why steer north? She'd be crazy to pass the convoy on the outside – which is what she's trying to do now – and then have to cut right across in front of the *Lion*."

"Maybe she's decided to make for Antigua," Southwick said doggedly. "She's a runner, so her master can make up his own mind."

"True – but what could have changed his mind in the last twenty-four hours? There'd be nothing for him in Antigua except transhipment cargoes which wouldn't interest a runner. The good freights are in Jamaica and he knew it when he asked to join the convoy."

"It's a puzzle," Southwick admitted. "But he's certainly going a long way round for Jamaica."

Again Jackson hailed. "Abreast her second ahead, sir."

Now the *Peacock* must be just about abreast the *Greyhound*.

"That frigate's lookouts," Southwick suddenly snarled. "They ought to be flogged."

Ramage decided to reserve judgment until he saw how well the *Peacock* showed up against the cloud when she came abreast of the *Triton*. But, he told himself quickly, if she gets as far as that, I'd better be doing something about it! For the moment I can risk leaving her, but not for long.

Yet why the devil were he and Southwick getting so worked up over a ship out of position? In a convoy this size it'd be usual for at least ten ships to be out of position by now, and half the convoy would be spread all the way to the horizon by dawn. Why were they so obsessed by this miserable runner? He could imagine the Admiral's scornful sneers to Croucher, his flag lieutenant and anyone else who cared to listen about young Ramage deciding to declare war on a merchantman that displeased him...Was he getting obsessed?

All captains risked getting obsessions – it was part of the lonely life of command. The Navy understood the problem and was patient with such men. One he knew of had an obsession about flags – couldn't bear the idea of any flag having a speck of dirt on it or the slightest worn patch. Another couldn't bear brickdust on board and the men had to use fine sand for polishing brasswork. Where does Lieutenant Ramage fit into all that? Oh, he turns a merchantman into a fleet of enemy ships...

"Deck there! – abreast the fifth ship!" Jackson called, and a few minutes later: "Deck there! – abreast the fourth ship."

Merchantmen out of position always dropped astern. But both times when the *Peacock* had been out of position she had forged ahead...He turned to Southwick.

"Fetch Jackson down, and send the men to quarters."

Dammit, he'd left it late now; minutes wasted with a lot of daft thoughts. He put his speaking trumpet to his lips: "Marines stand by on the larboard side with muskets loaded;

boarders muster at the main chains with pikes and pistols, but keep clear of the guns!"

"Deck there!" Jackson hailed. "There's another ship moving up the inside of the column!"

"The devil there is!" exclaimed Southwick.

"Tell us ship and position, blast you!" Ramage snarled.

"I'm just trying to make sure, sir," said Jackson's chastened voice from above them in the darkness. "I think it's the one that was ahead of the *Peacock* – I'm just trying to give an idea," he added hastily, knowing how Ramage hated indecisive answers that included the phrases "I think" or "about".

"Yes, it's her all right – the seventh, and now she's abreast the sixth ship, and the *Peacock*'s abreast the third."

"Leave him up there," Ramage told Southwick, who had quietly passed the order that sent the men running silently to the guns.

Southwick asked, "What do you make of it, sir?"

"Damned if I know," Ramage admitted frankly. "It's some monkey business, but exactly what, I can't think. That second ship's the one the *Peacock* went aboard last night – why, it's absurd!"

"At least we're up to windward," Southwick said.

This was Ramage's only advantage: he could wait until the last moment before doing anything; wait until there could be no mistake about what the *Peacock* and the second ship intended to do. What, exactly, did he intend to do? Strictly speaking he ought probably to drop down to the *Peacock*, close with her and ask her what she was up to. If there was trouble he would have to explain to a court martial why he had not done so.

But he didn't want to show his hand until the last moment. He was certain that the *Peacock* was up to something sinister and there was very little time left. His greatest ally would be surprise, if he could avoid raising the alarm. If he was wrong, and there was an innocent explanation of the *Peacock*'s manoeuvres, the damned ship could give the Admiral all the ammunition he wanted to fire the final broadside into the Ramage family.

And he knew that Southwick was thinking of that, too; aye, and Jackson as well, up aloft there. They were all on his side; *and they could all be wrong…*

The *Peacock* was closing fast: Ramage was startled when he looked over the *Triton*'s quarter with the night glass: even though it showed the *Peacock* upside down, she nearly filled the eyepiece.

"Quickly, Mr Southwick; check over the larboard side guns; I wasn't listening as they reported."

"Aye aye, sir; I was, though, and all is well."

Southwick disappeared forward and again Ramage turned towards the *Peacock*, at the same time hailing Jackson to come down: the *Peacock* would soon be close enough to hear any shouting on board the *Triton*. If only there was some moonlight, so he could get a sight of the *Peacock*'s decks. Were they empty of all but the watch?

The Master reported: "All loaded and the men hoping they won't have to draw shot and powder."

It was a childishly reassuring report: the only way of avoiding having the men drawing shot and powder from the bore of a gun was to fire it.

The *Peacock* was almost abreast the second ship: almost abreast the ship astern of the *Topaz*: in one minute's time he had to do something…ye gods, *do* something! And he still hadn't given it any real thought. Suddenly he felt cold as he remembered Goddard's warning at the convoy conference about the valuable cargo. He knew now what the *Peacock* was doing and it was probably too late. He was so frightened he froze; the worst kind of fear, the fear for someone else.

"Mr Southwick!" His voice was high and he hoped the men would not notice. "Mr Southwick – I'm laying us aboard that rascal!"

He put the speaking trumpet to his mouth: "Man the weather braces – tend the lee ones…Quartermaster, larboard four points…Ease away and haul in; run away with it, lads…right, tally aft those sheets…"

Why hadn't he shaken the reefs out of the topsails? He had thought of it earlier and decided against it for fear the *Peacock* would see men out on his yards, but he'd been wrong: he needed every square inch of canvas now to catch up.

As the *Triton's* bow swung round towards the *Topaz*, the great yards overhead slowly moved, keeping the sails filled. Men, one behind the other on the ropes like one side of a tug of war, hauled and strained.

Within a minute the *Triton* was steering for the head of the convoy. He could just see the *Peacock* silhouetted, larger and closer. The convoy was moving slowly to starboard; he now needed to steer a converging course, slightly crabwise to starboard.

Hurriedly he shouted once again the orders to trim the sails. A few words to the quartermaster and the *Triton's* bowsprit swung slightly to starboard, heading towards where the *Peacock* should be in a few minutes. Should be – damn and blast, he'd never make it under just topsails, but it'd throw the ship – and himself, if he was honest – into confusion if he set the forecourse now, and then tried to get it clewed up as he turned alongside the *Peacock*.

Last-minute rush and stupidity was what lost battles, and he was proving it…

With the wind almost dead astern, the *Triton* was at last picking up a bit of speed: the seas, too, were now dead astern, instead of being on the quarter, and that small fact added its quota to her speed through the water.

"Puzzle to know whether to raise the alarm or not," Southwick said, and Ramage realized that the old Master was thinking aloud, not asking a question. He was holding something out to Ramage – a cutlass.

As Ramage took it he noticed that Southwick had buckled on his own huge sword, a real meat-cleaver.

"You stay on board, Mr Southwick," he said. "No dashing over with a boarding party. That will be Appleby's job. Hear that, Appleby?"

"Aye aye, sir," the Master's mate answered cheerfully, waving his cutlass. "My party's all ready."

Since Ramage had guessed what the *Peacock* probably intended he had done all he could to counter it. But there was still just a chance that he was completely wrong and the *Peacock* entirely innocent.

There would be nearly a minute, as the *Triton* turned on to a parallel course, in which he had to decide whether he shouted a cheerful warning to the *Peacock*, or fired a broadside into her, killing a dozen possibly innocent men.

He didn't want to be babbling sail and helm orders while he made up his mind so he turned to the Master: "Mr Southwick, take the conn, if you please. Steer to converge on the *Peacock*. We'll luff at the last moment if she's not up to mischief; otherwise put me alongside her."

The Master said: "It'll be a pleasure, sir; leave it to me."

Leave the ship to me, he might have been saying, but don't make any mistakes with the thinking part. Ramage felt deep affection for the man, and wondered if anyone else could give so much and such good advice without speaking a word.

Ramage stuck the cutlass in the deck beside him and watched the *Peacock* through his night glass, cursing the inverted image. There were no more than three or four men on deck but suddenly the main and forecourse changed shape, like curtains being lifted to the yards.

"They're clewing up their courses!"

Southwick had spotted it too and Ramage put down the glass. The *Peacock* was less than a hundred yards from the *Topaz* and yet none of Yorke's people had shouted or fired a warning musket. They might have spotted her, but since they knew nothing of last night's episode they might not be suspicious. He pictured the officer of the watch idly watching...

Should he fire a shot to warn the *Topaz* or hold on and hope to surprise the *Peacock* by slapping the *Triton* alongside her?

He was just going to order the forwardmost gun to fire a warning when he saw sails moving beyond the third ship in the column. It was the *Peacock*'s next ahead and he'd forgotten all about her. He'd clean forgotten half the potential enemy force, but it didn't make much difference as it happened. There was nothing he could do about it: the *Peacock* would occupy all his energy.

Now Southwick was bellowing the order that would bring the *Triton* alongside the runner and was looking to Ramage for orders. Were they to open fire or not? Was he to crash the brig alongside, risk carrying away masts, and prepare to send a boarding party over as soon as the carronades had swept the decks a few times?

Ramage could not decide. All he could see were three or four men on the *Peacock*'s quarterdeck, and a few more men clewing up the courses. There was nothing really wrong with that and the *Peacock* still had fifty yards or so to go before she was abreast the *Topaz*. Then the distance between the masts changed slightly: the *Peacock* was turning to larboard: turning just enough so that a further turn of a few degrees to starboard could lay her alongside the *Topaz!*

But still nothing had happened that could tell him for certain that the *Peacock* was an enemy ship bent on attacking the *Topaz* rather than a friendly ship out of position on a dark night…

"Sir!" Southwick had been wailing the word for several seconds. He had to know now whether to luff up or lay her alongside: no further delay was possible.

"Put her alongside," Ramage heard himself shouting and, using the speaking trumpet, added: "Gun captains! Hold your fire until I give the order – then aim for the quarterdeck!"

The *Triton's* jibboom had been pointing just ahead of the *Peacock*, but in response to Southwick's orders it swung away to starboard and the merchantman moved round to broad on the *Triton's* bow. The combined movement of the two ships made it seem as though the *Peacock* was coming sideways towards the *Triton*; a fast-moving nightmare. Upside down in the night glass, black maggots swarmed suddenly over the *Peacock's* decks, and without consciously registering what he had seen, Ramage bellowed:

"Gun captains – fire as you bear!"

As the first carronade fired the flash lit up the *Peacock* like a flicker of summer lightning. With awful clarity he saw that the *Peacock's* decks were now covered with armed men. Scores and scores of them had been hiding below the bulwarks. As other carronades fired he saw more men pouring up from below, their cutlasses glinting in the flashes of gunfire. The *Peacock* was not yet alongside the *Topaz*, which he could just make out twenty or thirty yards beyond. Almost unbelievably the *Triton* had arrived just in time.

Just in time, if he could stop the *Peacock* being manoeuvred those last few yards to the *Topaz*. Nothing could save the *Topaz* or even the *Triton* from that swarm of men once the *Peacock* was alongside.

"Aim at the wheel!" he screamed at the men at the carronades. "Gun captains – the wheel!" In the flashes of gunfire he saw Jackson standing on the bulwark carefully aiming a musketoon, methodically aiming and firing it and passing it down to be reloaded, while another loaded one was handed up to him. Standing beside him on the bulwark, Ramage saw that the men in the *Peacock* were in confusion, and guessed her captain had been so sure he'd get alongside the *Topaz* before the *Triton* could reach him that he had all his gunners at the larboard side guns, ready to sweep the merchantman.

Not one of the *Peacock*'s starboard side guns had fired back at the *Triton* yet and Ramage decided to take advantage of the fact. Leaping down from the bulwarks he ran over to Southwick and shouted, above the thunder of the carronades: "Stay twenty yards off – I want to give them a good pounding with the guns, otherwise we don't stand a chance against all those men: they'll swarm over us!"

Southwick bellowed into his speaking trumpet, choosing moments between the guns firing, and as Ramage rejoined Jackson at the bulwark the brig settled down to a course parallel with the *Peacock* but twenty yards to windward. Ramage watched warily for the first sign that the *Peacock* was going to try to luff up and get alongside the *Triton*.

The gunners were settling into a steady rhythm and the flash as each carronade fired momentarily lit up the *Peacock*, like a furnace door being opened quickly and shut. The flashes showed the *Peacock*'s deck was now clearing: there were small dark piles of bodies where grapeshot had torn into her boarders, but the rest had dispersed to find some shelter. Ramage knew many must be crouching in the lee of the bulwark, waiting for the *Triton*s to board.

Suddenly Ramage realized the *Topaz* was no longer ahead of the *Peacock*. He glanced round in alarm and it took him several moments to realize that the *Peacock* must have come round to starboard a little – with the *Triton* conforming – and, sailing faster than the convoy, had left the rest of the ships astern. The nearest part of the convoy was now a good half a mile away on the starboard quarter. The *Topaz* was safe now, whatever happened to the *Triton*.

There was a flash from the *Peacock*'s side: one of her guns had been loaded and fired. Ramage heard neither the thud of a hit nor the noise of a shot passing close. As soon as all the *Peacock*'s starboard side guns were firing, it would be time to try the other tack.

He banged Jackson on the shoulder. "Tell Mr Southwick to make sure all the starboard side guns are loaded with grape, and to pass the word when that's done and he's ready to wear ship!"

Another flash from the *Peacock*'s side, and then another. Three guns manned and firing, and three more to go. With luck one or two had been damaged...

Jackson, pulling at his shoulder, reported that the starboard guns were already loaded and the Master ready to wear.

Another flash from the *Peacock*'s side warned him four guns were now manned. He knew it was time to attack from the other side...

He jumped down onto the deck and strode over to Southwick, but even before he could give any orders Jackson was beside him gesticulating. Ramage turned to see another ship coming up on the *Peacock*'s larboard quarter.

"The *Greyhound* frigate, sir!" Jackson yelled.

So there was no need to wear round to attack the *Peacock* on the other side.

As he watched the frigate, Ramage heard yelling and shouting coming from the *Peacock*; excited cries that carried over the noise of carronades and musketoons.

The shouting was in French, and he thought he could hear "Board her!" being constantly repeated. He went back to the bulwark and tried to concentrate his thoughts while, one after another, the carronades gave enormous, heavy coughs as they fired and then crashed back in recoil in a series of rumbles which shook the whole deck.

The stretch of water between the two ships, the waves slopping darkly but constantly reflecting the flash of gunfire, was too narrow. Too late, Ramage realized what was happening. The *Peacock*, sheering away from the approaching *Greyhound*, was running aboard the *Triton*.

"Stand by to repel boarders!" Ramage shouted at the top of his voice and at the same instant realized he was unarmed: the cutlass given him by Southwick was still stuck in the deck somewhere. He could hear the Master repeating his cry, but it was unnecessary: there was not a man in the *Triton* who did not realize there was no chance of the *Triton* avoiding the *Peacock* crashing alongside.

Ramage glanced back at the *Greyhound*: she was coming up fast – she had perhaps two ship's lengths to go before she was alongside the *Peacock*. A matter of minutes, almost moments. And in that time the bunch of cut-throats in the *Peacock* – obviously French privateersmen, although he hadn't the slightest idea how they got there – would have slaughtered every man in the *Triton*.

There was no point in standing up here on the bulwark like a pheasant on a gate, Ramage told himself; he could see all that was necessary from the deck. He jumped down and ran over to the rack of boarding pikes fitted round the mainmast. As he snatched one, the brig gave a sudden lurch: the *Peacock* had crashed alongside.

Boarding nets, Ramage thought with irritation: I didn't order them to be rigged up. But there was no sudden swarm of screaming Frenchmen over the top of the *Triton*'s bulwarks; instead the men at the guns continued sponging, loading, ramming, running out and firing into the French ship.

As he realized the enemy was not still alongside he saw Southwick was standing beside him, shouting something…"Managed to turn to starboard enough to dodge…Should I repeat it if the *Peacock* – "

"Yes, right now!" Ramage yelled as he felt the *Peacock* crash alongside once more and saw men holding on to her rigging, poised to jump and waving cutlasses that glinted in the flash of the guns.

Every available Triton was waiting at the bulwarks. Many had muskets, with cutlasses slung over their shoulders; others held boarding pikes, the seven-feet-long ash staves with long, narrow spear tips.

A flash and a noise like tearing canvas warned Ramage that a roundshot from one of the *Peacock*'s guns had missed him by a matter of inches. Then he saw, in the flash from one of the *Triton*'s guns, eight or ten Frenchmen toppling from the *Peacock*'s main shrouds. It took him a few seconds to realize that the *Triton*'s Marines were clearing the *Peacock*'s rigging by firing volleys from the musketoons. It said something for the coolness of the Marine corporal…

Suddenly there were twenty Frenchmen screaming and scrambling at the bulwarks where Ramage had been standing: they had all leapt at the same instant and, Ramage guessed, misjudged the distance slightly in the darkness. Instinctively Ramage lunged with the boarding pike, felt the wood jar his arms as the point came hard up against bone, and wrenched it back ready to stab again into the mass of men.

Jackson and Stafford were beside him, screaming like madmen and slashing with their cutlasses; a stream of blasphemy in Italian, the Genoese accent unmistakable, showed that Rossi was close by.

More Frenchmen were streaming on board and overrunning the carronades, and out of the corner of his eye Ramage saw Jackson slip. A Frenchman paused above him, bracing to slash down with his sword. Without thinking Ramage hurled the boarding pike like a spear and caught the Frenchman in the side of the chest. As he fell, Jackson got to his feet again and waved cheerfully before leaping at the nearest group of boarders.

Ramage caught sight of a cutlass lying on the deck, snatched it up and turned back towards the *Peacock*. There was a bellow of wrath a few feet away and he caught sight of Southwick, hatless and his white hair sticking up like a mop, slashing away with his enormous sword and driving three Frenchmen before him.

But there was something odd about the Frenchmen now; no more were boarding and the shouting was dying down. In fact, he suddenly noticed, many of them were scrambling back on board the *Peacock*.

Then the dull rumble of a heavy broadside warned him that the *Greyhound* frigate had just run aboard the *Peacock* on the larboard side.

All over the brig there were small groups of Tritons hacking and slashing away with pikes and cutlasses at groups of similarly armed Frenchmen, but there was something else happening. Ramage knew he would have to pause a moment before he could fathom what it was. The screaming Frenchman with whom he was fighting suddenly collapsed, stabbed by Rossi's pike, and Ramage leapt sideways and made for the mainmast. Standing with his back against it, cutlass in his right hand, he looked across at the *Peacock* and realized that all three ships, locked together, were slowly swinging. The "something else" that puzzled him was the change in movement as they swung broadside on to the sea in the lee of the *Greyhound*.

He stared at the *Peacock*'s masts, and then at her shrouds. There was no doubt about it – she was drawing away from the *Triton*. A moment later a group of Frenchmen noticed it and scrambled on to the bulwark to try to get back on board. But the gap was too wide: the *Greyhound* must have rigged grapnels from the ends of her yards and these were holding the *Peacock* alongside. The *Triton*, with nothing holding her against the *Peacock*, was drifting off to leeward.

There would be no more boarders now, and he must quickly rally the Tritons.

He ran to the wheel shouting, "Tritons! To me, Tritons!"

Other seamen took up the cry as they joined Ramage until it was a regular chant by thirty or more men, among them Southwick. Now he could clear the ship of the enemy, but as he was about to shout the orders he heard a terrible wail and saw that most of the remaining boarders had rushed to the larboard side and were looking at the *Peacock*, now ten yards away. Some of their shipmates appeared at her bulwarks and began throwing lines over the side. With that one Frenchman after another jumped into the sea and began splashing his way back to the *Peacock*.

Within a minute Ramage and Southwick were staring at each other in amazement: there was not one able-bodied Frenchman left on board the *Triton*.

"I want a dozen men to deal with the wounded," Ramage told Southwick, "and all the larboard side guns are to be reloaded. Let's get the ship under way again and give the *Greyhound* a hand."

Before all the wounded had been carried below and the sails trimmed, the firing from the *Peacock*'s guns had become sporadic. The thunder of the *Greyhound*'s broadsides continued for another four or five minutes before stopping abruptly, signalling that the *Peacock* had been captured.

An hour passed before Ramage, tacking the *Triton* up to windward again, found the convoy and got back into position. By then Bowen had reported the casualties to him. Six Tritons had been killed – all by the *Peacock*'s six-pounders – and, by what Ramage privately thought could only be a miracle, only five had been wounded. The French boarding party had left eight dead behind, but had apparently taken their wounded with them. Privateersmen, never giving or asking quarter, took care of their wounded whenever it was possible.

The *Topaz* was back in position, leading the column; but there were only six ships in the column itself. Ramage wondered what had become of the second ship that came up the inside of the column. As far as he could remember, he had not noticed it firing a single shot…But all that mattered was that Maxine's ship was safe.

CHAPTER EIGHT

As the grey dawn pushed the darkness westward away from the convoy, Ramage looked round the horizon anxiously until he sighted both the *Greyhound* and the *Peacock* over on the lee side of the convoy. It was still not light enough to distinguish detail, but since the *Peacock* had sail set, the Greyhounds must have had a busy night.

Ramage was weary. As soon as he could leave the ship to Southwick he had gone below to talk to the wounded, while on deck the dead were being sewn into hammocks ready for burial. After that he had gone to his cabin to write his report to Admiral Goddard – potentially the most dangerous part of the night's activities.

At daylight, with a clear horizon, the guns were secured and head-pumps rigged to scrub and holystone the deck. Large patches which had shown up black in the early light had finally revealed themselves as dried blood.

As they scrubbed, Stafford asked Jackson: "Will they take 'er into Antigua?"

The American shrugged his shoulders. "If she isn't damaged too much...otherwise Jamaica, I should think. Better off in Jamaica – big dockyard at Kingston."

"Better price in the prize court there, too," Stafford commented.

"Hmm, I hadn't thought of that. Still, we won't get much."

"Why?" Rossi demanded angrily. "We did all the fighting! But for us they lose the *Topaz*. The *Greyhound* – she is very late."

"All ships of war in sight at the time get a share," Jackson said.

"*Dio mio*, is not fair!" Rossi exclaimed, his accent thickening the more angry he became. "The *Lion* and the frigates – the lugger, too – why, is so dark they see nozzing! The *Grey'ound* – 'e only come after the flashes. Next time we write 'im a letter of the invitation!"

"Easy now," Stafford said mildly. "Listen, Jacko, I know that's the law, but why?"

"If another warship's in sight, it might affect what the prize did."

"Cor, wot a lot o' nonsense!"

"No it isn't. Could be you one day. Say the *Lark* lugger found a big merchantman and chased her. Not a hope of catching up, and precious little of capturing her if she did. Then we come over the horizon ahead of the merchantman and capture her. The *Lark* has a right to a share – after all, she found and chased the prize: but for her she might have gone in a different direction. And we'd deserve a share, because without us she couldn't have been captured. And if there was a third warship they'd probably deserve a share because that's another direction the merchantman couldn't have escaped."

"Yus, well that makes sense, Jacko; but this was in the *dark*."

"Dark or not," Jackson explained patiently, "the *Peacock* knew the rest of them were there. She wouldn't have tried to bolt across the bows of the convoy – she knew the *Lion* and *Antelope* were there. Nor astern, because of the *Greyhound* and *Lark*."

A few yards aft of the three men, Ramage and Southwick were also discussing the night's events, the Master saying vehemently: "I don't care what you say, I'm damned certain that the *Greyhound* was there only because she was trying to keep station on us; she wasn't bothering to watch the convoy. We could have gone ten miles ahead of the convoy towing a seine net and the Lord Mayor's carriage, and come dawn we'd have found the *Greyhound* six cables astern of us."

Ramage laughed and shrugged his shoulders. "Doesn't matter, really; the main thing is she was there when needed."

"If you'll excuse me, sir, you're generous to a fault. She was there all right, but by accident."

Ramage grinned. "I'll be more interested to hear how the *Peacock* talked her way into the convoy in the first place..."

"Haa!" Southwick snorted and waved towards the *Lion*. "Belike they'll have a good tale ready. And it wouldn't surprise me if we don't get involved in it; in return for saving his reputation, his High and Mightyship will somehow put the blame on us."

"Mr Southwick!" Ramage said reprovingly.

"Apologies, sir," the Master said hurriedly, realizing that Ramage wanted him to apologize because seamen nearby could have overheard his criticism of Admiral Goddard. "I'm sorry, that was a stupid remark."

An hour later, though, Southwick was more than ever convinced that the Admiral and his Flag Captain would make sure that none of the blame rested on their shoulders. He clattered down the companionway, acknowledged the Marine sentry's salute, and obeyed Ramage's invitation to come into the cabin.

"Flagship's just signalled, sir. You're wanted on board. The Captain of the *Greyhound* has just left the *Lion*."

Ramage patted the packet on the table. "I'm glad I stayed up late writing this. Have some coffee – there's some in that pot."

When Southwick shook his head, he added: "You ought to make the best of it while we are in the Caribbean: not often we get the real stuff!"

"Afraid I prefer my tea, sir; seems Frenchified, coffee."

Ramage looked up at him with pretended disapproval. "That sort of attitude won't make these planters rich – " he waved towards the chain of islands. "They depend on coffee, sugar and rum."

"The Navy's Board's a good customer for rum, anyway."

"It's just as well they are: I doubt the planters will ever lure the English away from their gin."

"The Admiral…" Southwick reminded him.

"Ah yes," Ramage said, with a flippancy he did not feel, "obviously a social invitation. He breakfasts later than I do."

He picked up the packet and reached for his hat and sword. "Well, Mr Southwick, if you'll heave-to the ship to windward of the flagship, I'll climb into my carriage and Jackson can drive me over to see the Admiral."

Rear-Admiral Goddard had been badly frightened and now he was furious. By contrast Croucher's thin face gave nothing away. Both men were trying to hide from Ramage that the attack on the *Topaz* was their main concern.

"Tell me again, Ramage: how did this begin?" Goddard said, tapping his knee with Ramage's report, which he had not yet opened.

"The ship's company had stood down from general quarters, sir," Ramage said. "I was on deck and looking casually round at the convoy with my night glass. I happened to glance at the *Peacock* just as she let fall her fore course."

"A great pity you hadn't seen her main course let fall," Goddard snapped.

"I did, sir; that was the movement that first attracted my attention. They were still bracing the yard round and sheeting home when I saw them set the fore course."

"We have only your word for that."

"Of course, sir," Ramage said, but couldn't resist adding quietly, "It's a pity we have no corroboration from the *Greyhound*…"

Croucher glanced at him quickly and Goddard looked away, saying, "Then what did you do?"

"Sent a man aloft with a glass. He reported she was hauling her wind. She then came onto a course parallel with the convoy's and about fifty yards to windward."

"But you didn't see fit to inform me," Goddard said.

"No, sir," Ramage said flatly.

"Note that, Mr Croucher. The Admiral's not important enough, eh Ramage?"

"I didn't mean that, sir. If you were informed every time a ship of the convoy was out of position, you'd receive a hundred signals a day."

"But this was an unusual circumstance."

"It didn't seem so unusual at the time: no one knew she was anything but an ordinary merchantman."

"If there was nothing unusual, why did you send a lookout aloft?"

A good question, Ramage thought to himself.

"I did say 'so unusual' sir. I sent a man aloft because I saw she'd set her courses, but – "

"Why had she set her courses?" Croucher interrupted.

"To attack the *Topaz*, sir," Ramage said evenly. "I know that now, but I could hardly be expected to know that at the time."

"Why not? She was the obvious target!"

"Indeed?" Ramage pretended surprise and could not resist adding: "I had no idea, sir, and as far as I knew the *Peacock* was an ordinary merchantman the Admiral had allowed to join the convoy."

Goddard waved a hand at Croucher, as if telling him to be quiet.

"You couldn't know," he said. "It wouldn't have mattered if the *Peacock*'s next ahead" – he broke off, realizing that was a bad example – "or any other ship for that matter – had been the target: you should have warned me."

Ramage could see the way that Goddard was shaping his defence. He would tell the Admiralty that Lieutenant Ramage had known all about the attack but had not told him. Very well, he thought, you have a fight on your hands, and here goes the first broadside: "I had already warned you, sir: I'd told you all I knew."

"You did what?" Goddard exclaimed.

"I warned you, sir."

"D'you hear that, Croucher?" he asked sarcastically. "Lieutenant Ramage had *already* warned me!"

Croucher knew what Ramage meant, and tried to tell the Admiral – "I think I underst – "

"But he says he *warned* me, my dear Croucher: have you ever heard such impudence?"

"The letter, sir," Croucher said lamely.

"The letter?"

Ramage said, "My written report, sir: the one I delivered yesterday morning."

"Oh that," Goddard said, dismissing it with a shrug. "You could hardly expect me to pay any attention to that, could you?"

"Yes, sir," Ramage said, his voice toneless, but rubbing the scar over his brow. "That's why I made it in writing and had it delivered on board…"

"Rubbish, pure rubbish; I don't even know where it is, now."

"I have a copy on board, sir," Ramage said unambiguously.

"You're not telling me your report said the *Peacock* would attack the *Topaz*, are you?"

Goddard bellowed with laughter, but Croucher's expression was wooden. Ramage had the feeling Croucher did not like the way the interview was going.

"No, sir, I merely reported all I knew. That was all anyone could know until the *Peacock* went alongside the *Topaz*."

"Balderdash, my boy; sheer balderdash. What the devil did you think the *Peacock* was going to do when she hauled her wind?"

"Possibly leave the convoy, sir. After all, she was supposed to be a runner from England to Barbados. She might have got impatient at the slow speed; she might have started to worry over this increasing swell and wanted to get into Jamaica quickly for fear of a hurricane."

"But she came right down the column."

"Yes, sir, and as soon as I couldn't find a reasonable explanation for her conduct, and when we sighted the second ship also coming up the inside of the column, we went into action."

"Much, much too late to do any good."

"Hardly, sir," Ramage reminded him politely. "We saved the *Topaz*."

"You were lucky, Ramage, and don't you damn well forget it."

"If you think – "

A knock on the door saved Ramage from an angry and insolent reply. Croucher called and a lieutenant came in to report to him.

"The *Topaz* left her position, and now she's close to windward, sir. She's not flying any signals but they're getting ready to hoist out a boat. I think…"

"Very well," Croucher said. "I'll be on deck in a minute or two."

As soon as the lieutenant had left Croucher looked at the Admiral questioningly, and he and Goddard walked out of the cabin, leaving Ramage standing by the desk.

Ramage was angry about the tone of Goddard's questioning – although it had been predictable – but, alone in the cabin, he found he had a vague feeling of uncertainty. Had he really been slow to guess the *Peacock*'s intentions? Should he have ignored the need for surprise and set off a few false fires to raise an alarm, or fired some rockets or a couple of guns?

If he had done so, and then found the *Peacock* was simply leaving the convoy, he'd have looked foolish, and Goddard could rightly have blamed him for giving the convoy's position away to the enemy. As he thought about it, he realized that his present uncertainty was not entirely due to the Admiral. He wanted to know what Yorke thought about it. Was he angry about the *Triton*'s late arrival? He might be. Yorke knew, as the Admiral did not, that Ramage was aware that the *Topaz* carried the "valuable cargo".

The more he thought about it, the more certain he became that Yorke – and the St Brieucs – must think he'd let them down. Originally they had been pleased to hear that the *Triton* was to be close to them, yet they'd been attacked from that very direction. Out of the darkness a ship full of privateersmen had appeared and as far as they knew Ramage had seen nothing until the last moment. To them it must have seemed lamentably late.

Perhaps Yorke was coming on board to make an official complaint. As the minutes passed, Ramage became more and more certain of it. He imagined a written complaint to the Admiral, signed by St Brieuc: Goddard would find that invaluable in hammering nails into Ramage's coffin.

Ramage suddenly sat down in the nearest chair: his knees no longer had any strength. The skin of his face was cold and covered in perspiration; his stomach felt as if cold water was swilling around inside it. The sun streaming in through the stern lights was now just a harsh glare; there was no joy or beauty in the blue of the sea or the sky: it was all without purpose. Doubts, questions, half answers and more doubts chased through his mind like mice in a treadmill; his hands were clenched as if to let go meant he'd fall into limbo. He had no idea whether time was passing quickly or slowly until he heard loud voices.

Suddenly the door was flung open by Croucher and Goddard strode in past him, looking back over his shoulder and saying angrily, "I resent the implication, sir; I resent it, I say."

"I've no doubt you do, Admiral; I think I'd resent it if you didn't."

Yorke's voice was calm but cold and Ramage realized the *Lion* must have luffed up, backed a topsail, let Yorke get on board, and got under way again without him noticing. He stood up but Goddard, whose face was swollen with rage and shiny with perspiration, did not notice him.

"Dammit, Mr Yorke; how was I to know the *Peacock* was French?"

"It wasn't hard to guess: every man in my ship was suspicious of her. She's obviously foreign built; those sails were never stitched in an English loft, and Lieutenant Ramage had warned you that she was behaving oddly the night before."

Ramage glanced up in surprise: how on earth had Yorke guessed that?

Goddard was equally startled. "Mr Yorke, you can't possibly know anything about Mr Ramage's activities!"

"But he did warn you, didn't he, Admiral? I heard his lookout hailing the deck the night before and I presume the *Triton*'s boat delivered his report yesterday morning. But why don't we ask him, since he's here?" Yorke's voice was mocking.

Goddard glanced round in surprise and Ramage realized that he was so disturbed by Yorke that he had forgotten his cabin was not empty.

"By all means. He did make some sort of report, but it was only vague suspicions."

"I fail to see how his suspicions could have been anything but vague, since he and the *Peacock* were at opposite ends of the convoy. But you failed to act on the report and you yourself had no suspicions at all. After all, it was you who let the *Peacock* join the convoy."

"Come now, Mr Yorke; how could you possibly know what action I took?"

"Come now, Admiral, I saw you signal to the nearest frigate to ask the *Peacock* if all was well on board. The master of the *Peacock* answered – quite truthfully, I am sure – that it was. My officers and I were expecting you to order the frigate to send a boarding party to investigate both the ships involved."

Ramage felt like singing: the sea was blue and so was the sky. Yorke might not be able to save him from Goddard in the long run. The Admiralty, Sir Pilcher Skinner, the Articles of War and tradition were agreed that, no matter what had happened, no admiral could be in the wrong if it meant putting a young lieutenant in the right. But Ramage valued Yorke's and the St Brieucs' verdict more than Goddard's or Croucher's.

Goddard sank into the chair Ramage had just vacated. He looked as though he had flinched from a blow, and the movement had toppled him over.

Yorke took a couple of steps towards him, holding out a white envelope with a heavy seal on it.

"This is addressed to you; it's from…It concerns my freight."

Goddard snatched it, broke the seal and started reading. Slowly his heavy jowls sagged; slowly the redness in his face turned to white. At last he seemed to realize that he was in for a terrible beating.

"This is ridiculous. Most unfair. Please, Mr Yorke, I'm sure that when you explain everything to M. St Brieuc he will see fit to withdraw this complaint and decide not to deliver the other letter he mentions."

"Which letter?" Yorke asked, and Ramage guessed that the question was put only so that he could hear the reply.

"The…the letter he has written to Lord Grenville. After all, the Secretary of State for Foreign Affairs is hardly concerned…"

"On the contrary, Admiral; when you think about it you'll realize that Lord Grenville is his only official channel of communication and is *most* concerned about his safety."

"I quite see that, Mr Yorke. My point is rather that I'm hoping you'll be able to persuade M'sieur – the writer of this letter – that there is no cause for complaint."

"With respect, Admiral," Yorke said, his voice still deceptively quiet, but choosing his words with care, "not only can I hold out no hope of so persuading him, but I'd be misleading you if I didn't warn you that I shall not attempt to do so since I fully agree with him."

119

"Come, come, Mr Yorke," Goddard said, his voice wheedling. "You know well enough that in battle chance plays a major part and..."

"In battle, yes," Yorke said, like a relentless prosecutor setting out an unbeatable case. "But you were not in battle. The battle is separate and there is no complaint about how it was fought, thanks to Mr Ramage here. It was the whole sequence of events from Carlisle Bay, when you took this French privateer – pirate is a more accurate description – under your wing and assigned him the most perfect position in the convoy for carrying out his plan."

A few minutes ago Ramage had listened to Goddard distorting everything so that the blame fell on the *Triton*; now Yorke was outlining the same facts so that all the blame was back on Goddard's shoulders, and with it the implication that there might be treachery involved in the *Peacock*'s presence in the convoy.

Goddard waved a helpless hand, physically as well as mentally beaten. Croucher looked away and Ramage wondered whether the wretched man was finally disgusted by his patron. With exquisite politeness, giving the impression that he had no idea the effect his words had already had on Goddard, Yorke said: "However, Admiral, there is one piece of good news that it will be an honour to give you."

Goddard's eyes lifted hopefully and Croucher turned back to look at Yorke.

"There is a second letter for Lord Grenville."

"Indeed, and what does that one say?" Goddard was trying to hide the hopeful note in his voice by being jocular.

"It will recommend to the Secretary of State that Lieutenant Lord Ramage be given 'signal recognition of his valour and alertness' – I am quoting the exact phrase in the letter – and asking Lord Grenville that the King should be informed. Our own King, I mean, of course."

Goddard glanced sourly at Ramage. "I am very flattered that this should happen to one of my young officers," he said heavily. "Naturally such recognition reflects on all the King's ships. May I be the first to congratulate you, Ramage? We are all very proud."

As Ramage clattered down the companionway to his cabin on board the *Triton*, acknowledged the Marine sentry's salute and ducked his head to avoid the low deck beams, he felt almost hysterically cheerful. He flung his hat on to the swinging cot and unbuckled his sword. Southwick followed him into the cabin and was waved to a chair as Ramage loosened his stock, sat at the desk and turned to the Master.

"Unbelievable, quite unbelievable."

Southwick grinned. "I thought as much, sir; I hadn't expected to see you quite as cheerful."

Ramage gave him an edited account of what had happened in the Admiral's cabin.

"Saw the *Topaz* go down to the flagship," Southwick said. "Must admit I thought the same as you: that Mr Yorke might try to lodge a complaint."

"Apart from us, the only one that comes out fairly well is the *Raisonnable*. The Admiral gave us the details of how she captured the second ship. I think what happened was that months ago the French heard the *Lion* would be carrying some very important passengers – people the Directory would like to get their hands on and silence forever. Unexpectedly, the passengers transferred to the *Topaz* – much more vulnerable than the *Lion* – before the convoy left Cork, and the French managed to send the *Peacock* to catch up with the convoy in Barbados, and join it.

"She had a couple of hundred extra men on board. Being in ballast she could carry plenty of water and provisions and they reckoned two hundred men would be enough to board the *Topaz* in the darkness, murder the passengers and escape again.

"In Barbados they found that joining the convoy was easy. The *Peacock*'s skipper is a renegade Englishman, by the way, and he called on the Admiral with false papers. Later he decided to improve on his orders and capture the *Topaz* as well, taking the prisoners into Guadeloupe alive as hostages. He'd have been richer by a good prize and seems to be a greedy man. He decided to change his tactics with the new plan. The night before last he ranged up alongside the next ahead in the convoy and put a hundred men aboard her – that's when we saw the two ships alongside each other. There weren't six men on deck so he captured her without a shout, let alone a shot.

"Now he had half his men in this ship – the *Harold and Marjorie* – and half in the *Peacock*, ready to take the *Topaz*. He reckoned he'd come up the outside of the column with the *Harold and Marjorie* on the inside, so he could board the *Topaz* from both sides."

"How the devil did he expect to get away with it?"

"Come, come!" Ramage chided. "He nearly did, and if you'd been him you'd have expected to get away with it too. He probably decided he had to do it last night or tonight because Guadeloupe is so near. And I suspect he was worrying about this swell. So out of the column they come, and in a very short time they're alongside. Or should have been.

"I think he reckoned the only real risk was the *Greyhound*. He didn't think we'd spot him against the masts and sails of the rest of the convoy, and even if we did he knew he could board us. Don't forget, he was counting on a hundred men and surprise: if we did go down to investigate, his men could suddenly leap up from behind the bulwarks and swarm on board – as indeed they did."

"But the *Greyhound*…"

"Say the *Greyhound* spotted him as soon as he let fall his courses and hauled his wind out of the column, he could claim to have seen a French privateer astern. A ship out of position in a convoy is irritating – but not usually a cause for suspicion…Once he knew the *Greyhound* hadn't spotted him, the *Harold and Marjorie* also left the convoy."

Southwick slapped his knee and said cheerfully: "But the *Peacock* didn't reckon on us pulling his tail feathers."

"The rest of the *Peacock* story is as we guessed it. The *Greyhound* seems to have been keeping station on us, instead of watching the convoy, so she wasn't too far away when we suddenly went down to the *Peacock*. The firing woke her up and she came down to help."

"What about the *Harold and Marjorie*?"

"The *Raisonnable* on the larboard quarter of the convoy saw the firing over this side and immediately cut diagonally across the convoy to get to it. Against the lighter northern sky she saw the *Harold and Marjorie* turning away southwards and obviously up to no good. The *Raisonnable* herself was against the dark cloud to the south – you remember how hard it was to see the convoy against it? Anyway, the *Harold and Marjorie* didn't see her until it was too late to dodge, and didn't realize she was a frigate. She opened fire – and that was all the *Raisonnable* wanted to know: no need for any more questions. She raked her a couple of times and the Frenchman had had enough."

"What about the renegade Englishman?"

"They can't find him on board the *Peacock*. He may have committed suicide – he must have known if he was captured he'd hang. But the French mate wanted someone to blame for the fiasco, so he has talked."

"D'you think the Admiral is going to leave us in peace now, sir?"

Ramage shrugged his shoulders. "Who knows..."

Southwick stood up. "I'd best be getting on deck. This swell is increasing quickly now..."

"I'll come with you. I want to time it. The trip in the gig gave me a chance to measure the height."

"Doesn't look too good," Southwick said gloomily as he led the way out of the cabin. "This high, wispy cloud to the east, and no Trade wind clouds. If it falls calm this afternoon..."

Ramage took out his watch and looked astern. The wind was light and made little more than wavelets; but beneath them, like large muscles rippling under the skin, were the swell waves. The crests were widely spaced and still fairly low; but they weren't as low as they had been yesterday. Whatever caused them was moving closer. Closer, but not necessarily towards them. It could move still closer without being a threat, just as one might pass a man on a road without bumping into him.

He looked down over the taffrail and the sun scorched through his clothes. The rudder post creaked gently as the man at the wheel kept the brig on course; the water was dark-blue and as he stared down at it, he had a feeling that it was bottomless: that it went down and down for scores of thousands of fathoms. Within a minute or two he had the rhythm of the swell waves, and he started to time the interval between each of a series of crests.

He shut the lid of the case and slipped the watch back into his pocket.

Southwick caught his eye and said quietly: "For what we are about to receive?"

Ramage shrugged his shoulders. "Keep your money in your pocket until you see if the wind drops later."

He went over to the binnacle box and picked up the biggest telescope, adjusted the eyepiece to a particular scratchmark that showed the correct focus for his eyes, and looked around the horizon.

Over on the starboard side, to the eastward, what were low dark smudges to the naked eye showed as high land with a few clouds. Guadeloupe and, on the quarter, Dominica. The small northern islands were still out of sight over the starboard bow – indication enough of the convoy's slow progress.

Light winds certainly made a convoy commander's task easier in one respect since it gave the masters of the merchantmen less reason for reducing sail; and there was nothing like an unexpected night attack for improving station-keeping! Southwick had already commented on the fact that by dawn several merchantmen had shaken out reefs during the night, a sure sign that the fireworks had bothered them. It's an ill wind, Ramage thought to himself.

He went down to his cabin again, found he'd forgotten to collect the master's log and sent his steward for it. Irritating how much paperwork was needed to keep a ship afloat, but at least the log served an obviously useful purpose. Every two months a parcel of documents had to be prepared for dispatch to the Admiralty and the Navy Board, and in every third parcel, among many other lists and reports, were the captain's journal and the master's log.

They were usually almost identical, which was hardly surprising since they were both based on the same source: the large slate kept in the binnacle box, and which was used to record wind direction, courses steered and speed and distances made good, either every hour or when any of them changed. An hourly diary of the ship's life, in fact.

Southwick took the slate down to his cabin every day, copied the details into his log and added other items of information concerning the ship and her crew, wiped the slate clean, and returned it to the binnacle box, where the quartermaster could reach it easily. Every day Ramage, like every other captain of a King's ship, took the Master's log as the basis for his journal entry, adding any other information likely to be needed for reference or required by regulations.

Since anything of major importance was the subject of a separate report, the entries tended to be brief. Ramage opened the drawer, took out his journal, glanced through Southwick's log, and then began writing, bringing the journal up to date from the last entry the previous afternoon.

"PM 3 wind SE by E, light, swell from E, ship's company employed a.t.s.r., convoy making 4 knots..." He hated abbreviations, but the phrase "as the service required" was used so often there was no choice. "Opened cask of salt beef, marked 54 pieces, contained 51," a common indication of the dishonesty of contractors. Then he settled down to the previous evening's events.

"7.45 sighted number 78 (*Peacock*) leave her position, subsequently opened fire on her to prevent attack on 71 (*Topaz*), 10.20 resumed original position, wind ESE, light..."

He read it over again. It was as brief as he dare make it, but there was almost bound to be a court martial, and as far as he could see it would be a matter of luck who would be accused. If Goddard had his way, it would be Lieutenant Ramage: if Sir Pilcher Skinner was intelligent and impartial, it would be Rear-Admiral Goddard.

Ramage was beginning to realize that the *Topaz* carried one of the most powerful of the French families in exile. A wise commander-in-chief would sacrifice a rear-admiral to placate such influential people, but from all accounts Sir Pilcher was not intelligent; he would probably agree with Goddard that a lieutenant was a more suitable sacrifice.

Ramage shut the journal, screwed the cap on the ink bottle and wiped the nib of his pen. If there was a court martial, his journal would be needed as evidence. All the previous entries were taciturn or lazily brief, depending on one's point of view. The words he had just written gave nothing away, but did not reveal too obviously that they'd been written with the possibility of a court martial in mind.

He found himself staring at the column of mercury in the weather glass. It had dropped slightly for the third day running. No longer was there the slight, twice daily rise and fall; now there was only the fall.

Within a few hours the whole sky was covered in a high haze which left the sun looking like a whorl of red paint made by the thumb of a violent and insane artist, and long high streaks of cloud started moving in from the east. The surface of the sea seemed oily and heavy with menace. The wind had died away fitfully until finally every ship in the convoy was lying lifeless, each ship's bow pointing in a different direction. Lifeless but not still: the swell waves persisted after the wind waves died away, still not high but long, measured from crest to crest. Ships lying west and east pitched heavily as the crests passed under them from stern to bow, or bow to stern; but ships lying north and south rolled violently without the wind pressing in the sails.

In every master's mind was the danger of his ship rolling her masts out; the whiplash movement of a ship swinging violently like an inverted pendulum put an enormous strain not only on the masts but on the long yards. The thick rope of the rigging vibrated as the loading alternated with the rolling.

Ramage sent for Southwick to come to his cabin and, when the Master arrived, looked up from the seat at the desk.

"I was just setting the men to overhauling tackles," Southwick said. "I don't think we've a lot of time left."

"That's what I wanted to talk about. As we are part of the escort I can't do anything until the Admiral hoists a signal. The signal might be later than we'd like so we're likely to have a number of things to do in a hurry.

"First will be small sails out of the tops. Then down t'gallant yards and masts. I want them properly lashed down on deck: assume a sea might sweep us clean. Studding sail booms down off the yards...spanker boom and gaff – down and well lashed below the bulwarks. Preventer braces on the yards...relieving tackle on the tiller, and make sure the spare tiller is where we can get at it...all the axes available. Issue tomahawks: they'll serve as small axes...Can you think of anything else?"

Southwick had been counting off the items on his fingers and shook his head. "No, but I wish we'd worked out something for the boats."

The boats, stowed over the hatchways, were hoisted in and out by tackles on the main yard. Ramage and Southwick had tried to devise a safe way of dumping them over the side in an emergency, but had been unable to think of anything.

"It shouldn't be too difficult to relieve ourselves of the carronades."

Southwick grimaced. "Hope we don't get as far as doing that: I reckon that's about the last goodbye to mother."

"Our fore and main trysails – I hope they're not as mildewed as those in most ships."

"The bosun's mate is going over them now. Material is sound enough; he's checking over the stitching and reef points. He's strengthening wherever he can."

"It's not being left to him to decide?"

"No, sir – I've just gone over both sails with him. We're laying a few more cloths on the tabling. Doubtful whether it'll do any good: just making tack, clew and head stronger than the rest of the sail."

"Well, if the roping holds, it makes it easier to mend. Just panels going!"

"Just panels." Southwick sniffed. "Finest and heaviest flax there is!"

"It might never blow, Mr Southwick, in which case we'll never know."

"I'd be happy to die of old age completely ignorant of hurricanes."

"Me too, but the longer we stay at sea, the more the odds turn against us."

Ramage picked up his hat and the two men walked back up on deck.

The sky to the west was a cold, coppery colour – a colour so unlike anything normally occurring in nature that its very strangeness was frightening. The reflection of the sky gave everything a coppery hue: the flax sails, normally raw umber with a touch of burnt sienna, the bare wood of the decks, the brasswork of fittings. Even the bright red, royal blue and gilt of the small carved crown on top of the capstan was distorted by the sun's strange lacquering.

Southwick sucked his teeth and shuddered. "Horrible. You can almost taste it. Like sucking a penny."

That's about it, Ramage thought, a colour that gives the impression of taste; a physical presence, like cold, only instead of chilling it frightened. There was a curious tension on board the *Triton* – something he'd never really seen before in a ship of war – it was not the same when they went into action. There was a slight rounding of men's shoulders as they walked the deck doing various jobs. They hadn't the jauntiness that was normally so obvious. Each man seemed in the grip of a private fear.

Up on the fo'c'sle, Jackson was working with Rossi, Stafford and six other seamen, stitching reinforcing patches into the fore trysail. The men were sitting on the deck, their legs under the sail, looking like old women mending nets on a beach. Each had a heavy leather palm strapped to his right hand to help drive the needle through the cloth.

Jackson leaned back and groaned. "My back…I feel like an old man."

"It's not me back; it's me 'and," Stafford grumbled. "This 'ere palm 'as blistered me 'and."

"Don't tell the bosun," Rossi said. "It is the proof you never do any work."

Stafford sniffed. "Ever been through an 'urricane, Jacko?"

When the American shook his head, another seaman said, "What d'you think it's like?"

"Windy," Stafford interrupted as he dug the sail needle into the material.

"Not in the middle," Jackson said. "They say it's flat calm in the eye and the sun shines."

"Ho yus," Stafford exclaimed. "An' all the women 'anging their washin' up ter dry, no doubt."

"Well, you'll soon meet one…"

" 'Ere, Jacko, you reckon – reely?"

Jackson nodded. "Yes – you'll see, it blows like the devil until you're in the middle; then the wind drops, it stops raining, the sun comes out and everything's lovely."

"You said the middle," Rossi said warily. "Then what happenings?"

"Well, just as soon as folk like Staff are out there hanging up their washing, it comes on to blow even harder from the opposite direction."

"*Accidente!* The *opposite* direction? But everything gets taken aback?"

"Precisely…"

All the men were silent for a few minutes, each alone with the mental picture of the wind suddenly gusting up and blowing on the forward side of the sail, instead of the after side, and pressing a sail and yard back against the mast.

As the pressure increased the ship would start going astern, starting a whole sequence of events: to steer the ship, the wheel would have to be spun the other way, and at the same time the pressure on the rudder would be enormous: pressure trying to wrench it off, pressure that kept on increasing. As it increased, so would the pressure on the sails and yards increase, and such pressure could be relieved only by the wind easing, the sail blowing out, the yard smashing in half or the mast breaking.

"She was caught aback and her masts went by the board."

It was a familiar description: each man could visualize the ship swept clean, her masts snapped off at deck level – by the board – and fallen over the side in a tangle of rigging, halyards, sheets, braces, yards…and there'd probably be death in the wreckage for many of them.

Beside each mast were piles of heavy rope. When Admiral Goddard made the signal for the ships under his command to prepare for a hurricane, the men would rig additional shrouds to support the masts, using these lengths of hawser.

Southwick and a couple of bosun's mates were already carefully checking over the lanyards of each pair of deadeyes. A group of men working unostentatiously – Ramage had given instructions that their activities should not be obvious from the flagship – were putting storm lashings on the guns.

Southwick met him abreast the mainmast on the larboard side. "Everything satisfactory, sir?"

"As far as we can go, yes."

The Master glanced round to make sure no seamen were within earshot. "Can't think the Admiral's been on deck today, sir."

"Nor Captain Croucher!"

"I was looking at the mules with the glass. Most of them are busy."

"Wait until they start sending down topmasts and yards…"

"Several are getting ready to."

"I wonder if the Admiral will tell them to stop," Ramage said, half to himself.

"I hope not: it'll take them several hours to get squared away. Except for the *Topaz* they are probably all short-handed."

"They'll manage," Ramage said, and wished he had not been reminded of the *Topaz*. She was his hostage to fortune at the moment. However competent Yorke was, he would still have preferred to have the St Brieucs on board the *Triton*…

The sun set in a wild, western sky. In the late afternoon the copper colour gave way to a dull and sickly yellow washed with an angry red as high clouds thickened and the wind came up, steadily freshening as the hours passed. The convoy soon got under way, but while all the escorts were busy trying to get the ships into their proper positions again the masters took little notice of orders or threats: most were already under double-reefed courses and their men were busy sending down topsail yards. The swell waves were slowly but inexorably increasing in height, like silent gestures of warning.

Slowly the wind backed from east to north-east, and then went north. Equally slowly Admiral Goddard was forced to keep edging the convoy's course round to the west as more and more merchantmen found it impossible to stay up to windward.

First one ship in the middle of a column would start sagging off to leeward, eventually sailing diagonally through the remaining columns. In turn one or two other ships, forced to bear away to avoid a collision, would be unable to get back into position and would themselves sag off.

Finally, to avert chaos, the *Lion* would bear away and hoist signal flags indicating the new course. The frigates, brig and lugger would repeat, then spend the next hour ensuring the merchantmen conformed, and just have the last one in position when the flagship would repeat the process.

Finally Southwick became exasperated. He took off his hat, ran his hands through his white hair and said to Ramage: "Never was an increment man, myself."

When Ramage looked puzzled, he explained: "The Admiral knows he's going to be steering south-west by midnight, so why doesn't he cut his losses and get on course now, instead of coming round by increments? And not only that, the sooner we get over to the westwards" – he gestured over the larboard beam, towards the middle of the Caribbean – "and give ourselves some sea room, the happier I'll be.

"Never liked the chance of a lee shore with this Caribbean weather," he continued. "That's one thing about European waters – may be cold and wet, but nine times out of ten, a gale or a storm comes from the south-west or west. Here it's any damned direction."

Ramage nodded but kept his fears to himself. His earlier suspicion that Goddard had lost his nerve was now confirmed. The Rear-Admiral was the kind of man who froze when he was frightened: instead of bolting or rushing around shouting, he withdrew into paralysed inactivity and indecision.

Southwick was right about the "increments" – but there was more to it than sea room. Nothing was really known about hurricanes, but men who had survived them talked and pooled their ideas, so that eventually an odd sort of pattern emerged.

In a lifetime at sea, Ramage's father had gone through two hurricanes, and Ramage could remember the old Earl's two pieces of advice. One was to prepare the ship early, so that men did not have to work aloft with the ship rolling heavily in a strong wind, which doubled and quadrupled the amount of effort needed. But the second point was the really important one; if the wind veered, steer to keep it on the starboard bow. The hurricane would probably pass southwards and the ship, altering course as required to keep the wind on the bow, would cover a semi-circular course to the north of it. But if the wind remained steady or backed – which it was doing now – it was vital to get the wind on to the starboard quarter, and keep it there, altering course as necessary. Then the hurricane would probably pass northwards. If you ran before the wind, the chances were that the middle of the hurricane would pass right over you.

Goddard's "increment" course meant that he was slowly doing just that. By trying to hold on to a predetermined course that would keep him as near to Antigua as possible, and being forced to bear away as the merchantmen sagged off, he would end up running before the hurricane…and running slowly before a massive hurricane meant that it was only a matter of time before it caught up.

If Goddard turned the whole convoy boldly on to a course of say – Ramage walked over and glanced at the compass – south-south-west, all the merchantmen would have the wind on their starboard quarters, and they would probably be able to keep it there even under storm canvas…

Every time a signal hoist was reported from the flagship, he looked expectantly at Jackson, and each time the American reported a course change of one point to larboard. One point! Eleven degrees fifteen minutes, or one thirty-second part of the circumference of a circle…It was like giving a starving man a single slice of bread: instead of saving his life, it merely emphasized how hungry he was and postponed the inevitable end. Altering course one point to larboard stressed the need for an immediate eight-point alteration.

"The wind will eventually do it for him," Southwick said bitterly, echoing Ramage's thoughts. "But we lose that much time – and mileage. And maybe our necks."

"Since we can't do anything about it, let's make the best of it."

He was startled by the harshness of his voice, and Southwick stared fixedly at the convoy. Ramage knew he was feeling the strain, but taking it out on Southwick was contemptible.

"It'll be dark in an hour," Ramage said.

"Aye, there's just about enough time to execute it if he makes a signal now."

Half an hour later the signals came in a series. Perhaps Goddard had been stirred into action as the sun sank below the western horizon – though it had been hidden before this by the ever-lowering cloud streaming in from the north, each layer a darker and more menacing grey.

Jackson called out the signals as they were made on board the *Lion* while Stafford and Rossi bent the flags on to the halyards and hoisted them, both in acknowledgement and also repeating them.

"Convoy flag and frigates' flag: *Strike yards and topmasts... Observe the Admiral's motions carefully during the night as he will probably alter course or tack without signal...*Frigates' flag: *Shorten sail and carry as little as possible without breaking the order of the fleet...Every ship to carry a light and repeat the signals made by the Admiral during the ensuing night...*"

Ramage picked up the speaking trumpet and, as Jackson called out the first signal, bellowed the order that sent the topmen running up the ratlines, not pausing until they were in the tops, where they scrambled into position to begin clearing away and lowering gear.

Ramage glanced at his watch, noted the time, and swore to himself he wouldn't look at it again until he heard Southwick give the order "Sway away".

He looked round the ship knowing that all the work to be done was going to take two or three times as long because of the darkness. The lateness of the signal made it obvious that the men were going to meet the coming dawn with precious little sleep.

"Mr Southwick – the hands will eat in two shifts, perhaps three, and pass the word that the tot will be issued late and may be poured with a heavy hand."

"Good idea, sir," the Master said. He lowered his voice, "The way things look, we may not have to account for any 'spillage and seepage'."

Ramage nodded and turned to Jackson. "Have you logged those signals, and the times?"

"Aye aye, sir. Specially the times."

Jackson's voice was expressionless; Ramage was probably the only man in the ship who could detect the judgment of the Admiral contained in the American's last three words.

Picking up the telescope and balancing himself, Ramage looked round at the convoy. The merchantmen appeared to be taking very little notice of the flurry of signals: each one had a cluster of men working aloft. Four had topsail yards upended and being lowered to the deck; a dozen would be lowering them any moment.

"They look odd now, don't they," Southwick said. "Like men with their heads shaved."

"They work fast enough at a time like this," Ramage commented. "Surprising how slow they can be with routine things like keeping their position."

"Yes, I'll be damned if I can understand it. After all, we're protecting 'em. We don't like escorting 'em any more than they like having us chase 'em up."

"Surely that's it," Ramage said. "Sending down masts and yards because bad weather's coming on – well, that's a natural piece of seamanship: they'd be doing that pretty smartly even sailing alone in peacetime. But cramming on sail to obey an order from an escort – that's not seamanship: that's being chased about by the Navy."

"Hadn't thought of that. Excuse me a moment, sir," he said hurriedly and lifted the speaking trumpet. "Aloft there, mainmast: Jenkins, unreeve that signal halyard. You'll have it a'foul o' everything in a moment!"

The fact is, Ramage told himself, the Master will make a better job of all this if I'm not on deck. As Southwick turned back, Ramage said: "I've some work to do below. Call me if…"

CHAPTER NINE

The night was the worst either Ramage or Southwick could remember. By midnight the wind had increased from a fresh gale to near storm force and the *Triton*, down to the storm canvas that Jackson and the men had been reinforcing, was labouring and plunging like a bull trying to get out of deep thick mud. Up to now the seas were not as big as either man had expected, but they would build up within a few hours and the wind would probably increase.

Throughout the night Ramage or Southwick had stood by the men at the wheel; down below more stood by at relieving tackles which had been clapped on the tiller. Up to now they had not been needed, but they could have the ship under control in a matter of minutes if anything happened to the wheel steering.

Until the rain started, the convoy – judging from the pinpoints of light displayed by each ship – was holding together better than either Ramage or Southwick had dared dream. Ramage flipped up the peak of his sou'wester and looked to leeward as he spoke to the Master.

"At least the water isn't too cold."

" 'Bout all that can be said for it, sir," Southwick bellowed. "Just as dam' wet as the North Sea. And twice as salty – my eyes are as sore as if I had sand in 'em."

"Mine too. Well, we haven't seen any rockets."

"Not for want o' looking. That's why I've got so much salt in my eyes. Can hardly believe it: all those mules so close to each other – in this weather."

"Well, they were until the rain started. Might be a different story now. Doubt if we'd see rockets with this visibility."

"An hour or so until dawn," Southwick shouted, and then added: "Listen to *that!*"

A prolonged gust seemed to pick up the *Triton* and shove her through the water like a goose landing clumsily.

Ramage tapped Southwick's arm. "We'll have to hand the main trysail, otherwise we'll never find the convoy at daybreak."

"At the speed we're making in the gusts it can only be astern!" Southwick yelled with a grim laugh, and strode off in the rain to call the watch.

A few minutes later, with the main trysail furled and only the fore trysail pulling – just a few square feet – the brig had not slowed down appreciably, and Ramage sensed that the wind had increased considerably even in that short time.

Southwick rejoined him, wiping the spray from his eyes, and said: "Gained nothing out of that. We'd have had to hand it anyway. If the wind pipes up any more, I reckon we'll be going too fast even under bare poles."

"Don't forget your mules will be doing the same," Ramage reminded him. "Probably been doing it for the past couple of hours."

"It's one way of making sure you don't get taken aback!"

Leaving Southwick beside the men at the wheel, Ramage walked aft to the taffrail, carefully timing his movements with the violent pitch and roll. Then he looked aft. The *Triton's* wake in the darkness was a broad band of turbulent and phosphorescent water stretching out astern over the waves like a bumpy cart track rising and falling over rolling hills. The seas were getting big. Certainly the darkness exaggerated them, but they looked like enormous watery avalanches rushing down on the ship from astern. Yet each time it seemed she must be overwhelmed, the stern began to lift and the wave crest slipped under the brig like a hand moving beneath a sheet.

He was frightened, but not by the size of the seas and the strength of the wind at the moment, even though they were higher and stronger than any he'd ever seen before. They didn't frighten him, but they gave him an idea of what the hurricane itself would be like, and that was frightening. A door opening slowly onto terror and possibly death.

What happened when the wind went over sixty knots? Men could only guess at the strength it finally reached. A planter in Barbados who had been in a hurricane had told him that the wind seemed almost solid in its strength, scouring paint off those houses it did not destroy and snapping mature palm trees a dozen feet from the ground. If the prospect was frightening for him, Ramage tried to imagine how frightening the present storm must seem to Maxine. At least he knew from experience what a well-found ship could stand, and from that experience he could also make a guess.

He went and stood with Appleby, who had just taken over from Southwick as officer of the watch. The young Master's mate was nervous and jumpy. Ramage talked to him for a few minutes and found he was not scared of the storm but slowly cracking up under the responsibility of handling the ship. In an emergency, Ramage realized, when a couple of seconds might make all the difference in avoiding disaster, it was unfair to leave the lives of the Tritons in Appleby's hands. On the pretext of making sure he had enough sleep for the coming day, Ramage sent the Master's mate below and took over his watch. From now on, until the hurricane blew itself out, he and Southwick would have to stand watch and watch about.

Dawn came slowly, as if reluctant to light up the terrifying scene. The surge of the seas was flinging the *Triton* around as if she was a chip of wood instead of a hundred-foot-long ship of war weighing almost three hundred tons. The wind and rain seemed solid, like an invisible maniac pushing with incredible strength, screaming with almost unbelievable shrillness, and making it hard to breathe.

As he clung on to the thick breeching of a carronade, Ramage wondered in the greyness, where the wind and spray and rain seemed one, how much of it the human mind could stand. His mind, anyway. Many men made of sterner stuff than he could probably endure a week of this; but he knew the prospect of another seven hours, let alone days, made him feel sick with anxiety.

If only the ship would stop this blind pitching and rolling for a minute. Any moment now one or both of the masts must go by the board; any moment one of these enormous great seas rolling up astern must smash down on the taffrail, pooping the ship, sweeping the deck clear of men, guns and hatch covers. She'd broach and then, lying over on her beam ends, she'd fill and founder, like a bucket tipped over in a village pond.

Water was pouring down Ramage's neck: the cloth he was wearing as a scarf was sodden and instead of preventing the spray on his face from trickling into his clothes, it seemed to be channelling it into torrents so that his clothes were soaked beneath the oilskins. He'd long since given up emptying his boots; he just squelched from one foot to the other. The Tropics, he thought viciously, are for pelicans and drunken planters. The former are adapted to the weather, and the latter can forget it in bottles of their own rum. And mockingbirds can just laugh it off and twitch their tails.

Suddenly he realized that the grey of dawn was spreading and he could make out the dark bulk of the wheel and the group of shadowy men standing up at it; the seas had grey caps and he could see more detail of their wild movements.

Southwick lurched over to him and he could see enough of his face to be shocked by its weariness. The Master seemed to have aged ten years overnight. The ends of his white hair hung out from under his sou'wester in spiky tails, giving him the appearance of an anxious porcupine, and the eyes and cheeks were sunken.

"Lookouts aloft, sir?"

"No," Ramage yelled back, "there'll be nothing in sight, and even if there was, we couldn't do anything except run before this weather."

"Aye, sir, that's my feeling."

But both men were wrong. Within twenty minutes, when they could see several hundred yards in the grey light, a lookout came scrambling back along the larboard side, clutching on to the main rope rigged fore and aft as though he was climbing.

"Larboard bow, sir," he gasped. "Ship, mebbe five hundred yards; a merchantman under bare poles I reckon, but I only saw her as we came up on the crest of a wave."

Ramage was leaning against the carronade in a daze caused partly by weariness and partly by the noise of the wind.

"Splendid," he said automatically. "You're keeping a good lookout."

As the man turned to go back Ramage beckoned to Jackson, whose eyes and nose could just be seen peering out from a glistening black cylinder. The American must have tarred his sou'wester and long oilskin coat very recently.

"Up aloft," Ramage shouted. "Larboard bow, five hundred yards, probably a merchantman. And have a good look round for anyone else. There's a glass in the binnacle box drawer – if you can use it."

In the five minutes Jackson was aloft it grew appreciably lighter, and the lighter it became the lower sank Ramage's spirits. He lurched to the taffrail, hollow-eyed and unshaven, grasped it with both hands and looked aft, forcing himself to stare at what frightened him.

The seas were so huge he knew he'd wronged many men in the past when they'd described such weather and he'd assumed – with smug superiority – that they were exaggerating. Even allowing for how cold and tired and hungry he was, and knowing this affected his judgment, he was certain that what he looked at was worse. Those men had been describing hurricanes, and he had to face up to the fact that the *Triton* was now in a hurricane. This was no brief tropical storm which seemed worse than it was because the preceding weeks of balmy weather had softened a man. Some time during the night, the storm had turned into a hurricane, just as earlier the gale had increased to a storm.

He stared at the waves, fascinated and yet fearful, like a rabbit facing a weasel. All his seagoing life he had dreaded this day. Here at last was what few sailors had experienced, and what fewer still had survived. In the Indian Ocean it was called a cyclone, in the Pacific it was a typhoon and in the Caribbean a hurricane. Like death, it went by different names in different languages, but was still the same thing.

The seas were so enormous he did not even try to guess their height, but he had to tilt his head back to be able to look up at the crests from under the brim of his sou'wester. They came up astern like great fast-moving mountain ranges, one steeply sloping forward edge threatening to scoop up the ship, the curling, breaking crest ready to sweep the decks clear of men and equipment. It was followed by another whose forward edge seemed almost vertical, like a cliff, and so sheer the *Triton*'s stern could never lift in time to avoid it crashing down on the ship, crushing it to matchwood. But, in a series of miracles, her stern did lift, and the crests did pass under her, producing even more prodigious pitching.

On and on came the mountains of water, each one fearful because its power was in itself, its own enormous weight set in motion by the wind. He watched each crest, a curling, roaring, hissing jumble of bubbling white water. The *Triton* was making about four knots with not a stitch of canvas set and her wake showed on each wave's face as a double line of inward-spinning whorls, like the hairsprings of watches.

Every few minutes an odd and often small wave, instead of coming up dead astern and meeting the ship squarely, ran in from a slight angle and she lifted slowly and awkwardly, the crest slapping hard on the quarter and squirting water up the space round the rudder post.

The quarter was where the danger was: all of Southwick's efforts with the helmsmen were devoted to making sure the *Triton* drove off dead to leeward, so every wave arrived squarely at the transom. A heavy wave catching her on one quarter, instead of rushing beneath the ship and lifting her squarely, would push the stern with it, forcing the bow round the opposite way. In a second the ship would broach, to lie broadside and vulnerable to the seas.

These seas were big enough, much more than big enough, to lift her up and throw her flat, so that with her heavy masts and lower yards lying in the water and acting as a weight on one end of a see-saw, she would not come up without the masts being cut away. Come up that is, providing the pathetically small shell of a hull did not fill with water…

A moment's inattention on the part of the officer of the watch or quartermaster; a momentary mistake by the men at the wheel or one of them slipping on the streaming, sloping deck and hindering his mates as they spun the spokes one way or the other and the *Triton* would broach. Or the wheel ropes would part, so that the thick tiller would slam across and splinter as the waves shoved the rudder hard over.

A shroud parting and a mast going by the board...The rudder itself being smashed...Springing the butt end of a plank below the waterline, letting tons of water pour in, or even springing one above the waterline, with these seas...A carronade breaking adrift from its lashings and crashing from one side of the deck to the other, smashing bulwarks and killing men...Each possibility flashed through Ramage's mind as fast as a fencer's lunge and riposte.

Suddenly he realized that in facing aft like this he was staring not at the sea but at fear. Nothing was to be gained by it, except perhaps, after thirty seconds or so, an additional warning about broaching. Making the seamen look aft for five minutes before a spell at the wheel would not encourage them to be more careful; they'd be so damned scared they'd probably make mistakes.

Jackson was tapping his arm to attract his attention above all the noise: that in itself was significant. Few seamen in few ships would risk doing that, however great the emergency, because they had been taught from their first day in their first ship that an unscrupulous lieutenant could turn it into "striking an officer...", an offence carrying the death penalty.

"Four ships!" Jackson shouted.

Ramage ducked down below the taffrail, motioning the American down beside him, where they were slightly sheltered from the howling wind.

"Are you sure?"

Jackson wiped his eyes with his knuckles; he too was tired, his face pinched with weariness and cold. Cold, in the Tropics…

"Certain, sir. One fine on the larboard bow, one on the starboard beam – I think it's the *Greyhound* – and two on the starboard quarter. The one on the larboard bow is close – the *Topaz*, sir, bare poles, and seemingly all right. Rest are maybe a mile off. Reckon there are several more ships around, but a mile's as far as I can see with this light and the rain and the spray."

So Yorke was all right, and Maxine…

"No sign of the *Lion*?"

It was an unnecessary question, since the American would have reported if he'd seen her, but Jackson shook his head. He had been with Ramage too long, and knew too much about the responsibility that rested on the young lieutenant's shoulders, to be impatient.

Looking at Ramage's haggard face in the half-light, the American was thankful, in a curious way, for his own limitations. Leaving aside his country of birth, which legally prevented it ever happening, he knew he did not have the capacity for command. It took a type of man that he understood but was not. The man who, presented with a terrible decision to make and limited time, went off to a quiet corner – and came back inside the required time with the decision made, much as another man might go below and change his shirt. No doubts, no asking other people's opinions, no delays, no second thoughts…and of all the leaders he'd met, Mr Ramage was the coolest of them all. Jackson knew he sometimes had second thoughts, not about the rightness of a decision, but more often because men – his own men – might get killed or wounded as a result of it. A youth who was a father to sixty or more men, all but a couple of whom were a good deal older than him.

That was where Mr Southwick was so good, Jackson realized: the old Master understood very well this humane aspect of Mr Ramage's personality, and the American had noticed he was usually around at the right moment – and with the right remark – whenever the situation arose. Ironical, Jackson thought to himself, that a young captain needed an older man to help him be ruthless when necessary. In Jackson's previous experience of young officers, the older men were usually trying to persuade them to be less ruthless; to be more careful of their men's lives.

Telling Mr Ramage it was the *Topaz* over on the larboard bow certainly cheered him up: Jackson was pleased with the way he'd done it – and pleased he was the one to pass the word. He still wasn't sure what it was all about, but the Captain obviously thought a lot of the ship – the people in her, anyway. Must have been a bad half an hour for him when the blasted *Peacock*…

When Ramage lurched over to the binnacle to discuss Jackson's report with Southwick, the American worked his way a few feet forward to the spot between the mainmast and the coaming round the wardroom companionway. There was precious little shelter anywhere on deck in this weather, he thought gloomily. Just that somehow the thickness of the mainmast, and the yard overhead, gave the impression of sheltering under a tree.

"Move over," Jackson shouted at the crouching figure of Stafford.

"Oh, it's you. Wotcher see up there?"

"The *Topaz* on the larboard bow, the *Greyhound* frigate on starboard beam and a couple of mules astern."

"The flagship?" Rossi asked. "Is sunk?"

147

"Not in sight, anyway."

"We can 'ope," Stafford said. "Well – 'ere, wotch it!"

He leapt up and a moment later a mass of water a foot deep swept forward along the deck.

Jackson and Rossi scrambled up, cursing, and Stafford, clinging to the mast, roared with laughter as water poured out of the bottoms of their trousers.

Jackson watched a seaman scrambling aft, working his way hand over hand along the lifeline.

"That's Luckhurst, one of the lookouts!"

With that he followed the man the last few feet to where Ramage stood with Southwick.

"Lookout, larboard bow, sir – reckon that merchantman over the larboard bow's in trouble, sir."

Jackson saw Ramage stiffen; at once, he noticed, the hand went instinctively to rub the scar over the brow, forgetting the sou'wester.

"What trouble, man?"

"Only glimpsed her, sir, just as we was on a crest: looks as though her main yard's come adrift."

Ramage nodded and signalled to Jackson, pointing aloft.

"Up, quick look at the *Topaz* and down again to report!"

It seemed to Ramage he had hardly had time to think of the problem, let alone work out the answer, before Jackson was standing in front of him again.

"Her fore yard's already down, sir, and the main yard's swinging on the jears: lifts and braces gone. Bowsprit end also gone. Men working everywhere."

"Does she look under control?"

"Four men at the wheel. I think she's under control – as much as anyone."

"Very well," Ramage said.

"Shall I go back aloft, sir?"

Ramage paused, looking up the mast. The wind was so strong it was a miracle Jackson could climb up. It was unbelievable he was volunteering again. "Yes, take a couple of men with you as messengers."

Jackson worked his way to the foot of the mainmast, stirred Stafford and Rossi with his foot and jerked his thumb upwards.

Cursing, the two men followed him, and a couple of minutes later the trio were trying to make themselves comfortable in the maintop with the mast gyrating wildly as the ship pitched and rolled.

As soon as he'd wriggled himself into position, Stafford looked round at the horizon, and, overwhelmed at what he saw, could only mutter, "Cor!"

By now it was quite light but the horizon was hidden by the rain and spray which reduced visibility to a few hundred yards. The sea was like nothing Stafford had ever seen before. It had no regular shape, nor did it seem to have regular substance: instead it twisted and curled like molten marble boiling in a huge cauldron.

Each man had to hold on with both hands and the wind was now so strong that it was impossible to breathe facing into it: they had to turn their faces to leeward, breathe and then look again. The noise in their ears was a combination of a high-pitched scream and a deep roar; a noise they'd never heard before and would never forget.

Their eyes soon became raw because the spray was so fine at this height that their eyelids did not close instinctively and there was no way of sheltering. Forced by the pressure of the wind to breathe through their mouths, their saliva began to taste salty.

Jackson carefully passed the telescope to Stafford and pointed to the *Topaz*, gesturing to Rossi to help hold onto the cockney so he could have both hands free for the telescope.

As soon as Stafford finished his examination, Jackson looked slowly round the whole horizon, making sure Stafford also saw everything he'd spotted, particularly another mule astern – making three – and two more on the larboard quarter. Then he signalled Stafford to go down and report to the Captain.

Six mules, including the *Topaz*, and the *Greyhound*. Jackson thought of the rest as he looked round again. Forty-four mules, a line-of-battle ship, two frigates and a lugger out of sight. He did not know much about navigation, but they couldn't have dispersed much in the few hours that had passed since the whole convoy was lying becalmed...Were these seven ships, and the *Triton*, the only ones to survive this bloody awful night?

By the time Stafford reached the deck his brain was numb from the noise and buffeting of the wind. He clutched one of the shrouds and looked around him, saw the Captain clinging to the binnacle, and gradually realized that Mr Ramage was waving to him; making sweeping movements with his arm.

Stafford seized the lifeline rigged along the deck and hauled himself aft. The wind had increased while he had been aloft he was certain. He was not holding the rope to keep his balance: he had to use it to move aft.

Stafford was exhausted by the time he crouched down beside the binnacle with Ramage, bellowing his report. Finally he reached the *Topaz*: "Main yard swinging but I think they're managing to rig new braces. Fore yard's gone over the side: it's smashed twenty feet of bulwark, starboard side. Jibboom's gone but the bowsprit's safe now from the look of it and – "

He broke off as Rossi appeared beside them. The Italian, white-faced from weariness and cold, reported that the main yard had fallen to starboard and parted several shrouds, and Jackson was afraid the mainmast would go by the board.

For a few moments Ramage looked at Rossi as though he was a ghost; then he nodded and stood up, looking over the larboard bow.

Stafford glimpsed a vague pale shape fine on the bow and nearer than he expected it, and pointed.

Ramage nodded and shouted: "One of you fetch Jackson down: nothing more he can do up there."

Then he inched his way to Southwick, who now had a rope round his waist, made fast to the wheel pedestal.

The need to break off every few seconds while Southwick – who was looking astern and watching every wave as it swept up to the ship – shouted and signalled orders to the helmsmen, gave Ramage extra seconds to think, but when he'd finished and stood there looking at the Master, his mind was empty of everything but the bare facts.

Finally Southwick gave his opinion in rushes between helm orders.

"Up to them…nothing we can do…couldn't even throw a heaving line over, even if we dare turn a point either side of the course…Only a matter of time before something like it happens to us…Every rope must be chafing badly…miracle anyone's afloat…If the *Topaz* loses her masts she probably stands more chance of surviving than with 'em – less windage. Up to us to stay afloat and pick up survivors after this has blown out…"

As he listened Ramage felt both relief and guilt: the Master was shouting aloud exactly what he thought himself. This had been his first reaction, and he'd discarded it. But he and Southwick were right: even if they saw the *Topaz* sinking, the

Triton could do nothing to help: it wasn't a question of wish, will or skill; it was physically impossible.

Southwick was shaking his arm.

"It's a good thing we're not closer: we couldn't avoid running aboard her if she was ahead."

The Master was right.

"I'm sure Mr Yorke understands. He knows he couldn't help us either."

The Master was right. The Master was right. The Master – Ramage felt as if he were falling, but it was only that he was so tired and dazed by the wind. He had almost gone to sleep as he stood listening to Southwick. Gone to sleep while Yorke was fighting to save the *Topaz*; sleeping while Maxine and her parents prayed for their lives; while…steady!

He took several deep breaths and knew he was wearier than he ever believed a man could be and still function. He knew now how unwise he'd been at the beginning of the hurricane: he'd stayed on deck far longer than was necessary – instead of getting some sleep. Now, when the lives of everyone in the *Triton* depended on his alertness, he was asleep on his feet. When had he last slept? Yesterday or last night or the night before? What day was it, anyway? He couldn't remember, but it hardly mattered. He had no idea of the time, but Southwick must be exhausted: he would have to take over the conn soon and give the old man a spell. As he shouted his intention, the Master answered: "Appleby, sir; let him stand a watch!"

"Not enough experience!"

"He'll be as good as you or me! He's fresh. We're both worn out: only a matter of time before we make a bad mistake."

"Very well, he can relieve you."

"Let him take the conn and I'll walk the deck for an hour," Southwick said. "I've had a lot more sleep than you."

Ramage shook his head, but Southwick bellowed: "You're asleep on your feet, sir. You'll make mistakes. The *Topaz* depends on you too and after an hour in your cot you'll be some use again..."

His voice and the noise of the wind and sea faded and again Ramage felt himself falling asleep and knew Southwick was right.

"All right, send for Appleby."

"He'll be glad, sir. It's too much to expect a man to stay below in this weather if he can't sleep."

It took Ramage ten minutes to get to his cabin and he found everything wet: drips from the deckhead showed how much the ship was working. The noise of the wind was too loud for the creaking of frames and timbers to be very noticeable.

He sprawled himself over the table, felt a tugging at one leg and looked down to see his steward trying to get a boot off. It was all such an effort; it was all so useless; anyway he was so tired...

Hours later his steward shook him awake. The cot was wonderfully warm and, although it swung so wildly it almost made him dizzy, the motion was definitely less than before and the wind less loud.

"Captain, sir, Mr Southwick's compliments and it seems to be easing up. I brought you some food, sir."

Ramage saw a big metal basin jammed in the seat of the armchair.

"And I've put some dry clothes out, sir."

The wind easing? The eye of the hurricane must be approaching!

Quickly he scrambled out of the cot, took the glass carafe of drinking water from its rack, poured it over his head and towelled vigorously. Then he dressed as the steward passed dry clothes to him.

As he began eating slices of cold meat, bananas, an orange, biscuit and a small carafe of fruit juice, he realized he had been so hungry he had a pain in his stomach. When he had finished he saw he had made very little impression on the food and he had a pain from eating too fast.

"Put it in Mr Southwick's cabin. Wedge it well," he told the steward, "so that..."

He broke off: stewards were experts in wedging articles so they did not capsize as the ship rolled.

He wrapped a thick towel round his neck and pulled on his oilskin coat. The steward handed him his sou'wester and Ramage ducked out of the cabin.

The wind had certainly eased a lot. Appleby was tired but alert; Southwick's eyes were bright though bloodshot from a combination of salt and weariness.

Southwick greeted him with a grin.

"The eye of the storm will give us a wink soon, sir."

"Thanks for letting me have a sleep first!"

They were in the eye now: there was no doubt about that. The rain had stopped, the wind was blowing now at about fifteen knots, and the cloud was breaking up overhead.

There was a curious noise, a distant roaring. He looked questioningly at Southwick.

"It's coming from all round us, sir. Heard it just as the rain stopped and the wind began to ease. Could it be the wind blowing outside the eye?"

Ramage found it hard to imagine, but realized they were inside a sort of cylinder forming the eye where the wind was little more than a breeze, and overhead patches of blue sky showed up, while outside the cylinder the wind would still be hurricane strength. The *Triton* would be back there as soon as the eye moved…Ramage reached for the telescope in the binnacle drawer and Southwick said: "The *Topaz* is still there, sir; nothing else has parted – not that I can see, anyway."

He could see the *Topaz* now, and more light was getting through as the blanket of thick cloud broke up overhead.

For a moment he was shocked at the way the merchantman was labouring. He watched her stern appear to dig into the forward side of a big wave, then saw the crest rushing forward, balancing the ship for a brief moment like a see-saw as the crest held her amidships, and then the bow dropping and digging into the after side as the wave swept on. Then he realized she was not labouring much more than the *Triton*; no more than one would expect with a heavy cargo down in the holds. In heavy weather it always looked as if the other ship was suffering more than one's own – but she rarely was.

Southwick should have a rest. He worked his way along the lifeline.

"Have a spell below."

"No thanks, sir; I'd sooner be on deck till this has passed."

"What, the hurricane?"

"No, sir, the eye."

"Don't worry, Appleby and I…"

"Not exactly worried, sir: I don't like the idea of being below while it's passing – I shouldn't sleep, and I'm learning something up here."

"I know what – "

Ramage broke off, appalled by the look on Southwick's face. The Master was staring over Ramage's left shoulder at something a long way off, and the only distant thing in that direction was the *Topaz*.

Swinging round, the telescope still in one hand, Ramage looked over the larboard bow, but stinging spray blinded him for a moment. He wiped his eyes and saw what by now he expected: the *Topaz* had been dismasted. She was just a stubby log, with her masts and yards lying alongside in the water in a tangle of rope and spars.

Gradually the wreckage, along the starboard side and acting as a sea anchor, made the ship swing round to starboard like a dog on a leash until she was lying broadside to the waves and rolling so violently it seemed she must capsize.

Plans flashed through Ramage's mind and were rejected as fast as a card player shuffling a pack. Finally one idea kept recurring. It was probably hopeless; but he tugged Southwick's arm, shouting: "Main storm trysail – can we hoist it?"

"We can try, sir."

"Do so, then."

As Southwick waddled forward holding the lifelines (the wind inside his oilskins inflating them like a bladder), Ramage doubted if the men could get it done in time. If they can get the sail hoisted, would the flax stand when the eye passed?

With the sail hoisted and holding, he hoped he could turn the *Triton* and heave-to near the *Topaz*. He was not sure there was really any point in doing so. It all seemed hopeless, almost stupid. There was no hope of passing a hawser to tow, and in this sea the idea of towing was ludicrous anyway. Could he take everyone off? The odds on a ship o' war surviving were slight; the chances for one of her boats was minuscule. But no one knew how long the calm of the eye would last. He might have half an hour.

Southwick was signalling and Ramage was surprised to see that he had a couple of dozen men on deck, each with a rope round his waist secured to something solid. The trysail was slowly going up the stay.

The *Topaz* was abeam: now every moment would put her that much farther to windward.

He turned to Appleby.

"I'll take over here: check that the men at the relieving tackles are standing by. Tell them to be ready for a turn to larboard. Then stand where you can see me and when I signal – I'll point to larboard with my arm – the helm goes over. Then we heave-to on the larboard tack."

Appleby staggered below and Ramage looked at the four ratings at the wheel. They were strong and steady men. He told them what to expect in a minute or so, saw Southwick looking aft and indicated by signs what he was going to do, and then noticed Appleby standing halfway up the companionway.

Ramage turned to look aft and suddenly realized that the distant roar of wind, which had been coming from all round the horizon, was now much louder from right astern. He couldn't work out the reason for it, and anyway he now had to wait for a smooth – a sequence of one or two, and hopefully three, waves less high than the others, so that he could start the turn.

From watching the tumbling waves astern he glanced up to see the main trysail was hoisted and sheeted home. It was tiny, only a handkerchief, but it had an immediate effect – he could see the wheel reacting to it. Then he looked aft again. The wave crest immediately astern was lower, and so were the ones beyond: he jerked out his left arm for Appleby's benefit, pointing to larboard, and bellowed at the men at the wheel.

They struggled and strained to turn it. After a few moments it became easier as Appleby passed the order to the men at the relieving tackles. The distant roaring was getting louder, and he glanced up to see that the few patches of clear sky had vanished: the thick low cloud was back.

The rudder, the wind on the main trysail – which was abaft the ship's centre of balance – and the wind blowing on her quarter, were all working together now to shove the *Triton*'s stern violently over to starboard and pivot the bow round to larboard. The seas, too, were now on the larboard quarter and adding their quota of thrust; in a few moments the *Triton* would be beam on to the seas and as she continued turning they'd be on the bow. There, with the helm hard over to counteract the main trysail, she should lie hove-to.

Ramage watched her turning, alarmed by the roaring, which seemed to be getting very near, and glanced back aft to see if – then the wind came: it suddenly increased and simultaneously veered twenty or thirty degrees: instead of coming from the quarter it was abeam; its sudden and enormous pressure was trying to capsize the brig. The eye had passed; they were back in the hurricane.

Looking astern, Ramage knew his manoeuvre was doomed. It was like staring up from a valley at the side of a mountain collapsing on to him: a series of great waves was sweeping down on the quarter. They might not have been bigger than the worst of the earlier waves, but because they were coming on the quarter and would catch the brig when she was completely vulnerable, halfway through her turn, they were potentially lethal. Catching the little *Triton* on the quarter, adding their quota to the beam wind on the spars and trysail, they would make her broach.

"Stand fast everyone!" he found himself bellowing, although only the helmsmen could hear him. As he looked forward he was glad to see that several of the men had already seen the danger and were grabbing rigging, eyebolts on the deck, the carronades or anything that was firm.

When the first of the great waves arrived, the whole larboard side, as high as Ramage could see, seemed to be a wall of water. He found himself fighting for his life, gasping, swallowing water, blinded by the salt in his eyes, coughing, winded by a tremendous blow on the chest, swimming upside down in the dark, suddenly snatched into light, drowning, kicking and struggling, clutching a thick rope with all the strength he had. He just managed to wrap his legs round the rope before there was the sharp cracking of breaking timbers. The rope he was holding went bar taut, then slack, and then taut again...The deck, already moving wildly under his feet, seemed to have slid up vertically and back again.

The sound of pouring water: a cataract, tons of water swilling and spilling...Still blinded by water, finding it hard to breathe, coughing and coughing, with water like acid at the back of his throat, he held on to the rope so hard it was part of his body. Such a bloody waste to die in a hurricane; just wind and rain and mountainous seas and achieving nothing; no enemy beaten, no prize. Just a bloody waste...

By now the noise was lessening and the cataract had stopped. He could hear the drumming of the wind, and miraculously, unbelievably, the ship was still afloat. Afloat but dead in the water, wallowing broadside on, as if pausing a moment before sinking. Perhaps he wasn't going to die after all. Perhaps there was a chance for the ship and for the Tritons.

He stumbled to his feet, shaking his head and blinking to get rid of the salt sting: until he could see he dare not let go of the rope. As he regained full consciousness he realized that he had nearly drowned while still on board. As his eyes cleared he saw that the ship was just a hulk covered in a complicated web of ropes. There were no masts, no yards and no wheel...Men were lying flat on the deck or crouched down, but the masts and spars were all in the water on the starboard side, attached to the ship by the web of ropes which had been shrouds and halyards, sheets and braces, lifts and purchases a few moments ago. It looked as if a giant in a fit of rage had plucked them out of the ship and flung them into the sea.

Muzzily he realized that the series of cracks and thumps he had heard were the masts going by the board as the ship…he began to reconstruct what had happened.

By a dreadful triple coincidence the *Triton* had begun her turn as the eye of the hurricane passed, bringing with it not just wind but those enormous seas which, coming up on the larboard quarter, had picked the ship up and shoved her stern round so hard she'd gone flat. That must have been when he thought he was sinking and drowning. In fact he'd been swamped but still on board, and probably flung against a shroud he'd managed to grab. That would be the thump on the chest, and the rope that was suddenly bar taut – the ship went over on her beam ends – and then slack as the shroud parted and the masts went by the board – or the masts went by the board and the shrouds parted – or the shrouds parted and…

Just before he passed out he was violently sick. When he came to a few moments later he felt fresher, the outline of the hulk was sharper and he could think again.

Instinctively he picked himself up and turned to the binnacle, meaning to use it as a rallying point for the men. The binnacle box was not there, nor was the wheel, nor were any of the men who had been steering. The capstan was still there, however, ahead of where the binnacle box had been, and ahead of the capstan was a three-foot-high splintered stump of what had been the mainmast, and beyond that a similar stump that had once been a foremast.

He held on to the edge of the capstan barrel and waved an arm at the men forward. Several were already making their way towards him, and the nearest was Southwick…

"Thank God, sir," the old man bawled. "Thought you'd gone!"

"So did I! And you?"

"Got wrapped round a carronade. Luckily it held when we broached and thank God the hatch covers held."

Ramage glanced at the hatchways – battens, tarpaulins and wedges all looked as if they'd just been fitted. The old man was dazed, and seamen were gathering round. Jackson, Stafford and others were holding axes they had collected from their special stowage places.

He shaped his hands into a speaking trumpet.

"Come on, men; we have to cut those masts adrift before they smash through the hull planking. Start with the mainmast: chop through the lanyards first!"

Several men scrambled over to the starboard side; others went to fetch more axes.

The wreckage of the masts, still tied to the ship by the rigging, made the *Triton* behave like a wild animal with one end of a rope round its neck and the other end tied to a stake driven into the ground.

The wind increased in strength every minute and the seas slowly drove the hulk round to starboard, radiusing on the wreckage. As she turned, more men crowded along the bulwarks, slashing away at the rigging.

Ramage found Southwick beside him and saw that the old man had recovered.

"Five minutes!" he said. "Then we'll get rid of the foremast. Sound the well – there must be a lot of water down there."

Southwick nodded but shouted back: "I don't think there's much, sir: the hatches held. She doesn't feel waterlogged."

Nor did she, Ramage realized; the dead feeling was caused more by the wreckage of the masts, whose weight still bore down on the starboard side.

Then Ramage remembered the *Topaz*. He had almost lost his sense of direction, first looking over the larboard bow. Of course he could see nothing, and the shock of thinking the *Topaz* had sunk was almost physical. Ramage turned away, not wanting to look at the area of surging water that marked where she had gone down. A moment later he felt Southwick tapping his arm and, glancing where he pointed, saw the *Topaz* less than three hundred yards away, dismasted and lying to the wreckage like a thick stick held in a millstream by pieces of string.

Southwick gave a tired grin. "Hope they realize we're standing by them!"

Ramage began laughing and knew he was close to hysteria.

He turned to the men chopping at the shrouds.

"Come on, men; lively there!"

Southwick beckoned to a couple of men and went below.

Relieved to find the *Triton* still afloat, Ramage began trying to relive the sequence of events that had led to the *Triton* broaching. Although he had at first thought his mind was clear, he found he was still dazed from the noise of the wind and tiredness. The *Triton* had broached because he'd handled her badly, and now he would not be able to help the *Topaz*. Even after the hurricane had passed he would not be able to be rowed over to the *Topaz* to discuss what Yorke might need, since the broaching had cleared the *Triton*'s decks of her boats as well as of everything else. The boats had been stowed, along with spare spars, over the hatchways.

The *Triton* and *Topaz* were now tiny, insecure and isolated islands in the Caribbean. Each had to be sufficient unto herself. He did not know what had happened to the rest of the convoy or how many men the *Triton* had lost when she broached. There would be time enough for checking on that, he thought bitterly; the most important job now was to safeguard the men left alive by making sure the ship stayed afloat. There was no chance of rescuing anyone who had been washed overboard. He was making a mess of everything and he knew it, but he seemed to be trying to think through a thick fog.

He imagined himself facing an examination board: now Lieutenant, you are commanding a brig, you've just broached, your masts have gone by the board, you've nothing suitable for setting up a jury rig, the wheel and binnacle were swept over the side, and you are still in a hurricane. What do you do?

To resign from the Service would be the most sensible answer, he thought, but the timing is inappropriate. Set the men to cutting the masts adrift to free the ship from the wreckage, at the same time sound the well and start men pumping if necessary. That's all being done. What next...?

With the wreckage cut away, the ship will need controlling, so check that the men at the relieving tackles are functioning, and see if the rudder and tiller are still working. If they are, then steer by using relieving tackles.

He did some quick calculations on what weight had been lost. The foremast, mainmast, yards, bowsprit and jibboom – about ten tons. Spare spars washed over the side – two tons. A suit of sails – just over a ton. Rigging and blocks – seven tons. Three boats – more than two tons. A total of, say, twenty-three tons. Later, if need be, they could get up the spare suit of sails and dump it. A couple of anchors and cables, powder and shot – it all mounted up when the displacement of the ship, fully provisioned at wartime allowance, was only 282 tons. Damn this screaming wind; it was so hard to think.

If the ship can be steered to leeward, well and good because it'll give me more time. Running off depends on which direction the wind flies to after the hurricane passes. If it comes from the west, the *Triton* and any other survivors from the convoy will probably end up ashore along the Leeward Islands; if it goes to the north, on the Spanish Main; if south, then ashore somewhere between Hispaniola and Antigua

According to all accounts it should blow from the south, but he could not rely on that.

Southwick interrupted his thoughts to report: "Fifteen minutes' pumping and it will be sucking dry, sir."

"Almost unbelievable!"

"Lucky the hatch covers held." The Master watched the men working with axes and added: "They'll soon be finished here. Let's hope we're clear of the wreckage before it smashes through the hull…"

Ramage saw a bosun's mate signalling to the men where to cut and realized that several ropes had been cut four or five times because it had been almost impossible to check where every rope went.

Southwick was soon back with a report, but his voice was so hoarse he could hardly make himself heard above the screaming wind.

"The relieving tackles?" Ramage asked.

"It's a shambles down there, sir, but the tiller's not damaged and the tackles held, though I don't know why. Wheel ropes parted each side where they go round the upper sheaves. The rudder's all right – the seaman in charge of the relieving tackle made fast with the tiller amidships. Did it on his own initiative immediately we broached."

"Remember his name and remind me later: I'll rate him 'able'."

"Deserves it," Southwick said. "Did you get hurt?" he asked suddenly.

"Only a crack across my chest."

"Thought so; you look sort of – well, crouched up. Like – "

"A wet hen!"

"Yes," Southwick laughed. "Haven't stove in a rib, have you, sir? Breathe in and out deeply. Any pain?"

Ramage shook his head. "No, it's just bruising."

"And the skin off the palms of your hands."

"And my shins. I should think everyone's suffering from that."

"Aye," Southwick said. "Rope is rough."

Ramage realized his hands were clenched, despite the soreness.

"Wind doesn't seem to be easing, sir," Southwick commented. "We're going to bounce around like a leaf in a stream when it does drop. It'll take six hours after the wind's gone for this sea to ease down noticeably."

Ramage knew he was not needed on deck at the moment: the men were working with a will, and Southwick could handle it. It was time he started looking at a chart: the ship should steer, running before the wind, maybe twenty degrees each side of it. Even at this stage it could make quite a difference to the *Triton*'s eventual destination.

He gave Southwick his orders and struggled below. When he reached his cabin he realized just how deafening the wind had been, and that his throat was raw because every word spoken for many hours had had to be shouted.

He pulled off his oilskins, took a dry towel from a rack and wiped his face and hands. The hands were painful now and he glanced down to see the skin pink, not quite raw, but worn smooth by the rope slipping.

It was hopeless trying to look at the chart standing up: without the masts steadying her and slowing the period of the roll, the brig was rolling even more violently. He flopped into the chair, and he couldn't remember it ever being so luxurious before.

He glanced through his journal, noted down the last position written in it, and did a quick calculation to bring it up to date. The answer could only be a guess. He unrolled a chart and marked an X on it with the date and time. By some miracle his watch had not filled with water and he wiped it with a dry towel.

The X on the chart was about 140 miles due west of Guadeloupe. That was the nearest land to the east. To the north – the chain of small islands running westward that became bigger the farther they went. The nearest land was the island of Santa Cruz, or St Croix, which was owned by the Danes and some ninety miles to the north-north-west. It was not very hospitable: the capital and harbour was on the north side of the island and thus out of reach of the *Triton* and *Topaz*. More promising was the island of St Thomas, beyond St Croix. Farther west was the small Spanish island of Vieques. Then came Puerto Rico, also Spanish, which stretched east-west for nearly a hundred miles.

To the south the coast of South America – the Spanish Main – was 400 miles away. There was nothing to the west for a thousand miles or more. If the *Triton* drifted mastless that far, her crew would die of thirst and probably starvation.

He tapped the chart with his pencil, trying to concentrate. With any luck he'd drift with the *Topaz*, and he wanted to answer the question "Where shall we try and make for?" before Yorke asked it after the hurricane. The short answer was, "It all depends which way the wind blows!"

If from the west, then Martinique: Fort Royal was on the west coast, with a wide entrance and therefore easy of access. If from the south, well, St Thomas seemed the best bet from a poor field of starters: its only merit was a big harbour that faced south. It was Danish and there would be all the nonsense of neutrality – although he could worry about that if and when the time came.

If from the east…Well, he must assume that whatever happened for two or three days after the lull – until the hurricane had passed on to scare some other equally deserving people – the wind would eventually go back to the east and the Trade winds would blow again. He tapped the pencil across the chart, following the course the convoy would have taken – there was a faint chance the *Triton* could make Jamaica, but could the *Topaz*?

Ramage read off some courses, rolled the chart up and put it back in the rack and pulled on his oilskins again. His clothes were soaking wet and beginning now to chill, but at least the sou'wester kept the wind out. He put his watch in the drawer: there was no sense in ruining it.

The wind had dropped a little: that much was obvious when he got back on deck. Had the seas eased slightly? Maybe not. However, the air wasn't full of flying spray and rain. It was all comparative; it just wasn't as bloody as it had been.

Southwick walked over, and handed him his telescope with a mock bow.

"One of the men just found it, sir, lodged under the starboard aftermost carronade!"

"How careless of me," Ramage said airily. "I also seem to have mislaid the wheel and binnacle."

"Ah," Southwick said, "I noticed that and I've shipped the spare compass." He pointed to a box secured by lines to a pair of ringbolts abaft the capstan.

"But – " Ramage began.

"Yes, they're iron," Southwick said hurriedly. "The carpenter's mate is going to fasten the box to the deck farther forward as soon as the hurricane stops. I've just lashed it down ready for him."

"Very well. By the way, did we lose all our signal flags?"

"No, sir." He gestured to the taffrail, where three men were rigging a short spar vertically. "I thought that might do for the moment as a signal mast."

Ramage nodded and, sighting the *Topaz*, was surprised to see how close she was. He went to wipe the lenses of the telescope and saw that Southwick had already done it.

The wreckage of the *Topaz*'s mainmast was almost completely adrift; the seamen were still hacking away vigorously at the rigging, while a few men were starting to work on the foremast.

She still had a wheel, in fact two seamen were standing at it, but no binnacle box. Several of her guns had gone, torn loose when the bulwarks were smashed. Pity to lose those splendid brass guns...Still, there were three or four left.

Both ships had nearly the same damage, except that the *Topaz* had a wheel. Ramage brushed that aside however, since the *Triton* could be steered with relieving tackles and would rig a second tiller on deck as soon as there was time.

Now a third man was standing beside the men at the *Topaz*'s wheel. It was Yorke, who raised a telescope and looked towards the *Triton*. Ramage waved, Yorke waved back and gave a thumbs-up sign. When Ramage waved back, Yorke began signalling again with his arm, making a complete sequence of movements, like an actor miming, and then repeating it when Ramage made no reply. Finally Ramage understood and gave a thumbs-up acknowledgment. Yorke went back to the men working on the wreckage and Ramage turned, to find that Southwick had been watching.

"Did you follow that?"

"Too far off, I'm afraid, sir. Eyes aren't what they were."

"The passengers are safe, his wheel isn't damaged, and he has nothing to use for a jury rig because, like us, he daren't risk keeping the wreckage alongside until the hurricane has passed."

By two o'clock in the afternoon the *Triton* and *Topaz*, each a hulk but cleared of the wreckage of their masts, were wallowing along within a hundred yards of each other while overhead the clouds began to lift as the wind eased.

"Just look at it," Southwick said angrily, pointing at the clouds. "If you didn't know, you'd think we were on the edge of a squall that'd blow itself out in half an hour."

"Except for these seas!" Ramage said.

Southwick nodded, and looked nervously at the *Topaz*. "I just can't get used to being dismasted. Feel vulnerable."

"Don't fret; I can't think anyone really gets used to it," Ramage said cheerfully. "Now, everything's settled, so why don't you get some rest?"

The Master looked around the ship, as if anxious to make sure nothing had been left undone.

"Rest, Mr Southwick," Ramage said finally. "I can make it an order, if you like."

"Sorry, sir," he said apologetically. "You're quite right. But you'll – "

"I'll call you if the weather worsens, but without sleep," Ramage added with intentional harshness, knowing it was one of the few ways of persuading the old Master, "you're no use to anyone."

Southwick nodded, excused himself and made his way below.

If only the damned seas would ease: the *Triton*'s motion was still violent. What had been forgotten? Ramage thought hard but nothing came to mind. His earlier idea of transferring everyone from the *Topaz* and abandoning her had been absurd: one glance over the side had shown the impossibility of that, apart from the fact that neither ship had a boat left.

He considered the possibility that another of the King's ships might sight the brig and take her in tow, but there was little hope of that: any ship within a week's sailing of this position was likely to be in as much trouble as the *Triton*, if not more. Nor were they now on any regular convoy track. Not even a privateer would come this way. The thought of a privateer brought him up with a start. It'd be a proud privateer that returned with the *Topaz* in tow. It would take practically no effort to capture her now, only patience. Wait for the weather to ease up, and then board her. Nor would the *Triton* be much more difficult; raking her by sailing across her bow and stern and staying out of the arcs of fire of her broadside guns...

Southwick was back on deck by five o'clock and cheerfully commenting on the speed with which the wind was dropping. The cloud was breaking up overhead, and the sea was easing slightly.

"Seems it goes quicker than it arrives!" Southwick said.

Ramage nodded. "I don't think the eye was in the centre."

"Couldn't have been, sir. It's cleared in – how long?" He scratched his head, a puzzled look on his face.

"Damned if I know," Ramage admitted. "We lost the masts about ten hours ago, I suppose. The hurricane began – hell fire, I can't remember. What day is it?"

Southwick shook his head helplessly. "We'll have to sit down and work it out, sir – and make up the entries for the log..."

By midnight the wind had dropped to a fresh breeze, stars were visible overhead through breaks in the cloud, and the seas were easing, although still running high. A muster of the ship's company showed four men missing, presumably lost when the brig broached. Considering the size of the waves and the speed with which it all happened, Ramage knew he had been lucky not to lose more. Six men killed by the *Peacock* and four by the hurricane.

Southwick, pleasantly surprised that only four had been lost, said cheerfully: "Think of it as fifty-one survivors, sir!"

CHAPTER **TEN**

Stafford was the first man to sight land a few moments before noon three days after the eye had passed. With all the watch gathered round and cheering, Ramage presented him with a guinea prize.

The cockney, in his usual breezy way, spun the coin and kissed it for luck and said to Ramage: "Permission to ask a question, sir?"

Ramage nodded, although guessing the question would probably verge on impertinence.

"Did you ever reckon you'd 'ave ter pay, sir?"

When Ramage looked puzzled, Stafford explained: "We was in the eye of the 'urricane when you said you'd present a guinea ter 'ooever saw land first. Didn't seem much chance we'd live long enough fer that, sir."

Ramage decided that it was not the time to tell the ship's company that the offer of a guinea prize was all he could think of to cheer them up when things looked desperate. Instead he just smiled knowingly at Stafford and said: "I even guessed where the land would be!"

Stafford looked startled. "Cor – where is it, sir?"

"One of the Virgin Islands."

"Virgins, sir? Wot, 'ere?"

Stafford's surprise was genuine and apparently shared by the rest of the men.

"Yes, several," Ramage said, without a smile. "British and Danish. No French or Spanish."

"No French or Spanish! D'yer 'ear that!" Stafford poked Rossi in the ribs. "Nor no Eyetalian virgins, either!"

Ramage gestured to Jackson: "Right, now; make a signal to the *Topaz* – *Land in sight to the north-west.*"

The *Topaz* acknowledged it promptly, and Ramage saw Southwick hunched over the compass.

Ramage walked over to take bearings of each end of the island. Radiating out from where the compass box was fastened to the deck, and looking like the spokes of a wheel, a series of thin grooves had just been cut in the deck planking, the thickest corresponding to the fore and aft line. It was Southwick's idea and was a crude pelorus: it allowed a rough bearing to be taken without lifting up the compass.

Ramage picked up the slate from its new stowage on the forward side of the starboard aftermost carronade slide, and after checking the time wrote: "12.03 p.m. Sighted one of Virgin Islands NW x W $\frac{1}{2}$ W, distant about twelve miles."

"Let's have a cast of the log," Ramage told Appleby.

Ten minutes later, as the Master's mate supervised the men stowing the reel again, be noted the *Triton*'s speed and the course being steered:

"Speed $1\frac{1}{2}$ knots, course north, wind south, fresh."

No log entry could describe seas that were no longer monstrous, clouds that no longer warned of unbelievable winds and rain the like of which few men ever saw and lived to describe. No log entry could tell how happy men were just to be alive, even though their ship was almost helpless, driven forward only by the pressure of the wind on the hull.

He looked over on the starboard quarter where the *Topaz* lumbered along, a great ox splashing through a muddy lane. She still looked smart, even without masts, bowsprit or jibboom. If spars suddenly went out of fashion, the *Topaz* would rate as an elegant ship. For that matter masts have gone out of fashion, he reminded himself, at least around here.

Landfalls were curious: one usually waited days, if not weeks; but once the low grey shape – it always *was* a low grey shape – was spotted, it became a matter of the greatest urgency to identify it. This was no exception: St Croix stretched for more than thirty miles athwart their course: they could pass either east or west of it to make for one of the other islands beyond. But if it was, say, Virgin Gorda, then they had to get to the westward quickly before they ran on to the reefs littering that end of the islands.

"You're smiling, sir," Southwick, who had just come on deck, said: "St Croix?"

"Virgins," Ramage said. "I was thinking that Columbus must have been in a whimsical mood when he passed through those islands and named them."

"How so?"

"Virgin Gorda, up to the east. It would have been the first of them he sighted. It means 'The Fat Virgin'!"

"He'd been at sea a long time?" Southwick suggested.

"No, not at that point, but the islands were being sighted thick and fast."

"Puerto Rico," Southwick said. 'That does mean 'Rich Port', doesn't it?"

"Yes."

"But why name a whole island 'Rich Port'?"

"He didn't – so the story goes: it was a mistake made in Madrid."

"How come, sir?"

"Because he sighted the island on St John's Day he named the island 'San Juan' after him. Then he found a deep bay on the north coast – a perfect natural harbour, and the soil was obviously rich. So he named the harbour 'Puerto Rico'."

"Ah," Southwick exclaimed, slapping his knee, "so when he reported back, some clerk got 'em mixed up!"

When Ramage nodded, the Master said: "But why have they never put it right?"

"The mistake probably arose in Court – Columbus reported directly to the King. Either the King did not notice the mistake, or would not draw attention to it later."

"I can't see anyone pointing it out to him, either!"

"Well, whatever happened it's been that way for three hundred years!"

Southwick pulled out his watch, looked first at the grey smudge ahead and then at the *Triton*'s wake, and sniffed disapprovingly. "Thirty minutes. Hasn't exactly leapt up over the horizon."

"We're not exactly galloping towards it!"

In an hour he'd know whether they would pass the eastern or western end. Two things could upset the calculations – a strong west-going current, and easterly winds: both would push the *Triton* and *Topaz* to the westwards. They needed the present southerly wind to continue, but it was an unusual wind. Almost certainly, once the effect of the hurricane had worn off, it would fly back to the eastern quadrant; the Trades would return.

An hour later Southwick took another bearing of the eastern end of St Croix. Even before he plotted it on the chart, Ramage knew they had no choice: they would pass the western end because the current was setting the *Triton* down to the west.

When he marked it on the chart, drawing in the *Triton*'s track for the last hour, it was increasingly obvious that it was going to be a struggle even to keep up to the east enough to be sure of making St Thomas, thirty miles beyond St Croix. To the westward of St Thomas, some seventy miles away, was Puerto Rico. Ramage had no wish to spend even a few weeks, let along months or years, in a Spanish prison…

Back on deck Southwick was pacing up and down and Ramage wondered what had angered him. Before he noticed the Captain had come up the companionway, the Master bent over the compass again, his eye travelling along one of the grooves in the deck planking and over the bow to the eastern end of St Croix. Then he saw Ramage.

"Should never have lost all the spars," he said wrathfully. "Not to be able to set up *any* sort of jury rig. Who'd have thought we'd have nothing left?"

"We couldn't have saved anything," Ramage said mildly. "I was damned glad to see it all go. I'd no wish to see a topmast surfing itself through our hull planking like a swordfish and sinking us."

"Well, no, sir, but if only we could set a stitch of canvas now we would weather the eastern end of that damned island. As it is, we'll be hard put to have it still in sight as we pass to the westward."

"No matter what jury rig you could contrive, Mr Southwick, don't forget you'd have to make a duplicate for the *Topaz*…"

"By jingo, yes! We couldn't leave her!"

"Well, then," Ramage said, shrugging his shoulders.

"But it doesn't stop me wanting to keep up to the eastward," Southwick said stubbornly. "It's only natural. All my life I've been trained never to lose an inch to leeward."

"Me too," Ramage said sarcastically. "I joined the same Navy. But we aren't trying to get the weather gage of a French squadron."

"True, sir. By the way, we opened another cask of salt pork today. Six pieces short."

Ramage nodded and knew Southwick's mood of depression had passed. When the Master mentioned such mundane things, all was well.

All was well, and some dishonest contractor to the Admiralty had made his usual illicit extra profit, by filling the cask with brine and a few pieces of salt pork less than the number he painted on the outside giving the alleged contents.

It was sometimes hard to think of the Navy as a fighting force, Ramage reflected; it seemed to be an enormous organization where contractors – whether supplying salt pork or beef, timber from the Baltic, rum from the West Indies, butter and dried pease, shirts for the pursers to sell or flax for the sails – made great profits selling items which were underweight or of poor quality.

If the contractors had to sell their wares in the market place, he thought bitterly, they'd starve. As it is they wax fat, presumably quietly paying the percentages required to ensure Navy Board officials look the other way, and attend banquets where they drink bumpers to the damnation of the French. In the meantime ship after ship, week after week, recorded in the log such entries as "Opened cask of beef marked 151 pieces, contained 147."

Now the spare tiller had been shipped on top of the rudder head, steering was a good deal easier. Certainly the long tiller sweeping across the after deck cut down the space the commanding officer had to walk, but he wasn't so sure whether, for a vessel of this size, the tiller wasn't really better than the wheel anyway.

The Italian seaman, Rossi, was taking a spell at the tiller with the coloured man, Maxton.

"No luff to watch," Ramage said.

"Does make no difference, sir," Rossi said.

"How so?"

"Habit, sir. All the time I keep looking here or here" – he pointed to where the luff of the mainsail would be on either tack with the wind close-hauled – "just as though the masts they still stand."

"No big t'ing, sir," Maxton said as if apologizing for Rossi's grumbling, and Ramage smiled to himself: it was a favourite West Indian expression. "But," Maxton confessed, "I keep forgetting and frightening myself when I see the masts are gone."

"You'll get used to it," Ramage said dryly.

"Do we…" Rossi stopped, embarrassed that he'd begun to ask a question, but continued after Ramage nodded. "Are we making for that island, sir?"

"No. We pass as close as we can. It has no harbours or bays we can use. We want another one north of it. Thirty miles beyond."

By nightfall St Croix was several miles to the east of them and with the night glass Ramage could just make out the high land behind Frederiksted, at the western end of the island. During the late afternoon they'd found the current sweeping athwart their course not only pushing them inexorably to the westward but increasing in strength the closer they got to St Croix. It was presumably the sea pouring into the Caribbean from the Atlantic through the Anegada Passage – there was a reference to it in the sailing directions. And it meant their progress was crabwise; a diagonal resulting from the south wind pushing them north and the current pushing them west.

Ramage was woken at four o'clock next morning: a wind change, the quartermaster reported. As he struggled into his clothes he reflected that any change could only be for the worse: the best wind for them was the one they'd had, from the south.

The deck was a vast and empty expanse in the darkness with a small group of men aft, by the tiller, and three or four men – the lookouts – up forward.

"It's backing, sir," Southwick said gloomily. "Dropped a bit and backed to south-east-by-south. The way it did it, I reckon it'll go round more."

Ramage pictured the chart in his mind. By now, the north-western corner of St Croix should be on the starboard quarter, St Thomas dead ahead, and the small island of Vieques, with Puerto Rico massive behind it, on the larboard beam.

Between St Thomas and Vieques, away to the north-west, was an island marked on the chart as "Snake or Passage Island", one end of a long line of coral cays reaching westward to Puerto Rico. But from St Thomas to Puerto Rico the sea was a mass of reefs, islands and rocks. In daylight, properly rigged, it was no great problem; at night a safe passage through there would be virtually impossible, whether one had masts or not...

If the wind went any more to the east they'd have no choice anyway. Without the means of steering, apart from making slight changes either side of the direction that the wind carried them, if they had to go through that passage they were done for. Avoiding the long and often unexpected reefs – for the charts were rudimentary – would mean tacking or wearing round, and probably beating to windward, and these were manoeuvres which were part of the past for both the *Triton* and the *Topaz*.

"We can only do our best," Ramage said to Southwick. "Same as before – keep up to the east as best you can."

He looked astern for the *Topaz*. That was one of the advantages of the Tropics – unless there was rain, it was very rarely completely dark. Almost always there was enough light to give a hint of land, or some other ship, at a useful distance.

The *Topaz* was on the same bearing and finding the same wind shift. So be it. Since he could do nothing about it, whether the wind backed, veered or went flat, he was going to get some sleep; he had been reminded of the dangers of the lack of it a few days ago.

He was woken again shortly before dawn when the ship's company went to quarters, and found it oddly comforting that he had not given the order to get rid of the guns after the ship broached: the *Triton* might not have masts, but no privateer would come alongside with impunity.

As daylight rolled back the horizons, Ramage was relieved to see that they had managed to stay up enough to the east to have St Thomas ahead, but frightened by the bewildering number of islands almost all round them, all with outlying coral reefs and shoals of rocks.

"Hopeless trying to identify them," he said to Southwick. "We need to spread out the chart and then mark 'em off!"

He sent Jackson down to the cabin to fetch it and stared at St Thomas again with the telescope.

"Like Tuscany," Ramage commented to Southwick, gesturing towards St Thomas.

"Dull," Southwick said. "Not a patch on Grenada."

Grenada and Martinique were Southwick's favourite Caribbean islands. He hated St Lucia because it was a wet island with an oppressive, sullen atmosphere and Antigua because it was arid and mosquito-ridden. On balance, Ramage agreed with his assessment.

Jackson arrived with the chart and at a gesture from Ramage spread it out on the deck, holding it down to prevent it rolling up again.

"Right," Ramage said. "St Thomas is dead ahead," jabbing a finger down on the chart. "Hmm – Puerto Rico looks a big lump!"

Over on the larboard beam they could see a large cone-shaped mountain which was the centre of a range at the east end of the island.

Ramage traced it on the chart. "Ah yes – *El Yunque*, 'The Anvil'. It looks tall enough!"

Southwick pointed to a nearer island almost in line with it. "Is that Vieques?"

"Yes, long on the chart, but looks deceptively short from this angle," Ramage said.

He slowly turned to the right. "That'll be Snake Island with all these little islands and cays round it – north of Vieques. You can just see it. Now look at the chart – see all these reefs – how they stretch on to Puerto Rico in a long line?"

Southwick measured, using two fingers as dividers. "Why, there's fifteen miles of them! The Cordilleras Reefs. And look at the rocks at the end. What does '*Las Cucarachas*' mean?"

"The cockroaches."

"Damned odd name." He looked round the horizon. "Ah, that's Sail Rock!" He pointed to a curiously shaped island sticking starkly up from the sea and, white in the sunlight, looking in the distance like a ship under sail.

Ramage took the slate and said brusquely: "Let's have some bearings noted down, please."

"Sorry, sir," Southwick said. "I got carried away!"

Even if the wind did not back any more, Ramage thought they would not reach St Thomas because of this west-going current sweeping towards the reefs round Snake Island. Maybe they'd only miss St Thomas by a mere couple of miles and take their chance among Savana Island, Kalkfin Cay, Dutchcap Cay, Cockroach Cay and Cricket Cay.

The upper edge of the sun's disc was just poking over the eastern horizon when his steward came up to announce that breakfast was ready. Jackson rolled up the chart and Ramage took it below.

They had left Barbados only a few days ago, though it seemed like weeks, and he still had fresh eggs to eat. The milk had lasted only twelve hours or so out of Carlisle Bay – something about the motion of a ship curdled the milk even faster than it curdled in a house on shore. His steward still had not got used to having a captain who demanded fresh fruit for breakfast when it was available, but although he did not approve, he served it. The other great advantage of being in the Caribbean was that the coffee was really coffee, not breadcrumbs roasted and boiled to make mud-coloured water.

As he cracked the shell of the first egg, Ramage had the curious feeling that he was being rushed like a twig in a flooded mountain stream, with events controlling him. He tried to think of the options open to him at this minute, but no more ideas came. The fact was that the *Triton* and *Topaz* were two ships without masts, and without masts they could move only in the direction the wind drove them. There was no point in trying to think of landfalls until he knew what wind and current were going to do. To plan was simply an exercise in futility and was spoiling his breakfast.

By nine o'clock in the morning, as the sun's warmth began to be felt, Southwick watched the seamen reeling in the log line and stowing the minute glass. He noted the *Triton*'s speed on the slate and turned to Ramage, shaking his head.

"It won't serve, sir."

"You're a late convert! I've already cancelled my rooms at whichever is the best hotel these Danskers have to offer."

"I was hoping we'd pick up an eddy current. We're only ten miles from St Thomas now."

Ever since dawn the west-going current had made the whole island appear to be sliding to the eastward, while the islands to the west – Vieques, Snake Island and, beyond them Puerto Rico – were creeping up on the larboard side from the westward, even though the *Triton* and *Topaz* were still steering directly for St Thomas.

It was hopeless trying to conceal from the ship's company that it was anyone's guess where the *Triton* would be cast ashore. Southwick had unrolled and folded his chart. Now, using the top of the capstan as a table, he was inspecting it.

"Could you spare a moment, sir?"

Ramage walked over, and Southwick, without saying anything, ran his finger in a gentle curve from where he had pencilled in the *Triton*'s present position, up to the north-west between St Thomas and Snake Island on out into the vast Atlantic. Ramage traced a sharper curve, landing them among reefs near to Snake Island.

"Can't be helped," he said briefly, knowing that any of the ship's company who overheard him would be none the wiser.

"But..." Southwick began helplessly.

Ramage pointed to the three or four soundings which showed depths of twenty and thirty fathoms.

"Around one hundred and fifty feet is too deep for good fishing," he said cryptically.

"Depressing, sir, I'd like some fresh fish."

He unfolded the chart and rolled it up, as if finally resigning himself to the impossibility of anchoring.

CHAPTER ELEVEN

"Not hard to see why it got its name!" Southwick said sourly, gesturing at the island. It did look like a snake lying coiled up, its head the top of the small, rounded mountain which seemed to be the centre of the island. But a look at the chart showed the real reason for the name: the island was shaped like a snake's head seen sideways and facing eastward with its mouth wide open. The mouth made a huge, almost enclosed bay, with the settlement of San Ildefonso on the east side of it and not even in sight of the open sea.

The island bore west now, and the *Triton*, followed by the *Topaz*, had just sailed and drifted a mile off Sail Rock and could make no better than west. The current was running north-west; the wind had continued backing and was trying to drive the ships south-west. The result was a compromise; a crabwise course of west.

"Should be able to separate the other islands and cays soon and identify 'em," Southwick commented. "In fact that headland over there on the north side – reckon that's Isla Culebrita."

"Probably," Ramage said, adding wryly, "but the fact is, for once we're not really concerned! We just need to know where we are once our keel touches."

"What's '*Culebra*' mean, sir? I see they give it as another name here on the chart."

"Spanish for 'snake'. No, 'serpent' would be more exact."

He looked at the chart and tapped the long shoal running diagonally up to the north-east, between them and the island, and nearly a mile offshore.

"*Arrecife Culebrita*...that's where we'll end up, Mr Southwick. You can take bets for positions from here" – he jabbed a finger on the southern end – "to here, by Culebrita. Three miles of splendid reef. Pity it's all underwater; otherwise we could have marched the Marines up and down it each day, and the ship's company on Sundays!"

"I don't trust this chart," Southwick said sourly. "It's a benighted mixture, a bit o' Spanish, a bit o' French, an' a ground tier of English. Between 'em they're bound to have missed a lot of isolated rocks – the sort that sink innocent ships."

"Well, tell the men; it'll get the job done all the faster!"

Ramage gestured forward where most of the Tritons were working hard with ropes, battens of wood, hammers and nails, making a raft from a dozen casks which had been brought up from below after being emptied of fresh water.

More men, working separately, were making a much smaller raft, where each alternate barrel was full of salt meat or fresh water. Yet a third raft, smaller still, was being made up of casks in some of which had been packed carefully wrapped muskets, powder, shot, cutlasses, tomahawks and a collection of tools supplied by the carpenter's mate.

"At least we're learning something about making rafts," Ramage said.

"An' keeping the lads occupied won't do any harm at this time," Southwick said.

"Well, if they're doing a good job they need only sit on their rafts and wait until the *Triton* breaks up underneath them. Then they can float clear with the band playing."

"D'you think she'll go that fast, sir?"

"No, not in this weather, but there's always a chance. Depends whether we hit an isolated rock and sink in five minutes, or scrape up gently on a nice coral reef and stay there for a year or more, a warning to Spanish fishermen of what happens if you eat meat on Fridays."

"Let's hope we slide on gently. I'd sooner transfer to our new estate at our leisure."

"Don't you think we should wait until the Dons send out written invitations?"

"No, sir!" Southwick said with mock alarm. "We don't want to put them to the trouble of rowing several miles to windward – why, it's four or five miles from San Ildefonso to the middle of the reefs."

"Then we'll call on them with banners flying and bearing gifts, Mr Southwick," Ramage said, in the ringing tones of some hearty politician. "By Jove, we mustn't risk upsetting his Most Catholic Majesty!"

"Doubtless a full dress occasion, sir; but using a raft instead of a carriage is going to wash the shine off our boots."

"Mr Southwick, if I dare mention more mundane matters than our proposed social engagements, would you care to place a man where he can give us a cast of the lead?"

"Indeed, sir; yours to command," he said, giving what he imagined was a flourish more suited to a Spanish courtier wearing an ostrich-feather plume in his hat.

In fact the depths were great enough to require the deep sea lead, and Ramage told the Master not to bother, since any accuracy with that required the ship to be hove-to.

"Have a man ready with the ordinary lead; he can try for soundings from time to time." With that, Ramage walked forward again to inspect the rafts. The Bosun was in charge of the construction of the large one and had already named it

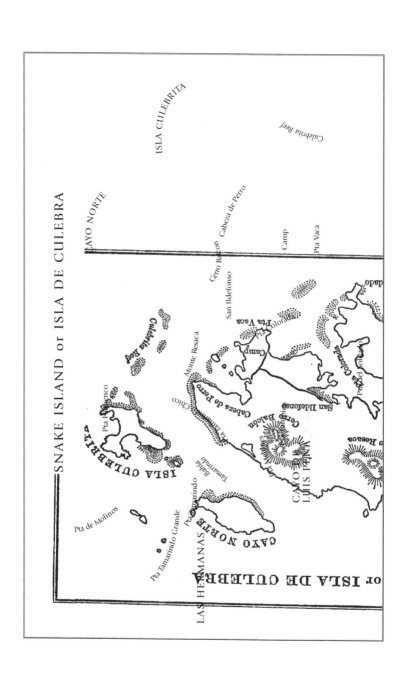

SNAKE ISLAND or ISLA DE CULEBRA

the *Gosport Ferry*, well known to most seamen who had ever been in Portsmouth. Jackson was supervising the muskets and tools raft.

"Breakers ahead!"

The shout came from the lookout at the bow and in a matter of moments Ramage was standing beside him. The man pointed to a line of lighter green water ahead and to starboard. Beyond, some waves broke on a shoal a foot or two below the surface and just visible as a dark brown mass.

Snake Island was still two or three miles ahead and Ramage shouted back to Southwick who was standing by the man at the tiller.

"Come over to larboard as much as you can: we might just scrape past south of them. Doesn't matter very much now the rafts are ready."

The last few words were for the benefit of the ship's company, and Ramage waited patiently to see what Southwick could do.

Slowly the bow came round a few degrees, and Ramage could see that unless the current eddied unexpectedly, they might just miss.

Damn! His memory!

"Mr Southwick! Make a signal to the *Topaz: Breakers ahead!*"

As seamen hoisted the flags from the staff lashed to the taffrail, Ramage saw that the *Topaz*, which had been in the *Triton's* wake, was already changing course to conform. Yorke and his officers did not miss much. The *Topaz* would definitely clear since she was beginning her turn a cable sooner. It was going to be close for the *Triton*, though. He stood at the stem with the lookout, who kept muttering to himself, without any sign of fear, as though trying to will the ship clear, "It's going to be close! It's going to be close!"

Stranded on this reef with the wind blowing fresh for twenty-four hours and knocking up a brisk sea would see the *Triton* reduced to splinters. The rafts would be useless since there was a second line of reefs beyond the first. If the brig was wrecked on the first reef the rafts would smash up on the second. He wondered if Southwick would notice: the Master had not pointed out the possibility when they first discussed making rafts.

Then Ramage saw that the *Triton* would pass clear. It would be close, but reefs were no exception to the rule that a miss was as good as a mile.

The little black figures on the reef were pelicans: one flapped into the air, incredibly ungainly until it was flying several feet above the water. A moment later it dived, suddenly closing its wings and splashing into the water.

"Like a round shot, sir!" the lookout commented.

"Yes. And they hit with such a bang I don't see how they avoid breaking their necks!"

He turned to call to Southwick and saw every man in the ship had stopped work and was standing staring at the reef. They were still shaken up. Guns blazing, cutlasses clanking, pikes jabbing, tomahawks thudding – these things were music rather than terrifying noises to the men. But the crazy, demented screaming of a hurricane; the penetrating hiss and bowel-shaking thump of enormous seas; the smooth curling of waves over sunken coral reefs were something different. Although the enemy couldn't frighten the Tritons, nature could.

He began walking aft, unhurried, and pausing at the big raft. He looked at the Bosun.

"Might be worth lashing a roll of canvas, or an old awning, on top there: the sun will bake us if we have to go far in the *Gosport Ferry*."

"Aye, aye, sir. I'll get up something for the other two rafts, too."

He walked a few steps to where the smallest raft was nearly complete.

"She can be launched whenever you're ready, sir," Jackson said.

"You heard me telling the Bosun about an awning?"

Jackson pointed to a bundle of canvas on the deck, secured to the raft by a line, and Ramage nodded.

All the men were back at work again, yet he was sure they had not yet passed the end of the reef. He walked leisurely aft to join Southwick, and from there saw that the reef was forty yards on the starboard bow.

Southwick mopped his face with a large green handkerchief, and said quietly: "I'm getting old for this sort of nonsense, sir. Being without masts in these waters is like riding a steeplechaser without a saddle."

"We're passing well clear."

"Yes, but I didn't think we would!"

Ramage saw a swirl in the water about two miles ahead and picked up the telescope. It was not just a single swirl: it stretched for a mile or more, tiny wavelets breaking on it, with a long band of dark brown just beneath the water.

A slowly shelving reef of coral? A sudden, sheer bank of rocks? Would the *Triton* run up gently, like a rowing-boat grounding on a sandy beach, or crash into it like a blind man walking into a low wall? The reef was long, and stretched athwart their course so there was no way of avoiding it. This was the *Triton's* grave and the only thing to do was to prepare for it.

He shouted for Jackson, and when the American arrived he said: "Make three signals to the *Topaz* – in this order: *Breakers ahead. Breakers to the south-west. Breakers to the north-west.*"

Southwick said: "That tells them the story!"

The shortcomings of the signal book always left captains trying to use their ingenuity to make their meaning clear. He hoped that Yorke would understand the signal was trying to tell him that this was the reef they would hit...

"Mr Southwick – please inspect those rafts. And make sure the men who can't swim have some wood to hold on to. Have the cooper stave a few barrels: the staves lashed together are just the right size."

Jackson, helped by Stafford, was hoisting flags and, as soon as the *Topaz* acknowledged them, hauling them down and preparing more.

How to lessen the *Triton*'s impact? That was important whether it was shelving coral or sheer rock. More important if it was sheer rock.

Let go an anchor just before they hit? It might work, swinging the ship round like a dog on a leash. But it needed perfect timing – and shallow enough water for the anchor to bite.

He gave Southwick orders to get ready to let go the starboard anchor.

There was nothing more to do until they hit – not on deck, anyway. He went down to his cabin with the signal book and quickly cleared the documents from his desk. Journal, orders, signal book, letter book, muster book...He put them in a box which had holes drilled in the sides and was weighted with a piece of lead, made specially for throwing secret papers over the side when there was a risk of capture.

Pistols. The pair of duelling pistols. He quickly loaded them, put them back in the wooden case, and slid that into a large canvas bag. He shoved clothing on top, and a pair of heavy leather boots, remembered his quadrant and put the box in another bag, then took the almanac and volumes of tables from the little bookshelf over the desk and added those to the items in the second bag. Without them he could not work out the sights. Pencils, a packet of paper, the chronometer and the miniature of Gianna.

He tied the necks of both bags and left them on his desk. After a word to the Marine sentry at the door, he went up on deck.

It was hard to believe that in half an hour's time this cabin and the ship would probably have ceased to exist. It seemed a long time since he had been given command of the brig. He'd sailed the ship more than five thousand miles since then, and she was covering the last couple of miles of her existence right now…

Although he did not know the exact figures, Ramage thought of what had gone into the building of the ship. About 350 loads of timber had been worked up at old Henry Adam's shipyard at Beaulieu, in Hampshire. About 130 tons of timber had gone into building her hull, along with eight tons of iron – wrought at the little ironworks at Sowley Pond – and nearly four tons of copper bolts. Her bottom – soon to be ripped out – was sheathed with nearly 800 sheets of copper, weighing more than three tons. Half a ton of mixed nails, nine thousand treenails, three tons of lead…All these were needed just for her hull. Two tons of oakum for hull and deck seams, seven barrels of pitch and seven more of tar, adding one and a half tons to her weight. The original three coats of paint put on by the builder weighed fifteen hundred pounds.

Once launched, the hull, weighing some 160 tons, was towed round to Portsmouth where she went alongside the sheerlegs to have her two masts put in. Then she had received her topmasts and yards. The standing and running rigging and blocks all added their quota of weight; by the time the sails were on board and bent on, the anchors and cables (totalling more than eleven tons), water and provisions, carronades, powder and shot, gunner's, bosun's and carpenter's stores, boats and ballast, the ship's total weight was nearly 300 tons. Of that, the ship's company and their sea-chests accounted for eight and a half tons.

All this timber, cordage and paint amounted to a brig named the *Triton*; to everyone but those who had served in her, she was a name in a list of the Navy, one of the smallest ships of war commanded by a lieutenant...

To those who served in her – or to the majority of them – she was home and, like a home on shore, she had a personality; something about her that distinguished her from all others, no matter how close the apparent similarity. She was a ship men would reminisce about twenty years later; a ship a man would suddenly recall by a trick of the memory, a smell, a noise, or some bizarre circumstance.

She had been in action many times – although only twice under Ramage's command. She was eighteen years old and had been blessed – with one exception – with good captains. But now her time was running out.

Nearly every man had a few personal treasures and his pitifully small store of clothing in a sea-chest. He called Southwick over.

"Give the men the choice. They can get their chests and bags up on deck if they wish. If we break up, they'll lose them anyway. If we hold together there'll be plenty of time to get them up from below. On deck they'll probably get swamped."

"Best not give 'em the choice, sir, begging your pardon. Having a lot o' dunnage on deck when we hit..."

"You're quite right; it could be dangerous. Very well, belay that."

What gives a ship a personality? What makes an inert mass of timber, canvas and cordage into an almost living thing which inspires loyalty and affection among such men?

He shrugged his shoulders – a gesture noticed by a puzzled Southwick – and decided to stop thinking about it. Since it had never occurred to him to think about it before, there was no point in trying to find an answer now.

"An anchor is cleared away, Mr Southwick?"

"Aye aye, sir."

"At least we won't have to watch out for the masts going by the board."

The Master chuckled. "We must count our blessings, sir."

Snake Island was closing quickly now. Ramage glanced at Southwick's chart to refresh his memory and then lifted the telescope.

On the south side and farthest from the *Triton* the island ended in Punta del Soldado, Soldier's Point, a row of high hills dropping gently to a low peninsula. Nearest, on the eastern side, there were three big hills with San Ildefonso out of sight beyond. There was a small mountain, Cerro Balcón, to the north, with a higher one beyond – Monte Resaca, more than 600 feet high.

As he looked through the telescope and saw his immediate future magnified in the circle of the lens, he wondered how many Spanish telescopes on the island were watching the two hulks coming down towards them and what orders the commander of the garrison was giving to his troops to secure the capture of the two crews…then he noticed that the wind was dying.

More than two hours passed before the *Triton* hit the first of the reefs. The sun was dipping towards the horizon as her keel caught the staghorn coral sticking up from the bottom like small trees. The impact broke off the tops of the coral and the ship drove on farther, swinging round broadside to the wind and waves and crunching across more coral. The splintering and groaning of timber warned that the rudder was being torn off. Two men had been at the tiller until, a few minutes earlier, Ramage had ordered them to stand clear. They watched open mouthed as it suddenly slammed over and broke off.

Then the ship stopped, heading north. Southwick had disappeared below at the first shock of impact, and Ramage waited impatiently for him to return.

He signalled to Jackson.

"Get both leadlines. Sound round the ship. Mind the lead doesn't get stuck in the coral. Aft, each quarter, amidships and either bow."

It was routine but really irrelevant. There was no question of ever refloating the ship so it would be of interest only to the court martial trying him for the loss of the ship. He realized suddenly that he had not thought of Jamaica, Rear-Admiral Goddard or Sir Pilcher Skinner for many hours.

Southwick returned to report that the *Triton* had not been holed and was not making water, and Jackson reported on the depths.

Both Ramage and Southwick then used telescopes to search carefully along the whole of the eastern shore of the island, looking for any sign of troops on horseback or boats putting out, but there was no indication anyone had seen them.

"Looks safe enough," Southwick said. "No patrols or sentries, and they can't look seaward from the village."

"A lookout wouldn't show himself."

"No, sir, but we've been in sight for hours. Plenty of time to get boats ready."

"They may be ready."

"Doubt it, sir: they wouldn't want to leave it until dark to try to get through the reefs to us."

"Less risk from the reefs at night than from our guns in daylight."

"True, sir, but all the same I'm sure we haven't been spotted."

Ramage shook his head, impatiently. "If I commanded a garrison here and I saw two ships drifting down on the island, I'd keep my presence secret."

"But why, sir? Surely that would mean the seamen would be more eager to land. I mean, if they thought there was no opposition…"

"And I'd have my men hidden, so when they stepped out of their boats or off their rafts, I'd shoot them down."

Southwick said ruefully, "You're right, sir. I only hope they haven't got a commander like you."

"There may not be a garrison here anyway," Ramage conceded. "I can't see any reason for one. I doubt if the Spaniards use the island. Just fisherfolk and some sheep and goats." And, he thought, frangipani and jacaranda, hibiscus and troupial birds singing…

As they talked they watched the *Topaz*. Yorke had very little steerage way; the merchantman would hit the reef more or less where the current decided. But, Ramage was pleased to see, it would be close to the *Triton*.

The *Topaz* grounded seventeen minutes after the *Triton* and one hundred yards farther north. She too let go an anchor and then swung broadside onto the sea, and by the time she had come to a stop, the two ships appeared to have reversed positions: the *Topaz* heading north seemed to be leading the *Triton*.

As soon as he saw the merchantman had settled, he shouted to Yorke through the speaking trumpet: "Welcome to the Triton Shoal!"

"Thank you," Yorke called back. "Sorry you beat me to it: I've always dreamed of naming a piece of territory."

"It's yours in fee simple, then," Ramage told him. "I'll put it in the log: 'Both ships grounded on the Topaz Shoal'."

Yorke swept off his hat in an exaggerated gesture. "Much obliged, m'lud, much obliged!" The two men, with throats getting sore from the prolonged shouting, discussed plans. Yorke agreed that the ship's company of the *Topaz* and her passengers should transfer to the *Triton* for the night and join them for the trip to the shore in the rafts next morning.

Ramage gave Appleby orders to set men to work chopping away a section of the bulwarks so that the rafts could be slid over the side, and as soon as he saw the axes at work he had a talk with Southwick.

"The weather looks reasonably settled now. I want to send the Marines and a dozen seamen on shore tonight with muskets to be ready to cover us as we land tomorrow morning."

Southwick nodded his head in agreement.

"They'd better start as soon as a raft is ready. I'm going to put Appleby in command of them."

"Oh, Appleby?" the Master said. "I was hoping – "

Ramage shook his head.

"Shall I tell Appleby, then, sir?"

"Yes. And tell Jackson and the master-at-arms to take three men at once to empty the spirit room. I want all the spirits brought here."

"The fish'll get drunk," Southwick commented as he went to find Appleby.

Ramage was thankful he could give the order about the kegs and barrels of rum stowed below without having sentries with muskets on guard everywhere. In all too many ships that went aground or started sinking, the accident was a signal for a number of the men to batter their way into the spirit room and drink themselves into a stupor. Often such men were the only ones drowned…He would keep a half hogshead of rum and the rest would be poured over the side.

There was a big splash, and Ramage saw the men had successfully launched the smallest raft and were hauling it forward, while a couple of men carried newly made paddles which had been lashed into bundles.

Damn, he'd given instructions for Appleby, but now he needed him to take the raft up to the *Topaz*. At that moment Southwick came bustling back.

"Appleby's mustering his men, sir. I've given the key of the spirit room to the master-at-arms. With your permission I'll leave with the raft to fetch the *Topaz* people."

Ramage eyed the old Master.

"I didn't know you liked these boating expeditions."

"Makes a change, sir. I can do with the exercise."

Ramage eyed Southwick's pronounced belly and nodded.

Two hours later, as darkness fell, most of the people from the *Topaz* were on board the *Triton*. A dozen armed men under a mate had been left to guard the merchantman. Yorke had suggested getting all the provisions and water they needed next day and then setting fire to the ships but Ramage demurred. Both wrecks were hidden from prying eyes on the Puerto Rico coast by the bulk of Snake Island, and they had such low profiles it was possible that passing enemy ships would mistake them for some of the many low cays scattered across the area. A lot of flame by night or a big pall of smoke by day would be visible from just about everywhere – St Thomas, Vieques or Puerto Rico.

"But what if they do see the flames or smoke?" Yorke argued. "They won't get anything because the ship will be destroyed."

"It'll tell them we're here."

"They'll know anyway: they'll see the wrecks."

"They'll see the wrecks," Ramage said patiently, "but at a distance they might well mistake them for cays or rocks. Don't forget, they won't be *looking* for wrecks."

"But supposing they do see them?"

"If they find two dismasted wrecks with no one on board, they'll probably guess it was the result of the hurricane and think the survivors were taken off at sea by other ships, leaving the wrecks to drift on to the reef. They'll probably pillage what they can and go happily on their way. But if they find the wrecks burned, they'll know people were here *after* the ships hit the reef; people who lit the match. They'll start searching the island – and they'll know they have two complete ships' companies to find."

"You're quite right," Yorke admitted.

"For the time being, my main concern is to keep us all out of the hands of the Spaniards: their jails are a little primitive."

"Agreed," Yorke said. "By the way, to avoid any embarrassment or misunderstanding – how do you want to deal with my men?"

"We may have to think in terms of weeks, or even months, on shore here," Ramage said tactfully.

"That's why I'm asking the question."

"Have you any doubts about them?"

"Yes," Yorke said frankly. "They're merchant seamen; I can't beat them on the head with the Articles of War."

"What do you suggest?" Ramage asked cautiously. He knew what would be best, but he wanted Yorke to mention it.

"Press 'em," Yorke said succinctly. "Put 'em down on the *Triton*'s muster roll. Twenty-eight more men to serve the King."

"You're sure about the mates?"

"Very sure: there's several months' pay due to them, so I've bought those two!"

"Fine," Ramage said. "I'd better press the men before I abandon the *Triton* officially. I haven't the faintest idea what the regulations are, but I think that's when the *Triton* ceases to exist."

"Look," Yorke said, his tone of voice indicating the seriousness of what he was going to say, "have you really thought about not burning the *Triton* and *Topaz*?"

Ramage nodded without saying anything.

"But you're taking a big risk, aren't you? You personally, I mean. When you face a court of inquiry, couldn't they claim you 'didn't do your utmost' to prevent your ship falling into enemy hands? I mean, they could claim the Dons could tow the wrecks off the reef and refit them."

"They could, and probably will. But the only way of destroying the ships is by setting them on fire. And that would probably lead to our being discovered by the Spaniards. Not us so much as the St Brieucs."

"You save them from capture only at the risk of your neck in fact," Yorke said.

"That's putting a melodramatic interpretation on it. There's no choice."

"They'll never agree to it."

"They've no say in the matter," Ramage said flatly and, since what had to be made clear could be said now without too much embarrassment, he added: "You're forgetting I'm in command."

"No I'm not," Yorke said amiably. "I've even brought my dress sword to wear when you are enthroned as Governor of Snake Island. It's just that I'm not forgetting Admiral Goddard's interest in your welfare."

"I appreciate that," Ramage said, "but he's in the happy position – if he's not drowned – of having me at his mercy whether I fire the ships or not! I can be damned if I do and damned if I don't, so that leaves me a completely free hand!"

Yorke laughed and then said quietly: "Whatever you decide, I'll back you with everything I've got. Everything."

An hour later, after Yorke had spoken to them all, the men of the *Topaz* were entered in the *Triton's* muster book and credited with the bounty paid to volunteers. They'll probably be better off on Snake Island than if actually serving in one of the King's ships, Ramage thought to himself. Surprisingly, the *Topaz* men had been cheerful at the idea of joining the Royal Navy, as if they thought it would cloak them with its authority and protect them if they were taken prisoner.

Ramage inspected the Marines in the darkness using a lantern, and made sure their muskets and powder supply were well protected from spray and that each had a paddle. Then he gave Appleby instructions to make the best of his way to the eastern side of the island, which could be seen as a black smudge. The minute he landed he was to secure the raft and have the Marines find the best defensive place nearby and occupy it, taking up the powder and shot.

As soon as they were sure they had not been spotted, they could sleep for the rest of the night, leaving two sentries on duty. And next morning at dawn, when he saw the rafts ready to leave the *Triton*, Appleby was to drape strips of canvas over bushes to indicate where he was. It was all so simple Ramage was afraid there would be some hitch.

In the meantime his steward had been busy preparing Ramage's cabin for the St Brieuc family. This had entailed slinging two extra cots from the beams overhead. Appleby provided one; Southwick gave the other.

As Ramage gave orders for a hammock to be slung for him on deck, from the taffrail to the bulwark, he looked up at the sky to the eastward. He could see all the stars; for the moment the weather looked settled. There was just a breeze, and the waves were normal; there was no swell. But this was the Tropics; the weather could – and often did – change within an hour. Still, long before dawn the remaining rafts would be launched and, with the men, passengers and provisions on board, would follow Appleby to whatever Snake Island had to offer.

CHAPTER TWELVE

Yorke had quietly prepared the St Brieucs, St Cast and Southwick for the landing: as the low waves curled and sucked, drifting the raft the last few yards and nudging it towards the beach, the young drummer, at a word from the Master, suddenly stood to attention and then played a ruffle.

Ramage jumped up, startled. At the back of the beach the Marines waited, and Appleby was at the water's edge.

In the silence that followed, as the raft came to a stop and several seamen leapt into the water to secure it, helped by some of Appleby's men, Southwick bellowed: "Drummer – the Governor's Salute!"

The little drummer, a look of intense concentration on his face, shy but proud of being the centre of attention, marched a few paces across the raft, turned and marched back, playing a spirited tune on his drum amid many twirls and flourishes of the drumsticks. Yorke, Southwick and the two Frenchmen now stood to attention and saluted, broad grins on their faces.

As soon as the raft was secured, Southwick roared to a startled Appleby: "Stand by: the Governor is landing! Why aren't your Marines presenting arms?"

The Master's mate quickly caught on and shouted an order to the Marines, then ran back up the beach and seized a short, thick branch of a tree which had been worn smooth and polished by wind, sea and sand. He marched back to the raft and, with the branch over his shoulder as a mace, stood at attention.

Southwick walked three paces to stand in front of Ramage, saluted again, and said in a stentorian voice: "Sir, your island awaits…"

Gravely Ramage returned the salute. "There's no gangway," he said with mock haughtiness. "However, our cause is just: I will get my feet wet."

He bowed deeply to Mme St Brieuc and Maxine. "Ladies, permit me to confer on you the freedom of the island!"

With that the mock ceremony was over; as seamen helped the women on shore, Ramage jumped down from the raft to question Appleby.

"We've seen nothing, sir. I did a reconnaissance myself last night with the corporal. I also sent men along the beach each way but there was no sign of boats or huts. So we just hauled the raft into shallow water and secured it."

"Very well," Ramage said. "From now on the Marines have the responsibility of guarding the passengers."

With that he signalled to Jackson. "Get three men and cut down some of these big palm fronds and make some sort of shelter for the ladies. The sun will be unbearably hot soon. Pick a spot that the breeze can get at."

Just at that moment one of the seamen gave a howl and hopped out of the water on one leg, cursing and swearing at the top of his voice.

A shocked Southwick was beside the man almost immediately, bellowing at him to be silent, and blushing at the thought that the women had heard the words which were simple, strong and unambiguous.

"What's the trouble?" Ramage demanded.

"Says his foot hurts, sir."

"Not used to walking on land?"

"Says he trod on a lot of sharp nails – by jingo, sir, he's got black spots all over the sole of his foot!"

"Sea urchin spines!" Ramage snapped. "Doesn't he have the sense to look out for them?"

But the man had never seen them before, and when Ramage saw how many there were along the beach just under the water, he shouted to all the men to stop and listen.

"Look down into the water," he shouted. "Can you see those small brownish-black discs on the sand – some of them three or four inches across? They're sea urchins. A small ball with hundreds of short spines sticking out all over like a porcupine. If you tread on one the spines stick into your foot and break off.

"They hurt like the devil for half an hour. After that it's not too bad. After a day or two you can forget 'em. But you can't get 'em out once they're in; if you probe around you break them up and they'll probably go poisoned. So leave them – they'll vanish eventually. It's a different story for Mediterranean urchins, but this is the Caribbean. And while we're at it, this is Snake Island but there are no snakes: the name comes from its shape. All you have to worry about are sea urchins in the water, and mosquitoes on land. And Mr Southwick and me. Right, carry on and be careful."

Southwick said quietly: "There is a way of easing the pain, sir! I wonder if you – "

"Yes, I know," Ramage said impatiently and added, lowering his voice, "The relief one gets from doing it is far less than the agony I'd experience in shouting at the top of my voice, in front of the ladies, that if you piss on where the spines are stuck in it'll take the worst of the sting out."

"Quite, sir," Southwick said, his face red. "I'd better keep an eye on the men with the provisions. The other raft will be here in a few minutes."

He pointed seaward to where the Bosun was conning the smaller raft carrying the muskets, carpenter's tools and powder in barrels. Seamen were hunched along two opposite sides wielding paddles.

Ramage nodded. "We'll see if the Bosun thinks Appleby can get back to the ship with the other raft before the wind springs up. We might as well ferry over as much food as we can. This island doesn't look as though it has much to offer. And we had better bring some water."

"Aye, it looks parched, and no streams on the chart. Not the place for them," Southwick said. "Probably a fresh-water well for the village, but – "

"If there's a garrison, they aren't going to offer to fill our casks…"

The Bosun was able to manoeuvre his raft in to the beach close to the big raft, and Ramage was thankful that there seemed to be a regular current crossing the outer reef on which the two wrecks were perched and which came to within fifty yards of this beach, so all that was needed was some vigorous rowing at the last moment.

Within fifteen minutes Appleby and the Bosun were heading back for the *Triton*, and with them was the mate of the *Topaz*: Yorke had given him instructions to collect some particular provisions.

Finally, with the last raft unloaded and the men carefully stacking muskets, shot and powder well back from the beach, Ramage had time to sit down on a rock and take stock.

Even though it was not yet eight o'clock, it was obvious that everyone's attitude towards tropical heat was about to change radically. The land was hot and humid; it was the kind of heat which had been there for centuries, as if during every moment of daylight the rock and earth soaked up and stored the sun's scorching heat like a vast oven. At sea there was no heated land; they had the full advantage of the cooling Trade winds.

For Ramage it was a welcome change after months at sea; there were compensations, like the mixed-herbs smell of the land, rich and intimate, and from where he sat he could see several frangipani bushes covered in white flowers. The rich perfume contained memories of all the erotic sensations he would ever know, but he did not go over to smell it. The memories were strong enough without any reminders.

The birds sang in clear tones, never shrill, always joyful and always a delight. At sea one forgot the sheer pleasure of watching the birds – he stared at a little dark green velvet hummingbird by a shrub, its wings working so fast they were almost invisible, and the bird motionless as it hovered. Then a sudden jink as it moved to investigate another part of the bush. Above it there was a golden-yellow flash as a troupial found all the human beings too alarming and fled along the beach.

He was torn between getting more stores on shore from the ship and setting up a base which he could probably defend, and going off for a reconnaissance of the island. He couldn't be in two places at once, but he did not want to trust anyone else with either job.

Jackson! He suddenly remembered a remark his cox'n had made a year or two ago in Italy when they were struggling over the Tuscan countryside, trying to avoid Bonaparte's cavalry who were busy invading.

"I was with Colonel Pickens at Cowpens, sir," the American had said, thinking that sufficient explanation as to why he knew a lot about soldiering. Well, the devil knew who Colonel Pickens was and what he was doing at Cowpens, but Jackson had obviously been a useful rebel during the American War.

Ramage called him over.

"Jackson, there's one village – maybe a small town – on this island, San Ildefonso. It's two or three miles from here, over these hills."

Ramage gestured to the north-west and bent down, drawing in the sand with his finger.

"There's an almost landlocked bay – entrance just beyond that headland – which forms the middle of the island. The village is on the east side, like so." He drew a small circle. "I want to know more about the village: if there's a garrison; if there's a quay, and any ships in; if there's a fresh-water well – and so on. How long – "

"Three hours, sir, if I can have a couple of hands," he said even before Ramage had time to frame the question. "Three hands, sir."

"As many as you want."

"I'd like Stafford, Rossi and Maxton," he said promptly, "and, sir, can I suggest something?"

When Ramage nodded, he said: "The Marines, sir, an' those red coats…Can't they just wear shirts and trousers? You can see the red two miles off, and in this heat…"

"You're speaking from experience about the red?"

Jackson grinned sheepishly. "Yes, sir. Many's the time I've sighted a musket on a Redcoat…"

Such is the absurdity of war, Ramage thought: now he's fighting for us and warning me about the red cloth.

"Very well, I'll deal with that. Take what weapons you want and be back as soon as – "

He thought a moment. There was no hurry. Better Jackson made a good job of it. "No, don't rush. Be back by sunset. Draw some rations and water from Mr Southwick."

Twenty minutes later Ramage saw the four men vanish into the low scrub at the back of the beach. Only two of them had muskets; the other two carried cutlasses, with pistols in their belts. It made sense: their task was to look and quit, not stand and fight.

He walked to the frangipani, pulled off several blooms, and went over to the palm-frond shelter in which the St Brieucs and St Cast were sitting.

"From the gardens of the Governor's Palace," he said to Maxine, giving a deep bow as he presented the flowers with an elaborate flourish.

"Please congratulate the gardener *en chef*," she said. "Oh – the *parfum* – smell it, Mother!"

St Brieuc said, "Thank you for our palace, too. No palace of stone and marble could be more welcome than this palace of palms!"

"We'll have something better ready for you by this afternoon," Ramage said.

"Believe me, its permanency is not important," St Brieuc said, "since we certainly never even expected to see land again. My wife was just commenting that she has never experienced such a fascinating twenty-four hours as those just past."

Ramage turned to her. "I'm sorry we've had you climbing in and out of wrecks like that, Madame, but it was unavoidable."

"Please do not apologize," she said, "I have enjoyed myself so much. And so has Maxine! This life we do not understand, but that does not mean we are not interested!"

Ramage bowed. "Unfortunately I can't make any promises for the future..."

"Mr Yorke told me about you deciding against burning the wrecks – I understand completely," St Brieuc said. There was a slight emphasis on the last word; a slight but significant inclination of the head.

Ramage found Southwick keeping the men busy rolling casks up the slope of the beach to the line of bushes, where there was both shade and concealment.

Suddenly a seaman yelled and sat down, clutching his foot. The devil take it, Ramage thought, not more sea urchins! He walked over to the man, looked at the foot and realized Snake Island had prickly pear cactus. Sticking in the man's foot was the land version of the sea urchin: a small green disc with spines radiating from it, like a flattened dandelion clock.

"Just give it a tug," Ramage said. "Mind you don't get the spines in your fingers."

"Aye aye, sir," the seaman said patiently, and Ramage felt he was being reproached for not including the prickly pear in his earlier warning.

By now Appleby was halfway back to the *Triton* with the raft. The sun was lifting high over the horizon but the breeze had not come up, and Ramage saw there was a chance they would reach the brig before it arrived. If only he could get a raft-load of provisions from the ship early each morning before the wind came up, he could last out here almost indefinitely.

Suddenly a thought struck him. He was loading casks on to a raft, whereas most of them, if they were pitched over the side, would float and eventually end up on the beach by themselves. Fishermen on Snake Island – if there were any – might find them but they would soon spot the wrecks anyway, so there was nothing to lose by pitching at least some of them over the side and letting the waves and current do the work. It was too late today, but as soon as the carpenter's crew had made a proper shelter for the St Brieucs, and a galley, they could make a rough boat which half a dozen men could use to get out to the wrecks each day.

A few minutes before noon, when the heat of the sun made men find shade before they stopped to talk, Southwick reported that the casks of provisions and water had been landed safely and stored at the back of the beach, covered with a topsail to serve as a tarpaulin, and the sail in turn covered with palm fronds to conceal it from prying eyes.

For the spare muskets, powder and shot, the seamen had collected small, flat rocks – there were plenty of them littering the ground – and built what looked like a large oven, between the provision store and the beach, for use as a magazine. It reminded Ramage of the donkey shelters so familiar in Italy. Branches served as roof beams, with canvas over the top, to weatherproof it. The men were now lining the walls and floor with canvas to keep out the damp.

Southwick was particularly pleased with its position; he had chosen it, Ramage was glad to note, midway between the provision store and the beach, so the Marine sentries guarding the store and the beach – which Ramage had decided was to be the place where everyone would live – did not have to march out of their way, and would pass it twice for every once they passed the store.

By designating a flat area at the back of the beach as the living quarters, Ramage was choosing one of the coolest spots around – it faced eastwards, wide open to the Trade winds – and a sudden outcrop of high rock on the west side protected them from the afternoon sun. Both wrecks were in sight and so was the entrance to the main bay, so that no boat or ship could leave or enter without being spotted.

The sun was still almost directly overhead when a Marine sentry came running up to him with a message from his corporal: five men were approaching from the west.

"Five?" demanded Ramage.

"Aye, sir, corporal was most definite that I told you five. Not four like left."

"But is it Jackson and his party?"

"Corporal didn't say, sir," the Marine said woodenly. "But they was a long way off."

"Take me to the corporal."

After calling to tell Southwick what he was doing and to stand-to with the seamen, Ramage hurried after the man, striding inland past the new magazine and provision store and then bending to keep below the tops of the bushes. They reached a small hill and the Marine gave a low whistle before scrambling up it. A few moments later Ramage found himself kneeling on the north side looking out over a narrow track that led away to the left and snaked down to enter a valley. Some five hundred yards away five men were walking along the track, making no attempt to conceal themselves. Quickly Ramage searched the ground on either side then, cursing himself for having forgotten to bring a telescope, settled down on his haunches to wait until the men got closer.

"Where are your men?" he asked the corporal.

"Six of them are just there, sir" – he pointed to a spot by the track in front of the hill – "an' we spotted those men some minutes ago, sir. Straightaway I sent the six men to prepare an ambush. They have their orders, sir," he said ponderously. "All good men."

Ramage nodded, but even at this distance the gait of one of the five men seemed familiar: he had the loping walk of Jackson. But *five* men?

After a couple of minutes the corporal took a deep breath and said, in what he obviously regarded as his official voice: "In my h'opinion, sir, 'tis Jackson returning with his party with another man h'identity h'at present h'unknown."

"I agree," Ramage said mildly. "I hope your men won't ambush him."

But the corporal's sense of humour had vanished years before, probably beaten out of him by the stamping of boots and the slamming of musket butts.

"They will ha'make the challenge, sir, h'and h'upon receiving the ker-rect reply, will h'allow the party to proceed, sir."

"Very well," Ramage said, and felt he had made the sort of reply that would never pass muster on a Marine parade ground.

Jackson's party had a prisoner with them, an old Negro.

"Leastways, not *exactly* a prisoner," Jackson was careful to explain as they walked back to the camp. "A sort of voluntary prisoner."

"They're common enough in the Caribbean," Ramage said sourly. "But first, is there any sign of a garrison?"

"No, sir. That San Ildefonso is just a small village – twenty-two houses, several collapsed – and almost deserted. Probably a dozen local people. Then there are about a dozen soldiers and twenty Negro slaves. The slaves dig trenches while the soldiers guard them."

"And then?"

"Then they fill the trenches in again, sir."

"Start again from the beginning," Ramage said, in despair.

The patrol, Jackson explained, had found the track almost as soon as it started out, and had followed it – not by walking along it, but keeping to the bushes about fifty yards away. It trended south and then one branch went between two high, cone-shaped hills and obviously led to the next bay to the west. The other continued along the valley towards the village.

They'd only just reached the fork – not quite a mile from the beach – when they heard men singing; Negro voices coming from high up, from a saddle between two hills.

Leaving Rossi and Stafford on guard at the fork, Jackson had taken Maxton with him to investigate.

"I found a trail where several men had gone up – several times. Leaves and branches broken off on different occasions. Maxie and I followed this track, sir. About a quarter of the way up the saddle, just off to one side, we found a trench on a flat bit under a calabash tree. Leastways, someone had dug a trench, and filled it in again."

"How big?"

"Big enough for a grave, sir."

"No marker – no stone to mark the head, or cross or anything?"

"No, sir. Anyway we went on up towards the singing. A sort of chanting, like you get when slaves sing as they work. Not very cheerful but musical.

"After another forty yards, on another little flat bit, we found a second trench. Same size, like a grave. This was on the right of the track – the other was to the left. Underneath another calabash tree, too, in the shade.

"Found two more trenches, same size, before we got up very close to the singing. This was actually right on the saddle, where there was a large flat bit and big rocks – twenty feet high, some of them, and plenty of bushes.

"Maxie and I managed to get close. Then I crawled up on a flat-topped rock that stood to one side so's I could look down on them. Two slaves were down in a deep trench digging away with pickaxes, two waited to take a turn, and four more waited with shovels – those long-handled ones.

"An officer stood right over them with three soldiers, and eight more soldiers stood round, and there were a dozen more slaves just standing about waiting.

"The guards weren't very strict. They seemed interested only in the grave. Especially the officer. Not the slaves with the pickaxes; just the hole they were digging; looking down into it."

"Your prisoner," Ramage prompted.

"Oh yes, sir. I saw one of the Negroes walk past the group of guards and – er, relieve himself – by a tree. Then another one used the same place.

"The guards didn't bother to move or watch him, so Maxie and I went round and waited until another came out. Maxie spoke to him quietly from behind a bush – they have a sort of patois. Next thing is the fellow wants to come with us. I guessed the Spanish guards would reckon he'd escaped, and it seemed to me you'd find out more from him than we could ever find out, sir. I had to make my mind up quickly, because it wasn't a chance we'd get again, so I hope I did right, sir."

"You did," Ramage assured him.

"The guards had six muskets between them. The rest had pikes and whips. Muskets not oiled – rust showing. Uniforms torn and dirty and old. Very long whips. The officer a dandy, sir; kept putting a lace handkerchief to his nose. Either got a cold or sniffing perfume."

By now they were approaching the camp and Ramage turned to Maxton.

"What language does this fellow speak?"

"Spanish, sir, and patois."

"Very well, we'll stop here before he sees the camp: I've some questions to ask him."

"He'll help, sir," Maxton said eagerly; an eagerness which Ramage realized was due to the fact the man was coloured, like Maxton. "His name is Roberto, sir."

Ramage motioned to the man.

"You are called Roberto?" he asked in Spanish.

The man gave a wide grin, nodding his head eagerly.

"Whose slave are you?"

"Of the Army, *comandante*," he said.

"What are you doing in the hills?"

"Digging trenches, *comandante*."

"That I know. Do you know why? You dig and then you fill them in again."

"Yes, we dig deep, as deep as a man is tall, and as soon as we get to that depth, the *teniente* orders us to fill it up again. 'Stop!' he says. 'Now fill it up.' "

"And then?"

"Then we go somewhere else and start digging again."

"What are you burying?"

"Burying?" the man repeated in surprise. "Why, nothing, *comandante*!"

"What are you looking for, then?"

Roberto shrugged his shoulders. "No one knows."

"Someone must!"

"*Si, comandante!* But not the soldiers or the slaves; only the *teniente*."

"How many soldiers are there on the island?"

"Those guarding us. I cannot count."

"No more? No garrison?"

The Negro shook his head.

"Where do the soldiers sleep?"

"In the village. Some empty houses. They have three. We slaves live in another one. They lock us in."

"And the *teniente*?"

"Yes, he has a house. His own."

"With sentries?"

"No, just his two servants. They are soldiers but they are servants, too."

Ramage began to get an idea, but for the moment Roberto could help no more. He stood up and signalled to Maxton.

"Look after him: is he likely to escape?"

"No, sir, he wants to stay with us. He reckons he's escaped from the Spaniards. He's grateful to us."

"Well, keep an eye on him. He could go back and tell the Spanish all he's seen. But don't say anything to him," Ramage added hastily. "Don't put the idea in his head!"

By the time they reached the camp the cooks had prepared a meal, and Yorke suggested they join the St Brieucs. Ramage accepted since he could tell them what little he had just learned. Before going over to the palm-frond shelter he told Southwick, whose relief was limited to having the seamen put away their muskets and start work again.

He found the St Brieucs and St Cast sitting comfortably in canvas chairs which the Bosun had brought from the *Topaz*, along with a small folding table.

One of the merchantman's stewards whispered to St Brieuc who, with all the aplomb of a host in a vast and elegant dining-room, said with a wave towards the table, "Luncheon is ready. If you will be seated..."

Chairs were moved, St Brieuc said grace, stewards served a hot soup and they began eating. Ramage was just about to speak when the realization of the taste of the soup overcame his preoccupation with the riddle of the graves. He looked across at St Brieuc.

"This is superb. We have the finest cook in the Caribbean, thanks to you!"

"*M'sieur le Gouverneur,*" St Brieuc said with a smile, "I told you this morning how happy we are. That was before our furniture unexpectedly arrived, and before we realized what culinary arrangements had been made for us."

Ramage nodded cheerfully. "I shall be inclined to agree with the first person that says my colony is the best administered in the Empire – British or French!"

"I say so!" Maxine exclaimed, and then blushed at her temerity.

"And I second mam'selle," Yorke said.

"Then I will deliver my report to the Governor's Council," Ramage said, and told them of Jackson's foray and his own interrogation of Roberto.

"These graves," Yorke said. "Are they burying something or looking? Hiding or seeking?"

"Seeking, apparently."

"How can you be sure?"

"The Negro doesn't know what it's all about. He would, if they were burying something."

"Not necessarily. The Spaniards could send the slaves away, put something in the grave, partly fill it, and then let the slaves do the rest."

Ramage shook his head. "No, I checked that. They finish excavating and start filling at once. The diggers don't even get up out of the trench before the order's given. If they were burying something, they'd keep whatever it was at the village with guards over it."

"Well, that's conclusive," Yorke commented.

St Cast said, as if thinking aloud, "When they fill the grave, the earth would be soft unless they stamped on it. Are they preparing those holes for subsequent use and just filling them temporarily?"

"There'd be no point," St Brieuc said. "Why fill? There's no risk of humans or animals falling in, and no need for secrecy…"

"I'm sure they're searching." Ramage said. "And they know it's hidden at a depth not more than a man's height – say five foot nine inches."

"They'd fill if they wanted to conceal what they'd been doing," St Cast said.

"Water!" Yorke exclaimed triumphantly. "They want to sink new wells!"

"Up a hill?" Ramage asked.

"Why not? I've seen many springs emerging from a hillside."

Ramage felt vaguely disappointed. It was such an obvious explanation. He had failed to think of it because, like a schoolboy, he had been making a mystery out of it…

After the meal, when they had left the table and were sitting round talking of their immediate future, Ramage was pleasantly surprised to find none of them in any hurry to get away from the island. The St Brieucs really were enjoying themselves.

Maxine's main regret seemed to be that she had no horse with which to explore the island. To Ramage's surprise, all three St Brieucs were emphatic in their relief that for an indefinite time they were free of what St Brieuc called "the overheated hypocrisy of the *salon*". For a moment Ramage thought about establishing a new little world free of Goddards and Sir Pilcher Skinners and Directories and gossip-ridden society and shoddy politicians…He was surrounded by men he admired, ranging from humble seamen to Southwick, from St Brieuc to Yorke.

Maxine seemed to be blooming. The delicate, drawing-room manner had gone, as though it had never been; in its place was growing confidence and assurance that was both startling and charming. She had not attempted to keep the sun off her hands and face while in the Tropics, and the result was she had a golden tan which added richness to her features.

Ramage wished he could invite her to gallop with him over the hills until their horses were exhausted. If he did, he thought, she'd seize his hand and run with him to the stables. She was like a delicate young plant that had suddenly grown, strengthened, and was now in flower.

As they all talked Ramage found himself catching her eye more frequently; talking to her secretly, without words. Finally he excused himself to check on the work of the *Topaz* seamen, who were making a tent for the St Brieucs from one of the ship's spare sails.

CHAPTER **THIRTEEN**

That night Ramage tried to sleep on the hard ground, fitfully slapping ants that crawled over him and mosquitoes that landed after flying round with an intimidating whine, and thought again of the graves.

Another half an hour spent questioning Roberto had left him no wiser. The Negro had told him all he knew, and it was precious little. There had been one piece of information which could be significant or utterly irrelevant; vitally important or of no consequence.

"Are the Spaniards short of drinking water?" Ramage had asked.

"Oh no!" Roberto had been surprised. "No, *comandante*, they have plenty. The well at the village is big and deep and the water is sweet. The *teniente*, they say, washes all over twice a day."

If they weren't short of water in the village, they wouldn't be trying to sink wells elsewhere...Yet the village was some three miles from where Jackson had found the graves.

Graves: he must think of them as trenches – graves summoned up a particular picture that might influence his thoughts and prevent a possible explanation coming to mind.

To start from the beginning again: why would a man dig a big hole?

221

To bury something; to look for water; to look for something that someone had previously buried. Hmm, Ramage thought to himself, I'll soon have myself convinced they're looking for Captain Kidd's hidden treasure; gold looted a couple of hundred years ago from the Spanish Main.

Looking for water seemed the most likely, once you agree that three miles is a long way to carry water – it would have to be in small barrels on the backs of mules or donkeys. Barrels leaked; water evaporated in the heat. Donkeys were probably scarce.

Yet would the Spanish *really* put a battery on this side of the island?

Extra water made sense if the Spanish were really interested in Snake Island, and they ought to be. If an enemy held Snake Island, with its enclosed bay large enough for a fleet to anchor even in a hurricane, it could dominate Puerto Rico. There was no port on the east coast of Puerto Rico. San Juan was far off along the exposed north coast, with a seventy-five mile beat to windward from there to the eastern end of the island. Snake Island was to Puerto Rico what Plymouth was to England, a good safe anchorage for the fleet and well to windward of what it was trying to protect. Perhaps the Spanish had finally woken up to this and the party of Spanish soldiers was making a preliminary survey.

He sat up and slapped off several ants in the darkness, and wondered if there was any point in moving somewhere else to sleep. The Spanish soldiers were far enough away and busy enough to be left for the moment, but he dare not risk leaving them for another day. If fishermen spotted the camp, rafts or wrecks, the alarm would be raised. He felt secure enough, however, now he knew exactly how many Spanish soldiers there were: his own camp was guarded by twice as many better armed seamen and Marines.

But a ship with provisions or reinforcements might arrive any day. And a ship would certainly spot the wrecks and probably the camp. Could he surround the Spaniards and make them surrender? Could seamen get through these bushes quietly and up that hill in broad daylight? Prickly pear cactus digging into the soles of their feet...No! Good seamen, every one of them; but apart from the Marines, Jackson was the only one trained for fighting on land. He must ambush them on the track leading to the hill.

The slaves would probably start digging early. Damn, he had to find out now, and organize the men. He scrambled up, not sorry to leave the hard earth and the hungry ants.

One of the Marine sentries patrolling the camp knew where Jackson was sleeping, and in a minute or two Ramage was kneeling beside the American and whispering: "Where's Maxton and that slave?"

Jackson gestured to his right. "Just over there, sir, by that bush."

"Come on!"

Jackson was on his feet in a moment, slipping a cutlass belt over his head.

"You won't need that!"

They found Maxton, who was sleeping beside Roberto.

"Roberto," hissed Ramage, "what time do the soldiers leave the village with you in the morning?"

"Just before daylight, *comandante.*"

Damn, Ramage thought, how long is "just before"? Try another tack.

"How far had you gone yesterday before the sun came up?"

"We reached the place where we were digging just before the sun came up, *comandante!*"

Ramage gave up: neither a Spaniard nor a Negro paid much attention to time; for a Spanish slave, time had no relevance at all. Early, anyway.

"Where do you think they will be digging tomorrow – at daylight?"

"That same hill, *comandante*. We've been digging there for many days. Many trenches."

"So I can be sure of finding them there at daylight?"

Ramage sensed, rather than saw, even though it was not a very dark night, that Roberto stiffened. Ramage thought he sensed fear and wariness.

"You're not taking me back, *comandante*?"

Ramage chuckled softly and touched the man on the shoulder reassuringly. "No, Roberto; you have been freed. Would your friends like to be freed?"

"Oh, yes, sir! Then they kill the *teniente!*"

"Why kill him?"

"A bad man, sir; every night he likes to have a slave tied to a tree and whipped."

"Punishment for thieving?" Ramage asked curiously.

"Sometimes, sir; but if no one has done anything wrong, he tells the guard to lash anyone to the tree!"

Ramage nodded his head slowly in the darkness. He could almost picture that lieutenant. Yet he was the only man on the island who knew about the trenches, and who might know when a ship was due with provisions.

"Jackson!"

"Here, sir."

"How many men will we need to ambush that party on the track before they get to the hill?"

"Twenty if you want to avoid bloodshed, sir; ten if it doesn't matter."

"Did you notice any good spots for an ambush? We don't have time to make much of a reconnaissance in the dark."

"No need, sir; I know just the spot. Made a note of it as we left. Just beyond the fork, sir. It's ideal."

"Very well; let's find the corporal."

Jackson gave a stifled groan. It was a masterpiece in its way. If Ramage had been liverish and reacted angrily, Jackson could have blamed the groan on an aching back; if Ramage was in a good humour he might well accept it as showing Jackson's contempt for Marines as land soldiers and choose seamen instead.

Ramage decided he was in a middling temper. He ignored the protest and decided to take eight Marines with twelve seamen to make up the rest of the party. The price Jackson must pay for his groan was to choose the seamen, tell them off for the duty, and have them mustered outside the camp at four-thirty, armed and equipped.

After finding the Marine corporal, giving him his orders and warning the sentries to call him at four o'clock, Ramage went back to the hard patch of ground by a large boulder where everyone in the camp knew they could find the captain in the dark, and flopped down. He'd never get any sleep tonight.

It seemed the very next moment that he was wakened by the sentry's hoarse voice whispering, "Captain, sir!"

He'd hardly sat up as the sentry left, before two men materialized from the darkness, one on each side.

"Morning, Governor."

One of them was Yorke, greeting him breezily and, as far as Ramage could make out as he rubbed the sleep from his eyes, fully dressed with a cutlass belt over his shoulder and carrying a musket.

"Morning," Ramage mumbled sleepily. "Bit early for social calls. Ah, Jackson?"

"Aye, sir. Glass o' lemonade and some biscuit, sir. Best I can muster. Lemons nice and fresh, though; clean your mouth out nicely."

"Thank you. Perhaps you can get a glass for Mr Yorke."

"He's already had one, sir."

"You have, by Jove!" Ramage exclaimed. "What gets you up so early?"

"Early bird catches the *culebra*," Yorke said airily. "Going out on a duck-shooting party."

"By God you're not!" Ramage exclaimed. "The sound of a shot will..." he broke off and laughed. "All right, I'm not awake yet. Sorry you didn't get a written invitation to my – "

Ramage drank the lemonade, using it to wash the dry biscuit down. The Navy Board's biscuit was best eaten in darkness: then one had neither sight nor sound of the weevils which, though perhaps nutritious, did not look appetizing.

"Well?" Ramage growled at Jackson.

"All the men ready, sir. The corporal's mustered the Marines."

"Come on," Ramage said to Yorke. "We'll inspect them. How did you know about all this?"

"The bustling before midnight. I had my spies make inquiries, and arranged to be called at the appropriate hour."

"With lemonade," Ramage said.

"Of course."

The corporal had the Marines standing in a double file and Ramage hissed at him just in time to prevent a stentorian bellow bringing the men to attention.

Ramage took the corporal's arm and steered him a few paces from the men.

"Corporal, this is going to be a completely silent operation. Any talking that's necessary will be in a low whisper. If any man makes a noise – and that includes stumbling and swearing – I'll have him flogged. Is that clear?"

"Yes, sir."

"Very well. Now tell each man individually. Whisper it!"

While the corporal passed from one man to another, hissing like an infuriated snake, Ramage inspected the seamen.

Six carried muskets and six had pistols stuck in their belts. The musketeers also had tomahawks tucked in their belts, while those with pistols carried cutlasses.

Almost inevitably, Ramage noticed, Jackson had chosen Rossi, Stafford and Maxton. But there were thirteen men.

He stood back and counted again.

"Jackson! How many men have you?"

"Er – twelve, sir."

"Count them!"

"I know, sir, it looks like thirteen."

"Looks? It damn well is. I mean, there damn well are!"

Bowen's voice said apologetically out of the darkness: "I invited myself along, sir. I thought you might need a surgeon. Gunshot wounds and that sort of thing…"

His voice trailed off lamely as he sensed Ramage glaring at him.

Ramage realized that Yorke had already been quick to slip behind him, perhaps guessing there was going to be trouble, and he was irritated at the way Jackson, Yorke and Bowen seemed to be taking over the operation.

"Mr Bowen," Ramage said sarcastically, "in planning this expedition I considered whether I would need coopers, caulkers, carpenters, cooks, topmen, fo'c'slemen or loblolly men. I decided we could do without them. I also considered whether we would be plagued with croup, canker, black vomit, malaria or clap. I decided we wouldn't, so we do not need a surgeon."

"Aye aye, sir. I apologize. I'll go back to the camp."

Bowen sounded so crestfallen that Ramage relented.

"Well, you'd better stay with us now you're here," he said huffily. "I don't want you blundering round the camp in the dark waking everyone up."

With that he went over to the Marines, inspected them closely, warned them again of the need for silence and then gathered Jackson, the corporal, Yorke and Bowen round him.

He was in a bad temper. He'd slept heavily and it always took him time to wake up properly, and almost invariably he became bad-tempered. To be honest, he was jumpy at the prospect of unaccustomed soldiering. But now was not the time for honesty. He could indulge in the only pleasure open to a leader – being bad-tempered.

"We'll be in two parties, seamen and Marines. I shall command the seamen, and since Mr Yorke has graced us with his presence, he can command the Marines.

"That doesn't mean, corporal, that you aren't responsible for any clumsiness or stupidity on the part of your men. Mr Bowen will also go with the Marines," he added as an afterthought: Yorke and Bowen were smart enough to make sure the Marines did the right thing.

"No muskets or pistols to be loaded until we are in the ambush position. No talking. I want to avoid any unnecessary killing so use common sense. The Spanish lieutenant must be taken alive. Any questions? Carry on then."

He went over to the group of seamen, followed by Jackson.

"Right, follow me. Walk in pairs. And if you trip up and break a leg, do it quietly!"

Jackson automatically went ahead as their guide, walking in a loping stride, not fast and not slow, just confident, the gait of a man who knew where he wanted to go and knew he could get there. From the way Jackson covered the ground he seemed to belong there, like a fox. Yet he also seemed to belong in a ship.

It was still dark – as dark as an ordinary tropical night ever was. The Southern Cross to the south, in this latitude, four quite undistinguished stars. The Plough ahead of them to the north, and the Pole Star, a bare eighteen degrees above the horizon. All the other familiar constellations were brighter than they were in northern latitudes, as though they were nearer.

A seaman stumbled behind; some small animal scurried away; a land crab scampered across the track. Soon Ramage thought he could see a little farther; the blackness had a hint of grey and his eyes seemed out of focus. From long experience he recognized the first hint of dawn. The track was curving to the left. Ramage hoped the Marines would do a good job, if only to show Jackson.

Now the muscles in the front of his shins were hurting – they were unused to walking far on land. He started thinking of blisters on his heels; a thought banished by the thought that a musket ball in the gizzard would be a more likely ailment before the sun set again.

Jackson had slowed down to let him catch up.

"The fork's about thirty yards ahead, sir."

Ramage waited while the two files of men caught up and stopped.

The land on the left of the track sloped gently upwards towards the saddle; on the right it was level.

He decided to put the Marines farther along the track, nearer the village, so that the Spaniards passed them on their way to the trenches and were captured by the seamen. The advantage was that if the Spaniards bolted from the seamen's ambush, they'd run back along the track towards the village and be trapped by the Marines. Would the Marines have enough discipline to let the Spaniards pass the first time without opening fire? With Yorke and Bowen among them he knew he could depend on it. He explained it to Yorke and the corporal, and then they filed off into the deep greyness.

Ramage was pleasantly surprised at how quietly they moved: they were out of earshot almost as soon as they were lost to sight. The Marines, like the seamen, would stay on the left, or western side of the road. That way each would know roughly where the other force was and, more important, neither would fire – if shooting was necessary – towards the hill.

Quickly he and Jackson led the seamen into the bushes and positioned each of them two or three yards back from the track. Each was shown where the man on either side was stationed; each was warned what could happen if anyone forgot.

Finally Ramage walked along the track with Jackson to take up his position. He found a large, straggling divi-divi bush which would hide both him and Jackson, and sat down, sore-footed and tired, with the American beside him. He took one of the two pistols from his belt and, after checking it was not loaded, squeezed the trigger to make sure the flint was sound. It made a good spark. From his coat pocket he brought a metal powder horn and shook a measure of coarse powder into the barrel, using the rammer to push down a wad on top of it. Then he took a lead ball from his pocket and turned it between finger and thumb to make sure it had no dents or bumps, that it was perfectly spherical and would fly true. He put the ball in the muzzle and rammed it home firmly with another wad on top. Finally, using the fine powder at the other end of the divided powder horn, he held the pistol tilted to the left and shook a small amount of powder into the pan. Carefully he made sure the touch hole running from the pan into the bore of the gun was full of priming powder, and then flipped the steel down to cover the pan. He blew gently to get rid of loose grains of powder, and put it on the ground beside him while he loaded the other pistol.

Finally, with both pistols loaded, he was able to relax. It needed only a slight movement of each thumb to cock the hammers; it needed only a gentle pressure on the trigger to fire.

As they sat there, cautiously and silently fighting off attacks by the now only too familiar red ants, whose bites were like jabs from red-hot needles, Ramage and Jackson looked along the track, watching as approaching dawn extended the visibility. They could identify a particular bush five yards away, and then within minutes distinguish details of its leaves and branches. The overall grey of land and sky began to turn into pale but individual colours: the yellow blossoms of a shrub here, white blossom of a different shrub there. The green of odd blades of coarse grass, then the deeper green of bushes.

Jackson nudged Ramage's knee, and then Ramage too heard a distant clink of metal and voices; faint but deep, a descant even, and musical like distant murmurings. He realized it was the sound of slaves quietly singing and chanting as they walked.

He felt no tension now, only relief that his decision to believe the slave Roberto was likely to prove a right one. Now the only risk was that they'd arrive at the ambush before there was enough light to see properly.

Jackson seemed to guess his thoughts, whispering: "The track slopes downhill for a mile, sir. That's why we can hear them so well. They won't be here for fifteen or twenty minutes."

It seemed a long, long wait as it became gradually lighter. Ramage was surprised how noisily he breathed. On board the ship he had not noticed it, but out here, in the dawn silence, the air seemed to hiss and snort as it went up and down his nostrils. He tried breathing only through his mouth, but his throat began to dry and he was afraid of starting to cough. His heart seemed to be beating abnormally loudly. His stomach gurgled. The devil take it, was his body always as noisy as this?

The singing had faded for a few minutes and he worried in case the Spanish officer was taking the men to a new site, but Jackson explained that the silence was due to the road curving as it came up the hill, and masking the sound. Then Ramage could hear them again, suddenly louder.

Quickly he stood up with a pistol in each hand, and a moment later heard twigs breaking to his right: a careless seaman, but no matter; the singing of the Negroes should help drown any such noise.

Then he swore under his breath as he remembered he hadn't warned the seamen that he would challenge the Spaniards in Spanish: he suddenly had a mental picture of the seamen firing at the source of any Spanish voice.

Jackson, sensing his sudden tension, whispered a question and Ramage explained.

"It's all right sir," the American said, "I told them before we left the camp."

Ramage felt both relief and irritation – the American seemed to think of everything.

The Negro singing became louder and Ramage could see a cluster of men walking along the track towards him, three or four abreast, not in formation. The nearest were wearing hats – Spanish soldiers. After a gap, two or three men, then another gap. They were spread out over a much longer distance than that covered by the seamen; a column twenty yards long. The seamen were spaced a yard or so apart. He should have thought of that…

It was not yet fully daylight. Dawn had reached that deceptive stage when small boulders seemed large, bushes took on the shape of mythological beasts and all clouds looked stormy.

He had made the mistake so it was up to him to sort it all out…

And here came the first men…twenty yards…fifteen…two tall and one short…ten yards…muskets over their shoulders, strolling rather than marching…five yards…

Ramage stepped out in front of them, a pistol in each hand. His stomach shrivelled…it seemed to be so vulnerable. A man behind the leaders might fire at them with a pistol.

The leaders stopped suddenly, startled. Their bodies seemed frozen as if each had managed to stop just in time to avoid treading on a snake and was now too frightened to move.

Those behind bumped into each other; a querulous voice said: "*Que pasa?*"

Ramage spoke in Spanish clearly and sharply.

"Let no one move. A hundred English guns are pointing at you from the bushes. Let the *teniente* come to the front!"

Nothing happened.

A Negro moaned; an eerie, frightened and frightening moan.

"If the *teniente* steps forward, he will be safe. If I call my men to find him, many of you will probably be killed, including the *teniente*."

Ramage felt like giggling. Creating a hundred men in the bushes by a quirk of his imagination and a flick of his tongue was great fun; like this it would be easy to manoeuvre armies.

Still there was no movement.

Ramage moved a step forward and gestured with his pistols to the middle of the three leaders, cocking each one, the twin clicks loud, sharp and ominous.

"Is the *teniente* with you?"

"*Si señor.*"

"Oh, he just lacks *cojones*, eh?"

"*Si señor – no! No, señor!*"

Ramage conjured up a blood-curdling laugh. "He soon will, if he doesn't step forward!"

With that he saw men moving aside and a tall, slim man walked to the head of the column. He stopped before he was abreast of the three leaders and stared at Ramage.

"Who are you?" he demanded querulously in Spanish.

Ramage turned to Jackson and said in English: "Remove his sword. Don't be too gentle."

The Lieutenant protested in the peevish voice of a shrewish young wife. He protested but, Ramage noted, not too much.

As soon as Jackson was holding the sword, Ramage said to the Spaniard: "Tell your men to lay down their arms."

He did so with remarkable alacrity as Ramage watched warily. Muskets came from shoulders and were put on the ground. Other weapons, which he could not recognize in the dim light, were dropped.

"Tell the slaves to stand still and the soldiers to walk forward and stand ten paces behind me."

As the Lieutenant gave the order Ramage stepped back off the track and, led by the three in front, the soldiers began walking.

Suddenly there was an urgent, high whistling noise and as Ramage jumped back, startled, there was a flash and bang of a pistol going off almost beside him and something snakelike writhed for a moment on the ground in front of him.

A few feet away, among the group of soldiers, there was a dreadful gurgling and Ramage realized it came from a soldier lying on the ground, a long stick-like object clutched in one hand. Then, with his ears ringing from the sound of the shot and dazzled for a moment by the flash, he saw that Jackson had fired. The whistling had come from the tail of a whip wielded by the Spanish soldier and intended to strike him down.

"Stand still," he shouted in Spanish. "No one move, or you all die!"

What a splendidly melodramatic language is Spanish, he thought to himself as he called in English down the track: "Mr Bowen – there's work for you here."

Then, realizing he was needlessly handling everything with only Jackson's help, he said briskly: "Tritons! Take the soldiers prisoner!"

As the seamen rustled from the shrubs he called to the slaves to stand still.

Five minutes later, with it getting lighter every second, the Lieutenant was standing to one side with Jackson behind him on guard, a pistol in each hand. The Spanish soldiers were in single file, each man tied to the next by a rope from one ankle. The slaves were in a group, chatting excitedly.

Bowen walked up, wiping his hands on a cloth.

"It's no good, sir, he's dead."

"Too bad," Ramage said, remembering the whistle of the whip and trying to guess what it would have done to him if the thick tail had hit him. He walked back to the dead man and picked up the whip.

It was the vilest thing Ramage had ever seen, designed as an instrument of torture, a means of punishment, a weapon. One heavy blow could cut a man almost in half. The whole whip was made of finely plaited leather; the handle, some five feet long, was as thick and rigid as a broom handle and then tapered to the tail, which was at least eight feet long, and little thicker at the tip than a piece of thin codline.

He loosened the dead man's grip, picked up the whip and found he was trembling with rage as he remembered the slave Roberto describing how the *teniente* sent for a slave if none was due to be flogged for punishment. He heard the echo of the *teniente*'s querulous voice a few minutes ago. He remembered the *teniente*'s reluctance to leave the anonymity and safety of the column and come to the front and accept his task as leader.

Bowen sensed his rage, gestured at the whip and said quietly: "It's a habit that's catching, sir."

Ramage pitched the whip away.

"Thank you," he muttered, and started walking back to the camp, calling orders to the corporal for bringing in the prisoners and slaves and burying the dead man.

Back at the camp he washed and shaved and had breakfast alone. The whip episode had left him in a fury. He imagined soldiers whipping slaves out of sheer boredom, or for slight infractions. The Navy's cat-o'-nine-tails was hardly a toy but it was used for punishment only in specific circumstances. Only the captain of a ship – or a court-martial – could order its use. There were some bad captains – like Pigot of the *Hermione*, who was so addicted to the cat his crew mutinied and murdered him – but such men were rare, and held in contempt by their fellow captains.

By comparison to these whips, the cat-o'-nine-tails was a bundle of shopkeeper's string; by comparison a flogging round the Fleet – the harshest sentence, apart from death, that a court could award – was merely painful. With this whip the lowest soldier could, with one or two blows delivered as a whimsy, punish a man as severely as a naval court martial. With three or four blows he could kill, and from what Roberto had said, he was only blamed because it meant a slave less to work.

Ramage was not looking forward to interrogating the contemptible *teniente*, who was being guarded by the inevitable quartet of Jackson, Stafford, Rossi and Maxton. He had thought some time ago that he might be accused of favouritism, because he often gave them special tasks, but the quartet was popular among the men. They had been with him in so many situations, ranging from the desperate to the bizarre, that each knew how the other's mind worked. In emergencies this saved valuable seconds.

Ramage tucked a pistol in his belt, jammed his hat on and strode across the coarse grass and prickly pear to the provisions dump, where Jackson had the prisoner. The sun was getting heat in it now and the glare made him frown. The dry air reminded him of the smell of hay.

He found the four seamen standing round the Lieutenant, who was sitting on a tree stump the picture of petulant dejection. At Ramage's approach he tried to stand up, but Ramage told him to remain seated – he wanted to avoid any of the usual polite formalities.

"Your name?"

"*Teniente* Jaime Colon Benitez."

"Your regiment?"

"The first battalion of the Regiment of Aragon."

"What are you doing on this island?"

"Commanding a platoon of men."

"Obviously. What were your orders?"

"They are secret," Colon said contemptuously, as if while sitting on the tree stump he had recovered his courage.

"Very well," Ramage said, apparently accepting the reply. "Where is the headquarters of your regiment?"

"San Juan – at El Morro."

"The rest of your battalion is stationed in the fortress?"

"Yes. A few platoons such as mine are detached."

"When did you arrive here at Culebra?"

"Three weeks ago."

"With your orders?"

"With my orders."

"Since which time you have dug graves."

"Graves? How absurd!" Colon was contemptuous again, as though the word summoned up thoughts of tradesmen and other things with which no one of Colon's breeding would associate but which an Englishman like Ramage could not understand.

"Trenches, then."

"I'm not prepared to discuss it."

"Of course not," Ramage said easily. "Because of the nature of your orders."

"Precisely. They are secret."

"But I can find them at your quarters – the house in the village – and read them."

"Oh no you can't!" Colon exclaimed triumphantly. "They were verbal. The Colonel was most emphatic that nothing was put in writing. Because of the need for secrecy," he added, his voice dropping conspiratorially.

"Ah yes," Ramage said sympathetically. "It is dangerous to confide matters of such secrecy to paper."

"It certainly is!"

"Very well. Let me see now, I want to make sure I have all your details correct."

He repeated the man's name, regiment, and the fact he was based at El Morro, in San Juan.

Colon nodded and said: "That is correct. You speak Spanish very well – with the accent of Castile."

Ramage inclined his head in acknowledgment, and then said: "My apologies: there are one or two other details I need. Then no more questions."

"I will do my best to accommodate you," Colon said airily.

"Thank you. When is the next ship due with provisions from Puerto Rico?"

"I can't tell you that."

Ramage nodded his head regretfully. "Now, the last question: of the trenches you have dug, which is in the prettiest position – the most tranquil?"

"What an absurd question!"

"But important," Ramage said gently.

"Well, I don't really know. None is in what a civilized person would call an arbour."

"Nevertheless, you must express a preference."

"Well, I haven't one, I hate them all," Colon said impatiently, as though bored with trenches as a topic of conversation.

"I must press you to answer," Ramage said, with a slight edge to his voice. "Just one."

"No! Not even one."

"Well then," Ramage said, in a more reasonable voice, "may I ask which place in the whole island you regard as the most tranquil, trench or no trench?"

Colon gave a contemptuous wave with his hand. "The whole place is ghastly; I hate it."

He stamped his foot and said almost hysterically, "I hate it! I hate Puerto Rico! I hate the Tropics!"

"Do you?" Ramage said sympathetically. "Well now, you are putting me in a difficult position. I wish you'd just tell me of a tranquil place for a trench."

"Do be quiet about trenches!" Colon said peevishly.

"Graves, then," Ramage said.

Colon's eyes opened wide. "I don't like the way you said that!"

" 'Graves'?" Ramage repeated with feigned surprise, shaking his head. "What's wrong with that?"

"You said it in a threatening manner."

"You can't accuse me of threatening you," Ramage said in a hurt voice, "I'm trying to arrange that everything is as you would wish it for your removal."

"My *removal*?"

"A polite euphemism for death," Ramage said flatly, and Colon fainted.

"Quick," Ramage said to Jackson. "Have you a piece of line or a belt? I want a garrotte."

" 'Ere," Stafford said, holding out a length of cord. "Can I be carrotter, sir?"

"There'll be no garrotting as such, but you can pretend. Tie a knot in one end and keep running it through your fingers. Look fierce!"

"Aye aye, sir."

"Look," Rossi said, taking the line expertly and tying one end in the form of an eye. "Put your left wrist in there. Now – the line goes over the head of the victim; up comes your left wrist; a jerk back hard and upwards with the right hand, so; knee in the back, like thees, as you jerk; and – "

"Rossi!" Ramage said, grinning at the Italian's professionalism and enthusiasm, "give it back to Stafford, he's coming round."

Colon moaned weakly and Ramage signalled to Jackson and Rossi, who lifted the man up, shook him and sat him back on the tree stump.

It was, Ramage noticed, the charred stump of a tree that had been hit by a bolt of lightning.

"Do you feel better?" he asked.

"You murderer!" Colon blurted.

"I'm not – yet!" Ramage said, and Colon fainted again.

"Gawd," Stafford grumbled as the Spaniard slid to the ground, "I'd 'ave to be quick to give 'im the carrot."

"Garrotte," Jackson said automatically as he bent over Colon. "By the way, sir, what do we want to know?"

"About the trenches. Why he's digging them. He says his orders are secret."

"Does he speak English, sir?"

"I didn't ask him, but he probably does."

"If he does, why don't you leave him with your barbaric crew?"

"None of that, Jackson!"

"No, sir, we won't touch him; but I guarantee he'll talk. In fact we'll have him singing."

Ramage nodded. "No violence, though."

"Guarantee not to touch him, sir."

"No need for guarantees; just remember, 'moderation in all things'!"

"Aye aye, sir; my grandfather always said the same thing."

As soon as Colon recovered and had been propped up on the stump of the tree once again, Ramage carefully arranged his face to look as brutal and ruthless as possible, and said icily: "Do you speak English?"

"A little."

"Now you have one last chance to tell me about the graves."

"Never," Colon said, with little conviction, and added despairingly, "They are not graves."

"I am busy," Ramage said haughtily. "I take my farewell. My men will deal with you."

The effect on Colon startled Ramage and the seamen: he gave a tragic and despairing moan, slid forward from the stump face down on the ground, his hands clutching at Ramage's feet.

"No," he whispered, "I cannot tell – "

Ramage, embarrassed, hurriedly stepped back, glanced at Jackson and said with as much melodrama as he could muster: "Farewell, *señor*; if you cannot tell, you cannot live…"

With that he turned and hurried away.

Only a fool never knows fear, he thought; but I'm damned if I can understand a man too craven to hide or control it. Colon believes he has only a minute or so to live. So far as he knows, I've given orders for him to be killed. A minute or so isn't long to clench your teeth, stand up and perhaps shout defiance. It's something you owe yourself, and surely it makes the going easier than weeping and tearing your hair out.

He hadn't gone twenty yards towards the camp before he began worrying about Jackson. Would the American be able to make Colon talk? Supposing Colon kept up his refusal? Was he prepared to die with the secret? Because that wretched example of foppery held the key to…to what?

He stopped walking and stared at the distant horizon, his eyes out of focus and his mind racing.

Whatever Colon was up to with his gang of gravediggers and platoon of armed sextons was absolutely no concern of his, except for the potential threat of the soldiers to the men of the *Triton* and *Topaz*. His only responsibility was the present safety of the two ships' companies and subsequent rescue.

Back at the camp Southwick was ready with reports on the day's activities so far: Appleby had gone off with the raft and was more than halfway to the wrecks; carpenter's mates from both ships had gone with him to find suitable timber for building a boat; his calculations on the provisions landed so far, and based on the regular Navy issue, showed that they had food for three months.

Ramage walked with Southwick round the provisions store, hidden under its tarpaulin and palm fronds, nodding to the Marine sentries, and then went on to inspect the magazine. The men had made an excellent job of building it, using the same method as Cornishmen had used for centuries to make their drystone walls.

In a couple of centuries' time, Ramage thought, someone is going to examine the remains of this little magazine and, knowing nothing of the hurricane, the *Triton* and the *Topaz*, wonder how a small building using such a remote system came to be erected on Snake Island. A building with such a tiny doorway that the men or women who used it would have to have been midgets...

At that moment he saw Jackson approaching; looking cheerful, almost smug.

"I think he's ready to tell you all about it, sir," Jackson said in reply to Ramage's inquiry. "I can't speak Spanish, as you know, but he made himself understood."

Ramage glanced at Colon and saw his dejected, hunchbacked walk, the reluctant, foot-dragging steps.

"What did you do to him?"

"Well, sir..." Jackson began sheepishly, "we didn't lay a finger on him..."

Ramage eyed the seaman, and then laughed. "Lieutenant Colon will tell me all about it."

Jackson's face fell. "Honestly, sir, we didn't touch him. Just a bit o' play-acting by Staff and Rosey."

A few moments later Colon was led up by a gleeful Stafford, Rossi and Maxton.

Southwick looked curiously at Colon. He had shown little interest in Ramage's description of the morning's ambush, but that was his way of showing disapproval at not being put in command.

Colon had eyes only for Ramage and began speaking as soon as Stafford signalled him to stop walking.

"I wish to tell you," he said, words tumbling out as if he was trying to make an urgent plea as the guillotine blade fell. "I will tell you everything. But I want a guarantee. Your word of honour – "

"A guarantee about what?"

"That they won't garrotte me!" he said, pointing to the seamen. "Slowly," he added with a shudder. Stafford's pantomime seemed to have been extremely effective. But again Ramage thought of this man sending for a slave to be whipped for his pleasure.

"You aren't in a position to demand guarantees. Tell me about the graves."

"Not graves!" Colon exclaimed almost tearfully, as though using the word to describe the trenches would eventually change their purpose. "Trenches."

"Holes," Ramage said, suddenly exasperated. "You shouldn't waste time fussing about the precise choice of words. Tell me about the holes."

"I want a guarantee."

Not at all sure he could muster a blood-curdling laugh without breaking into a giggle, Ramage merely said contemptuously, "A beggar doesn't make demands."

Colon stared at the ground. Ramage looked directly at Stafford, let his eyes drop to the cord the cockney was still holding and then looked back and forth along the ground in front of Colon.

Stafford understood the signal immediately and began to walk around, slapping the cord impatiently against his leg and whistling cheerfully through his teeth. He looked the picture of an impatient killer, as though, as he might phrase it, in a hurry to use the "carrot".

Colon glanced up nervously, looking first at Stafford and then at Ramage, who said nothing. Apart from the sharp slapping of the cord against Stafford's leg, his whistling, and the distant boom of waves hitting the outer reefs, there was silence.

To Colon, though, it seemed to be a silence filled with terrifying fantasies; he was perspiring and pale, clasping and unclasping his hands.

"The orders you received," Ramage prompted.

Colon looked up and Ramage was reminded of an animal trapped in a snare.

"You can guess," Colon said.

Ramage was puzzled for a moment and then wondered if there was more to Colon than he thought. Was the man hoping Ramage would guess, so that he would not actually have to use words to reveal his orders? A legalistic interpretation of "reveal"? Ramage decided that as long as he found out what the holes were for, he didn't give a damn, so he gave Colon a little help.

"I presume you were looking for something."

"Of course."

"The only things of value likely to be on this island are water and pirate's treasure."

Suddenly Colon became animated: his head came up, his shoulders straightened, both arms came up as though he was greeting a long-lost friend.

"Precisely! And there is plenty of water in the village..."

"So you are looking for treasure."

Colon did not answer; instead he grinned happily. Ramage was too excited now for the long-winded method he'd been manoeuvred into. Treasure! Presumably treasure looted from the Spanish Main, so who would be in a better position to know about it than the Spanish!

"You have a map?"

Colon shook his head.

"You're not just digging at random?"

Colon nodded.

Is this clown being legalistic again? Ramage wondered.

"You *are* digging at random?" Ramage asked.

Colon nodded vigorously.

"Anywhere on the island?"

Again Colon nodded.

"You'd better find your tongue," Ramage said. "Don't forget that now I have guessed about the treasure, you aren't revealing that!"

This seemed to reassure Colon.

"Anywhere," he said. "Just selecting likely places and digging."

"Are the holes all the same depth?"

"Oh yes, no more than the height of a small man."

"Why that limit?"

Colon shrugged his shoulders. "Orders. The Colonel said it wouldn't be deeper than that."

"How did he know?"

Ramage had the impression that Colon was slowly becoming conspiratorial in his manner; as though he had secretly abandoned the Colonel and the service of Spain, and was giving clandestine help to the British.

"There was a report."

"What report?" Ramage said angrily, getting impatient as he levered the facts out of Colon a few words at a time. "Come now, tell me all you know, otherwise you'll be pegged out to dry like *boucan*."

His exasperation gave his words just the right ring; Colon went white again and Ramage expected him to faint. Pirates and privateersmen haunting the Caribbean islands pegged out raw meat to dry in the sun to preserve it, calling it "boucan", and became known as *boucaniers*, or buccaneers.

Ramage turned to Jackson and said in English: "Use your cutlass to clear some of this – " he pointed to the low shrubs. "Level a space about seven feet long and five feet wide. In front of this chap."

Jackson gave an impressive salute and began a series of low, sweeping strokes with the cutlass blade.

Colon watched, as if hypnotized, and when Jackson had finished and kicked the branches clear, Ramage turned to the Spaniard and said abruptly: "Pegged out there. You were saying?"

"The report," Colon said hurriedly. "A family here, on this island. No taxes – they had not paid taxes. It was a long fraud on the government. The *Intendente* was going to put father and son in prison and confiscate their land. To save themselves the father offered to tell the *Intendente* about the treasure if the tax was forgotten."

"How did he know about treasure?"

"He is a descendant of a pirate. There are many such families."

"But treasure? Not every pirate family – "

"This one knew," Colon said contemptuously.

"How could the *Intendente* be sure?"

"A week in the dungeon at El Morro and everyone tells everything," Colon said. "That much I can assure you."

"We can do quite well here, and in less time," Ramage said dryly. "Now, tell me all you know about it."

"Well," Colon said nervously, "treasure is buried here *somewhere*. They've known that in San Juan for scores of years. They've looked for a map and they've watched the people, hoping that the family that knew would one day start to dig."

"Did they?"

"No. In fact they didn't know the details. Only the depth."

"And what is the important clue?"

"I was going to tell you about that," Colon said quickly. "Everyone says it's important, but no one understands it."

"Say it!"

Colon recited:

> " *'By the sound of the sea*
> *and my memory,*
> *Three times three*
> *A tree above.'* "

"And no one knows what it means?" Ramage asked.

"No one!"

"What else should you tell me?"

"That's all," Colon said, and Ramage felt he was telling the truth. "That's all, and now you can kill me."

The voice was so lugubrious that Ramage laughed, and then realized Colon interpreted the laugh as agreement.

"I'll wait a while," Ramage said. "I may think of some more questions. By the way, the family that knew the poem?"

"They are still in jail at El Morro."

"And the other islanders?"

"They know nothing."

He gave Jackson instructions for guarding Colon and he and Southwick went back to the beach. There they found Yorke, St Brieuc and St Cast and walked along the beach with them. After describing the so-called clue he said, "You can all exercise your brains on that. As soon as one of you tells me what it means, we can start digging for the treasure."

"If it really is a clue," Yorke said doubtfully.

"I'm inclined to think it is," St Brieuc said. "The Spanish are not stupid. They're close to the treasure. If they believe it, then I think we should."

"They were digging on level patches," Yorke said. "That's something we can do anyway. There can't be so many in a hilly place like this. Plenty of flat fields, of course, but I think the Dons know it's a small flat area up in the hills. If we try those we don't waste time while we work on the clue. We want to get to windward of the treasure before the provision ship arrives."

Ramage had quite forgotten to find out when the ship was due. He excused himself and went off to question the *teniente* again. He found him much more cheerful, and quite prepared to talk. The next ship was due on the first day of the month. That was the regular date, though it was sometimes a day or two late.

While considering the problem of keeping Colon a prisoner without a building to lock him in, Ramage remembered that there were houses in the village…Houses and a well.

The Marines and a handful of seamen could stay here in the camp to guard the provisions and magazine and the rest of them could move to San Ildefonso. The slaves seemed quite cheerful with their new status, which could be best described as freedom with limited liberty.

CHAPTER FOURTEEN

By nightfall most of the survivors of the two ships were in occupation of the village. The powder and muskets had been moved and the St Brieucs and St Cast were given the best house while Ramage, Yorke, Southwick and Bowen shared another. The senior petty officers shared two more which left four unoccupied and in various stages of disrepair for the seamen. Ramage was surprised at the lack of enthusiasm for them.

"Those houses," he asked Jackson. "What's wrong with them? Why don't the men use them?"

Jackson looked blank and Ramage said irritably, "I've given them four houses and told 'em to decide among themselves, you know all that!"

The American said apologetically, "Sorry, sir, I didn't quite follow what you meant. The men are grateful, sir, but they'd sooner sleep out in the open."

"You mean that what is good enough for the officers isn't good enough for them," Ramage said acidly.

"Oh no, sir!" Jackson exclaimed in alarm, "it's not that at all. Sleeping in hammocks slung from trees in the Tropics with all the birds singing and the strange flowers and all that – why, sir, they're like kids at Michaelmas Fair. They're loving it. They've been betting on hummingbirds, putting their money on which particular blossoms on a tree get visited in a set time."

"Oh," Ramage said lamely. "I'm glad. I hope they won't forget how to sling a hammock afloat."

"They'll be ready to go to sea when the time comes, sir. It's just something completely new. Even the men from country places are finding it so different, sir."

Supper was served in the largest room in the house taken over by Ramage, and he decided that he would eat his meals with the others simply because the alternative was too complicated.

They were halfway through the meal when Ramage said: "Has anyone thought of an explanation of the mysterious clue?"

No one had.

"What do you propose to do?" Yorke asked.

"Well, the provisions ship isn't due from San Juan for another three weeks. I might as well keep the men busy digging holes as doing anything else."

"The wrecks, sir," Southwick reminded him.

"Of course. The most important jobs are protecting ourselves here, guarding the provisions, bringing over the rest of the powder, and getting more supplies from the wrecks before they break up, just in case we don't get off the island for a while. That means I can use the slaves and some seamen just to dig. The dons dug only one hole at a time."

"I'm not surprised," Bowen said. "If that Spanish officer wasn't there, the moment the treasure was found, it'd vanish into thin air!"

"Exactly," Ramage said. "And because we have more reliable people to take charge, we can cover more ground."

"Count me in," Yorke said.

"I hope you won't forget me, sir," Bowen said. "I should regard the discovery of pirate treasure as the climax of my medical career."

"Medicine and piracy go hand in hand," Southwick teased.

"Exactly," Bowen said. "Didn't you notice the alacrity with which I volunteered?"

"I wonder what language the clue was composed in," Yorke said.

"Why not Spanish?" Ramage asked.

"I just can't see a pirate not making it rhyme. I was wondering if it was originally in English, poorly translated, and now translated back, slightly differently from the original."

"I should have thought of that before," Ramage said, feeling his face redden. "The Spanish weren't the pirates; they were the victims. The clue certainly wouldn't have been in Spanish."

"Let's translate it again," Yorke said cheerfully.

Ramage sent his steward for pen, ink and paper, and when he had written a translation of the Spanish phrases, he read them out aloud:

> "By the sound of the sea
> and my memory,
> Three times three
> A tree above."

"Let's take the first line," he said. "I want ideas reflecting treasure and poetry!"

Yorke said, "It's wrong, I'm sure. It's isolated from the next line, whereas it probably ran on originally."

"What was the man trying to describe?" Bowen asked.

"It's a distance," Southwick said. "Buried within sound of the sea."

"You're right," Ramage exclaimed. "Let's look at the second line for a moment. It's ambiguous. It could be 'my memory' or 'remember'."

" 'Remember me'?" asked Yorke.

Ramage nodded, wrote it down and then said tentatively, "It could begin, 'Hear the sea and remember me...' "

"That's more like it," Bowen said. "Now, how did the third line go?"

Ramage read it again, and the surgeon said: "Three times three, eh. Nine paces, or perhaps three pieces of something in three places?"

"Three pieces...I'd have expected it to be 'Three by three' in that case," Yorke said.

Ramage scribbled it down, and read the fourth line, adding, " 'A tree above' could also mean 'underneath a tree', or in the shade of it."

"What have we got now, sir?" Southwick said, running his hands through his white hair. "My memory isn't very good for poetry."

Ramage continued changing a word here and there for a moment, then said: "How does this sound?

" *'Hear the sea*
and remember me;
Three by three,
Beneath the tree.' "

"Well, we can hear the sea," he continued. "Then we have to remember this chap – presumably remember his treasure. Then 'three by three', or 'three times three'. Trees in three groups of three...A hill with three groups of three big rocks on its slope – plenty around here, I've noticed…Three groups of three peaks among the hills?"

"Not trees, surely," Southwick said. "They grow quickly or get blown away in a hurricane. Or burned down – I've seen traces of big fires here, probably started by lightning. And hills – they're not precise enough."

"Not trees," Yorke echoed. "Too obvious. The family here who knew the rhyme would have spotted anything like that. They've probably been looking for a trio of anything for a century or more."

"Can you hear the sea from where the Spanish party was digging when Jackson found them?" Bowen asked.

"Barely," Ramage said. "On a still night with a heavy swell on the reefs…"

"So either the Spanish don't realize the significance of 'The sound of the sea', sir, or they discount it," Bowen said.

"Yes, but obviously they have plenty of time. I didn't ask this fellow Colon how long he expected to be here, but the provisions ship is due monthly. Now, we have enough slaves to make up five parties of four. Plus four seamen to each party. And one officer."

By the time they went to bed the leadership of each party had been decided. At dawn next day they marched out along the track towards the camp. Ramage had decided to continue in that direction because Colon had covered all the flat areas flanking the track from San Ildefonso to the point where he was captured.

By nightfall the parties had returned to report that they had dug an average of twelve trenches each and found no sign of anything.

"Sixty damned trenches," Ramage said crossly to Southwick, "and not a trace…"

"Don't think of it like that," the Master said soothingly. "It means three hundred and sixty a week which is about a year's effort for that Spanish lieutenant."

Southwick's mathematics were comforting, but whoever buried the treasure did not envisage scores of men digging for weeks: he meant someone who learnt the poem and solved its riddle to be able to go straight to the treasure.

At supper that evening he discussed the day's digging with the other men. He felt they did not share his sense of urgency; to them three weeks seemed time enough. It probably was but, as he pointed out to Yorke, "We can't be sure a ship won't arrive unexpectedly. If it does we have to capture it, and if it's suitable, sail away in it, treasure or no treasure."

"We ought to proceed with scientific precision," Yorke said mockingly. "If one or two people who know the poem just walked around the island looking for possible sites and checking the 'three by three' part, we might save a great deal of time and effort."

After supper when the table had been cleared, Ramage spread out some paper and made a rough sketch of the section of Snake Island he already knew. He shaded in the area the men had worked on during the day, and those where Colon's men had been unsuccessful.

"Which would you prefer?" he asked Yorke. "Search or dig?"

"Search!" Yorke said promptly.

For three days they searched the island, Ramage taking Jackson, Yorke accompanied by Stafford and Bowen with Rossi. Slowly they worked their way over the lower foothills on the east and north-east sides of the island. From Cabeza de Perro, the headland on the east side of where the rafts had landed, Ramage was sure they were getting warm: just opposite, half a mile away, was a small island, Culebrita, with another to the north-west. There were two sections of beach which fishermen obviously used as landing places, and there were several flat areas like platforms close by in the low hills. But there was nothing near the platforms that answered the "three by three" description.

Late in the evening Ramage and Yorke were sitting on the low wall outside their house and looking down at the reflection of the stars on the mirror-like surface of the bay.

"It could take a year," Yorke said.

"It could," Ramage said stubbornly. "But that wasn't the intention of whoever hid the treasure."

"I've been trying to picture him," Yorke said. "After all, who buries treasure, and why?"

"People like us a century or so ago."

"How do you mean?" Yorke asked, and suddenly sprang up and gave a bow. "Madame."

Maxine had walked to the wall from her parents' house.

"Are you talking about affairs of state, or may I sit and listen?"

Yorke left Ramage to reply.

"You are always welcome; I'll get you a chair."

She gestured for him to remain seated. "I will sit on the wall with you."

She sat between them and arranged her skirt. Then she turned to Ramage and gave an impish smile.

"We're trying to look into the mind of the corsair who buried the treasure," Ramage said.

"How fascinating. Please continue, I shall feel important if I can help."

They had been talking for several minutes when Maxine asked Ramage to repeat the clue. When he had done so she commented: "I would expect five lines. *Peut-être...*did someone forget a line?"

"By jingo!" Yorke exclaimed. "I think she's right."

And Ramage knew she was. Colon had fooled him.

"If you'll excuse me for a few minutes," he said.

He collected Jackson and Stafford, gave them instructions and took them to the hut being used as a prison. In a sudden fit of pique Colon had refused to give his parole, so Ramage had to keep him locked up and guarded.

Jackson led the way, carrying a lantern, reassured the sentry and followed Ramage into the room.

Colon, eyes blinking in the light, looked wary.

"The poem," Ramage said abruptly. "You forgot to tell me one of the lines. I hope you made no other mistakes."

Colon shook his head. "I told you everything."

"I saved your life," Ramage said.

"Do you usually murder prisoners?"

"Listen carefully," Ramage said, not troubling to keep the bitterness from his voice. "Since the Inquisition, you people have had a bad reputation where prisoners are concerned. Now, think like a man. If I fell into your colonel's hands, and he discovered I knew a poem which was the clue to the whereabouts of a treasure trove...you know what he would do!"

"He would behave like a gentleman."

"Rubbish!" Ramage exclaimed angrily. "He would torture me, and you know it – just as the *Intendente* tortured that family in the first place. You can even guess *how* he would torture me!"

Colon's silence told Ramage he had been lucky in choosing the Colonel as an example.

"Now," Ramage said ominously, "all I have to do is to imitate the Colonel. Then you can have no complaints."

Colon was beginning to perspire. Tiny beads of sweat mottled his brow and upper lip. His eyes jerked from side to side so much that Jackson stood with his back to the door.

"Send these men outside so that I can talk!" Colon whispered.

"They speak no Spanish."

"How can I be sure of that?"

"You can't," Ramage said unsympathetically. "You have to take my word for it."

"I will tell you," Colon said. "I told all of it except for the first line."

"Well, go on," Ramage said when the Spaniard paused, and then saw he was concentrating, as if anxious to get it right this time.

"You see the three,
By the sound of the sea
And my memory,
Three times three
A tree above.

"That's all, I swear," Colon said. "It makes no sense with or without. It is useless. The finest brains in Spain have tried to solve it. And there's the legend that the treasure lies no deeper than the height of a small man."

"Is there anything more to tell me?"

"No, *señor*," Colon said, "I swear it."

At last, Ramage thought, he was speaking the truth.

Leaving Jackson to lock the door, Ramage strode back to his room with the lantern, took out his copy of the earlier version of the poem, and then began changing the new version to fit the modified translation. He wrote:

"You see the three
and hear the sea
and remember me.
Then three by three
Beneath the tree."

He could hear Maxine and Yorke talking quietly outside, and he joined them. They both turned towards him expectantly.

"You were right, Madame, and thank you."

"Presumably you now have the missing line?" Yorke asked.

Ramage nodded. "It doesn't help much," he said, and repeated the poem.

"You stand somewhere and you see three things and hear the sea," Maxine said, as if thinking aloud. "Three what? Trees, hills, capes?"

"Headlands!" Ramage exclaimed. "Quick, let's look at the chart!"

They went into the house and Ramage unrolled the chart, but it was too small in scale to be of much use.

"A local fisherman?" Yorke suggested.

There was a chance. He called for his steward and sent him to find the slave Roberto. He would know the most reliable fisherman.

Half an hour later a thin, middle-aged and frightened fisherman stood before Ramage, wide-brimmed straw hat in his hand. The man's skin was the colour of mahogany, the result of a coloured forebear and a life spent under a tropical sun.

"Please be seated," Ramage said quietly, indicating a canvas-backed chair.

The man sidled towards the chair, as if fearing some trap, and finally sat down.

"I wish for your help," Ramage said in Spanish. "A small matter concerning the island."

The fisherman stared at him.

"The names of the bays and headlands," Ramage said. "You know them all?"

The fisherman nodded.

"That's all I want to know," Ramage said. "Just the names."

"Where do I start?"

"The entrance of this bay. Imagine we are sailing out of it and round the island with the sun. Round by the west."

"Dakity," the man said. "Ensenada Dakity, that's the first, it's a bay. Then Malena next to it. Then Punta del Soldado – that's the tip of the island. There are no more names until you get to Punta de Maguey, and Punta Tampico, with Bahia Linda in between."

As the fisherman paused to think, Ramage knew he was wasting his time; but since the fisherman was now reassured it was easier to let him go on than to shut him up.

"Punta Melones, that's next. No, Bahia de Sardinas first, then Melones. Then Bahia Tarja – that's a long bay, all the way between Punta Melones and Punta Tamarindo Chico.

"It's very rocky off Tamarindo Chico, but it has lobsters. Then comes Bahia Tamarindo, Punta Tamarindo – that's the other end of the bay – and then Punta Tamarindo Grande. There are no more names for a long distance, until you get to Punta Noroeste – "

Yorke interrupted to ask Ramage: "Didn't he just give three or four places with the – "

"I'm letting him go on so he doesn't guess we attach importance to them."

Yorke nodded, and Ramage waved for the fisherman to continue. Name after name followed – Molinos...Flamenco

…Manchit…Playa…Larga…Perro…Manzanilla…Vaca…Mosquito.

Finally the fisherman intoned, "Punta Carenero, Punta Padilla, Punta Cabras – and then you are back here."

"Thank you," Ramage said. "They have interesting names. Why do you suppose Punta del Soldado was so named? A garrison perhaps?"

"Yes, long ago," the fisherman said. "My grandfather mentioned it."

"And Bahia de Sardinas – good for sardines, no doubt?"

The fisherman snorted. "Never one in *that* bay!"

"No more than there are tamarinds in Bahia Tamarindo!"

"Ah," the fisherman said knowingly, "plenty of tamarinds there, just at the back of the beach. Beads," he said. "I collect the pods and we empty out the seeds. Then I soak the seeds in boiling water until they get soft and I can stitch them. Make necklaces for the lady?" he asked, looking at Maxine. "Would she like to buy them? I can make to whatever pattern she wishes."

Quickly Ramage seized the chance, speaking to Maxine in French as though asking her a question. Then he said to the fisherman: "The señora would like to buy. She wishes me to go to the bay tomorrow to select the seeds."

"Certainly," the fisherman said, "I have no seeds in stock. How many necklaces does the lady require?"

"Many," Ramage said. "For herself and her mother."

"Ah," said the fisherman, "it will be a pleasure."

Ramage told him to report next morning at dawn, and the man left after bowing to Maxine with the natural manners of an honest man.

Yorke raised his eyebrows. "Reveal to us the secrets of the Tropics, O Governor with the Spanish tongue."

Maxine laughed when Ramage drew himself up and took a deep breath, like a politician about to harangue a crowd.

"Tamarind," he said gravely. "Vote for the tamarind, known to our Spanish brothers as the *tamarindo*, and our French sister as the *tamarin*."

"It has our vote," Yorke said equally gravely. "But what we want to know now is, will it win the election; will it reduce taxes and bring us peace and prosperity at no effort?"

"We'll know by tomorrow," Ramage said, and explained what the fisherman had told him. "There are three 'Tamarind Points' – and that's unusual anywhere – with a 'Tamarind Bay' for good measure."

"Why three points?" Yorke asked.

"Well, the one in the middle is plain Punta Tamarindo, with Bahia Tamarindo to the south down to Punta Tamarindo Chico. *Chico* can mean 'small' or 'short'. The one to the north, Punta Tamarindo Grande, is just the big one."

"And now..." Yorke asked.

"We sleep, and at dawn the fisherman takes us there to gather tamarind seeds."

"Oh good, I must admit I was running short of them," Yorke said.

"I guessed that," Ramage said. "By the way, the trees are the wild tamarind. The seeds can be strung together as beads, or shaken as a musical instrument."

Next morning Ramage, Yorke, Jackson and Stafford stood on Punta Tamarindo while the sun rose behind them. The air was dry and aromatic and already the heat had set the shrubs buzzing with insects, while hummingbirds inspected the blossom. The fisherman tapped Ramage's arm.

"It is beautiful, eh?"

Ramage nodded, and the man pointed to a cone-shaped island in front of them.

"Cayo de Luis Peña," he said. "Just goats there now. Good fishing – grouper, snapper, lobster…And the little cays beyond – Las Hermanas. And beyond them, towards Puerto Rico, I don't know their names. There" – he pointed to the long, low island to the south-west – "that is Vieques. The priest lives there," he added. "He visits us twice a year."

Ramage nodded, wondering when to steer the conversation back to where they stood, but the fisherman needed no prompting. He pointed southwards, to their left.

"There, Bahia Tamarindo. The water – have you ever seen it so blue? Then Tamarindo Chico at the end."

"The point beyond Chico?"

"Ah," the Spaniard said, with the pride of a shopkeeper displaying an item he knows a wealthy customer will not only admire but buy at the right price. "That is Punta Melones and in line beyond it, the most distant of all, Punta del Soldado."

"Beautiful," Ramage said.

The fisherman turned to the north, pointing to his right. "Tamarindo Grande," he announced. Ramage nodded appreciatively and, turning to Yorke, said in English: "Any comments on the scenery?"

"Yes. For what it's worth, Tamarindo Grande, the Melon – or whatever it was the fellow called it – and Punto del Soldado are in line. Two miles from each other and a geometrically precise straight line passes through the western tip of each one."

"And that," Ramage said, "seems to put paid to our 'three by three'."

Yorke shrugged his shoulders.

The fisherman had walked fifty yards away and was beginning to pull the long, flat pods from the tamarinds, crack them open and shake the seeds into his sack.

Ramage and Yorke looked around the short headland. There was a scattering of trees, the most prominent being a tall, lacy-leaved casuarina, and they strolled towards it.

"Seven trees," Yorke said. "The significant thing is that seven has no possible connection with three, or three times three!"

"I know," Ramage said. "I'm getting to the point where things only exist for me if they're in multiples of three."

Yorke laughed and bent down to pick up a large seashell. It was sun-bleached and worn by the sea and the sand.

"How do these things get up here?"

"Birds, probably," Ramage said. "They find them alive and bring 'em ashore to eat the animal inside."

"It's a pretty shell."

"A flame helmet."

"What is?" Yorke asked in surprise.

"That shell. A type of conch – you've seen the natives eating the Queen conchs. They cut a small slot here" – he pointed to one end – "and that severs the animal's anchor so they can pull it out. The birds haven't learned the trick. This one is a cousin of the Queen conch. You can see it's shaped something like a helmet."

"Haven't seen one before," Yorke said, turning it in his hand. "I'll take this one back and present it to Madame."

The fisherman joined them, his sack of seeds slung over his shoulder.

"You take him back with you," Ramage said. "Jackson and I will just have a look over the other two Tamarinds."

Yorke said doubtfully: "I've got a feeling the trio of tamarinds is just a coincidence."

Ramage grimaced. "We might as well clutch at a tamarind as a straw..."

With that Yorke, Stafford and the fisherman began the long walk back to the camp while Ramage and Jackson went northwards to Tamarindo Grande. It was barren; just a few trees and boulders. Then they walked back past Punta Tamarindo to Tamarindo Chico.

Jackson kicked a small stone in anger.

"It isn't as though the Spaniards *deserve* to find it, sir!"

"No more or less than us," Ramage said mildly.

"I suppose not. Do the admirals get a share, sir?"

That's an interesting point, Ramage thought. "I've no idea. Probably not treated like prize money."

"But it's the same thing, isn't it, sir?"

"It most certainly isn't! Only a ship can be condemned as a prize. You wouldn't get a penn'orth of prize money for capturing this island, for instance."

"Not even a reward, sir?" Jackson asked hopefully.

"You might get something. Don't spend it until you've received it though, just in case!"

In silence the men started back to the village.

As he walked down the slope to the houses Ramage heard the sound of women's laughter and found Yorke and St Cast sitting with the St Brieucs on the balcony of their house.

Maxine waved gaily when she saw Ramage and beckoned to him to join them. He would have preferred to go to his own room and sit alone for an hour or two: the visit to Punta Tamarindo was a bigger disappointment than he cared to admit. He'd spent the night and all the time they were walking there thinking that the three headlands called tamarind must fit the poem. His hopes had strengthened when he found three headlands in line, and now he felt flat. His feet were sore from the long walk; his eyes ached from the sun's glare; his mouth was dry and gritty from the dusty tracks, and mosquitoes and sandflies had bitten him freely.

"Come!" Maxine called "We have *limonade* ready for you."

As she stood facing him, her eyes sparkling and her hands outstretched, he wanted to take her in his arms. Instead he climbed the steps to the balcony, bowed to the St Brieucs and nodded to the others.

"Such a long face!" Maxine exclaimed.

"Someone knocked his sandcastle down!" Yorke said.

Maxine looked puzzled. "Sandcastle?"

"Mr Yorke likes talking in riddles."

She shrugged her shoulders. "*Alors* – he has given me a beautiful present."

Ramage was jealous but said quickly: "Don't tell me what it is – I'll guess. Now, let me see – a coronet studded with diamonds and rubies?"

She shook her head and laughed. "Not exactly."

"A tiara, then – of gold, mounted with a huge emerald and one hundred perfect pearls."

She shook her head again. "No, it is *much* more beautiful."

"A miniature of me."

She laughed so loudly her mother looked shocked and her father delighted. St Brieuc glanced at Ramage, as if encouraging him to go on making her laugh; she needed to laugh much more.

"That would be 'a pearl beyond price' – isn't that how you say it? No, it is a seashell."

She waved the flame helmet which Yorke had cleaned and polished.

"It is wonderful – look, if I hold it to my ear I can hear the sea!"

Ramage froze for a moment, and then reached out for it.

"Give it to me please," he said harshly.

He put the open part of the shell to his ear and sure enough there was a hollow noise, like breakers on a distant beach. Even as he listened, he saw the startled look on Yorke's face give way to deep thought and that in turn was replaced by an almost disbelieving grin.

Before either of them could say anything, St Brieuc whispered, "That's it, 'The sound of the sea...' "

Then Maxine, who had been startled by Ramage snatching the shell from her, gave a quick curtsey and said, "A *shell* without price, anyway!"

They all laughed and for several minutes they chattered excitedly, passing the shell from one to another. As they talked Ramage kept trying to fit this particular shell into the hunt for the treasure.

St Brieuc put it into words, saying in his quick yet authoritative voice: "We must not forget this is only one shell. I presume that there are thousands more in the sea."

And they all looked crestfallen.

"We're letting the treasure hunt get on our nerves," Ramage said. "I am, anyway."

"Me too!" Yorke said. "I have to admit it's exciting. Even if we find nothing, I've enjoyed it so far. What small boy hasn't played pirates and searched for treasure?"

"Quite," Ramage agreed, "but at the same time I'd like to be one of the few adults who actually *found* it!" As he spoke he saw Maxine watching him speculatively, as though weighing him up. Their eyes met and Ramage wondered, yet again, what her husband was like.

Within a week of the landing from the rafts, life on Snake Island had settled into a pleasant routine. The seamen of both ships enjoyed the treasure hunt – they were so eager to join one of the digging teams that Southwick grumbled that if there had been any miscreants he'd have made them part of the raft's crew.

After a day's digging, several of the men spent an hour or two each evening tidying up the ground round the houses. They cleared out some of the shrubs to give more space to the frangipani, now coming towards the end of its blossom, and a dozen other and smaller flowering trees, shrubs and bushes. They had made crude tables and forms and set them under the shade of a big flamboyant which towered over them like a scarlet umbrella. The paths leading from house to house had been lined with small rocks which had been painted white. Slowly San Ildefonso was being transformed into a neat hamlet.

Ramage saw that the men, starved for years of the sight and sound of life on land, were making up for it by getting the feel of the soil; watching and helping it to produce beauty. Southwick, in his quiet, fatherly way, was helping them. Appleby was told to bring over paint, nails, a few planks of timber chopped from bulwarks, so the men could make more furniture.

Much to Bowen's delight, St Cast had proved to be a fine chess player, and Appleby brought the surgeon's chess-set back from the wreck so the two could play a few games each evening.

The St Brieucs had settled into life in the tiny village of San Ildefonso as if they were in a comfortable château on the banks of the Loire. Early in the morning, before the sun was too hot, or in the late afternoon, he saw all three of them walking slowly along one of the beaches of the great inland bay as if they were inspecting their estates. They were enchanted by the flocks of small white egrets which flew out every evening to sleep on a small cay in the centre of the bay, and came back with descriptions of strange birds and butterflies, chameleons and insects.

Ramage intended to let Appleby make two more raft trips to the wrecks. After that they'd have more than enough provisions. The idea of putting partly filled casks over the side and letting them float ashore had been highly successful. The cooper had also taken the opportunity of cleaning water casks and floating them over empty, and now they were stored by the well, ready to be filled when the supply ship arrived. Ramage was determined they should not be short of water and provisions on the voyage to Jamaica.

The slaves had proved a cheerful crowd of men, and most evenings they sang the songs of Africa or danced round a fire, to the delight of the seamen, who were soon learning the steps of the dances and joining in with clumsy enthusiasm.

It amused everyone to refer to Ramage as "The Governor". St Brieuc quietly promoted the idea and it certainly made things a lot easier for Ramage. He was the youngest of them all, except for Maxine, but as Governor he could give orders without affecting the social side of their lives together.

Ramage was talking to Jackson one morning when the American asked: "Did the fisherman make a good job of the necklaces?"

"Excellent. They were a great success."

"That Tamarind Point business was a big disappointment, sir."

Ramage nodded. "Tamarinds, and flame helmet s – I don't care if I never see any more!"

"Flame helmets, sir?" Jackson asked. "What are they?"

Ramage described the shell to the American.

"I remember it now, sir."

"Yes, if only there'd been three of them," Ramage said

absent-mindedly as he recalled Maxine's "I can hear the sea",

and their brief excitement.

"There were, sir," Jackson said. "Three of them in a straight

line. Mr Yorke picked up the nearest one. Didn't you see the

others?"

CHAPTER FIFTEEN

It promised to be a very long night. Taking a party of seamen to Punta Tamarindo to dig by the light of lanterns might attract the attention of the local folk and, for the moment, the less they knew the better. They knew the English dug trenches in daylight, but this was merely copying the Spanish. To dig by lantern light might suggest urgency...

The heat in Ramage's room was stifling. The wind had dropped with the sun and the offshore breeze had not materialized to make the night pleasantly cool. It had become the sort of tropical night that was a test of endurance. Ramage forgot nature's glorious riot of colours, the startling flowers, the scarlet of the flamboyants and the exciting blue of the sea. He even forgot the temperature during the day, when the breeze and the shade made it perfect.

In the misery of a windless night in the hurricane season, he hankered for the cold nights of the northern latitudes. Chilblains and colds, the sniffing and sneezing, the layer upon layer of clothing needed to keep not just warm but to avoid being frozen, were overlooked and he realized for the first time just how much life in the Tropics was governed by the wind. The thermometer could be showing eighty degrees and it could be two o'clock in the afternoon. If the Trade winds were blowing, the temperature was ideal. With no wind eighty degrees became uncomfortable: clothing was soaked with perspiration and energy destroyed by heat and humidity.

There was a gentle tap at the door and Ramage reached down for the pistol by his bed.

"Who's there?" he whispered loudly.

"It's Yorke."

271

"Come in," Ramage said and added as he saw the door open into the starlit room, "What's the matter, can't you sleep?"

"No – I keep on hearing the sound of the sea in that damned helmet shell. You know, I don't enjoy these waiting games; I'm far too impatient!"

"Nor do I," Ramage confessed. "I'm just lying here waiting for the hands of my watch to get moving."

"What time do we start off for Punta Tamarindo?"

"Five o'clock. Takes about an hour to get there. I want people to think we are just digging trenches somewhere else for a change."

"Who knows," Yorke said lightly, "that may be all we are doing."

"It probably is. Best to think of it that way."

"Why don't we go and dig?" Yorke said impulsively. "Just a few of us. We needn't make any noise, and Punta Tamarindo must be one of the most isolated places in the Caribbean anyway."

Ramage swung his legs off the bed and began dressing without a word.

Within fifteen minutes, having left a disapproving Southwick in command at the village, Ramage and Yorke were leading a party of ten seamen and four Marines along the track round the edge of the great inland bay. They cut through a long valley almost to the coast on the north side of the island before swinging in a half circle to skirt a ridge of three high hills that separated Bahia Tamarindo from the rest of the island.

The seamen, far from truculent at being roused out after a day's digging, were excited; but for the need for some secrecy, Ramage guessed, they'd have been singing like a party of Cornish miners on their way to the local fair.

They reached Punta Tamarindo in little more than an hour, and leaving the seamen and Marines waiting twenty yards back, Ramage took Yorke and Jackson to the casuarina tree.

Jackson, carrying the lantern, quickly found the shells.

"There's one, sir, and there's the other. That's where yours was lying. You can see the impression in the earth – it's deep. Wonder there wasn't a scorpion under it."

Three flame helmets in a row. All with the pointed end facing inland, towards the root of the tree, and the round top towards the sea.

"If you were using them to show a direction," Yorke said, "I assume you'd point them that way." He pointed towards the tree.

A tree and three shells in line, each shell two paces – he stepped it out – from the next one, the shells pointing in the same direction.

> *"You see the three*
> *and hear the sea…"*

Which three? The three headlands or the three shells? In a logical sequence, one would need to see the three headlands, and then "hear the sea" in the shells. But the poem certainly did not sound like that…

> *"…and remember me.*
> *Then three by three*
> *beneath the tree."*

"Three by three" *must* refer to the shells, and the one in the first line meant the headlands. But, he thought, exasperated by the whimsicality of the poem, what do the last two lines *mean*?

Three by three...well, the first three must be the line of shells. But what other symbol of three showed where to dig?

"Well," Yorke said impatiently, "have you made up your mind where to dig?"

Ramage swallowed hard to avoid making a brief and bitter reply. Yorke's tone implied it was only Ramage's tardiness that kept the men's spades from the treasure.

"Yes," he said, "and you have the honour of digging the first spadeful."

"Oh thanks!" Yorke said, his old enthusiasm bubbling again. "Hey! Stafford! Bring me your spade!"

Yorke spat on his hands with a flourish. "I'm never sure what that does, but all the best labourers do it. Now," he said, "where do we start?"

"I've no ideas," Ramage said. "We've got to start somewhere!"

Yorke looked around at the area lit by the lantern. "It'd take a few days to clear the soil here to the depth of a man..."

"I know; that's why I was hoping we'd get another clue. 'Three by three...' "

"Three paces from the shells?" Yorke said hopefully.

"Which way, and measured from which shell?"

"Yes," Yorke said. "It doesn't sound like our piratical poet to leave it so vague."

Ramage gestured to Jackson. "Start the men digging a narrow trench along here." He indicated a line through the shells. "Two feet deep."

To Yorke he said, "We have to move the shells. We'd better set up some sticks showing where they were."

Within fifteen minutes the seamen were digging vigorously, and from the intersection of lines of sticks stuck into the ground at the edge of the light thrown by the lantern, it was easy to see where all three shells had been.

Within an hour the seamen had cleared a trench some eighteen feet long from the tree to well beyond where Yorke's shell had been placed. There was just earth and small stones – the soil, heavy and red, was spread thinly over the rocky island.

As the men stood back from the trench Yorke said: "How about making a geometric pattern?"

"Why not?" Ramage said. "It's a matter of chance. We'll start with a line perpendicular to this trench. Jackson! Same length, which means nine feet either side of this point, where we found the first shell, making a cross."

Yorke gestured to the perspiring men, faces shiny in the dim light of the lantern, their bodies making grotesque shadows. "The gravedigger scene in Hamlet," he said. " 'Alas poor Yorick…' "

"How old d'you think that tree is?" Ramage asked suddenly.

"No idea. A casuarina, isn't it? Use them out here to shelter houses from the wind – plant a row of them. That means they grow quickly, like firs. A hundred years? No more."

"That means the tree probably has nothing to do with all this."

"Almost certainly. Why?" Yorke asked.

"I've been wondering about these shells. After all, anyone could kick them around, and that would spoil the whole thing."

"I wonder when anyone last stood here?"

"I agree; but how could a pirate be sure that bushes would not grow here and hide the shells?"

"Don't forget he was trying to *hide* his treasure," Yorke said.

"Yes, but I wonder why?"

"Oh – being pursued…or used this island as a base, then suddenly his ship's destroyed – a hurricane for instance… Marooned here and dying of starvation – or even old age.

Buries his treasure and before he dies he carves the poem somewhere..."

Ramage nodded. "That sounds quite possible. Henry Morgan was around here a hundred years ago. 'The Brethren of the Coast' – wasn't that his gang?"

"Yes. He was Governor of Jamaica, too, wasn't he?"

"I think so. Still, Jamaica was remote then. I suspect that in those days the Governor wasn't quite the law-abiding person we think of now!"

"A shell!"

The yell came from a seaman, and Ramage bellowed: "Don't touch it!"

Jackson seized the lantern and ran to where the man was working at the landward end of the trench.

"I didn't pick it up, Jacko," the man said excitedly. "Look, there it is!"

Jackson crouched down with the lantern and Ramage could see it clearly. It was a flame helmet, and it pointed directly at the tree.

Ramage looked at Yorke. "Geometry!" he said, "or trigonometry. Or just a man that liked patterns!"

"The direction it's pointing," Yorke said. "It must be significant!"

"Jackson – a new trench," Ramage snapped. "Start here and go in a straight line to the foot of the tree. With a bit of luck you'll find more shells."

He turned to face the seamen. "File past in a moment and look at this shell. As you dig a new trench from here to the tree look for more shells. Try not to dislodge one if you find it. Or if you can't stop yourself in time, see which way the sharp end is pointing."

Like a bunch of small boys let loose on a row of ripe strawberry plants, the seamen marked out a straight line and began digging again.

"I begin to have a faint hope," Ramage said quietly to Yorke, his words hidden from the men by the noise of their cheerful chattering.

"When I find I might be within a few feet of a million pounds in treasure trove," Yorke said, "I have no difficulty in fanning faint hope into a roaring furnace!"

The two men stood, each wrapped in his thoughts, each glancing from one seaman to another, each willing one of the men to leap up with an excited shout.

He's a cool one, Yorke thought to himself as he watched Ramage, who was blinking occasionally, his face a sharp profile against the lantern light beyond. In the past couple of weeks he's fought off a French privateer that damn nearly captured the *Topaz*, survived a hurricane and become the ruler of a small island. The curious thing is that whatever he's doing, he looks as though he's completely at home and perfectly accustomed to it. Bringing the *Triton* alongside the privateer, handling the brig in the hurricane, having rafts made ready when both ships hit the reef, taking over on the island, acting as jailer for the Spaniards, a graceful host to the St Brieuc party, managing the seamen from both ships – and a congenial friend to Yorke himself. It was an impressive list.

As leader of a treasure hunt, he had imagination, patience and determination and behaved as though his profession in life was hunting for treasure...

One of the reasons why Yorke enjoyed being with Ramage was that his sense of humour seemed to expand and grow sharper the more serious the situation. Perhaps when everything was going perfectly, with no problems or crises on the horizon, Ramage might become a humourless and boring companion.

Probably not boring, because he had that essential curiosity – almost nosiness – about life and everything that comprised it that always made him stimulating company. Flame helmet shells, odd and archaic – almost bizarre – words in English and Spanish that he delighted in using not to show off but because he assumed everyone else would share his delight in them; information about local customs, picked up on his travels.

He seemed to Yorke a lonely man. Lonely on board, of course, because the maintenance of discipline required all captains to be lonely, but probably lonely in his private life as well, if only because the chances of finding people who understood his complex personality were slim.

Yorke had the feeling that the St Brieucs wished Ramage was their son, or perhaps their son-in-law. They often spoke of Maxine's husband, but casually, as one might refer to a favourite horse. A bond of the physical body, not the soul. Maxine never mentioned him at all. She might be breaking her heart over his absence, or it might not be as unwelcome an absence as her husband might hope. Had Maxine fallen in love with Ramage? He felt a twinge of jealousy but did not know the answer.

Everything here revolved round Ramage, but what was his future? Witty, charming, impatient, brave to the point of foolhardiness, and almost damnably handsome. With his family's wealth and position, Ramage could live an enjoyable life in England but like his father and grandfather, he had gone to sea. After what had happened to the old Earl, any sane youngster would have resigned his commission. For him the dangers to his life came as much from men like Goddard as from hurricanes or battles. He must really love the sea because –

A seaman yelled and Yorke pulled himself together and glanced across at Ramage. He was standing transfixed, his mouth open and his eyes out of focus...

Like Yorke, Ramage's thoughts had been far from Punta Tamarindo.

"Flame helmet, sir!" Jackson called briskly. "Same depth as the last one and pointing in the same direction."

Yorke joined Ramage where Jackson was bent over with the lantern.

Ramage pointed. "Spaced the same distance apart. Two paces. And..."

He gestured along the first trench, and then from the first shell in the second trench to where they now stood.

"The third shell should be here – " He walked two paces.

" – Jackson!"

The American grabbed a shovel and began scooping the earth away in layers, careful not to disturb a shell if he came across it.

After a few minutes he suddenly stopped, dropped the shovel and began scooping with his hands. He glanced up.

"It's here, sir."

The silence was frightening. Yorke had the feeling that every man believed for the first time that he was standing inches from a fortune.

Ramage signalled to the Marines to go over to the tree.

"Jackson, Stafford," he said as he joined the Marines. "I want you Marines facing outwards, kneeling and ready to fire, and beyond the light of the lantern. Your job is to guard us against an attack by outsiders. Keep absolutely quiet and don't look back at the lantern, because you'll lose your night vision. Get your backs against bushes or a big rock, otherwise you'll be silhouetted against the lantern. Challenge twice, then fire if you get no reply. Any questions? Carry on."

Ramage took his pistols and gave them to Jackson, and said quietly: "I'll be occupied with this digging. Stand beyond this tree, and cover us. I can't think any one of the men will be silly, but if there's treasure, the sight of gold can upset a man. Hide yourself somewhere within range. No need for anyone to know where you are. Mind the Marines, though..."

With that, Ramage said to Yorke: "Any suggestions where we dig now?"

Yorke looked bewildered. "Along the present trench – or, rather, continue the same line, I imagine."

"Perhaps," Ramage said softly, and Yorke thought almost triumphantly, "but I like triangles – they have three sides! Project the line of the first three shells and then the line of these three and you have two sides of an isosceles triangle. Almost two sides, rather. Look" – he swept with his hand – "how about that for the apex?" He was pointing to a spot five feet from the trunk of the tree.

Without waiting for an answer he walked to the spot, sighting along both trenches. He ground a heel in the earth and then beckoned to the nearest seamen.

"Dig here. A big hole. Pitch the earth well clear."

To Yorke, he said: "I'm going to make a guess, which is a silly thing to do at this stage."

Yorke waited, and when Ramage said nothing, prompted him. "Well? Why not turn it into a bet – then one of us stands to win *something!*"

"I was hoping you'd say that. Let's bet on the age of this tree!"

"Fifty years," Yorke said promptly. "And fifty guineas backs my guess."

"Ah," Ramage said. "Can I bet that it's more than a hundred – or more exactly, dates from when the treasure was buried?"

"Done," Yorke said.

Ramage was reminded of quiet days at home in Cornwall, watching a dog digging at a rabbit burrow. The determined dog panting with excitement; the earth flying up between its back legs. Already the hole had taken shape; already the excavated earth was making small heaps.

He walked over to the diggers. The hole was now in shadow and two feet deep. He could see wooden veins which were the roots of the tree, and hear the occasional thud and judder of a spade bouncing off a thicker root.

Then they were down to three feet and the roots were thicker and closer, springy and harder to cut. They were going to need axes – and daylight. He gave the orders to stop digging and picked three men to go back to the village for axes, first calling to the Marine sentries to let them pass.

"We've lost a lot of sleep," Ramage commented to Yorke, "but so far we haven't got anything except experience."

Yorke did not reply. He was feeling depressed. The prospect of digging under the tree seemed hopeless. Although he would never have said anything to Ramage, he began to think the treasure hunt was over. It had been great fun and a test of their wits, but somewhere a series of coincidences had entered into the game.

One of the seamen who had not yet scrambled out of the hole gave an excited yelp and lifted something up. As the dim yellow light of the lantern shone on it, the rest of the men gave a groan in which there was disappointment and superstitious fear mixed in equal proportions.

Ramage took it from the man, looked at it, and said casually: "A human femur – the thigh bone. You'll probably find the rest of the skeleton there."

He walked to one side and put the bone down carefully.

"Put the rest here when you find them. We'll rebury them later."

He turned away. He had carried his disappointment off well. Yorke would probably guess at it, but not the men, not even Jackson.

After all this work, they had found a grave. Presumably it was the grave of some pirate leader – someone famous enough to have his grave on an almost deserted island marked for posterity with a tree, seashells and a poem.

Everyone – himself included – had assumed that whatever was buried was treasure. Plates of solid gold, and cups and chalices; thick and heavy bracelets of silver inlaid with gems...No one had thought of bare bones. Yet the poem could just as easily be an epitaph:

> "...and remember me
> ...beneath the tree."

CHAPTER **SIXTEEN**

Everyone at the camp was very sympathetic and understanding; infuriatingly so in fact. What annoyed Ramage was that everyone had pretended to be surprised. Ramage was sure that – with the exception of Maxine – they had thought all along that he was on a wild goose chase, but encouraged him out of politeness. Metaphorically patting him on the shoulder as he tried, and now patting him on the head as he failed.

He sat in his room, his journal open in front of him, his body rigid with tension. It was unlikely any of them would have got any of the treasure anyway, so why had he become so obsessed with that damned poem that he slipped back into the world of an excitable schoolboy? He felt humiliated.

There was a knock at the door and at his call, Maxine entered.

"Nicholas," she said hesitantly, "my father – "

"Wants to see me?" Ramage was already on his feet and moving towards the door.

"*Non!*" she said, smiling and gesturing him to sit down again. "My father knows I am visiting you."

"Oh," Ramage said lamely. He always found it embarrassing when a woman visitor indicated that her reputation would – or would not – be compromised by being alone with him. "You are a welcome visitor."

He escorted her to the only other chair in the room and she sat with a movement which was both feline and regal; a movement that transformed this shabby, hot and dusty room into an elegant salon.

As soon as he sat down she looked directly at him, making no attempt to disguise the fact that he attracted her. She was deliberately setting aside the fact that she was a young married woman, that her husband was thousands of miles away, and that she was alone in a room with a young man. She was conveying frankly and with superb taste, that she knew she was a beautiful woman attractive to men, and surely he knew he was attractive to women, so why did not they accept the facts without gaucheness.

"You are very upset," she said.

He shrugged his shoulders. "Disappointed, perhaps. Natural enough, surely?"

"Yes, very natural, *mais* – that is not all you feel…"

She spoke quietly, but with certainty, choosing her words carefully and concentrating on her accent. She was not anticipating that he would tell her she was wrong, and, he realized, he was not going to.

"Not finding a king's ransom in treasure when you thought you were standing on top of it…" he said lamely.

"You feel you've failed."

"And I have too!"

She sighed. "You men! You are more frightened of the word 'failure' than of all the devils in hell!"

"Failure is more apparent," he said dryly.

"But it is *not* failure! If you had orders from your Admiral to find the treasure and you could not find it, that would be failure only if it was known for certain the treasure *was there*."

She slapped her hand on to her knee for emphasis. "It isn't failure if there is no treasure. If someone told you to fly up to the moon on the back of a goose, the fact that you could not would not be failure!"

"Yes, but it's different for – "

There was a loud, rapid knocking on the door.

"Come in!" Ramage snapped, annoyed at the interruption.

An excited Jackson stepped inside the door, but the moment he saw Maxine he stopped in embarrassment.

"Sorry, sir – "

"Carry on, Jackson."

"It's about the digging, sir…"

"Go on – there's no need for secrecy."

"Well, sir – " Jackson broke off, and Ramage saw it was not because of Maxine. Something disagreeable had happened, that much was clear from the American's slightly sheepish manner. But something else had happened, too, which had brought him hurrying back from Punta Tamarindo, where he and half a dozen seamen were supposed to be filling in the trenches.

Ramage began tapping the table with his fingers, and Jackson started again.

"After you left with Mr Yorke, sir, we got to thinking about the skeleton, sir."

"Come on, Jackson, out with it, do you want me to wheedle every word out of you?"

"The skeleton was neither right under the tree nor clear to one side, sir."

"I can't see – " Ramage's voice broke off, because suddenly he could see that the position of the skeleton was odd. If the tree marked the grave, it should have been directly over the body, but it was to one side, four feet down, and only the side roots had grown through it. The tree had been planted – or the seed began growing – after the body was buried. Did it matter? But Jackson had not finished.

"Stafford and me tried to work out why. We couldn't think of anything, so after you'd gone we decided to do some more digging. The rest of the lads were keen, sir."

"Where did you dig?"

"All round the tree, sir, in a big circle and we found lots more skeletons."

"Did you, by Jove!"

"Yes, sir, eight so far and still more coming up."

Maxine sighed. Ramage glanced at her and saw she was as white as a sheet. In a moment he was at her side, holding her against him by the shoulders.

"Breathe deeply," he said quietly. "I'm sorry, we are crude oafs."

"*Non*," she whispered, "it's not the talk of bodies and skeletons; I just started thinking of...things. I'm all right now."

Ramage gestured to Jackson to leave the room and as the door closed he turned to Maxine and took her in his arms. It began, he realized later, as a gesture to reassure her; but she closed her eyes and raised her lips and a moment later they were clinging to each other as desperately as if they were drowning.

"Oh, Nicholas," she whispered, what seemed an age later, "I've wanted to kiss you for so long..."

"We must be careful – people will..."

"I don't care," she said. "And my father and mother have guessed already."

Ramage thought of her husband. Had she forgotten? And what did her parents think, now they had guessed? They could hardly approve of their married daughter having an affair with a lieutenant in the Royal Navy.

"Kiss me again," she whispered, "and then you must go to Jackson. But, my darling, don't let this treasure hunt dominate your life."

He held her tightly. "I've found my treasure!"

"It took you long enough," she said.

An hour later Ramage and Yorke were standing on the edge of a large semi-circular hole, the tree forming the centre of the radii. The skeletons had not been moved; the seamen had simply started digging again to the side as soon as they had found one and cleared away the earth.

"Look, sir," Jackson said as he jumped into the hole and moved from one skeleton to another, pointing. The top of each skull was badly damaged.

"A shot in the back of the head," Ramage said.

"Yes, sir. And their arms are together."

"Hands tied behind them, shot in the back of the head, and pitched into a big open grave," Ramage said.

"That's what we thought," Jackson said. "But we can't understand why, sir."

Ramage began thinking aloud for Yorke's benefit.

"A mass execution, but who were the victims? Perhaps pirates, if one band attacked another, or if the members of a band quarrelled? Or a party of slaves who were killed to ensure the secrecy of some work they'd been doing?"

"Slaves," Yorke said, as if to himself. "Made to dig their own grave."

Ramage nodded. "It would make more sense because we'll find at least twenty skeletons if this is a circular grave. To tie up and execute twenty pirates would probably mean at least twenty more."

"But *why* do it?" Yorke said softly. "It doesn't make sense. There's no point in leaving a poem as a clue to a mass grave."

Ramage stared at Yorke. Perhaps there was treasure as well as skeletons. Most people would not dig below the level of the skeletons: one glimpse of a human bone and a man would be reluctant to disturb a grave. That was why he had stopped the original digging and left the men to fill in the trenches after the first skeleton had been found.

He was reluctant to let all the old excitement well up again after his recent disappointments but perhaps those two converging lines of shells did mark something else...

When he pointed to the spot, Yorke nodded.

"I don't understand what the devil it's all about," Yorke said, "but I think we should carry on digging there."

Ramage told Jackson to set four men to work and he and Yorke settled down to the worst wait of all.

The men had to chop more than they had to dig, and the roots of the tree snaking down into the earth were springy yet unyielding. More than an hour had passed before one of the men, digging with a pickaxe in a corner of the hole, gave a grunt and, turning slightly, struck again with the pick.

"Jacko!" he called. "Wot abaht this?"

Ramage, talking to Yorke five yards away, noticed that the man's voice was puzzled: whatever he had found it was not a skeleton.

Jackson jumped lightly into the hole and crouched down. Ramage walked deliberately slowly towards them and heard the muttering of voices. Then Jackson leapt out of the hole, knelt before Ramage with a flourish, and opened both hands. In his palms were several coins which shone dully.

Gold doubloons, dollars, pieces of eight and reals...He rubbed a dollar to make it shine. The Spanish "cobb" of seaman's slang and recruiting posters. He nodded and passed it to Yorke.

"Are there many?" he said in an offhand voice.

"Hundreds, sir – all spilling out of a rotted wooden box."

"I'm so glad," he said in the same offhand voice. "You'd better send Stafford to fetch more Marines; we need a strong guard on here, and ask Mr Southwick to tell our guests we have – er, had some success."

It was remarkable how calm you could be when you succeeded.

The next eight days were so unreal that Ramage felt he was not just dreaming, but dreaming of a dream. Most of the seamen had been moved up to Punta Tamarindo, slinging their hammocks between trees, to save the long walk every morning. Under the casuarina tree seamen dug carefully, while on the landward side of the open space the carpenter's crew worked with saws, hammers and nails making strong crates in which to stow the treasure.

The coins were sorted into different denominations, put into canvas bags made from sailcloth – "a quarter o' the size o' a normal shroud" as Stafford commented – and sewn up. Each bag was then put into a wooden crate and pummelled until it took up a square shape. Then the lid of the crate was put on and nailed down securely.

Ramage limited each crate to half a hundredweight, and after the money had been checked by Southwick, the details of the contents were painted on the outside. A pair of long poles secured along the sides enabled two men to carry the crate comfortably like a stretcher, and it was taken away to be stowed. One of the houses in the village had been nicknamed "The Treasury" and was closely guarded by the Marines.

The gold and silver plate and ornaments – they ranged from dishes to candelabra – were dealt with in much the same way. They took up larger crates since they were bulkier and lighter than coins, but every item was described in an inventory kept by Southwick. When they did not know the name or purpose of a particular vessel or ornament, a small sketch was added with the main dimensions and weight.

As the totals of coin, plate, ornaments and jewellery mounted in what came to be called "The Treasure Log",

Ramage was thankful that the men still regarded the digging and packing as a great game.

He had talked to Southwick and Yorke about a potential danger: the survivors from the two ships numbered some seventy-five seamen, but there were only three King's officers and a dozen Marines. If the seamen from both ships decided to keep the treasure, killing officers in their beds at night would present no problems. With the officers dead, the corporal of Marines would be a fool if he tried to stop his men joining the seamen…

The three of them had watched closely, but there was not the slightest hint of an intention to plunder on the part of the crew of either ship. Ramage was reasonably sure that by now the men had a few gold coins sewn into the waistbands of their trousers: he secretly hoped that they had, since it was unrealistic to begrudge a man ten guineas when ten thousand were his for the taking.

Yorke had agreed that as far as they were concerned no treasure was "dug up" until it was noted in the log as it was lifted out of the hole. What men did with odd coins when they were in a hole six feet deep and eight feet square was not their affair. There was a limit to what they could hide each time since none of them wore more than a pair of trousers. He only hoped the diggers shared with the rest of the men.

From the time the treasure was first found, St Brieuc had been urging Ramage to take special precautions against the seamen mutinying. He was so alarmed and so certain they would all be murdered in their beds that Ramage had asked Yorke to give him and St Cast a brace of pistols. St Brieuc had accepted gladly and then, four days later, returned the pistols to Yorke, explaining that having them about the house upset his wife and daughter. As Yorke told Ramage, it was a signal that St Brieuc now agreed with them that the men were "safe".

Teniente Colon frequently asked to see Ramage, but when the guard took him pencil and paper, with instructions to write his message, he wrote nothing, so presumably he was simply curious to know if any treasure had been found.

Ramage did not care whether Colon knew or not, but had neither told him nor given the Marines instructions that he was to be kept in the dark. It was interesting that the Marine guards had said nothing to him even though Colon often tried to strike up conversations with them in his halting English.

Two days before the supply ship was due from San Juan the last of the treasure had been brought to the surface and packed, and the skeletons reburied. Ramage read a burial service, the ground was smoothed over, and the working party marched away from Punta Tamarindo for the last time.

"I wish we'd been here when it was buried," Yorke commented. "Intriguing not to know exactly what happened."

Ramage shrugged his shoulders. "We might have ended up in the grave. I'm more interested to know *why* the owner decided to bury it. I'm sure we've guessed correctly that the hole was dug by slaves or prisoners, and that they were killed and buried here as well to ensure secrecy."

"Why the poem, then?" Yorke persisted.

"*That's* the puzzle. How about pirates trapped here because their ship hit a reef, and hurrying to bury their treasure before being captured. Perhaps they were put in prison and never came back...and one of them made up the poem..."

"Or one of them stayed behind on the island – Colon said something about an ancestor having a copy of the poem."

"An ancestor...one of the original pirates who stayed or came back...we'll never know."

That night at dinner Bowen asked the question on nearly everyone's lips.

"Any idea of the value of it all, sir?"

Ramage shook his head. "I don't know the current price of gold."

St Cast glanced up. "I can help there. Last February I was realizing some assets in London, and I can remember the prices quite well. Bar and gold coin was £3 17s 6d per fine ounce, and Portuguese gold was the same. That's troy measure, of course," he added. "A troy pound is over half an avoirdupois pound. Eight-tenths, if I remember correctly."

Southwick was scribbling with a pencil.

"A pound of gold avoirdupois is worth at least £100," Southwick said. "In other words, over £11,200 a hundredweight avoirdupois."

"How much does all the treasure weigh?" St Brieuc asked.

Ramage said: "We haven't totalled it all up yet, but we've estimated there's more than five tons of gold, and roughly a ton of silver."

"A ton of gold," Southwick said, "is worth nearly a quarter of a million pounds."

"Nearly?" Yorke repeated.

"About £224,000. So our five tons totals roughly £1,120,000..."

Southwick caught Ramage's eye. "It won't rate as prize, sir, I'm sure of it. The Crown will claim it all, and no shares for anyone."

"I told you that when we started digging," Ramage said heavily. "It's a pity we didn't let the Spanish find it, and then capture the ship they used for carrying it away..."

"Why?" asked St Cast.

"That would have made it prize money...in which case I would have received two-eighths. Southwick and Bowen would share an eighth, and the seamen two-eighths."

Southwick threw down his pencil in disgust. "It would have meant £280,000 for you, sir," he told Ramage, "while Bowen and I share £140,000 equally. Phew," he whistled, "I've just realized young Appleby would have an entire eighth share, £140,000: no other principal warrant officers, lieutenants of Marines, chaplains and so on to share with him..."

Yorke began laughing. "Actually I come off best. Since I'm not entitled to anything I haven't just lost either £280,000 or £140,000!"

CHAPTER SEVENTEEN

Stafford marched up, halted and saluted smartly. "A dozen bleedin' cabbyleeroes, all present an' ker-ect, *señor!*"

Jackson, resplendent in the Spanish lieutenant's uniform, looked down his nose at Stafford and the dozen seamen now dressed in the uniforms of the Spanish soldiers.

"Hmm," he said airily, "none of you'd pass muster as the King's Guard in Madrid; but out here I can't be so fussy!"

The seamen laughed cheerfully; then Jackson said quickly: "Right, straighten yourselves up, you bedraggled dons; here comes the Captain."

Ramage came out of the house, jamming his hat squarely on his head and walked over to where Jackson had the seamen formed up in two ranks.

Jackson, enjoying playing the role of the *teniente*, saluted and said: "Garrison all present and correct, sir."

"Very well," Ramage said, and slowly walked along the first rank, inspecting the men as Jackson followed a pace behind.

From the house fifteen yards away they certainly passed for soldiers. Even at ten yards they looked smart enough – but close to they looked exactly what they were, British sailors dressed up in Spanish soldiers' uniforms.

Suddenly Ramage said: "Stafford, march to the door of my house and back."

As the seaman left the front rank, Jackson said: "I'm afraid they all walk like that, sir."

"It's a bit late to do anything. Stick broom handles up the back of their jackets!"

"Maybe in twenty minutes, sir..."

"Don't bother; just don't let them march!"

The crew of the supply ship might expect trouble but Ramage doubted if they would. Her captain would certainly see the wrecks on the eastern reef and be curious, but if he saw the gold and red flag of Spain flying from the flagpole in front of the houses at San Ildefonso and the garrison standing waiting on the wooden jetty with their lieutenant he would probably think all was well.

Ramage had discussed it a dozen times with Southwick and Yorke. Since he commanded a small transport, the Spaniard was unlikely to be very intelligent, and anyway no other plan had been thought of. If the Spanish captain got suspicious at the last moment, it would be too late. Four of the *Topaz*'s brass six-pounders covered the jetty from carefully concealed positions beside the houses. Even before the transport tacked off Punta del Soldado to make the last long board up to the narrow entrance to the bay, the guns had been loaded with grape and aimed at different points near the jetty. If anything went wrong, a command from Ramage would send the dozen seamen disguised as soldiers bolting from the jetty, out of the line of fire; at a second command the four guns would fire at the ship.

The ship was a day late. She had been due the previous afternoon but lookouts on Punta del Soldado had not sighted her until ten o'clock this morning, slowly beating her way up to Snake Island from Cape San Juan, the nearest point of Puerto Rico. It had been a long and tedious turn to windward, with the tacks to the north shortened by the almost continuous line of cays and reefs between Cape San Juan and Snake Island.

There had been plenty of time to prepare: to relieve the real Spanish soldiers of their uniforms and dress up a dozen laughing, joking seamen so that tunics, breeches, hats and boots were the best possible fit.

Jackson, in Colon's uniform, had come out best: the men were of similar build. Ramage grinned to himself as he recalled Colon's expression when, having suffered the indignity of being made to remove his uniform by a none too gentle Jackson, he had watched the American dress up in it, with Stafford providing a ribald commentary.

The island had a perfect anchorage, with the bay shaped like a bottle, the narrow entrance, or neck, facing south. With the Trade winds always blowing from the easterly quadrant, any ship entering could be reasonably sure of a commanding wind. Leaving might be a different story: a south-easterly wind could mean towing out, using the boats for a few hundred yards. But few ships sailing from Snake Island would be likely to be in that much of a hurry.

Ramage caught sight of a distant white shape beyond the entrance to the bay and walked up to the house, where he was met by Southwick.

"Just spotted her," Ramage said. "She's rounded Punta del Soldado and is getting ready to ease sheets to reach in."

"Everything is fine here, sir."

"Your Castile Yeomanry," Yorke commented, "may not be smart enough to be His Most Catholic Majesty's palace guards at the Escorial, but from a distance they'll pass muster as the garrison of Snake Island."

"I'll remuster them as the Snake Island Volunteers," Ramage said. "Recruiting starts in the morning. Subalterns' commissions are selling for five hundred guineas."

Yorke whistled. "A stylish regiment, hey?"

"We can afford to be fussy about who we accept," Ramage said airily, and then suddenly stiffened as he saw Maxine watching from the window of her house.

"I thought I gave an order that the St Brieucs were to be escorted inland until the ship arrived."

"You did," Yorke said wearily. "There is a slight difficulty in making the youngest member of the family obey it."

"What about the parents, and St Cast?"

"They're already a couple of miles away, escorted by a couple of mates and six of my seamen."

"But why wasn't Maxine...?"

"Ask her yourself," Yorke said.

Ramage blushed and turned to look to the entrance of the bay again. The ship's hull was lifting appreciably over the curvature of the earth: she had a couple of miles to go. There was no need for the men to stand in the heat of the sun providing they formed up before the Spanish captain could see their rolling gait, and Ramage told Jackson to march them to the shade of the houses.

Jackson looked uncertainly at Ramage.

"March them," he repeated. "I heard one or two of them laughing at Stafford's attempts."

So they marched.

"Hogarth ought to be here," Yorke said, "with his easel placed on this balcony. Only his brush could do justice to it!"

" 'The Rakes' Progress'," Ramage said. "Not the kind of rake he had in mind, nor the progress, but it'd be a fitting title."

An hour passed before the ship, a beamy schooner, finally stretched through the bottleneck entrance to the bay, and Jackson's soldiers returned to the jetty.

No one seemed to know why the troops met the schooner, but Ramage was relying on the slave Roberto's description of how the last supply ship had been greeted. She had arrived a few days after the frigate that brought Colon, the soldiers and the slaves from San Juan, and Roberto had mimicked Colon's annoyance at having to stop the slaves digging so that the soldiers could be at the jetty.

Roberto was unable to offer any explanation, however. The soldiers did not help unload; the slaves did that. The soldiers neither fired a salute nor presented arms when the ship came alongside. Roberto added that they ran off the jetty at the last moment "because the captain of the ship is not very skilful and he hit the jetty so hard that everyone thought it would collapse".

Apparently Lieutenant Colon sat on the balcony of his house, watching. Lines from the ship to secure her alongside were handled by the men in the ship, who jumped down onto the jetty. Once the crew had shouted abuse at the soldiers and later the captain had had words with the *teniente*. They had shouted at each other for half an hour and after that they never spoke to each other again.

They asked Roberto what sort of ship she was but he shrugged his shoulders. Two masts, the body was black with a red stripe all round it, like a belt. He had only been in two ships in his life, the one that brought him to Puerto Rico (a slaver) and the one that brought him here. The ship was called *La Perla* – "The *teniente* mentioned her name when he was swearing at the captain."

The slave's information was reassuring: there was no Spanish military or naval custom which, if ignored, would arouse suspicion. Ramage wanted no mistakes made: if even one of the *Topaz*'s guns had to open fire, it would mean damage to the schooner and might even put her permanently out of commission.

Once inside the bay, the schooner moved fast: her captain had to harden in sheets to get up towards the jetty, and then for a reason neither Ramage nor Yorke could subsequently explain, he bore away and then suddenly luffed up head to wind, dropping his foresail, mainsail and headsails. But she was carrying too much way: as the seamen hurriedly tried to furl the sails, the captain ran from side to side of the quarterdeck, screeching at the two men at the massive tiller. At the last moment they heaved it to larboard as the schooner came directly towards the jetty and the houses.

"Try prayer," Yorke advised.

"Miracles," Ramage said. "He – we – need lots of miracles."

A minute or two before the schooner was due to hit the jetty her bow gradually began to come round to starboard. Ramage shouted to Jackson to clear his men out of the way – security was not necessary now. Jackson could have been conducting a band playing "Heart of Oak" without being noticed. Ramage began running down the slope from the house, followed by Southwick and Yorke.

At that moment the schooner passed clear of the end of the jetty and her bow slid up on the sandy beach at the water's edge.

Ramage, Southwick and Yorke all stopped, looking up at the masts now towering above them. "Bolt!" Southwick shouted and they spread out in all directions to avoid being crushed if the masts fell over the bow, broken like twigs by the force of the impact. But there was no splintering wood and snapping rope rigging. The screeching of the Spanish captain, who appeared to have gone berserk, was the only sound to be heard.

Ramage turned back and began running for the beach, again shouting for Jackson who had vanished with his seamen. He had no idea how to regain control of the situation. His splendid plans took no account of the potentially lethal effect of bad seamanship.

The only way of getting on board the schooner now was by wading and clambering up over the bow. He waved to Southwick and pointed to the gun positions.

"One round to one side to scare 'em!"

He and Yorke stood at the water's edge looking up at the schooner's bowsprit and jibboom jutting out above them.

"I could strangle him," he said thickly. "The damned incompetent idiot!"

"Saves anchoring or wearing out ropes," Yorke said, "but of course, you get your feet wet going on shore!"

Ramage was trembling with rage. Where the hell was that damned American with his men?

"Jackson!" he bellowed. "Jackson, blast you!"

"Here, sir!" the American called. Ramage and Yorke looked round and saw nothing.

"Up here, sir!" said Jackson, peering down from the schooner's bow.

"What are you doing up there?" Ramage asked weakly.

"You said to board and – "

A tremendous explosion behind them sent Ramage and Yorke flat on their faces in the sand; then, as the noise echoed and re-echoed across the bay and among the hills, sending up flocks of squawking white egrets, Ramage realized what it was.

"Your bloody brass ordnance," he said to Yorke, standing up, and brushing sand from his breeches. "God, what a mess!"

"I don't know," Yorke said coolly. "Prize captured without a shot fired until after it was secured!"

The schooner was *La Perla*, built at Rota seven years earlier of Spanish oak and larch. Yorke commented to Ramage that one advantage of having the ship run aground was that inspecting her lines was so much easier.

The ship's company had put up no fight and Jackson's description of how they captured her was one that Ramage could dine out on for years. They had realized *La Perla* would miss the jetty and run up on the beach, so that they were there to meet her, waiting on her starboard side and had been hidden from Ramage and Yorke.

As soon as she came to rest they had splashed out, slung their muskets over their shoulders and climbed up over the bow, using the bobstay and anchors to get a foothold. The Spanish sailors had been very courteous, assuming they were Colon and his men.

"They helped every one of us over the bulwark," Jackson said. "One of the fattest men I've ever seen gave me his hand as I jumped on deck. As long as no one spoke there seemed no hurry so I began strutting up and down as though I was disgusted with the Captain and impatient with my soldiers.

"The lads were busy getting their muskets unslung, and without me saying anything, Staff and Rosey stood side by side, and the rest of the lads took the hint and formed up in one rank. So there we were, sir, my dozen lads standing to attention and me marching up and down in front of them.

"The Spanish sailors weren't taking much notice, of course, and the Captain was still screaming at the helmsman. I couldn't help thinking that if I didn't do something we'd be there for hours. So I stood to attention and just as I was going to say 'Tritons, take possession of the ship', both Staff and Rosey started laughing – seems I was puffing out my chest like a Spanish customs agent.

"With that we took the ship and then I heard you calling me, sir."

La Perla's regular task was delivering provisions to Spanish garrisons, the majority of them in Puerto Rico itself. There were no troops on the island of Vieques, Ramage was surprised to learn. The skipper of *La Perla* was indignant that Snake Island, or Culebra as he called it, had a garrison since it gave him another forty miles to beat to windward. Otherwise he left San Juan and went round to Ponce on the south coast and then on to Mayaguez at the western end of the island.

Refloating *La Perla* took four hours. At first Ramage thought they would have to use her small boat, take out an anchor astern and haul her off. Fortunately, just before he gave the order the wind freshened. As usual, it was easterly and the schooner's bow, at right angles to the beach, headed east.

The Tritons went on board, clambering up over the bow, while the Topazes guarded *La Perla*'s former crew. Soon Southwick and Ramage were standing on her quarterdeck looking over each side.

Ramage nodded his head to the southward, where some seamen were taking soundings from *La Perla*'s only boat.

"Looks clear. We've got plenty of room. Then wear round and come alongside."

If *La Perla* had run up on mud, it would have gripped her hull with all the suction of an octopus. The thicker the mud, the harder the schooner would be held. Luckily it seemed to be a sandy bottom.

Ramage walked the length of the schooner, noting her general shape, the point of maximum beam and, without realizing it, working out her probable underwater shape and the exact point the hull would pivot under the pressure of various combinations of sail.

The seamen reported the depths they had found to Southwick.

"Straightforward, sir," he said. "I reckon we're only short of six inches of water forward..."

Which meant, Ramage noted thankfully, that with the angle *La Perla* made to the beach, and the direction of the wind, hoisting the headsails and sheeting them aback would give the schooner's bow a hearty shove to starboard, pivoting her so she was pushed off the beach. Then the big foresail and mainsail – already hoisted and just flapping – would be sheeted in and *La Perla* would be under way again.

It was a straightforward operation, though not a routine one, and the schooner refloated at the first attempt. He sailed her across the bay and back to get the feeling of how she handled, and then brought her alongside the jetty without any fuss.

The men worked in shifts for the rest of the day unloading surplus provisions and making room for the large number of people *La Perla* would now be carrying to Jamaica.

Most of the provisions were familiar to the British seamen, but there was much more rice than they expected, and many sacks of a kind of bean they had never seen before. One of the men was incautious enough to take a bit from one of a string of onions and let out a yell as he began gasping for breath, his eyes watering.

"Don't steal the grub," Jackson told him unsympathetically, "but if you do, keep your thieving hands off the garlic."

With everything prepared for the voyage to Jamaica, Ramage began to have misgivings. The risks were ones he accepted for himself and his men without a moment's thought; but with *La Perla* ready to sail, he found himself worrying more and more about the St Brieucs. Was he justified in taking chances with their lives, particularly since St Brieuc was a man valued by the British Government? The least he could do was warn them.

That evening he invited St Brieuc, St Cast and Yorke to his room for a talk, but when they arrived and sat down, looking at him expectantly, he found it hard to explain.

"The voyage we start tomorrow…" he began lamely.

The three men waited, all attention.

"There are risks…"

303

St Brieuc sensed his discomfort and said lightly, "We are becoming accustomed to them. They add a zest to life!"

Yorke came to Ramage's help. "These are different. I think our 'Governor' has privateers in mind."

St Cast turned to St Brieuc and smiled. "I suspect he is more worried about us than the treasure – a flattering thought!"

"He is constantly preoccupied with our safety," St Brieuc said, as though Ramage was not in the room. "I think he should worry more about the treasure – I'm sure that would be the Admiralty's view."

Ramage wondered if St Brieuc had guessed his thoughts and given a subtle hint.

"Either way, the privateers concern me," Ramage said. "I want to be sure you understand the risks."

"I assume it is considerable," St Brieuc said, "since all the islands between here and Jamaica are held by the Spanish or French."

Ramage nodded. "It is considerable, but I'm damned if I know how to describe it. If I told you there were probably six privateers between here and Jamaica, you'd conclude it was dangerous. If I said a dozen, a score or a hundred, you'd reach the same conclusion..."

"The figures mean nothing," St Brieuc said, "since we have no standards to apply. Surely the point is, would you risk making the voyage with the treasure if we weren't here?"

"Yes, but that's not – "

"Yes, it is the point," St Brieuc interrupted quietly. "You worry unnecessarily about us. If we stayed here, I think it would be only a matter of time before Spanish soldiers arrived to hunt us down – don't you agree?"

Ramage nodded.

"So if we stay here, we are certain of ending up in a Spanish prison – or worse."

"Fairly certain." Ramage thought a moment, and corrected himself. "Absolutely certain."

"What are the chances of *La Perla* being captured by a privateer?"

Ramage shrugged his shoulders. "What was the chance of us being caught in a hurricane? One in a hundred, one in five…hard to say."

"As far as privateers are concerned," Yorke commented, "I'd put my money on not more than one in ten."

St Brieuc smiled at Ramage, a friendly but worldly smile. "You think of yourself as a gambler, young man?"

"I suppose so. Not with money, but in action one has to…"

"Take an old man's advice, then – confine yourself to the odds in battle. Never go near the gambling tables!"

Ramage grinned. "You seem very certain I'd lose."

"I am, and you've just proved it. You say that if we stay on the island we will be captured. We are one hundred per cent certain of losing, in fact. But if we sail with you in *La Perla*, we face only a one in five chance of capture. Although I'm the most timid of gamblers, I know which I choose!"

"Although mathematics aren't the 'Governor's' strongest subject," Yorke said dryly, "I think he is being unfair to himself!"

"Yes," Ramage said ruefully. "I had in mind that if you stayed here and *La Perla* reached Jamaica safely, a frigate would come back and rescue you. I'd leave enough men to guard the Spaniards."

St Brieuc's eyes twinkled. "Your heart is ruling your head. Doing that increases the odds against us. If we stay here, and *La Perla* is captured by a privateer, we still end up in a Spanish prison. If she reaches Jamaica, we have to wait for the frigate to get back. Head winds all the way, and perhaps another hurricane…What might the Spanish have done in the meantime? No, please take us in *La Perla*. I understand your concern, but quite apart from the mathematical aspect which shows the odds are in favour of making such a voyage, we have complete confidence in you."

Yorke nodded in agreement.

"Now that's been decided," St Cast said conversationally, "how long do you think it will take for the Spanish in San Juan to do something about Snake Island?"

"Three weeks at the outside," Ramage said. "Once a passing ship sights the wrecks on the reef and reports them in San Juan, the naval commander will send a frigate...Apart from that, *La Perla* will be reported overdue at Ponce within a week. Since Snake Island was her first port, they'll start investigating here. Because of Lieutenant Colon's mission, they're probably sensitive about Snake Island anyway."

"The minute we leave," Yorke said, "Colon will try to raise the alarm. Some men could reach Puerto Rico in a fishing boat – it's not that far."

"Southwick has collected the boats and they are being burned in the morning, but if Colon has any sense, he'll set fire to the grass and bushes on the hills, and hope someone in Puerto Rico takes notice of the smoke."

"We're lucky to have *La Perla*," St Brieuc commented.

"Yes, we stand more chance of reaching Jamaica with her than if we had the *Topaz*," Ramage said. "Not so comfortable, admittedly, but safer."

St Brieuc looked puzzled.

"Ships," Ramage explained, "are rather like human beings: you can learn a lot about them from their appearance. *La Perla*'s hull and rig is clearly Spanish. She could never have been built in England."

Yorke nodded in agreement as Ramage continued: "At first our main danger will be of capture by Spanish privateers or ships of war between Puerto Rico and Santo Domingo. Later there's a danger of French ships from the western end of Hispaniola and finally a slight risk of Spaniards from Cuba.

"A Spaniard seeing *La Perla* sailing close to his own coast and flying a Spanish ensign would assume she was Spanish. And so would a Frenchman. They'd have no reason to think anything else."

Yorke looked keenly at Ramage. "A few miles off the coast past Puerto Rico and all the way to the western end of Hispaniola, then a dash down to Jamaica?"

Ramage nodded. "As close to the coast as we dare."

"Supposing the French want to board us to check up?"

Ramage shrugged his shoulders. "Let them. We have all the ship's papers and unless the Frenchman commanding the boarding party spoke fluent Spanish, which is unlikely, I think I could pass myself off as a Spaniard. I might even do it with a Spanish privateer – the accents vary enormously from province to province."

St Brieuc nodded. "You could, I am sure. When you were talking to that wretched man Colon I remember thinking I would not have thought you were English."

"The point is," Ramage said with a grin, "would you have thought I was Spanish? Anyway, have either of you gentlemen any suggestions for improving my plan?"

All of them shook their heads.

"Right," Ramage said, standing up, "then we sail for Jamaica tomorrow morning as soon as the breeze starts."

After dinner Ramage felt Maxine's foot touching his under the table, and a moment later she said casually to her father, "Nicholas and I are going to have a last walk along the edge of the bay."

"Don't make yourselves sad," he said. "When your mother and I went along there this afternoon we felt quite doleful."

"We always seem to be leaving places we love," Maxine said bitterly as she stood and took Ramage's arm. "We won't be long."

She knew now that she loved him, and she was on the verge of accepting that it was hopeless. Obviously he loved someone else; only that could account for his stiffness. She still wanted him to herself for half an hour tonight; for half an hour when he would not be preoccupied with privateers and hurricanes and hunting for treasure.

By now they were picking their way along the short stretch of sandy beach beside the jetty. The schooner was a dark shape against the stars, and the air was alive with the high-pitched, rapid croaking of tree frogs.

She held her skirt clear of the ground with her left hand and clutched his arm tightly with her right, and pictured in her mind the way he would be frowning as he looked at the ground to make sure she did not trip. Then, out of the corner of her eye, she saw his right hand move up to his brow. He was rubbing those scars!

It took another ten minutes before they reached the spot she had chosen. It was another small beach with several boulders on it, one of which made a natural seat.

"Here," she said, "let us sit for a few minutes and thank Culebra and say goodbye."

He sat and she realized there was no energy in him. It was as though he was suddenly completely exhausted.

She turned and looked at him.

"You are tired," she said. "It has been a terrible month."

He shook his head. "Not terrible. Exciting, yes."

"The hurricane, the treasure hunt...yes, exciting enough," she said.

"And you," he said, reaching for her hand. "I wish I had met you a long time ago."

"Why 'a long time ago'?"

"Before you were married," he said shyly.

Suddenly she shivered and knew an instant later that he had noticed it.

"I'm sorry," he said quietly, "that was a tactless thing to say."

She reached up and held his face with both hands.

"Yes, a tactless thing to say...what do you know of my husband?"

"Nothing, apart from his name and the fact that you obviously love him." He said it gently, almost sadly.

"Do you know how much I love him?" she whispered.

"You never talk about him – as though remembering him makes you unhappy."

"It does, very unhappy. But Nicholas, not for the reason you think." She was still whispering, and her hands moved back so her fingers were twined in his hair, gently pulling him towards her.

"Not for the reason you think," she repeated. "No – the memory of him makes me unhappy because I hate him. I wish he was dead!"

From the way he suddenly gripped her shoulders she knew he had not understood, and she startled herself with the harshness of her voice and her words as she continued. "You are afraid of making a cuckold of the man who betrayed me, my mother and my father to the agents of the Directory?"

"Here!" she said, and took one of his hands. She pulled at the front of her dress and guided his hand down over her breast. "There – and there – and there: you feel the scars? My husband caused them. The torturers of the Directory actually used a red-hot poker. They wanted to know where my father was."

"And you said nothing," he said, bemused both by what she said and the fact his hand was not only still on her breast but that she was pressing it to her, and he could feel the nipple stiffening under his palm.

"They let me go and then followed me secretly because they thought I would lead the way to my father. It was in Paris," she said, "but I was looking for my husband, because I wanted to kill him. My parents were in Brittany and escaped to London, and I managed to follow them. And now," she added simply, "I am here."

"I was so jealous," Ramage said. "And I – "

He was going to say that although he was in love with her he did not even know her real name, but managed to smother the sentence by kissing her.

By nine o'clock next morning the light breeze that had been blowing from the north most of the night veered to the east and freshened, and Ramage waited impatiently as *La Perla's* boat was hoisted in after returning from across the bay.

Jackson left the group of seamen and came over to Ramage to report.

"Where did you leave them?"

"The headland you pointed out, sir; Punta Colorada. Over there, on the western side of the entrance."

"Any tracks or paths there?"

"Didn't see any, sir. Plenty of trees and bushes. Not hard to get through. Maybe three hours or so back to here."

"They gave no trouble?"

"No, sir. The Lieutenant complained about the long walk back."

Ramage grunted sourly. "He's lucky!"

"We told him that, sir."

The problem of what to do with *Teniente* Colon and his troops, and *La Perla*'s master and crew, had been solved by locking the soldiers and sailors in the large house with the bricked-up windows used as the slaves' barracks, and taking Colon and the Master to the other side of the bay with the one key that would open the enormous padlock on the door. The prisoners were crowded, but Ramage had little sympathy for the soldiers.

The slaves had been given the choice of joining the Royal Navy or staying on Snake Island. Five, including Roberto, had volunteered. The remainder preferred the known life of slavery to the unknown perils of the Navy.

As soon as the boat was secured, Ramage gave a swift series of orders that saw *La Perla*'s lines taken in, headsails hoisted, the big foresail and even larger mainsail set and the schooner reaching smoothly down the bay towards the narrow entrance. The wind funnelling round the hills was freshening every minute, but inside the bay the water was flat, its surface only pewtered.

Southwick turned to Ramage and nodded: "She goes well."

"We've trimmed her too much by the bow!"

The Master walked to the bow and peered over the lee side; then came aft and looked over the taffrail at the wake. He waved the two men away from the big tiller and took it himself, holding it firmly but with hands sensing the feel of the rudder in the water.

He told the two helmsmen to take over the tiller again, and said to Ramage: "Two tons. Sorry, sir."

Ramage laughed cheerfully. "You're allowed ten tons of leeway with a new ship!"

"Don't worry, sir," Southwick said, mollified as soon as he realized that Ramage's original remark was intended as a comment, not a criticism, "I'll have her trimmed as soon as we get round the point. I made allowances for doing that."

Ramage slapped Southwick on the back – the first time the Master had ever known him do that to anyone – and exclaimed: "Mr Southwick, do you realize the significance of what you've just said?"

The Master looked startled. "No, sir! I made allowances for trimming her. I mean," he added hastily, "I had the holds loaded so I could shift – why, of course, the treasure, sir! The coins are the easiest to move."

"Exactly! How many masters in the service use gold and silver as ballast?"

Southwick grinned delightedly. "Good Heavens, I didn't think of it that way! I'll put it in the log – 'Shifted so-and-so tons of Spanish doubloons to trim the ship.' That'll make a good yarn to tell in Portsmouth!"

By ten o'clock La Perla had passed out through the entrance, eased sheets for the reach along the edge of the reefs down to Punta del Soldado at the south-western corner of the island, and rounded it to bear away before a soldier's wind.

To the westward, Puerto Rico was shimmering in the heat with the island of Vieques a long, low shape to the southwest. If Snake Island, Vieques and Puerto Rico formed three sides of a square, the fourth was made up of an almost impassable barrier of small cays stretching in a long line between the northern ends of Puerto Rico and Snake Island.

Without the Spanish charts Ramage could not have risked the passage between Vieques and the cays, but he guessed La Perla would use that channel on her way to Ponce, and to pass south of Vieques might arouse suspicion.

The sun, climbing high now, would be almost directly overhead in a couple of hours. Streaks of pale green, and brown marks in the sea – like dirty fingermarks on a bright-blue enamel dish – showed where reefs lay just below the surface waiting to rip the bottom out of an unwary ship. Some of the shoals rose above the surface to expose coral whitening in the sun, making islets for the dozens of solemn and dignified pelicans soaring, diving lazily, or watching indifferently as *La Perla* passed within a few hundred yards.

"Feels strange, doesn't it?" Ramage commented to Yorke, nodding towards the Spanish ensign.

"It certainly does. A trifle florid, isn't it?"

The horizontal stripes of red, gold and red were rarely seen at sea by British eyes.

"It's legal, I assume?" Yorke asked. "I mean, if we get taken by a Spanish ship of the line, we won't be hanged as freebooters or pirates or anything?"

"Perfectly legal," Ramage said. "You have to hoist your own flag before you open fire on someone, that's all."

"Barbarous!" Yorke said with a shudder.

"You're looking at it only from the point of view of a potential victim."

"True enough; I was born a potential victim!"

"It looks different if you use it as a trick to capture a prize."

"I'm a peace-loving man," Yorke said. "With an inborn respect for flags."

"So am I," Ramage said blandly. "I just don't believe everything I see!"

By late afternoon *La Perla* was passing through the channel between Vieques and the south-east corner of Puerto Rico. Punta Tuna on the starboard bow was the last piece of high land they would see until they had passed westward along the length of Puerto Rico and crossed the Mona Passage to sight the eastern end of Hispaniola.

Just before darkness Ramage searched the horizon with his telescope. There were no sails in sight. Lookouts along the coast should be quite happy: *La Perla* had left Snake Island

according to schedule, making for Ponce. What they would

not know was that the schooner would pass Ponce in the

darkness, and unless the wind dropped away in the night,

would be beyond Puerto Rico and out of sight by sunrise.

CHAPTER EIGHTEEN

Ramage always found Jamaica one of the most exciting of tropical landfalls, with the peaks of the aptly named Blue Mountains showing up fifty miles away. They were sighted low on the western horizon just before sunset on the fifth day.

Responsibility for the safety of a small schooner with important passengers and laden with a king's ransom in treasure meant that Ramage, Southwick and Yorke did not have more than two hours' uninterrupted sleep after leaving Snake Island. Once across the Mona Passage, with Hispaniola a few miles on the starboard beam, the lookouts had done little else than hail "Deck there!" and report a sail in sight.

Each time Ramage had to thrust aside his training as a naval officer and try to think with the mind of the fictitious Spanish captain that he had become. If anyone boarded them he had to remember that he was ostensibly on passage from Puerto Rico to Havana, Cuba, with provisions for Havana's garrison and seamen intended for a frigate being commissioned there. It sounded likely, and only four ships had inquired – one Spanish and two French privateers, and a French national sloop. Ramage was thankful not to have sighted a British frigate; he was in no mood to be delayed while he tried to persuade some sceptical post captain of the truth of his improbable story.

He had ordered Southwick to reduce sail for the rest of the night to ensure that they arrived off Morant Point, at the eastern end of Jamaica, soon after dawn.

The St Brieucs were on deck at sunrise, eager for their first good look at the island they had many times despaired of ever seeing, and Maxine's excitement was catching. "It is so green – and so mountainous!" she exclaimed to Ramage.

"When Columbus was describing it to Queen Isabella, he crumpled up a piece of paper and threw it on the table."

"Where is Port Royal?" she asked.

"Just to the right of the highest peak. But there's not much of it left after an earthquake and a hurricane. Kingston is the main harbour now."

By nine o'clock, Southwick came down to Ramage's cabin to report that he could just distinguish the eastern end of the Palisadoes, and Ramage went on deck to find Yorke helping Maxine with a telescope and trying to tell her what to look for.

"You see how the land runs east and then curves south?" Ramage said. "Well, Kingston is in the elbow. The Palisadoes is a long spit running parallel with the land like a trigger, with Port Royal and the entrance to Kingston Harbour at the tip."

"Towns!" Maxine said contemptuously. "You talk of towns, with all this to look at? Just look at those mountains! And the mist in the valleys. It's magical!"

Yorke grimaced at Ramage as Maxine moved the telescope to range over the rest of the island.

"Just look!" Maxine said excitedly. "All the little ships – and canoes close to the beach."

"Local fishermen," Yorke murmured.

"All the houses with pointed roofs!"

"Cattle mills," Ramage said. "They use cattle to work the machinery to make sugar."

"And tall chimneys with smoke coming out of them!"

"The chimneys of the boiling houses," Ramage said.

"What are they boiling?"

"The sugar cane. Extracting the molasses."

"Tell me how they make sugar," she demanded.

"I don't know," Ramage said firmly. "All I do know is it makes a terrible smell."

"Excuse me, sir," said Southwick, "but I can't make out the pilot schooner – permission to fire a gun?"

Ramage nodded: both inshore and ahead of *La Perla* there were now a dozen or more vessels, ranging from small droggers bringing cargoes of sugar, molasses and rum into Kingston from a dozen coves and bays round the coast, to large schooners arriving from many different countries.

As soon as the gun boomed out, they saw a schooner close inshore suddenly making sail and then heading towards them.

"Ha! They take their time," Southwick grumbled.

"Don't forget *La Perla* isn't one of the King's ships," Ramage said. "As far as they're concerned she's just another little schooner with heavily patched sails."

"Wait till they see that!" Southwick said, gesturing to the British flag that now streamed out above the Spanish, indicating that she was a prize.

"The pilot won't be impressed," Ramage said. "He'll have seen too many captured ships of the line brought in."

Ten minutes later both *La Perla* and the pilot schooner were lying hove-to as a small canoe brought the pilot on board. As he watched, Ramage thought for the first time in many hours of the problems that probably awaited him in Kingston.

First, the hunt for the treasure, then the reception of *La Perla*, and finally the voyage itself, had given him other things to think about. Now he had to face the fact that Rear-Admiral Goddard was probably in Kingston. A ship of the line like the *Lion*, if properly handled, should survive a hurricane. By now, though, the Admiral might well have given up hope that Ramage had survived to face whatever had been prepared for him.

The pilot scrambling nimbly on board was a muscular young Negro dressed in white canvas trousers, a gaudy blue and yellow shirt and a narrow-brimmed straw hat which many coats of black varnish had made as a rigid as a cast-iron cooking pot.

He stared at the British flag over the Spanish ensign and looked slowly round *La Perla*.

"Come on, Blackie!" Southwick said impatiently.

"Harry Wilson, if you please, sah."

The Master sniffed. "Very well, Harry Wilson, as soon as your canoe is clear of our bow we're getting under way again."

The man sniffed in turn, implying that his talents were wasted on such a small vessel.

"A nice little ship," he said conversationally to Ramage, who had not yet changed back into uniform. He caught sight of Maxine, raised his hat and gave a deep bow. He then turned back to Southwick. "A sound little ship. You must have a nice captain to send you off in command of the prize crew."

Ramage looked steadily at Southwick, defying him to squash the pilot.

Getting no reaction from Southwick, Wilson turned to Ramage. "Who is she prize to?"

"The *Triton* brig."

"No trouble finding a buyer here; she's a nice size. A schooner like this sold a month ago for fifteen hundred pounds."

"Good, we can do with the money," Ramage said as Southwick relieved his annoyance by bellowing the orders that got *La Perla* under way again.

Yorke had been standing by the taffrail. He was no stranger to Kingston and was finding it pleasant watching and knowing the navigation of the ship was no responsibility of his.

The pilot glanced at both Ramage and Yorke once or twice, obviously puzzled. He recognized the bearing of an officer, but the only man on deck wearing a uniform was Southwick.

"You know Kingston?" the pilot asked Ramage.

"No."

He had been in and out several times when he was a young midshipman, but did anyone really know Kingston? The life in the big houses was considerably more luxurious than that in the great houses in London, since few people in England could afford such an army of servants. But what was life like in the tiny shacks in the mountains, where the thumping of voodoo drums was as commonplace as the sound of tree frogs?

"These batteries," the pilot said, pointing to the harbour entrance. "Blow you out of the water! Boom boom – then no more of your little ship."

"You're safe enough here," Ramage said in a suitably awed voice.

"We need them!" the pilot said, peering over the side at the shoal only twenty yards to windward. "Privateers...the Spanish at Cuba...just pirates. Channel narrow here – you wouldn't get far without a pilot, mister."

He pointed to the land on the starboard side and the dozens of cays and reefs on the larboard bow. Apart from an occasional almost casual direction to Southwick, Wilson then lapsed into a sulky silence and Ramage walked back to join Yorke at the taffrail.

The Palisadoes, with the harbour and town of Kingston behind it, was now abeam as *La Perla* sailed along parallel with the shore and a mile off. Half an hour later as the pilot gave directions for the schooner to turn north to anchor off Port Royal, Ramage signalled to Southwick that he would take the conn. At the same time, Yorke began to point out various sights to Maxine.

"The remains of Port Royal," he said, pointing to the western end of the Palisadoes. "You see the hill on the side? The big battery up there is called the Twelve Apostles. Now – it's just coming clear of the point – you can see Fort Charles: the low, red brick walls are all that's left. And beyond – Gallows Point!"

Maxine shuddered.

"You'll see the bodies still hanging from the gallows – mutineers from the *Hermione* frigate!"

"*Mon Dieu!* How long have they been there?"

"A year or two. They're wrapped in chains, a warning to other seamen…"

Southwick was on the foredeck making sure everything was ready for anchoring, and Yorke excused himself and walked over to Ramage.

"Everyone with a telescope is watching us by now," he said quietly.

Ramage nodded. "And they won't make head or tail of it!"

"Just another prize sent in by a frigate?"

"Yes – the only interest will be in guessing how much she'll fetch."

By now the pilot was standing by the main chains, apparently in a huff, so no one could hear them talk.

"M'sieur St Brieuc was right," Yorke said quietly. "You are going to take his advice, aren't you?"

"I suppose so," Ramage said reluctantly. "I haven't really made up my mind."

"You're leaving it rather late!"

"I know," Ramage said glumly. "I hate getting them involved in this sort of nonsense."

"Involved? See here, Ramage!" Ramage was startled by the harsh note in Yorke's voice, "They owe their lives to you." He held up a hand to silence Ramage's protest. "That's a fact. Certainly once, with the *Peacock* attack, and probably twice, getting us all ashore at Snake Island and then to Jamaica!"

Ramage shrugged his shoulders, but Yorke persisted.

"Anyway, he's going to involve himself, whether you agree or not. If you were simply a lieutenant with no problems he'd be grateful and want to show it. He's doing no more because it's you."

"All right!" Ramage said wearily, "I'll do as he says. I appreciate his suggestion."

"Is your report all ready?"

"Dozens of reports," Ramage said sourly. "I seem to have been scribbling ever since we passed Puerto Rico. There's a lot to be said for losing your ship and escaping in an open boat – you don't have pen and paper, then."

Yorke laughed. "The Navy floats in ink, and ships are built of paper."

"And their guns fire broadsides of pens," Ramage added.

"So M'sieur St Brieuc will keep out of sight until tomorrow," Yorke said as a statement of fact.

"I suppose that's all right," Ramage said doubtfully. "This damned protocol. Who does he report to, anyway?"

"The Lieutenant Governor. His letters are addressed to him."

Ramage gave a sigh of relief. "That's a help. I should have guessed that."

"What do you do now?" Yorke asked.

"As soon as we anchor and clear Customs here at Port Royal – the manifest won't mention the bullion – we'll shift into Kingston and I'll go on shore and report to the Commander-in-Chief if Goddard isn't there."

The two men stood looking round them as *La Perla* completed the last few hundred yards into the anchorage, and then Ramage saw Jackson running aft along the deck towards him.

"The *Lion*'s here, sir!"

Ramage looked in the direction the American was pointing.

She was little more than a hulk in Kingston harbour, and partly hidden by merchantmen. There was a lighter each side of her, and only her mainmast was standing.

Ramage put his telescope to his eye and the circular magnified picture revealed the story. "Foremast and mizzen gone by the board," Ramage said loudly, knowing that every man on board was curious. "Mainmast fished in two places. Bulwarks stove in on both sides. Jibboom gone, and the bowsprit fished. Several port lids torn off."

Yorke grunted. "We weren't the only ones in trouble, then!"

Then Ramage saw the stream of water frothing across the deck and over the side.

"And leaking badly; they're pumping."

"Flag, sir?" Jackson asked.

"No – the Admiral must be on shore."

"No sign of the others, sir," Jackson said quietly.

Ramage swung the telescope round the anchorage to confirm that there was no sign of the three frigates and the *Lark* lugger that had formed the escort.

Ramage shut the telescope. He'd never recognize the merchantmen and he would know soon enough how many had survived when he went on shore.

At least he didn't have to alter the address on his reports. He had made them to Rear-Admiral Goddard, but he'd hoped…Anyway, instead of reporting to the Commander-in-Chief, he had to report to the Rear-Admiral, the new "second-in-command of His Majesty's ships and vessels...at and about Jamaica".

After the customs officers cleared *La Perla* at Port Royal, Ramage took the schooner round Gallows Point, at the end of the Palisadoes, and beat up through the ships anchored in Kingston Harbour.

"One thing about coming in with a ship like this," Southwick commented. "You can choose where to anchor, instead of being ordered to a particular berth!"

Ramage nodded. He was anxious to anchor abreast of the town of Kingston, since *La Perla*'s boat was too small to make a two-mile row anything less than a test of endurance.

Yorke examined the *Lion* carefully through a telescope as the schooner tacked across her stern.

"She was lucky to get in," he commented. "I'll bet there are ten men at the pumps night and day."

As soon as *La Perla* luffed up and anchored, she was surrounded by bumboats, each improbably named and gaudily painted with sails made of sacking and pieces of canvas crudely sewn to shape. Each was manned by an energetic and flamboyant Negro shouting at the top of his voice, anxious to carry the captain on shore or bring out supplies. While the schooner's sails were being furled, the bumboatmen were yelling to Southwick – apparently assuming that because of his bulk he was the purser – and giving him a string of prices for everything a ship and her crew could possibly need, from fresh fruit to women.

When they saw *La Perla*'s boat being hoisted out they groaned with pretended dismay and then began describing the superior speed, safety and comfort of their respective craft.

Ramage went below to the tiny cuddy he shared with Yorke and changed into one of his best uniforms. By the time he had dressed he was soaked with perspiration – there was barely room to crouch in the cuddy, let alone stand up. Giving his stock a last twitch to straighten it, he picked up his sword, his best hat and the heavily stitched canvas pouch containing his reports.

Before going on deck he went to the St Brieucs' cabin. None of them had come to watch the ship coming into Kingston and he was disappointed. He knocked, called out his name, and heard St Cast telling him to enter. Maxine had been weeping. Her eyes were red and as Ramage looked at her, too startled to look tactfully away, she gave a dry sob.

St Brieuc said quickly: "Don't worry, my lord. My daughter is both sad and happy and so is my wife." Ramage saw that she too had been crying.

St Brieuc went on quickly to avoid an embarrassing silence, "We are sad at the prospect of leaving you, even though it will probably not be for a day or two."

Ramage was too dumbfounded to do anything more than stand there, holding his sword and hat.

"And a little worried too until you return to tell us how the Admiral receives you. Sir Pilcher, I mean."

"Goddard," Ramage said without thinking.

"He is here?"

Ramage pulled himself together, unable to take his eyes off Maxine.

"The *Lion* is. She's badly damaged, but safe."

"And the others?" Maxine asked.

"I don't know about the merchantmen, but none of the escorts are here." Hastily he added: "If they weren't damaged, they might have sailed again already."

She did not believe him and began sobbing again. So Ramage bowed helplessly and left.

Jackson was waiting in the boat and within five minutes the men at the oars were pulling clear of the schooner and heading for the shore.

Ramage saw none of the local boats, which had given up hope of passengers from the schooner and were speeding back to the shore, nor did he notice the curious eyes watching from nearby merchantmen. He did not notice the heat, the dust, the noise or the smell as they arrived at the jetty. He was thinking about Goddard, who had survived but could not know that Ramage had done so as well. The moment the Admiral discovered that Ramage was alive, something unpleasant would happen. Ramage could not think exactly what it would be because there was such a wide choice.

The heat and noise hit Ramage like a blow as he reached the top of the stone steps of the jetty and began walking to Rear-Admiral Goddard's house. The streets were crowded. Goods landed from the merchant ships were being carried to the stores and warehouses in heavy drays, light carts and on the backs of stubborn donkeys. Cheerful Negroes pulled and pushed, shouting and singing at the top of their voices and good-naturedly jostling each other; coloured women walked with grace and elegance, many of them carrying large baskets balanced on their heads with as much dignity as a dowager arriving at a court ball in a tiara.

Rear-Admiral Goddard's house was some distance from the jetty, a big and cool stone building with a red roof and whitewashed walls, standing in the centre of a walled garden. Wide, covered balconies ran all round the ground and upper floors, reminding Ramage of a square, two-tiered wedding cake.

An old coloured man with grey hair was sweeping leaves from the withered apology for a lawn. The heat of the sun had scorched the grass brown, and in places the hard ground showed enormous bald patches, criss-crossed where the earth was cracked, as though wrinkled by age.

The Marine sentry saluted, but the coloured butler who came to the door when Ramage jerked the brass bell handle left him standing on the top step while he went back into the building. The Admiral seemed to have given standing orders about how to deal with young lieutenants who called at the second-in-command's residence without orders or invitation.

At last the pimply young lieutenant he had last seen at the convoy conference on board the *Lion* at Barbados came to the door.

"Good afternoon," Ramage said coolly. "Have you got any spare handkerchiefs?"

The lieutenant looked blank and Ramage could not be bothered to explain.

"Admiral Goddard, please. Lieutenant Ramage to see him."

"I – er, we thought you'd...Yes, well, he'll be busy for about fifteen minutes. Come this way."

Nervously he led Ramage to a waiting-room, ushered him in like a doctor's assistant, and left.

A cool room in a cool house, and somewhere to sit down. The door was slatted like a large, partly-opened venetian blind. The roof over the outside balcony shaded the room. The legs of a small, round mahogany table stood in shallow metal trays of water as part of the ceaseless war against ants that had to be waged in the Tropics.

Ramage put his hat and sword on the table and opened the canvas pouch to check over the documents he'd written using his knee as a desk while crouched in the cuddy on board *La Perla*. On the top of the pile was his report to the Admiral describing the loss of the *Triton*. He made that a separate report since he would have to face a routine court of inquiry which always followed the loss of one of the King's ships. He had been careful to cover the period from the onset of the hurricane up to the dismasted *Triton* running on the reef at Snake Island. It described building the rafts and using them to ferry men and provisions on shore, and it stopped there.

The second report covered the capture of *La Perla* and the voyage from Snake Island to Jamaica. It was a brief three pages of writing. Every word was true, yet it did not tell the whole story. It did not mention that he had fallen in love with Maxine, for instance, nor that Sydney Yorke, who had become a good friend, was ruefully envious of her attitude to him.

The third report, marked "SECRET" and sealed with wax, dealt with the treasure. With it was a complete inventory, "Treasure Log", a detailed list of the contents of the crates, a stowage list and a diagram – recently amended by Southwick after he shifted some to trim the schooner – describing in which holds the crates were stowed in *La Perla*.

As he put them back in the pouch, carefully keeping them in the same order, he thought about how little of an episode an official report really described. The report on the treasure was probably the most detailed and complicated he'd ever written, but it told nothing of the days and nights when he thought he'd never work out the meaning of the poem, the misery and disappointment they had felt when they found the first bones; the ghoulish effect of digging up skeletons by lantern light, or the excitement when Jackson leapt out of the trench with the first coins...

He heard voices outside the front door and heavy boots clumping up the carriageway from the gate. Impatient at the long wait for the Admiral, he walked to the window and looked out. Five Marines armed with muskets, one of them a corporal, were standing sweltering in the sun, and the pimply lieutenant was whispering to the corporal.

Ramage sat down again, and a moment later the lieutenant, perspiring freely, came in to say abruptly: "Follow me: the Admiral will see you now."

The room was large and heavily shaded by partly closed shutters. A large desk stood in front of the windows and beyond it, where the breeze cooled him, the Admiral was lounging back on a settee.

He looked as hot, uncomfortable and petulant as he had when Ramage first saw him at the convoy conference with the pimply Lieutenant passing him fresh handkerchiefs. Now his face was slack and drawn, as though heat and worry were making it difficult for him to sleep through the sweltering Jamaica nights. He looked, Ramage thought, like a rich nabob fearful that someone is about to tell him he is bankrupt, that his wife has cuckolded him, or perhaps both.

Ramage stood stiffly, holding his sword scabbard with his left hand, hat tucked under his left arm, and grasping the canvas pouch in his right hand.

"Good afternoon, sir."

Goddard just stared at him.

The room was silent except for the distant high-pitched laughter of Negroes and a faint ticking somewhere, showing that a death-watch beetle was at work. The settee creaked as Goddard moved slightly, and in spite of the open door and window, the room smelled musty, like a family vault.

Ramage stared at a point a foot above Goddard's head and listened to his heavy breathing; the man was far too fat for the Tropics.

"Where have you been?" the Admiral inquired finally, in a tone of voice that suggested that he would have preferred to ask: "Why have you come back from the dead?"

"The *Triton* went on a reef, sir."

"I'm not surprised. Some strange and unexpected current, no doubt, that swept you onto a reef not shown on any charts? The standard excuse."

"Yes, sir."

"You admit it, eh?"

"Yes, sir."

"By God!"

The Admiral was dumbfounded. His questions had been hopes put into words. This was what he hoped to prove against Ramage and now Ramage was admitting it.

"You're under close arrest, Ramage."

"Yes, sir."

"Damnation, is that all you have to say? A bloody parrot!"

"Yes, sir."

"Are you being insolent?"

"Oh no, sir!"

"Don't you want to know the charges?"

"If you wish, sir."

Of course he wanted to know the charges but he would be damned if he'd give Goddard the satisfaction of knowing it.

Not attempting to keep the note of triumph out of his voice the Admiral said: "Articles ten, twelve and seventeen. To which will now be added number twenty-six."

"Ten, twelve, seventeen and now twenty-six, sir," Ramage repeated calmly.

"So far. There may be more after I've read your report. You have it ready?"

"Yes, sir."

"Give it to Hobson as you go out."

Ramage flushed. "Yes, sir. May I send a message out to the former master of the *Triton* on board the little schooner we came here in?"

Goddard was not interested. "Of course," he said, and waved his hand in dismissal.

Lieutenant Hobson was outside the door.

"Your escort is waiting," he said triumphantly.

Ramage put his hat down on a chair and opened the pouch. He looked through his reports and took out the top one.

"For the Admiral."

Hobson took it as though snatching a hot chestnut out of the fire.

Ramage unclipped the scabbard of his sword and handed it to Hobson. "You'd better have this. And pass the word that the Admiral's given permission for me to send a message out to my ship." With that he picked up his hat and walked swiftly to the front door. "Come, corporal, let's not hang about in the sun!"

Ramage strode down towards the gate, squinting in the bright sun, and it was several moments before he heard shouted orders and the hurried thumping of boots, and then the corporal's voice pleading: " 'Old 'ard, sir! Yer'll get us inter trouble if the h'Admiral sees!"

Ramage slowed down to let the Marines form up round him. "Step out, corporal, it's a lovely day."

The corporal was clutching Ramage's sword.

Ramage put the pen down and screwed the cap on the inkwell. He folded the sheet of paper and cursed himself for not asking for wax. He decided to enclose it in another blank sheet folded into an envelope and trust that if whoever delivered it was nosy he wouldn't understand the significance of what was written.

Although addressed to Southwick, the letter was meant for Yorke, and knowing he wouldn't seal it Ramage had written with deliberate ambiguity:

"I have been put under close arrest on charges presumably arising from the *Peacock's* attack on the *Topaz*. Articles ten, twelve and seventeen. More charges are likely, relating to the loss of the *Triton*. I have not yet received the precise charges nor been told the date of the trial. Unless it is necessary I'd prefer nothing went on shore yet from *La Perla*, particularly talk, but if you happen to call on me at the Marine barracks, bring my razor and fresh clothing."

Yorke and St Brieuc would realize that Ramage wanted them to stay out of sight. Southwick would understand that the treasure must stay on board under guard and under conditions of secrecy.

Ramage got up from the table in his small and hot room – the quarters intended for a Marine subaltern – and banged on the door.

The Marine corporal, a red-faced, plump and cheerful Londoner, unlocked it and came in.

"Can you see this is delivered to *La Perla* schooner – the Spanish prize that came in earlier today?"

"Yes, sir! Saw you come in, sir!"

"What ship?"

"*Lion*, sir."

"You came in with the convoy?"

"Yessir!"

"How was the hurricane?"

"Cor!" The corporal rolled his eyes and kicked the door shut with his heel. "Confidenshurally, sir, it was 'orrible."

"Windy, eh?"

"The wind warn't too bad," the corporal said ambiguously, dropping his voice. "T'was storm *aft*, sir."

Ramage looked puzzled and the corporal winked, repeating "*Aft*, sir."

"Two hands at the wheel?"

It was the best Ramage could do on the spur of the moment. The corporal, for reasons Ramage could not guess, was friendly, and the way gossip spread he probably knew even more than Ramage himself about the circumstances leading up to the arrest. If the corporal wanted to pass on information, it was up to Ramage to make it easy for him.

"Two hands at the wheel?" The corporal thought a moment and then nodded his head vigorously. "And hauling in different directions, sir!"

Ramage nodded sympathetically. "That's how masts go by the board."

"Indeed they do! Killed eleven men. The mizzen mast did for the master, two midshipmen and eight of the afterguard."

"The Captain wasn't hurt?"

"No, thank Gawd! We'd have drarnded if 'e'd gom. 'Mazing sir, 'ow it took 'im."

"What took him?"

"Losin' the masts. He was a noo man. Ordered – " he broke off, paused and then plunged on, using emphasis to make his meaning clear. "Ordered *everyone* off the quarterdeck who wasn't on watch. Everyone," he repeated. That included the Rear-Admiral. "Then 'e did what 'e wanted, an' that's 'ow we got 'ere. Later we met a frigate orf the Morant Cays an' she towed us in."

The corporal looked at Ramage.

"You don't remember me, do you, sir?"

"I thought your face was familiar."

"The *Belette*, sir. 'Afore I got promoted. When you was wounded. My proudest day, sir. You was wonderful, sir; I'll never forget 'ow you took command. Cor, yer looked dreffel wiv that cut on yer 'ead!"

The corporal's eyes widened. "Why, sir, yer got *two* scars there nar!"

"St Vincent," Ramage said briefly. "The French seem to like my head!"

Satisfying though it was to know the corporal was friendly, and grateful as he was for the information about Captain Croucher's troubles with the Admiral, he wanted his letter delivered to *La Perla*.

The corporal took it. "Mr Hobson passed the word, sir. I'll send my best man out wiv it. Oh – it ain't sealed, sir."

"I've no wax. Can you get any?"

"Aye, sir, no trouble at all."

"Just seal it and give it to your man."

"Leave it ter me, sir," the corporal said, flattered at Ramage's trust in him. He returned in a few minutes to report the letter sealed and on its way to *La Perla*, and apologizing for having to shut and lock the door.

An hour later there was a peremptory rap on the door which flew open to admit a shrivelled little man who strutted like a bantam cock and wore tiny, steel-rimmed spectacles that stuck on his nose like a price label.

"The deputy judge advocate!" he announced in a high-pitched voice that fitted the body like a squeak would a rusty hinge.

Ramage remained seated, eyed the man and said: "What about him?"

"I *am* the deputy judge advocate."

"Your manners are certainly familiar; what's your name?"

"Harold Syme," he said, oblivious of Ramage's snub. "I have come to serve you with the charges."

Ramage held out his hand for the papers. Puzzled at Ramage's silence, he began fumbling in the leather bag which had been tucked under his arm.

"The charges are exhibited by Rear-Admiral Goddard. They are capital charges."

Ramage gestured impatiently with his hand.

"Deliver any documents necessary, please. I am busy."

"Busy? Why – "

"I will let you have the names of my witnesses in due course," Ramage said. "The documents?"

The man burrowed into his case, took out several papers and handed them to Ramage as if they were delicate, breakable objects. Ramage tossed them carelessly on the table.

"I have to read the 'Letter to the prisoner' to you."

"I can read," Ramage said. "Please have some wax sent in."

"What do you want wax for?"

Ramage gestured to the writing materials on the table. "To seal my letters from prying eyes."

"Really! Do you suppose I would – "

"The thought occurred to you, not me. Good day to you, sir," Ramage said, and began unscrewing the inkwell.

"Mr Ramage, how – "

"I'm preparing my defence. Do you want it said you deliberately hindered me?"

After a pause the man strutted from the room, calling loudly to the corporal that he was leaving.

As the door slammed, Ramage opened one of the letters. It was Rear-Admiral Goddard's report to Sir Pilcher, dated two weeks earlier, soon after the *Lion* arrived. He began reading, underlining with his pen the words which were taken directly from the various Articles of War.

"I beg leave to inform you that Lieutenant Nicholas Ramage, commanding officer of His Majesty's brig *Triton* while escorting ships of a convoy under my command, on the occasion of one of the ships being attacked on the night of the 18th of July last, by a French privateer, <u>did not make the necessary preparations for fight, and did not in his own person, and according to his place, encourage the inferior</u>

officers and men to fight courageously and furthermore the said Lt Ramage upon the same occasion did withdraw or keep back and did not do his utmost to take or destroy the enemy ship which it was his duty to engage; and furthermore the said Lt Ramage upon the same occasion, being the commanding officer of the ship appointed for convoy and guard of merchant ships, did not diligently attend upon that charge according to his instructions to defend the ships in the convoy, and did neglect to fight in their defence: in consequence of which I am to request you will apply for a court martial on the said Lt Ramage for the said crimes,

I am, &c,"

By the time he finished reading Ramage felt coldly angry. The moment Admiral Goddard had mentioned the numbers of the Articles of War he'd guessed the charges would revolve round the *Peacock* attack. It hadn't been clear – since the Articles ranged widely – that he was in fact accused of one thing only: cowardice in the face of the enemy. Charges arising from the loss of the *Triton* were presumably being kept in reserve.

Ramage gave a bitter laugh. At least once a month, on a Sunday, during the whole of the time he had been at sea, he had heard the Articles of War read to the ship's company. For the past year or two, as commanding officer, he had read them out himself, noting the fact in the log to show that the regulations had been carried out. In his imagination he could hear himself reading loudly, trying to make his voice heard above the noise of wind and sea...

"Article ten...shall not encourage...officers and men to fight courageously...shall suffer death...Article twelve...Every person in the Fleet who through cowardice, negligence or disaffection, shall in time of action...not do his utmost to take or destroy every ship...shall suffer death...Article seventeen...running away cowardly, and submitting the ships in their convoy to peril...be punished...by pains of death, or other punishment, according as shall be adjudged by the court martial..."

There was a devilish skill about it all. As far as Admiral Goddard knew, the *Topaz,* and presumably the *Greyhound* frigate, had been sunk in the hurricane, so the only surviving witnesses to the *Peacock's* attack were the *Lion's* officers and Ramage's own men. It wouldn't be hard to guess which a court would believe.

It was difficult to guess precisely what Goddard was going to accuse him of doing to constitute the actual act of cowardice. Yet the limits were solely the limits of Goddard's imagination and ingenuity, since as far as he knew Ramage was the only person who could challenge him. Few courts would believe a young lieutenant's pleas of innocence against the charges of a Rear-Admiral who was also second-in-command on the station, especially when the charges were ones of cowardice.

Well if the heat of Jamaica made him feel drowsy, or he began to get bored with the trial, he had something to make him concentrate. All he need remember was that if the court did find him guilty under either of the first two Articles, it had no alternative but to sentence him to death. Articles ten and twelve were among the few which presented a court with a nice, simple equation: guilt equals a sentence of death. The third one, Article seventeen, gave a "death or" choice.

His thoughts were interrupted by a knock at the door and the cheerful voice of the Marine corporal.

"Mr Southwick to see you, sir, with your lawyer."

"Bring them in."

Thoughtful of Southwick to find a lawyer, but at a court martial one was better off without one. The "five or more" captains forming the court usually knew little or nothing of the law, and were often antagonized by lawyers.

It was Yorke who came in with Southwick. He was dressed in a drab black suit, had his shoulders hunched and was carrying a stove-pipe hat and a large leather briefcase. His hair was combed diagonally across his brow and the whole effect was to age him ten years and make him look convincingly like an attorney.

Southwick grinned and said, "I've brought you a lawyer, sir; he says he'll be happy to conduct your defence for one hundred guineas!"

"Too much!" Ramage said, "offer him fifty!" By then the door was shut and locked again.

Ramage waved the two men to the chairs round the tiny table, and Southwick said: "What are they trying to prove against you, sir?"

"I don't know the details, but cowardice is the main charge."

"Cowardice..." Yorke repeated quietly. "It's a wicked charge. Cowardice is one of those words that – well, you can be found not guilty of murder and that's the end of it; but if you're found not guilty of cowardice there's always a – well, a stigma. Cowardice over what?"

"The *Peacock* business."

"The *Peacock*?" Yorke was genuinely dumbfounded. "But how can they?"

Ramage shrugged his shoulders. "Probably blaming me for the attack on the *Topaz*."

"But you prevented it! No harm was done to the St Brieucs! Everyone knows what happened. You gave the Admiral a written report, didn't you?"

Ramage decided that the time had come to tell Yorke the facts of life where people like Goddard were concerned. He tapped the table with the quill pen.

"The court reminds you, sir, that your claim that no harm was done to the St Brieucs can't be substantiated. As far as this court is aware, they were drowned in a hurricane. The *Topaz* was lost in the hurricane, with no survivors. The three frigates and the *Lark* lugger were lost too. The Admiral has given evidence on oath that he received no written report from the accused. The Admiral has produced evidence from among his own officers that the *Triton* held back because the accused was safeguarding his own skin."

"It's wicked!" Yorke said.

"It's almost as ruthless as business," Southwick said unexpectedly. "All this gammon goes on because men are struggling to get power, which means struggling for promotion and interest. To a serving officer, promotion means profit, more pay and more opportunity. It's the same for a businessman," he continued as patiently as a vicar talking to his flock. "A businessman's profit isn't promotion and interest, it's money. But he's often just as ruthless in trying to get it."

"I suppose you're right," Yorke finally admitted. "It's just that business seems more subtle and less cruel – less blatant!"

"It might seem like that to a businessman," Ramage said, "but not to a naval officer! Southwick was just comparing the two so that you'd understand. He's crediting you with sharp business instincts and thinks that if you can see how getting promotion in the Service and making a profit in business are alike, you'll be better able to look into the Admiral's mind. It's the same – perhaps worse – in politics."

Yorke nodded "I do understand. But Goddard can't really hope to prove any of this."

"Why not?" Ramage asked.

"My evidence alone would…"

Ramage shook his head, knowing it was absolutely vital that Yorke fully understood the significance of what he was about to say. *"Your evidence might never be given!* That's why Goddard is in an almost perfect position. He has the rope all ready to drop round my neck!"

The harshness in Ramage's voice left Yorke looking dumbfounded. "But surely he can't stop me giving evidence?"

"If he discovers you and St Brieuc are still alive, he'll immediately drop these charges."

"But how could he discover that in time to make any difference?"

"You have to get on board the *Arrogant* to give your evidence. From the moment he spots you in court, he needs only a couple of minutes to announce that the prosecution is withdrawing the charges."

"What if he does?" Yorke demanded. "Surely that means you're safe!"

"No, it doesn't," Ramage said impatiently. "It means that he withdraws the charges on which your evidence has any bearing, then substitutes something else."

"Oh, come now," Yorke protested. "You're getting overwrought. What can he substitute?"

"Losing the ship," Southwick growled. "That could put a rope round Mr Ramage's neck!"

When Yorke glanced at him for confirmation, Ramage said: "He'd forget all about the *Peacock* attacking the *Topaz* – that means dropping the charges under Articles ten and twelve. He might well chance leaving the *'running away cowardly'* to show I deserted the convoy – you couldn't disprove that. He'd then concentrate on my losing the *Triton* – Article twenty-six, *'…no ships be stranded, or run upon any rocks or sands, or split or hazarded…upon pain that such as shall be found guilty therein be punished by death, or such other punishment as the offence…shall be judged to deserve.' "*

"But they can hardly hang you for losing the ship in the circumstances."

"Possibly not," Ramage said, "but if you add that to a charge of *'running away cowardly'* I think you'll see the noose tightening round my neck."

Yorke sat deep in thought, rubbing his knuckles against his forehead. Finally he looked up and said carefully: "I want to make sure I understand the situation correctly. First, at the moment you are charged with cowardice over the *Peacock* and *Topaz*, and Goddard thinks he can prove it – and get you hanged – because he doesn't know St Brieuc and I survived. But you know you can prove you're innocent because you have our evidence."

When Ramage nodded, Yorke continued, still speaking slowly: "Proving yourself innocent – with our evidence – means you prove Goddard to be a liar who has perjured himself to try to get you hanged. That would be enough to ruin his career – and end his vendetta against you once and for all, I imagine?"

Again Ramage nodded.

"But we're agreed that Goddard would drop the cowardice charges – the main ones, anyway – if he knew St Brieuc and I were alive and going to give evidence. You've said it would take him only a couple of minutes to do that, once he sighted us. Is that an exaggeration?"

"I doubt it. Depends how quick-witted he is."

"*Can* he withdraw the charges just like that? I mean, would the court allow it?"

340

Ramage shrugged his shoulders. "He can certainly withdraw the charges, but I can't say for certain that the court would agree. After all, the court is simply a group of captains."

"You're taking a devilish risk, Ramage. After all, our evidence will come after the prosecution's case. Suppose he has time to withdraw the charges, and the court agrees? You still face another trial on the charge of losing the *Triton*. Why take such a chance on the *Peacock* affair? Why let Goddard bring up the main cowardice charges? Why not let him know we're alive, so that he drops the *Peacock* affair and goes for you on the loss of the *Triton* – and perhaps *'running away cowardly'*? After all, you can fight him on both those charges without taking any risk on Goddard or what the court might decide?"

Southwick was nodding his head in agreement with Yorke. "I have to take the chance," Ramage said flatly. "It's the only way of ending this vendetta. If I don't, it'll drag on for years. Anyway, he'd get me on losing the *Triton*. Maybe I'd dodge the noose, but I'd be finished in the Service."

"You'd be finished even if the court found you not guilty," Southwick said as if thinking aloud.

"Would you?" Yorke asked sharply.

"Yes. Don't forget there are never enough ships to go round. That means no one gets a command if there's the slightest doubt about him."

"And favouritism," Southwick murmured.

"True enough. If you're out of favour with the local admiral – or the Admiralty – you'll be left to rot on half pay for the rest of your life."

"I still think you're mad," Yorke said doggedly. "You're staking everything – including your life – on slipping me and St Brieuc into court and getting one or both of us giving evidence before Goddard has time to withdraw the charges. What's to stop him withdrawing the charges after we've started giving evidence? Or even after we've both told everything we know? Have you thought of that?"

Ramage nodded wearily. "Yes, I've thought about it until my head spins." Yorke was trying to be helpful, and he deserved an explanation; but Ramage already knew he was taking an enormous risk, and having decided to take it he didn't want to discuss it because further talk only mirrored and enlarged his fears.

"I'm counting on several things. The main one is the natural curiosity of the court. By the time you and St Brieuc arrive, all the prosecution evidence will have been given on the assumption that you are both dead. I'm hoping that whatever Goddard tries, the court will want to hear what you have to say. It may lead to them deciding against allowing Goddard to withdraw the charges, and that means the court is bound to find me not guilty.

"Almost as important," Ramage continued, "are the minutes of the trial. Don't forget that as far as the Admiralty is concerned, all that happens in a trial is what is recorded in the minutes. Even if the charges are withdrawn, the minutes have to go to the Admiralty. With a little luck, those minutes might say enough."

"If only we knew who St Brieuc really is," Yorke mused. "I wonder if there's any need for secrecy now…The point is, if he's really influential, would Goddard be forced to carry on? Be too frightened – or too flustered – to withdraw the charges?"

"I've thought of that, too. All I know is that Goddard is scared of him."

Southwick coughed politely. "Supposing the gentleman is important, sir. Suppose the Admiral does withdraw the charges. Would the French gentleman be sufficiently important to write to the Admiralty – or the Commander-in-Chief – and tell them what he knows?"

Both Yorke and Ramage stared at the Master.

"He might be!" Yorke exclaimed.

"What matters," Ramage said, "is whether or not Goddard – and the court – *thinks* he is! Well, you've earned your tot for today, Mr Southwick!"

But a moment later Yorke was again looking gloomy.

"It's still a fantastic risk, Ramage. Listen, why don't you take advantage of what Southwick's just suggested, only modify it. First, let it be known that St Brieuc and I are still alive, so that the *Peacock* cowardice charges are dropped. Let Goddard bring up a charge over the loss of the *Triton*. And ask St Brieuc to write a report for the Admiralty?"

Ramage shook his head. "For a start, anything St Brieuc wrote would then seem vindictive: in effect he'd be denying charges which Goddard hasn't made – "

"But he has – dammit, you have the wording in front of you!"

" – which Goddard hasn't made *in court*. Until they're made in court they don't exist, at least, not in this sense. All St Brieuc could write is that Lieutenant Ramage didn't behave in a cowardly fashion over the *Peacock* attack, and My Lords Commissioners of the Admiralty would reply, 'Who the devil said he did?' "

"That sounds likely enough," Yorke admitted. "It's just that it's almost as though you're staking everything on the turn of a card."

"I am," Ramage said. "That's what I've been trying to tell you. If I can't completely smash Goddard on the *Peacock* charges, I'm finished. He'll keep hammering away at me. If not this week, then next. If not this year, then in a couple of years' time. Don't forget, this isn't the first time he's tried."

"We'll all do our best," Yorke said soberly. "We'll keep out of sight in *La Perla*, even though she's like an oven in this sun."

Ramage nodded gratefully. "I'll try and get the trial brought on quickly. I don't think there'll be much delay."

After Yorke and Southwick had gone, Ramage went through the rest of the documents left by the deputy judge advocate. The second in the pile was from the man himself, a routine letter to the prisoner.

"Sir Pilcher Skinner, Vice-Admiral of the Blue and Commander-in-Chief of His Majesty's Ships and Vessels employed at or about to be employed upon the Jamaica Station, having directed a court martial to be held on you for cowardice in action, tomorrow morning at half past eight o'clock on board His Majesty's ship *Arrogant*. I am to acquaint you therewith, and enclose for your information Rear-Admiral Goddard's complaints against you.

"You are therefore desired to prepare yourself for the same, and if you have any persons to appear as witnesses in your behalf, you will send me a list of their names that they may be duly and speedily warned to attend the said court martial."

A corresponding letter would have been sent to the Rear-Admiral by the deputy judge advocate asking for the list of prosecution witnesses Goddard wanted to call "in support of the charges".

Half past eight o'clock tomorrow morning! Ramage snatched up the pen and quickly scribbled a letter to the deputy judge advocate saying he wished to call the former Master of the *Triton*, Edward Southwick, and the Master's mate, George

Appleby. He was just going to sign it when he decided to include Jackson and Stafford. He would not call them, in fact, but it would give them a day or two on board another ship, and they deserved a change. He added a postscript: "In view of the fact that I have been notified that the trial starts in sixteen hours' time this is my first list of witnesses: a second list will follow later."

He called the corporal, sent off the letter, and was told he was being transferred to the *Lion* in half an hour. Before that the corporal had to hand over responsibility for his prisoner to the *Lion*'s Marine lieutenant, who would act as provost marshal. " 'E'll be glad o' the four bob a day," the corporal said. " 'E's got four nippers."

A good thing some deserving soul was gaining by his arrest, Ramage thought sourly, as he wrote a quick note to Southwick.

"My trial fixed for half past eight tomorrow morning on board the *Arrogant*. Assume haste is due to the fact captains now available have to sail soon. I have asked for you, Appleby, Jackson and Stafford as witnesses. Please bring my journal, your log, the *Triton*'s muster book, *La Perla*'s log, particularly for the period under my command. Also bring with you personally a dozen circular samples of the ballast. Ask our friends to come on board the *Arrogant* at exactly half past ten tomorrow morning. They should insist on seeing me and if necessary send in visiting cards."

Early that evening Ramage was taken out to the *Lion*. Captain Croucher, presumably on orders from the Admiral, had given instructions to the Lieutenant of Marines acting as provost marshal to take a large escort which would have been more suitable for bringing a wild elephant on board.

He had been led from his room by the corporal, whose sheepish manner showed his own view, to find the lieutenant with a dozen Marines. He read Ramage his warrant in a loud voice, with a crowd of gaping seamen for an audience.

Amid much stamping of feet, thumping of muskets and clouds of pipeclay they had marched to the jetty, where the *Lion*'s yawl waited. Her masts were not stepped, so Goddard intended that she should be rowed through the anchored ships. No one was to be deprived of the sight of Lieutenant Lord Ramage sitting in the stern sheets, with the citizens of Kingston protected from robbery, rape or arson by a dozen alert Marines with bayonets fixed while the provost marshal held Ramage's surrendered sword across his knees.

The *Arrogant*, where the court martial would be held in the morning, was a seventy-four anchored half a mile to windward of the *Lion*. Her yards were perfectly square – her master would have made sure of that within a few minutes of anchoring. The enormous fore and main yards projected several feet over the side of the ship.

There, within an area of a few square feet, his immediate future would be decided, for the trial would be held in the great cabin. If the five or so captains at a court martial decided on a death sentence it would be carried out just under the fore yard on the starboard side.

First, a yellow flag would be hoisted at the *Arrogant*'s mizzen peak and a gun fired, signalling that an execution was to take place. A rope would be rove from a block near the outboard end of the yard. The end of the rope with a noose in it would come down vertically to where the prisoner was standing. The noose would be slipped round his neck, and they would be thoughtful enough to arrange the knot so it was comfortable – he had heard that executioners tended to be apologetic and excessively polite as they set about the preliminaries of their trade. A black hood would be put over the prisoner's head, and there he would wait in the darkness and it would seem a lifetime before he reached eternity.

The other end of the rope would lead down at an angle from that block to a point almost abreast the mainmast. Twenty or so seamen would be holding onto the rope and facing aft. On the deck immediately below where the prisoner was standing a gun would be loaded with a blank charge. Finally the word would be passed to the captain of the *Arrogant* that all was ready: the noose would be in position round the prisoner's neck, and so would the hood. The seamen would have tailed onto the other end of the rope.

When the *Arrogant*'s captain gave the word, the gunner would apply a steady pull to the trigger line of the gun; the flint would fly down to strike a spark which would ignite the fine powder in the pan. The intense flame would spurt through the touch-hole and in turn ignite the powder in the breech of the gun. In a fraction of a second two pounds of exploding gunpowder would vomit flame, smoke and noise from the muzzle.

At the same instant someone would signal to the men at the rope and they would suddenly run aft. In a moment the prisoner's body would be jerked many feet up into the air by its neck, and it would all be over.

Hanging...It was better known to seamen as being "stabbed with a Bridport dagger", a reference to the Devon town's fame for the quality of rope it made. A great leveller. Many men had probably been hanged from the larboard fore yardarm of the *Arrogant*, but probably none from the starboard yardarm. Seamen were traditionally hanged on the larboard side; the starboard side was reserved for officers. Ramage shuddered. He was glad the trial was unlikely to develop quite as Goddard planned.

"Ramage!"

He looked up and realized that the yawl was alongside the *Lion*. He had been so lost in thought that he had not heard the orders to the men at the oars. Now the lieutenant acting as provost marshal waited impatiently.

As Ramage moved across the boat to climb up the ship's side he was reminded of a farmyard at home. If one of the hens had a cut or a sore, all the other hens pecked it. Human beings often behaved in the same way. As far as the Marine lieutenant was concerned, Ramage was the hen with the wound. Peck, peck, peck.

He was taken directly to a cabin – some wretched lieutenant had been displaced on his behalf. The Marine officer reminded him pompously that he had been appointed provost marshal and was responsible for guarding him.

"Make a good job of it," Ramage said, irritated by the man's patronizing manner. "It's worth four shillings a day to you."

"I have my duty!"

"Then guard me well: I'm a desperate man. Any moment I might jump over the side and elope with a mermaid."

The lieutenant looked at him blankly and left hurriedly. For a moment Ramage felt guilty about teasing him, but did the hen that pecked deserve any sympathy if the pecked hen suddenly pecked back?

An hour later Southwick arrived.

He had brought a uniform, fresh underwear, several pairs of silk stockings, a pair of highly polished boots and some carefully ironed stocks.

"If there's anything else you want, sir, tell me. Your steward reckons that will do for a couple of days."

"The trial will only last a day, and after that…"

"After that you'll get a new ship, sir," Southwick said stoutly.

"I hope so," Ramage said, realizing that the old Master was more in need of comfort than he was himself.

"I received your note, sir, and it's all arranged. The timing is important, I take it?"

"To the minute."

"Jackson's timed the boat from *La Perla* to the *Arrogant* by a route with no prying eyes to spoil the effect!"

"Good."

"I was worrying about the ballast, sir. Nothing laid down in the regulations, sir, Admiralty or Customs," Southwick said euphemistically, looking round and frowning, to indicate he was worrying about eavesdroppers and pointing to the pocket of one of the jackets he had brought with him.

"Exactly, so we needn't worry. With the charges I face, forgetting to fill in a form won't matter!"

"I suppose not," the Master said. "Will the 'ballast' help, sir?"

Ramage shrugged his shoulders. This was something he hoped he would be able to decide tonight, lying in his cot. Most of the time so far he had been receiving Admiral Goddard's broadsides; he needed the peace and quiet of his cot to decide where his own salvoes would be aimed. Did anyone get a share of the treasure trove, or did it all go to the Crown automatically? He could not find out without giving the game away.

Southwick said goodnight and Ramage sat at the tiny table to draft some headings for his defence. The trial was being brought on so quickly that he could demand a postponement to have more time. Obviously the charges against him had been prepared many days ago, when there seemed a chance that the *Triton* would limp in after the hurricane. That accounted for the speed with which the deputy judge advocate had produced the documents. A postponement would not help him, however, since it only increased the chances of Goddard discovering that Yorke and the French party were still alive. If he did, the charges would be changed.

He decided that he needed no notes, wiped the pen, folded the single sheet of paper and put it in his pocket, undressed and flopped down on the cot. He had eaten nothing since lunch, but felt too weary to try to get anything now. A moment later he was asleep.

CHAPTER **NINETEEN**

Ramage woke with a steward standing beside his cot, a lantern in one hand and a tray in the other.

"Dawn, sir," the steward said cheerfully. "Wind from the north at five knots, and no cloud. Plenty of mosquitoes, though."

He hung the lantern from a hook in a beam overhead.

"I'll put your breakfast here on the table, sir. There's a jug of hot water for shaving and I'll go and get you some more water for washing. My hands were full."

Ramage grunted, rubbed his eyes and wondered why the officers for whom the steward worked had not trained him to bring washing and shaving water first, and breakfast later. He sat up and carefully swung himself out of the cot. The cabin was airless and hot, and his body felt greasy. His teeth seemed coated with wool, his mouth tasted as though he had been sucking a penny and he had a headache.

The steward brought in a basin of water, soap and towel, and Ramage had a brisk wash, then lathered his face and shaved with great care, using a broken mirror held to the bulkhead by three bent nails. He rinsed his face, wiped it, and slowly dressed, smoothing the wrinkles from the silk stockings, pulling on his breeches and tucking the tail of the shirt in with as much deliberation as a dowager dressing for a court ball. By the time he had tied his stock, combed his hair and sat down to his breakfast he had succeeded in keeping his mind closed to the thought of the forthcoming trial.

He sipped the coffee, almost cold by now, nibbled at some bread and left the rest of the food. Finally, he put the tray down on the deck and took the pen and paper out of his pocket.

He wrote "Defence" across the top of the page and underlined it carefully. No thoughts came to him, so he wrote out from memory the tenth Article of War, pleased that he could even remember all the capital letters.

"Every Flag Officer, Captain, and Commander in the Fleet, who, upon Signal or Order of Fight, or sight of any Ship or Ships which it may be his Duty to engage, or who, upon Likelihood of Engagement, shall not make the necessary Preparations for Fight, and shall not in his own Person, and according to his Place, encourage the inferior Officers and Men to fight courageously, shall suffer Death, or such other punishment…a Court martial shall deem him to deserve; and if any Person in the Fleet shall treacherously or cowardly yield or cry for quarter, every Person so offending…shall suffer death."

Good stirring stuff, Ramage thought bitterly, but what the devil had it to do with the fact that he had successfully beaten off the *Peacock*'s attack on the *Topaz*?

Of course, it had none; but the Admiral was accusing him of not engaging the *Peacock*. Everyone would have to admit that in the darkness they saw the *Triton*'s guns firing. By skilful questioning the Admiral could make the officers serving on board the *Lion* admit that they could not be sure how close the Triton was and that some of the flashes could have been from the *Greyhound* frigate. Did the *Triton*'s crew fight courageously? Only the *Triton*'s officers and men could answer that one, and who would believe their evidence? Obviously they would say that they had for fear they too would be charged under the past part of the same Article.

He began writing again, this time the twelfth Article of War.

"Every Person in the Fleet, who through Cowardice, Negligence, or Disaffection, shall in Time of Action withdraw or keep back, or not come into the Fight or Engagement, or shall not do his utmost to take or destroy every Ship which it shall be his Duty to engage, and to assist and relieve all and every of His Majesty's Ships, or those of His Allies, which it shall be his Duty to assist and relieve, every such Person so offending...shall suffer death."

Well, that was really the trump card. It was the one under which Admiral John Byng had been accused in 1756; the one under which he was shot on the *St George*'s quarterdeck.

The first Article was obviously intended to muzzle the *Triton*'s officers – to discredit their evidence, anyway. The second was the one with which Goddard planned to hang him. Ramage remembered they'd intended to hang Admiral Byng, until the old man protested at the indignity and traded the rope for a Marine firing squad...

It had been dark and the officers in the *Lion* could be made to say the *Triton* attacked the *Peacock* dangerously late and at long range. "Or keep back", the Article said. Engaging from a safe range was "keeping back". That was all Goddard had to prove, and without evidence from the *Greyhound* or the *Topaz* it wouldn't be difficult.

If Ramage managed to slip through all those traps there was still the twenty-seventh Article. He wrote down:

"The Officers and Seamen of all ships, appointed for Convoy and Guard of Merchant Ships, or of any other, shall diligently attend to that Charge...and whosoever shall be faulty therein, and shall not faithfully perform their Duty, and defend the Ships and Goods in their Convoy, without diverting to other Parts or Occasions, or refusing or neglecting to fight in their Defence, if they be assailed, or running away cowardly, and submitting the Ships of their Convoy to Peril and Hazard...be punished criminally according to the Quality of their Offences, be it by Pains of Death, or other punishment, according as shall be adjudged fit by the Court martial."

Having written the three Articles, Ramage took a fresh sheet, once again wrote "Defence" across the top and once again found himself staring at the single word on the page several minutes later.

He needed a walk round the deck in the fresh air. Perhaps a look up at the *Arrogant*'s starboard fore yardarm would sharpen his wits. He banged on the door, called the sentry and told him to pass the word for the marshal.

The Marine lieutenant was there, opening the door, before the man had time to call.

"What do you want?"

"Good morning," Ramage said politely.

"Oh – good morning. You..."

"Want some exercise."

"You can't – "

"Then send for the surgeon."

"Why, you're not ill – are you?"

"I'll want a certificate to postpone the trial."

"What on earth are – "

"I have a splitting headache and I can't work on my defence."

"Your defence!" the man sneered. "It shouldn't take very long to write *that* out!"

"The surgeon," Ramage said and sat down abruptly.

"Oh, very well! Half an hour's walk, then."

Up on deck it promised to be a fine day; with luck the Trade winds would set in early and keep a breeze blowing through the great cabin. As Ramage paced up and down, with the marshal following a few steps behind, he looked round at the anchored ships.

At least five captains would be cursing at the thought of having to spend the day sitting at his trial – a minimum of five were necessary to form a court martial – but the thought gave him no satisfaction and he paced up and down. He watched seamen go to the flag locker, secure two sequences of flags to the signal halyards, and then hoist them smartly after tying them into neat bundles.

Ramage watched idly as the first bundle reached the block and one of the seamen gave a sharp tug on the halyard to break it out.

Automatically Ramage read the signal. Number 223. He couldn't remember the exact wording, but it was to the effect that flag officers, captains, commanders and anyone else concerned in the court martial that had been ordered were to report on board the ship whose name would be pointed out. A few minutes later the signal was hauled down and another one run up. The flags breaking out gave the Arrogant's pendant number.

Then, showing they had been ready, the Union flag streamed out from the *Arrogant*'s mizzen peak, indicating that a court martial was to be held on board.

His own court martial! It seemed unreal, remote and so distant from its cause, that wild night when the *Triton*'s carronades were cutting swathes through the boarders covering the *Peacock*'s deck, and Jackson was blazing away at her helmsmen with a musketoon. In reality the court-martial flag now flying from the Arrogant had its origins in the trial of his father. Linking that trial and this was one man, Jebediah

Arbuthnot Goddard, then a captain and now Rear-Admiral of the White.

He pulled out his watch. A minute past seven. The trial began in an hour and a half.

Ransom, the provost marshal, who had been standing against the taffrail, came up to Ramage.

"Come on, back to your cell."

"Cell?"

"Cabin, then."

"Do you have to be so obviously crude and unpleasant? I've not been found guilty yet."

"You will be," Ransom sneered.

"If I'm not, you'd better watch yourself," Ramage said angrily. "You're behaving more like a jackal than a gentleman. Just make sure the body's dead before you get to work."

"Carrion," Ransom said viciously, "all carrion!"

At that moment someone called Ransom's name. The voice was contemptuous, and it sounded familiar. Ramage looked round to see Captain Croucher standing watching, his eyes glittering like a lizard's under the jutting eyebrows. He looked angry and Ramage turned away so that neither man should think he was trying to eavesdrop. Croucher made no particular attempt to keep his voice low, however, and Ramage heard a few words here and there.

"...think you're doing?...you can at least try...gentleman ...only accused...even if condemned...might...your turn one day..."

A chastened Ransom came back. Croucher had frightened him.

"My lord," he said, "we'd better go below."

"I don't use my title," Ramage snapped. "You know that!"

"Er – yes, as you please."

Ramage went down to the cabin puzzled by Croucher's behaviour. Clearly the man had overheard Ramage's exchange with Ransom, but why was Croucher, of all people, concerned about the way Ramage was being treated by the acting provost marshal? He was not a man to do another a good turn unless he had a reason. Had Goddard's behaviour in the hurricane brought about a change of heart?

An hour later the *Lion*'s yawl was alongside the *Arrogant* and Ramage climbed up the side and stood watching as Ransom scrambled after him, carrying both their swords. When he finally managed to get on board without falling, Ramage could not resist saying: "Next time you're appointed a provost marshal, don't let the prisoner surrender his sword until you're both on board the ship where the trial's being held. You might drop it and find yourself being sued for a hundred guineas for a new one."

The Marine lieutenant flushed, and one of the *Arrogant*'s lieutenants, obviously the officer of the day, said unsympathetically, "He's right, you know; only a fool goes up a ship's side with two swords, and you seem to be clumsier than most!"

He turned to Ramage.

"The presence of our military friend here makes me think you are probably the unfortunate fellow inscribed on my list as 'Lieutenant Ramage, the prisoner'."

Ramage grinned and gave a mock bow. " 'Lieutenant Ramage-the-Prisoner' at your service."

The lieutenant marked his list and turned to the provost marshal.

"And you, my nimble friend, are probably the King's bad bargain herein listed as 'Lieutenant Ransom, acting provost marshal upon the occasion', and if you'll but nod your head,

I'll bestow a tick against the name as a slight token of my approval."

Ransom nodded dumbly, overwhelmed by the lieutenant's bantering manner.

"Well," the lieutenant continued, "you have committed the ultimate social solecism by arriving too early for the ball. Numerous brave and distinguished post captains must first board us, not to mention an admiral named God Ard, or should it be 'ard God?, and dance the opening minuet before you'll be allowed to blunder on to the floor and fall flat on your face because you've got your sword caught between your legs. Ah me," he said, with a delicate yawn, "what pitfalls face an acting provost marshal. You'll have earned your four shillings a day by the time the sun sets."

He turned to Ramage: "If you're planning to escape, be pleased to wait until after the end of my watch: t'would be a pity if my remarkably promising career was brought to an untimely end for failing to stop you. The Navy can't afford to lose brilliant young men like me."

"How could you possibly think I'd be so thoughtless?" Ramage said. "Only a bounder would escape before the forenoon watch."

"I'm glad you see things my way," the lieutenant said, "such a pleasure to deal with a gentleman: we seem to be getting such a poor class of fellow these days, don't you agree?"

"Indeed," Ramage said gravely. "Very poor."

"Yes, a sad business. What did you say your name was?" he asked the Marine suddenly.

"Alfred Ransom."

The lieutenant turned to Ramage in mock despair. "*Alfred* – you see what I mean? And where the devil did you get that surname? Was your grandfather a kidnapper? Or just a plain moneylender whose rates of interest made his unfortunate clients think of ransom?"

Before the Marine had time to answer the lieutenant waved him away. "Go and walk round the belfry – here come some of Mr Ramage's judges. Captain Ormsby, closely followed by Captain Robinson of the *Valiant*, are about to grace us with their presence."

Ramage and Ransom walked the *Arrogant*'s deck for more than half an hour as the captains arrived from their ships. Rossi was acting as coxswain of *La Perla*'s little boat and brought over Southwick, Appleby, Jackson and Stafford. As the Italian called out orders for the boat to leave the *Arrogant*'s side he caught sight of Ramage and, still looking ahead, said loudly in a broad Neapolitan accent, "*Sta tranquille, comandante!*"

Ramage smiled down at him, and then looked over at Jackson and Stafford. It was unlikely that they had ever been so smartly turned out before; Ramage had the feeling that everyone on board *La Perla* must have sorted through his wardrobe to find the best shirts and trousers for the two men.

The court martial was due to open in fifteen minutes, and Ramage saw the *Lion*'s launch coming from the shore. The fat figure in the stern sheets was unmistakable.

The lieutenant at the gangway turned to Ramage and, waving at the launch with his list, said: "The last guest invited to your reception."

Ramage nodded. "Thanks for your help. You have an invitation?"

"No, but I may drop in."

"Do, it passes away an idle hour or so."

With Rear-Admiral Goddard waddling aft and entering the great cabin, the court was within moments of assembling.

"Come on, Ramage, they've passed the word for us."

The seven captains ordered to the trial had gone into the great cabin and read out the dates of their commissions. Captain Napier, commanding the *Arrogant* and appointed president of the court, had seated them round the table in order of seniority. Syme, the fussy little deputy judge advocate, would have all his papers sorted out, quills sharpened, inkwell full, spectacles polished and Bible and Crucifix ready for administering the oath. Rear-Admiral Goddard was in there, with his faithful Hobson, ready to act as prosecutor. Croucher was there too, among the witnesses.

It was supposed to be a big day for Goddard. As far as he was concerned it would be the end of a vendetta, the end of a very long-drawn-out act of revenge against Admiral the Earl of Blazey. The night before, Ramage had wondered how he would feel walking these last few feet into the cabin. What he felt was anger. Anger that had come in the past few moments when he reflected that Goddard was not attacking him but his father. By attacking the Earl's son he was dealing the old man a blow against which he had no defence. Goddard was an assassin moving out silently in a dark Neapolitan street and striking with a stiletto…A cowardly blow, an unnecessary blow and perhaps a lethal blow. Goddard hoped that getting the son hanged for cowardice would shame the father into an early grave – the mother, too. Death before dishonour, or if not before, then dam' soon after. Every man's weakest point, his Achilles' heel, was his family. That was something Goddard had known all along.

Men like the Marine lieutenant, trotting along behind now and puffed up with the importance of being "provost marshal upon the occasion", were the jackals, content with snapping at the scraps. The Goddards of this world were the hyenas; bigger and more vicious, and although not brave, so greedy that occasionally they would leap on a badly wounded animal and drag it to the ground.

The sentry at the door of the great cabin snapped to attention and as Ramage removed his hat before going through the door Ransom pushed him aside, chest stuck out, shoulders back, Ramage's sword tucked under his left arm like a telescope, and marched into the cabin. Exasperated, Ramage stopped outside the door and watched Ransom striding in, straight to the two empty chairs, one for the prisoner and one behind it for the provost marshal.

Eight captains, counting Croucher, an admiral, the deputy judge advocate, several lieutenants, Southwick, Appleby, Jackson, Stafford and various other witnesses, watched as Ransom marched. He halted, stamping his feet, and turned to direct his prisoner to the chair.

The Captain seated at the head of the table raised his eyebrows.

"Pray, what are you supposed to be doing, lieutenant?"

Ransom looked round wildly. "My prisoner!"

"You are acting as the provost marshal?"

"Yes, sir!"

"Well, your prisoner appears to have eluded you."

"I – well, sir, he was…I have his sword!"

"We need the prisoner, lieutenant," the Captain said. "You are from the *Lion*, I assume?"

"Yes, sir," Ransom stammered.

"I thought so," Napier murmured. "Run along and fetch your prisoner."

Ramage, standing just outside the door, was puzzled by Napier's reference to the *Lion* – it seemed a calculated snub to Croucher…He stepped into the cabin before Ransom was halfway to the door, gave a slight bow, and walked deliberately to the empty chair as if Ransom did not exist.

Syme, the deputy judge advocate, had stood up and half turned to watch him. Goddard was looking away, pretending complete indifference.

"Sit down," Captain Napier said, "I want to sort out some papers."

The President was giving Ramage a minute or two to get his bearings. A long table covered with a green baize cloth ran almost the width of the cabin, and eight men sat round it. At the head was Napier, with Syme opposite him at the foot. Three captains sat down one side and three the other, and Ramage knew they were sitting in order of seniority left and right of Napier, with the juniors at the bottom, next to Syme. Ramage's chair was four feet from the table on Syme's left. An empty chair, for witnesses, was four feet from Syme's right hand. Clear of the table and over on Captain Napier's left sat Rear-Admiral Goddard, as prosecutor, with Hobson in another chair just behind him.

Standing in a group behind Admiral Goddard were the witnesses: Croucher, Southwick, several lieutenants – presumably the *Lion*'s officers – and, not looking at all ill-at-ease, Jackson and Stafford.

Captain Napier took out his watch, put it down on the table in front of him, rapped with his knuckles and said in a clipped, incisive voice: "Gentlemen, it is half past eight o'clock: the court is in session. Admiral" – he turned to Goddard – "can you see that all the witnesses for the prosecution are here?"

Goddard nodded indifferently.

"Mr Ramage – are your witnesses all here?"

"All the witnesses I was able to assemble in the time available, sir."

"Very well: I shall ask that question again when the court is sworn and it can be noted in the minutes."

Ramage looked at him and thought that Captain Napier had a real interest in administering justice. Admiral Goddard was staring at Napier with the look a man might give his wife at a reception if she suddenly announced that she had discovered certain of his defects. Ramage had a feeling that Captain Napier's name must be near the top of the captains' list, so near that he could soon expect his flag. Too senior and self-confident to be unduly impressed by Goddard.

Napier rapped the table again. "Carry on, Mr Syme."

The deputy judge advocate stood up, adjusted his spectacles, picked up a single sheet of paper and, after looking round at all the captains, began reading Sir Pilcher Skinner's order for the court martial. Then he read: "By Vice-Admiral Sir Pilcher Skinner…Commander-in-Chief of His Majesty's ships…at Jamaica…a court martial to try Lieutenant Nicholas Ramage, of his Majesty's late ship the *Triton*, on various charges laid by Rear-Admiral Goddard…I do…hereby authorize you to execute the office of judge advocate upon the above occasion. For which this shall be your warrant."

Syme looked round, as if half expecting someone to challenge it.

"This is addressed to Harold Syme, esquire," he added pompously.

Napier nodded, and the man reached down for another page.

Napier was a tall man with iron-grey hair, an aquiline nose and eyes revealing a shrewd sense of humour. He had an indefinable air of authority and Ramage guessed that he was a man who commanded without ever raising his voice.

Syme began reading again, this time the seven names, listed in seniority beginning with Napier, of the men forming the court. He glanced to the left or right as he reached each name; Captain Lockyer, a plump, fatherly man who reminded

Ramage of Southwick, sat on the President's left, and Captain Robinson, sandy-haired, red-faced and looking young despite his seniority, sat on his right. Woodgate sat next to him and Hamilton sat next to Lockyer. Ramage looked at Hamilton again. He was a nondescript man except for his eyes. They were spaced wide apart and blue and they looked shifty. Ormsby, at the end of the table on the President's left, was young and obviously flustered. The single epaulet on his right shoulder showed he had less than three years' seniority. Innes, opposite him, also had less than three years' seniority and was a plump young man who looked as if he was more at home astride a horse on the hunting field than commanding a ship of war.

Now Syme picked up the Bible and walked round the table to Napier. Putting the Bible in front of him he said, his voice taking on a monotone in deference to the solemn occasion: "Place your right hand on the Holy Evangelist and repeat your christian and surnames."

Napier stood and said: "James Royston Napier."

Syme then read out, phrase by phrase, the oath by which Napier swore "I will duly administer justice according to my conscience, the best of my understanding and the custom of the Navy in like cases…"

After Syme had administered the same oath to the other six captains, Napier administered an oath of secrecy to Syme, who then went back to his seat.

As Napier looked round the cabin, he had as much moral authority over its occupants as a judge.

"Read the charges, Mr Syme, slowly and *audibly*."

Syme looked up indignantly, stung by the instruction, but he obeyed. As he read, Ramage looked across at Goddard. The man wiped his face once, then sat with his hands clasped, staring at the deck a few feet in front of him.

Ramage saw a squalid opportunist grasping plump hands together like an ingratiating undertaker. The man had risen quickly in the Navy and had enormous "interest". One day he might well achieve the highest rank – providing he never had to lead a fleet into action. He was not a man that lowly lieutenants would choose as an enemy…But, Ramage thought ruefully, the choice had not been up to this lowly lieutenant; Goddard had chosen him.

Napier turned to Goddard as Syme finished his reading.

"Your first witness, sir?"

Goddard pointed to Croucher.

"All other witnesses leave the court," Napier said, waving to Syme.

Syme motioned Captain Croucher to the chair on his right as the rest of the witnesses left the cabin. A dozen other people, among them the lieutenant whose breezy manner had so cheered Ramage at the gangway, sat at the back of the cabin.

Croucher gave his name and took the oath without once glancing at Goddard.

Syme looked severely at both Goddard and Croucher, as though they had never attended a court martial before, and said: "You must give me time to write down each question before it is answered. And then give me time to write down the answer."

Goddard gestured to Hobson, who was holding several sheets of paper in his hand.

"The first questions are written down."

Goddard and his cronies seemed to have prepared the case well. If the prosecutor had the questions written on slips of paper which were passed to the deputy judge advocate to read aloud the accused had to answer at once. If the prosecutor spoke the question so the deputy judge advocate could write it down and then address it to the accused, it gave the prisoner time to think about his answer. With the question already written down, the deputy judge advocate need only number it, make a note of the number in his minute of the trial, and ask the question at once.

Hobson went over to stand by Syme, handing him a page with the first question. Before the deputy judge advocate had time to read it, Captain Napier said: "Has the accused all his witnesses available?"

"No, I have only those immediately available."

Ramage had already thought through the probable sequence of question and answer, and now that the court was sitting there was little Goddard could do even if he suspected that there was some sort of a trap behind Ramage's carefully chosen words.

"What do you mean by 'immediately available'?" Napier asked.

"Only those that could attend the court when it opened, sir."

Syme jammed his spectacles back on his nose. "All those on the list you gave me are present," he said angrily.

"Quite," Ramage said.

"What do you mean by that?" Napier asked.

"In view of the gravity of the charges I face, sir – all of them are capital – and my present lack of witnesses, I hope that the court will be indulgent should any other witnesses become available."

Would Napier just leave it at that or demand more details? Ramage tried to look nonchalant.

"Very well. Carry on, Mr Syme."

"I haven't noted all that down yet," Syme said sourly, and Ramage guessed that the deputy judge advocate had been so absorbed in what was being said that he had forgotten to write.

Hobson handed him the first page.

"Were you," he asked Croucher, "commanding the *Lion* on the eighteenth day of July last when, during an attack upon a ship of the convoy, His Majesty's ship *Triton* did – "

"Stop!" Napier snapped. "Strike that from the record." He looked directly at the Admiral. "The prosecution is no doubt aware of the meaning of the phrase 'leading question'?"

When Goddard said nothing, Napier said quietly: "The court requires an answer. First," he said to Syme, "note my question in the minutes."

When he saw Syme had written it, he motioned to Goddard. "The prosecution understands," the Admiral said grudgingly.

"Very well. The deputy judge advocate will read written questions carefully before speaking them aloud. Carry on."

For a moment or two Ramage wondered why Napier was on his side and then realized that he was not. He was just conducting the trial impartially. Ramage's only previous experience of a court martial was the one staged – and "staged" was the right word – by Croucher, in Bastia. There the President had used his position to twist everything in favour of the prosecution.

Goddard decided to abandon the written questions, frame new ones, and speak them aloud.

"What were you doing on the eighteenth day of July?"

"I was commanding His Majesty's ship *Lion*."

"What were your duties?"

"Flying the flag of the Rear-Admiral and escorting a convoy from Barbados to Jamaica."

"Was there any unusual occurrence that night?"

"Yes, a French privateer attacked one of the ships."

"What was that ship's position in the convoy?"

"Leading the starboard column."

"Where was the *Lion* at this time?"

"In her proper position ahead of the centre column of the convoy."

"Which of the King's ships was closest to the merchantman that was attacked?"

"The *Triton* brig."

"Who commanded the *Triton*?"

"The accused."

"How was the attack made on the merchant ship, and what was the merchantman's name?"

"The ship was the *Topaz*. The privateer came up from astern, following the line of ships, and went alongside the *Topaz* and attacked her."

"Was there any chance," Goddard asked, "of the privateer being seen from the *Lion*?"

"None," Croucher said. "It was a dark night and she was a mile or so away, and hidden against all the ships on the northern side of the convoy."

"Was a ship responsible for that section of the convoy?"

"Yes, the *Triton*."

"Did she prevent the attempt?"

"She eventually fired from a distance."

"At what distance, and from what bearing?"

"From perhaps a mile. From the starboard bow of the convoy."

Ramage wondered if he would remember all the discrepancies.

"For how long did the *Triton* engage the privateer – or, at least, fire on her?"

"For perhaps a quarter of an hour."

Napier said: "Can you be more precise?"

"For a quarter of an hour."

"Did the privateer capture the *Topaz*?" Goddard asked.

"No, the *Topaz* drove her off with her own guns, and the *Greyhound* frigate came up and captured her."

"What, to the best of your knowledge and belief, would you have expected the *Triton* to have done?"

"Hauled her wind and come up to the privateer before she reached the *Topaz*."

Captain Robinson raised his hand.

"Are you aware of any reason why she did not do so?" he asked.

"None. Nor did the prisoner subsequently give any."

"Answer only the question you are asked," Napier said. "Strike the last part of that answer from the minutes."

Goddard wriggled impatiently and, at a gesture from Napier, continued the questioning.

"From your long experience as an officer and from your knowledge of the circumstances, did the action of the prisoner lead you to any conclusions?"

Hmm, thought Ramage, very neat. It's probably phrased illegally but none of us knows enough of the law to challenge it. Napier is frowning but obviously not sure of his ground.

"Yes," Croucher said, almost whispering, "he fell under the tenth, twelfth and seventeenth Articles of War."

"Can you be more specific?"

Croucher shifted from one foot to the other as though Goddard was forcing him to give the required answers.

"He kept back from the fight: he did not engage the ship he should have engaged; he did not do his utmost. He did not defend the ships of the convoy."

Captain Innes, sitting nearest to Ramage, turned to Croucher.

"You have deposed that the *Triton* did open fire."

369

"Yes," Croucher said.

Goddard asked: "In the time available – from the time of sighting the privateer – could she have closed the range?"

"Stop!" Napier said crisply. "Strike out that question."

Ramage stood up. "With respect, sir, I don't object to it."

"Good heavens!" Napier exclaimed. "Very well, carry on."

Croucher said: "Yes, she could have closed the range."

"No more questions," Goddard said.

"The court has some questions before the prisoner examines the witness. You said the *Lion* was a mile ahead of the convoy?"

"About a mile, to the best of my knowledge."

"And ahead of the centre?"

"Yes."

"How many columns of ships were there in the convoy, and how far apart?"

"Seven, and two cables apart."

"So the front of the convoy extended two thousand four hundred yards?"

"That is correct."

"And the *Triton* was 'perhaps a mile' on the starboard bow of the convoy?"

"That is correct."

"Thank you." Napier said.

Napier's spotted a discrepancy, Ramage thought, cursing his mathematics. As Syme began reading back the evidence, Ramage pencilled a right-angled triangle on a piece of paper, wrote in "*Lion*" at the apex, "centre ship" at the right angle, and "*Topaz*" at the other end of the base line. One mile from the *Lion* to the centre ship; twelve hundred yards from the centre ship to the *Topaz*. The hypotenuse would be the distance from the *Lion* to the *Topaz*.

He drew a second triangle, substituting the *Triton* for the *Topaz*, so the base was the distance from the centre ship to the *Triton*. The hypotenuse was the distance from the *Lion* to the *Triton*. Bully for Pythagoras. A mile and a quarter from the *Lion* to the *Topaz*; roughly two miles to the *Triton*. Two? He checked his figures again. A few yards short of two.

"The prisoner may examine the witness," Napier said.

Ramage stood up.

"Could you tell the court the position assigned to the *Triton*?"

"Abreast the *Topaz* and two cables off."

"If the *Triton* was as far out of position as a mile off, why did you not make a signal to her?"

"I could not see her in the darkness!"

"So you did not know she was there?"

"No," Croucher said indignantly, not noticing the infuriated look on Goddard's face.

"But you have already told the court where the *Triton* was. How did you see her and estimate the distance?"

"From the flash of the guns when she opened fire."

"Would you agree that the distances," Ramage asked, glancing at his notes, "were from the *Lion* to the *Topaz* roughly a mile and a quarter, and from the *Lion* to the *Triton*, about two miles?"

"Without pencil and paper, I cannot."

Napier said: "If the witness will accept the court's mathematics, those distances agree approximately with the evidence the witness has already given."

"I'm grateful," Croucher said.

"When the *Triton* opened fire on the privateer, what was her rate of fire?"

"Slow and sporadic," Croucher said uncertainly. "Single guns."

"How slow, would you estimate?"

"Two or three guns a minute. Less, perhaps."

"But you saw the flashes and you knew they were the *Triton's* guns?"

"Of course."

"Can you, under oath," Ramage said deliberately, emphasizing each word, "explain how you estimated the distance of two miles in the dark with such certainty when you only had 'slow and sporadic' flashes to go by?"

"Experience, of course. I have served at sea for many years," Croucher said stiffly.

"Would you care to describe your previous experience in estimating distances under such circumstances, and what proof you subsequently had that such estimates were correct?"

Goddard leapt to his feet.

"Impertinence," he shouted. "Sheer damn'd impertinence. The accused is impugning the honour of one of the most experienced – "

"Order!" Napier snapped. "You will not make further interruptions of that nature. The question is perfectly in order. It is a very important point, and the court is trying to get at the truth of this matter."

The seven captains round the table looked at Croucher.

"One can never subsequently check one's estimates; that's absurd. But after being in action many times…"

Ramage waited, but when Croucher said no more he knew there was no need to labour the point.

"You referred to a privateer," he said. "Could you tell the court the nature of this vessel?"

Once again Goddard was on his feet. "This is absurd! She was full of Frenchmen and – "

Napier rapped the table and Goddard broke off.

"This is the second time the court has had to warn the prosecution…"

Goddard sat down like a sulky schoolboy, and Napier continued: "The witness will answer the question."

"She was a fairly large ship. She came up from astern – "

"What was the position you had assigned to her in the convoy?" Ramage interrupted quietly, and saw the heads of all seven captains jerk up in surprise.

"She was the eighth ship in the starboard column."

"The last ship in the column led by the *Topaz*?"

"Yes."

"When did the ship join the convoy?"

"I ought to explain that – "

Napier rapped the table. "Please just answer the question; you are not allowed to make statements."

"I can't be forced to incriminate…" Croucher began unhappily. He broke off as Goddard stared at him coldly. Slowly, as though they were the guns of a broadside, the seven captains turned to look at Goddard, those sitting with their backs to him swivelling round in their chairs.

"Do you wish the court to be cleared while this point is decided?" Napier asked Goddard.

"I don't know what the witness is talking about," Goddard said.

"Very well," Napier said crisply, and turned back to Croucher. "You will answer the question."

Croucher took a deep breath. "She joined the convoy in Barbados."

"A British ship?"

"No. Yes, I mean…"

Robinson held up his hand.

"The court understood you to say she was a French privateer."

"Well, she was!"

"But you have just said she was a British ship."

"We thought she was," Croucher said desperately. "She had all the correct papers. Her master claimed she was a runner and wanted to join the convoy to Jamaica. He said the route to Jamaica was thick with privateers!"

Captain Innes began laughing until he saw Napier frowning at him and gesturing to Ramage to continue. Ramage took out his watch and looked at the time, then asked: "Was any report made to you or to the Admiral about the behaviour of this ship at any time before she attacked the *Topaz*?"

"Yes," Croucher said grudgingly.

"Was this report in writing or verbal?"

"In writing."

"Do you have the report with you?"

"No."

"Do you recall what it said?"

Napier interrupted. "I'm not too sure whether the court ought not to insist on this report being put in as evidence."

"It is available, if required," Goddard said.

"Very well. Continue."

"It said, to the best of my recollection, that the ship – the *Peacock* was her name – had ranged up abreast her next ahead in the previous night."

"Did it say any more?"

"Well, it hinted that something might be wrong."

"Who made that written report?"

"You did."

"And what was the distance of the *Triton* from the ship ahead of the *Peacock*?"

"Well, the ships were a cable astern of each other. Six cables."

"So in the darkness the *Triton*'s lookouts had spotted a suspicious movement twelve hundred yards away."

"I suppose so."

"What action was taken over this report?"

"A frigate was sent to investigate," Croucher exclaimed triumphantly, glad to have some positive evidence to give.

"What did she do?"

"She reported that all was well."

"I asked what she did, not what she reported."

"Well, she went close to the other merchantman and hailed her."

"Do you know now who in fact answered the frigate's hail?"

"Yes, a French prize crew."

"How did a French prize crew come to be on board her?"

"They had been put on board the previous night by the *Peacock*."

"Thank you," Ramage said heavily. "You gave evidence that on the night that the *Peacock* attacked the *Topaz*, the *Triton* engaged her. Do you think the *Triton*'s fire drove off the *Peacock*, or contributed to her capture?"

"Not that I know of," Croucher said. "It was the alertness of the *Topaz*'s own officers and the bravery of her own crew with the assistance of the *Greyhound*."

"How can you be sure?"

"The captain of the *Topaz* boarded the *Lion* the next day and made a report to the Admiral."

"In writing?"

"No, verbally, I understand."

"Do you have my written report on the episode?"

"No," Croucher said nervously, glancing at Goddard. "You made no such report."

Ramage's jaw dropped. He looked over at Goddard, who was staring at him, his eyes hate-laden and triumphant. So he had managed to persuade Croucher to condone the deliberate suppression of evidence.

"Did you make any charges or remonstrances when I came on board the *Lion* on the morning after the attack?"

"You know very well that the Admiral did. And I gather that Mr Yorke, the Master of the *Topaz*, did so as well."

Napier was watching Ramage, expecting a protest from him about hearsay evidence, but Ramage rubbed the scar over his brow and could not resist asking: "Did Mr Yorke make any specific accusations of cowardice?"

"I was not there," Croucher said lamely. "But I gather he was very bitter against you."

"He accused me of cowardice?"

"So I was told."

"And anything else?"

"I understand that he said you'd nearly been the death of his passengers, and that he was going to complain to the Commander-in-Chief."

"Did he?"

"No. They were all drowned in the hurricane."

"Did Mr Yorke make any written accusations of cowardice?"

"The Admiral thought it unnecessary. There was no hint that such a tragedy would overtake them. It could have been done on arrival at Kingston."

"Did the captain of the *Greyhound* frigate make any written report about the *Peacock*'s attack?"

"He probably did, but it was not delivered to the flagship."

Ramage glanced at his watch again to have time to think. Croucher puzzled him. The man seemed nervous, many of his answers were qualified and the quick glances at Goddard seemed to indicate that he was giving evidence against his will and trying to say the minimum that would gain him Goddard's approval. Had Croucher at last seen the Admiral for what he was? Had his behaviour in the hurricane finally sickened him? Plenty of questions, Ramage thought sourly, and damned few answers...

"I have only two more questions. From what you saw, from your own professional knowledge and experience, do you consider I was guilty of cowardice during the attack by the *Peacock*?"

"I was too far away to see everything."

"Do you consider the accusation of cowardice made against me by Mr Yorke of the *Topaz* was justified?"

"From what I have heard of the incident, yes."

"Thank you. I have no more questions."

The seven captains were looking at Ramage as though he had gone mad. The deputy judge advocate's pen had been flying over the paper and he had been feverishly pushing his spectacles back as they kept sliding down his nose.

Croucher looked uneasy. His earlier doubts about his estimate of distances were of little consequence but Ramage's questions had brought out how little he knew from his own experience and how much he had heard from Goddard.

Syme began reading back the evidence and Ramage sat down and pulled out his watch again. Syme had five minutes to get through it and have Croucher sign it as a correct record of his evidence.

At that moment there was a knock on the door and Ramage realized that he had not decided exactly how to handle the next episode. Napier looked up angrily, signalled to the provost marshal, who went to the door, had a whispered conversation with someone outside, shut the door again and marched over to the President.

He placed a letter before Napier and whispered something. The President waved him away and opened the letter. Three small white cards dropped out, and Napier, obviously puzzled, glanced at them before reading the letter. He then looked up at Ramage, and folded the letter and cards.

Syme finished reading the evidence and Napier glanced at Croucher.

"You may remain in court if you wish," he said.

He has guessed, Ramage thought to himself; or if he has not guessed, he suspects!

"Mr Ramage," Napier said, "you mentioned earlier that you might have further witnesses. It appears they have arrived. This has come for you, and the court agrees to your receiving it."

He held up the letter, and Ramage walked over to collect it. Goddard was lolling back in his chair, completely satisfied with the way things were going and making little effort to hide his boredom. He began polishing his nails with an ivory-backed strip of chamois leather, and Croucher moved to the back of the cabin and took the chair offered him by a lieutenant.

Ramage went to his place and sat down before reading the letter. Unsigned, it said simply: "Three witnesses of extreme importance to the defence are waiting to give evidence."

He read the names on the visiting cards. The first said "Sydney Yorke", the second was larger, and embossed on it was "Le Duc de Bretagne", the third said, "Le Comte de Chambéry".

Ramage felt his head spinning. So the man calling himself "St Brieuc" was the Duke of Brittany, one of the most powerful men in France before the Revolution, a close friend of the late French King, and now the leader of the French refugees in London. "Valuable cargo" indeed! Goddard must have known his real identity – which meant that Goddard too was fighting for his professional life!

Sir Pilcher must be wanting to know why the Duke of Brittany had left the *Lion* – which survived the hurricane – and sailed on the *Topaz*, which foundered. Even if Sir Pilcher could be satisfied, the Admiralty – and the Government – would be ruthless. He imagined the Foreign Secretary's angry notes to the Admiralty – "Why did the Duke leave the *Lion*? How was it that a French privateer was allowed to attack the *Topaz*? With a hurricane coming, why was the Duke not made to return to the *Lion*?" Goddard could hardly tell the truth: that it had started because of something offensive he did or said to the Duke's daughter. He needed a scapegoat – and he had chosen the "cowardly" Lieutenant Ramage...

Ramage tried to decide which of the three men to call first. Better start with Yorke, because...he suddenly realized he had made a terrible mistake; a mistake so obvious that, his body rigid with fear, he could hardly believe it.

He had told St Brieuc – the Duke, rather – and Yorke to come at half past ten on the assumption that the prosecution case would be almost over by then. But the case was going so slowly that several prosecution witnesses had still to be called. He would not be able to call the defence witnesses before tomorrow morning, at the earliest. With the Duke, the Count and Yorke already on board the *Arrogant* – and Captain Napier had seen their visiting cards – it would be impossible to keep their existence secret for another ten minutes, let alone twenty-four hours. Without a surprise confrontation, he was lost...unless – he realized there was just one chance of springing his trap.

He stood up suddenly, with everyone except Goddard watching him.

"If it pleases the court, in view of the evidence given by the last prosecution witness, I feel that one of my witnesses is really more suited to be a prosecution witness."

Napier sat bolt upright, as though Ramage had suddenly stood on his head.

"A *prosecution* witness?"

"Yes, sir."

"I hope you know what you are doing!"

"Yes, sir."

Goddard stood up suspiciously.

"Who are you proposing as a prosecution witness?"

Ramage passed Yorke's card to Syme who, without glancing at it, walked over to give it to Goddard.

"On second thoughts, sir," Ramage said to Napier, "the second of my witnesses is also better suited to the prosecution's case – I am assuming of course, the court wishes to get at the truth of the charges."

Napier raised both hands in a despairing gesture, as if it was all beyond him.

Ramage handed the Duke's card to Syme, who dutifully gave it to the Admiral.

"Is that all?" Napier asked.

"The prosecution could have the third witness if it wished, sir."

There was a gasp from several people and Ramage looked round at Goddard. He had collapsed across his chair; his face was grey and he seemed to be panting for breath. The swine is having a fatal convulsion, Ramage thought coldly; he'll escape me yet!

Croucher ran from his seat to help Hobson, who was trying to lift Goddard's bulk squarely onto the chair.

"Send for the surgeon," Napier snapped.

Goddard was clutching his chest and fighting for breath and Croucher ripped at the stock, finally untying it. The seven captains watched without leaving their seats and on deck Ramage heard men shouting, passing the word for the surgeon.

The Admiral was gasping for breath, as though being strangled, and Ramage suddenly pictured himself, a noose round his neck, being hanged from the fore yardarm. If the sudden jerk did not break his neck, he too would be fighting for breath just like that. He glanced at the captains seated round the table. Their faces were impassive; each had seen death too often to get excited.

At that moment the surgeon arrived with his assistant and went straight to Goddard, who was by now ashen-faced but conscious, taking great gulping breaths and making an effort to sit upright. Croucher whispered something to the surgeon who, without bothering to examine the Admiral, went over and spoke quietly to Captain Napier, who nodded.

The surgeon gave brief instructions and his assistant, Hobson and two other officers who had been sitting at the back of the court, lifted the Admiral and carried him from the cabin.

As soon as the door shut behind them, Napier rapped the table.

"The court stands adjourned until tomorrow at half past eight in the forenoon. The accused will remain in the custody of the provost marshal."

Ramage stood up wearily as Ransom tapped him on the shoulder. The cabin was hot and his clothes seemed to stick to his body like wet pastry. His sword was still on the table. He'd gambled, and unless Admiral Goddard died between now and this time tomorrow morning, Ramage feared that he might have lost. As he followed Ransom out of the cabin, he admitted to himself that he ought to have followed Yorke's advice.

The little cabin on board the *Lion* was like an oven, although the door was open. Even the canvas stretched over battens to form bulkheads seemed to exude heat. Ramage had stripped off his shirt and sat in his breeches, naked from the waist up.

An hour after Ransom had brought him to the cabin and shut the door, giving loudly spoken orders to the Marine sentry, he had been surprised when a lieutenant came with a message from Captain Croucher to the effect that he was to be treated as a prisoner at large. It was a pleasant gesture, even if in practice it meant simply having the door open and no sentry outside. If he wanted to he could roam the ship – but that meant having every man on board staring at him, and Ramage preferred to stay in the cabin.

He was just mopping the perspiration from his chest with a towel when one of the ship's lieutenants appeared at the door. "Visitors for you, Ramage."

A moment later he saw Southwick and Yorke peering into the darkness of the cabin, their eyes still dazzled by the bright sun on deck.

"Is this a cabin or a clothes locker?" Yorke inquired quizzically.

"Stay out there a moment while I get dressed," Ramage said shortly. "I'm a prisoner at large, so we can take a turn on deck."

Five minutes later the three men were standing on deck in the shade of the awning, looking across at the town of Kingston and thankful for a gentle Trade wind breeze that did its best to keep them cool.

"He went on shore after about an hour," Southwick said without any preliminaries. "Just him and that whippersnapper Hobson. He'd got his colour back. Couldn't have been anything serious, otherwise they'd have kept him on board the *Arrogant,* or the surgeon would have gone with him in the yawl."

"Sounds as if it was a touch of the vapours," Yorke said blithely. "Had an old aunt who had an attack like that just as the Bishop of Lincoln was getting out of his coach to kiss her hand. One of the horses broke wind, and she thought it was the Bishop."

"Must be the same sort of thing," Ramage said. "It happened just as Goddard read the name on your visiting card."

"Whatever it was," Southwick said sourly, "it wasn't fatal, and that's all that matters. What's the next move, sir?"

"When the court convenes again tomorrow morning, Goddard will withdraw the charges. We've been over all that once."

"But will he get away with it, sir?" Southwick asked.

"I'll bet the deputy judge advocate is looking up all the precedents he can find, and Admiral Goddard is probably talking it all over with Sir Pilcher Skinner."

"Curious thing is that no one's come to *La Perla,*" Yorke said. "Once the secret was out the Duke sent a formal letter to the Governor, telling him that he'd arrived but was staying on board until your court martial ends, in case he can be of help."

"That's kind of him," Ramage said. But he knew there had not been time enough for anyone on shore to react to the news that, far from being dead, the Duke of Brittany was in the anchorage on board a tiny captured Spanish schooner.

Yorke glanced around to make sure no one was within earshot.

"Listen, do you really think Goddard will withdraw the charges now? What's to stop him going ahead, and as soon as the Duke and I have given our evidence, just get up and say it's all been a mistake? That if he'd been able to talk to us earlier, the charges wouldn't have been laid? That it simply *appeared* Lieutenant Ramage had behaved in a cowardly way, but now of course…and so on?"

Ramage suddenly realized that neither Southwick nor Yorke knew the extent of the evidence given in court that morning.

"If you were going to give evidence tomorrow, I suppose I shouldn't tell you this," he said, "but since you won't, I can talk freely. Captain Croucher this morning gave evidence on oath – in answer to questions from Admiral Goddard – that after the *Peacock* attack, you went on board the *Lion* and accused me of cowardice."

"Good God, what a lie! I can prove – "

"But you won't be giving evidence," Ramage said. "Not only did you accuse me, but to my face and in front of Admiral Goddard, and in – "

"But that's monstrous!" Yorke exclaimed angrily.

" – and in addition you said that I'd nearly caused the death of your passengers and they were complaining to the Commander-in-Chief."

Yorke had gone white, and leaned back against the breech of a gun. He seemed almost stupefied at what he had heard, and it was a minute or two before he spoke.

"I begin to understand what you were talking about yesterday. I thought you were – well, overwrought. These men can do anything they please!"

Ramage shook his head. "No, not quite. But Goddard has got to get this trial stopped for the simple reason that he can't risk having you and the Duke prove that he and Croucher not only perjured themselves, but actually conspired together to bring false charges against me for which the only penalty was death. The only way of stopping you both is to stop the trial."

"But the Commander-in-Chief..." Yorke said lamely.

"I'm sure the Commander-in-Chief is just as anxious as Goddard. Don't forget that he signed the order for the trial. Don't forget Goddard is his second-in-command. Don't forget that any scandal concerning Goddard also reflects on Sir Pilcher..."

"But the Duke will tell the Governor what happened!"

"And the Governor will forward any letter to London without comment. Once the Government know the Duke is alive and safe, they won't give a damn about the affair of some wretched young lieutenant!"

"The Duke would never allow that," Yorke said firmly.

"The Duke won't have any say in the matter. It's what the Admiralty decides that matters to me, and I can tell you the Admiralty won't want a scandal; certainly not one concerning the Commander-in-Chief and his second-in-command."

"What are you going to do, then?"

"Listen politely to what's said in court tomorrow, and prepare myself for another visit from the judge advocate so that I can read the wording of the new charges over the loss of the *Triton*."

"Well, what can we do?" Yorke asked soberly.

Ramage held up his hands helplessly. "I wish I knew."

"Perhaps Mr Yorke and the Duke ought to come over to the *Arrogant* when the court convenes tomorrow," Southwick said quietly. "Just in case, sir. After all, you never know."

Ramage gave a cynical laugh as he rubbed the scar over his brow. "I think we know well enough. Still, if they wish..."

"We'll be there," Yorke said. "The Duke is a very angry man."

"So am I," Ramage said. "After all, it's my neck we're trying

to save!"

CHAPTER TWENTY

The Marine sentry outside the *Arrogant*'s great cabin saluted smartly as Ramage followed Ransom through the door next morning. Although the early sun was bright and the sky clear, the ship still felt cool and, as he had done from the time he woke at dawn, Ramage tried to shut out all thought of the trial. He had slept badly – hope was hard to sustain in the darkness. Lying in his cot, a thousand pictures sped one after another through his mind; wild pictures that at any other time would come only with a high fever. Croucher standing on the *Lion*'s quarterdeck and giving the order that would run Ramage to the fore yardarm with a noose round his neck; his father receiving the news in Cornwall of his trial and execution; the Duke comforting a weeping Maxine...But when sleep finally came it was soon chased away by a bleary-eyed steward with the inevitable weak coffee.

He had washed, shaved and dressed with great deliberation, studying every movement. He found it was the only way of preventing his mind racing back to the trial, and was surprised how many everyday things were done without conscious thought. Shaving the left side of his face before the right, putting the left leg into his breeches before the right, slipping his left arm first into his jacket. Did left-handed people use their right hands and legs in the same way?

In the great cabin nothing had changed from the previous day: Napier was already seated at the head of the table with the other captains in their places; Syme was shuffling papers at the foot of the table; Admiral Goddard was sitting in the same chair with Hobson just behind him. For a moment Ramage found it hard to believe that the previous day's events were anything more than a half-remembered dream.

Napier glanced up, nodded briefly as Ramage sat down, and then tapped the table.

"The court is in session – are there any witnesses present who have yet to give evidence?"

He glanced round but no one spoke.

"Very well, the deputy judge advocate will read the minutes so far, and then we will proceed, since everyone has already been sworn."

As Syme reached for a small pile of papers on the table in front of him, Admiral Goddard stood up and coughed. His face glistened with perspiration; his eyes darted nervously from side to side. Captain Napier glanced up questioningly.

"The prosecution – " Goddard paused for a few moments, as if out of breath. "The prosecution wishes to state – with the court's permission, of course – that it withdraws all the charges against Lieutenant Ramage."

For a moment there was complete silence in the cabin; a silence in which every one of the seven captains turned to stare at the Admiral, and Syme's spectacles slid almost to the end of his nose.

Even as he jumped to his feet Ramage realized that Goddard had taken the court by surprise; Napier must have kept the contents of the letter to himself.

"Sir, I must protest!" Steady, he told himself; that was too loud, too sharp, too aggressive. "Capital charges have been made against me, and much of the prosecution's supporting evidence has already been given. I submit the prosecution cannot now withdraw the charges without one word of my defence being heard!"

Napier held up his hand. "The court will be cleared. The prosecutor and the prisoner will remain."

As soon as everyone else in the cabin had left, Napier turned to Goddard.

"The court wishes to know your reasons for withdrawing the charges."

Goddard shrugged his shoulders and wiped his lips with a handkerchief.

"The charges were drawn up upon assumptions which have subsequently proved to be incorrect."

"What assumptions?" Napier asked.

"On the assumption that there were no survivors from the *Topaz*."

"What?" Napier exclaimed in surprise. "Do you really mean that there was only one assumption?"

"No, of course not," Goddard said hurriedly. "That was merely one of the assumptions."

Napier turned to Ramage. "What do you say to this?"

"Has the prosecution questioned any of the survivors of the *Topaz*, sir?"

Napier looked at Goddard. "Have you?"

"Well, no, not yet."

Ramage shrugged his shoulders and, looking directly at Napier, said quietly: "Then how can the prosecution possibly know that any survivor's evidence could alter the case, sir? I am accused of cowardice in action – how can the fact that the *Topaz*'s people weren't drowned possibly affect that accusation?"

"Really!" Goddard exclaimed angrily. "That isn't the point at all. The prosecution has every right to withdraw the charges if it wishes!"

Napier looked questioningly at the deputy judge advocate. "Can it? What are the precedents for that, Syme? I've never met such a case."

Syme took off his spectacles nervously.

"I – er, I can find no exact precedent, sir. Yesterday, out of curiosity, I tried to find a similar case – simply out of curiosity, of course – and the nearest seemed to be the case of Admiral Keppel."

Napier looked puzzled. "I fail to see the connection."

"When charges were brought against Admiral Keppel by Vice-Admiral Sir Hugh Palliser, it was debated in both Houses of Parliament. However, the Admiralty insisted that they could not interfere; that once the accusations had been made, they were obliged to act ministerially, not judicially. They had to accept the accusations and give orders for the trial."

"That hasn't the slightest bearing on this case," Napier said crossly.

Ramage took the opportunity of reinforcing his objection. "It can't be anything but an injustice, sir, if an officer is charged with these most terrible offences, and the trial is ended the moment the prosecution's case is completed, before the accused can say a single word in his own defence. Whatever the court might rule, the fact is the charges will be talked about by every officer in the Service. But since the defence was never heard, the stigma must always remain!"

Napier turned towards Goddard. "What has the prosecution to say to that? The court feels the prisoner has made an important point."

The Admiral waved his hand contemptuously towards Ramage. "It is up to the prosecution to decide, otherwise the whole discipline of the Navy would be in the hands of dissident seamen!"

Ramage suddenly spotted the flaw in Goddard's argument, and felt himself growing cold with anger. Goddard was recovering his poise; subtly he was changing his role from Ramage's prosecutor to the Admiral who was second-in-command on the station, treating these captains as the subordinate officers they would once again become the moment the trial was over. Very well, Ramage thought; the moment has come to shake that poise; to frighten Goddard.

"With respect, sir," he said to Napier, "a great deal of evidence has already been given on oath, written in the minutes and signed by the witnesses. All that evidence was intended to prove that I acted in a cowardly fashion. If that evidence is true, then I am a coward and deserve to be sentenced to death. If it isn't true, then the witnesses have perjured themselves in an attempt to have me hanged. Since the prosecution brought the charges against me, the only possible reason for the prosecution to withdraw the charges now must be that it *knows* the evidence is not true and that its witnesses have perjured themselves."

"There was only one witness," Napier said, as if thinking aloud.

"This is scandalous!" Goddard shouted. "Since when has it been a defence to accuse the prosecutor of perjury?"

"He wasn't accusing you," Napier said quietly. "He referred specifically to evidence that has been given."

He waved to Syme. "What do the Court Martial Statutes have to say about perjury?"

The deputy judge advocate hurriedly picked up a volume in front of him, looked at the index and then flicked through several pages.

"Section seventeen, sir – I'll read the relevant part. '...*All and every person...who shall commit any wilful perjury...or shall corruptly procure or suborn any person to commit such wilful perjury, shall and may be prosecuted in His Majesty's court of King's Bench, by indictment or information...*"

"Hmm, most interesting," Napier commented. "This court, in ruling on the prosecution's application, must be careful not to cast doubt on anyone's reputation. Well, the court will now deliberate. The prosecutor and prisoner will wait outside."

Goddard strode out of the cabin, followed by Ramage. Ransom was waiting just outside the door and moved over ostentatiously to stand beside Ramage.

Ramage rubbed the scar over his brow. He felt dazed, as though someone had flashed a bright light in his eyes. As he tried to recall everything that had been said in the past few minutes, he could only remember Napier's comment when Syme finished reading the reference to perjury – "...must be careful not to cast doubt on anyone's reputation..."

That, he realized, could mean that Goddard's reputation – or, to be fair, the reputation of the second-in-command on the Jamaica Station – must be safeguarded. So the court would probably decide in Goddard's favour: the prosecution would be allowed to withdraw the case.

What would happen to the minutes? He had told Yorke that whatever happened they had to be sent to the Admiralty, but now he was far from sure. After all, withdrawing the charges presumably meant there had never been a trial in the legal sense, so no minutes would be required. In fact, he suddenly realized, Goddard must be sure that withdrawing the charges meant that all records of the whole business vanished automatically.

Ransom was pulling his arm. "The court is in session again," he hissed. "Come on!"

Napier's face was expressionless, and when Ramage glanced at the other captains they were all staring at the table in front of them or looking round the cabin. Their faces revealed nothing: there was no indication of whether they would toss the victor's laurel crown to the prosecutor or to the prisoner.

He glanced at Goddard. The plump cheeks, thick lips and folding chins were placid and smug; for once the eyes were looking up at the deckhead, fixed and not flickering back and forth. He was almost smiling. Somehow Goddard was sure he had won…

Fear soaked through Ramage like fog forming in a forest; slow and almost imperceptible, yet irresistible. It was the creeping fear that dissolved energy and left the victim lethargic, accepting his fate. It was quite different from the fear of the moments before battle which sharpened the senses and strengthened the muscles.

Once again Napier rapped the table. "The court is now in session," he announced.

He looked at Syme, who was waiting with pen poised to take down his words.

"The court has considered the prosecution's application to withdraw the charges against Lieutenant Ramage, and it has considered the prisoner's application that the trial should be continued to give him an opportunity of making a defence."

He paused and glanced round the court. His voice was neutral. He'd make a good judge, Ramage thought.

"The court can find no precedent for accepting either application."

Again the pause to allow Syme to write. It'll go on for days, Ramage thought; I'll just sit here and wait and wait…

"Whatever the court decides will thus set a precedent for the future."

Go on, for God's sake, Ramage said to himself; you can't set a precedent for the past.

"The court has considered whether or not the prosecution, in making the charges in court, has started a judicial process which can logically and legally end only when the court, having heard all the evidence in support of the charges and all the evidence of the defence against them, has returned a verdict."

Ramage leaned forward slightly. Was there a slight chance?

"On the other hand, it has had to consider the position of the prisoner. He is charged with capital offences, and he has a defence against them. A defence which he no doubt considers will result in a verdict of not guilty. Yet the court has to decide whether the prosecution's withdrawal of the charges is not tantamount to a clear verdict of not guilty. The prosecution is saying, in fact, that at first it thought the prisoner was guilty of certain charges, but has now decided he is not."

There's not the slightest chance now, Ramage thought. Those captains must know of the vendetta – it's been common knowledge for several years – but they're ignoring it. Or perhaps they genuinely believe what Napier has just said. But they are forgetting the stigma and the gossip; they're forgetting the new charges that will follow. They're taking the safe course – and who could blame them?

Still speaking in the same tone, Napier said: "After mature consideration, the court rejects the prosecution's application. The trial will continue and the prosecution will call its next witness."

It took Ramage several seconds to appreciate what Napier had said. He glanced at Goddard. The Admiral was staring at Napier, his features frozen. Then slowly the muscles of his face went slack and the flesh sagged. Ramage realized that Goddard was staring not at Napier but at the prospect of complete professional ruin.

Napier and the other six captains had obviously tried to reach a just decision. Although they knew Goddard would be their senior officer again the moment the trial was over, and able to ruin each and every one of them in pure revenge, they had made a decision which would stand the scrutiny of the Lord Chief Justice of England.

Napier turned to Goddard and said crisply: "Everyone is still on oath; call your next witness, please."

Goddard lurched to his feet. "Call Sydney Yorke," he whispered.

Yorke walked in, as debonair and nonchalant as the day Ramage first saw him on board the *Lion* at Barbados, and as he took the oath Ramage wondered what questions Goddard could ask him that would back up any part of Croucher's evidence.

Ramage guessed that Yorke's attitude would be offhand and flippant. This always angered Goddard, and making the Admiral lose his temper was the best way of provoking him into some damaging admission, or throwing him off his stride.

He looked at Goddard curiously. There was something strange about the man now that he was standing: his movements, such as they were, seemed jerky, like a wooden soldier. His eyes were remote, almost glassy, as though staring at alarming sights beyond the confines of this stuffy cabin. He looked like a man paralysed by fear.

Napier asked patiently: "The prosecution is ready?" When Goddard remained silent, he went on: "The court has some questions to ask. We might take those first."

Yorke bowed, unaware of what had happened, but obviously puzzled by Goddard's behaviour.

"You were the master of the *Topaz* merchantman?"

"Master and owner."

"You were commanding her in a convoy escorted by the *Lion* and the *Triton* brig on the eighteenth of July last?"

"I was."

"Tell the court what happened that night."

"My ship was attacked by a French privateer, the *Peacock*, which was sailing in the convoy and masquerading as a merchant ship. Fortunately Lieutenant Ramage had suspected this ship because of something she had done the previous night. The result was that he was able to board the French ship before she could capture us."

"Where was the *Peacock* at this time?"

"Almost alongside the *Topaz*. Or, rather, the *Triton* ran aboard her a few moments before she ran aboard the *Topaz*."

"Could you have beaten off the attack without assistance?"

"Indeed not!" Yorke exclaimed. "The *Peacock* had more than a hundred men on board – quite apart from a hundred or so on another ship she had captured the night before. We had no warning, so there was only the usual watch on deck."

"We haven't questioned you about the other ship: please confine your answers to the questions asked."

Yorke bowed.

"You went on board the flagship the next day?"

"Yes."

"Tell the court the purpose of the visit."

"To protest to the Admiral about his carelessness in allowing a French privateer to join the convoy openly; to protest that this privateer had been allowed to capture another merchant ship and, while she was still in the convoy, turn her into another privateer; to tell – "

Syme was waving frantically, "Give me time to write!"

Yorke waited until he saw the man's pen stop.

" – to tell the Admiral that in the view of the Duc de Bretagne, whose care was his special responsibility – "

"Do you know that for a fact?"

"I suppose that's hearsay," Yorke said cheerfully, "but it's easy enough to check."

"Confine yourself to fact, please."

"Very well. To convey M. le Duc's protest to the Admiral and to inform the Admiral that it was M. le Duc's intention to make sure that Lieutenant Ramage's gallantry was given the highest reward – by writing to the King. That letter is written, incidentally, and ready for the post."

"Tell the court how you came to be here." Goddard had found his voice at last.

Yorke shrugged his shoulders. "The *Topaz* was dismasted in the hurricane at the same time as the *Triton*. By good fortune, the two ships managed to stay together. Eventually they drifted onto a reef."

"And then?" Napier prompted.

"Lieutenant Ramage managed to get everyone on shore by rafts."

"What land was this?"

"Snake Island, at the eastern end of Puerto Rico."

"What happened to the ships?" Goddard asked harshly.

"They were abandoned."

"Badly damaged?"

"Dismasted, certainly, and stranded. But not badly damaged."

"You saw the wreck of the *Triton* with your own eyes?"

"Yes."

"Did the accused destroy her to prevent her falling into Spanish hands?"

"No," Yorke said cheerfully. "In fact he decided not to set fire to either ship."

"Do you know why?"

"He didn't want to alarm any Spanish garrison there might be on Snake Island."

"Was there such a garrison?"

"Oh yes, a dozen men, and a lieutenant."

"And the brig wasn't destroyed for fear of a dozen Spanish soldiers?"

"Well, not exactly," Yorke said vaguely. "We captured the soldiers. But the smoke might have been seen from Puerto

Rico where I assume there are a few thousand soldiers. It was the treasure as much as anything else that made us think the Spanish would be vigilant."

"The *treasure*?"

"Yes, you see, the garrison was digging these holes all over the place."

"Holes?"

"Well, trenches, really," Yorke said in an offhand voice. "They looked like graves. There was one big grave, too. Lots of skeletons."

"Skeletons, Mr Yorke?"

"Yes. Dead people. They'd been murdered, you know. I found it all most depressing – you would have too, I'm sure. All shot in the back of the head. A bullet makes a frightful mess of the cranium, you know."

"But who were they?" Goddard stammered.

"No idea, I'm afraid. All in a circle, like signs of the zodiac. Pirates…slaves…who knows? Their hands had been tied together. Perhaps to stop them dipping into the treasure."

"The treasure!" Goddard exclaimed, as if suddenly remembering it after being diverted by the skeletons. "What is this nonsense about treasure?"

Napier interrupted: "Pray, what has all this to do with the charges against the accused?"

"Dunno!" Yorke said blithely. "The accused went off on a treasure hunt, and I thought Admiral Goddard seemed interested."

Napier looked at Goddard. "Do you think this forms part of the prosecution's case?"

"How do I know!" Goddard said angrily. "If it pleases the court, I think the matter should be investigated."

"Very well…The court will inquire. Mr Yorke, what led you to think there was treasure on the island?"

"Not me, Mr Ramage."

"Describe the events in your own words."

Yorke glanced at Ramage, who gave an almost imperceptible nod.

"The Spanish soldiers were guarding slaves who were digging trenches all over the island. Lieutenant Ramage, who speaks Spanish, discovered they were looking for treasure."

"Did they have some sort of chart showing where it might be?"

"No, there was just a poem, a sort of riddle, which was supposed to give clues to its whereabouts."

"Did you manage to solve the riddle?"

"Mr Ramage did."

"And then what happened?"

"We set the men to work digging."

"With no success, it would seem?"

"Oh no," Yorke said languidly, "I think it was quite productive really. We found various boxes of treasure: old Spanish coins, metal ornaments and plates – that sort of thing."

"Of no great value, then?"

"They seemed valuable to me, but then I'm a poor man! It weighs very many hundredweights and was mostly gold."

There was a silence in the cabin until Napier asked, in an awed voice: "Where is it now?"

"On board *La Perla*, a Spanish schooner."

"I assumed you had removed it from Snake Island," Napier said.

"Lieutenant Ramage did."

"But you said it was on board *La Perla*."

"*La Perla* is at anchor half a mile from here: Lieutenant Ramage captured her and sailed her here as a prize."

"Clear the court," Napier snapped. "The court stands adjourned. The prisoner will remain behind."

When everyone but Ramage, Syme and the seven captains had left the cabin, Napier said harshly: "See here, Ramage, the court doesn't take kindly to you turning the proceedings into a circus."

"I'm on trial for my life, sir."

"I know that, dammit; but this treasure business. Is it as much as this fellow makes out?"

"More, sir. About five tons. With gold at three pounds, seventeen and sixpence a fine ounce, I estimate it as worth well over a million pounds."

Napier held his hands palm upwards. "You don't help your own case, doing this sort of thing. Good God!" he exclaimed, "We must get a Marine guard on it!"

"There are a hundred seamen and Marines guarding it now, sir."

"But – who's in command of *La Perla*? Your master is on board here as a witness."

"The Master's mate, sir."

"Tons of gold and silver, and a master's mate in charge! You're mad, Ramage! The whole damn ship's company could rise on him and sail out of the anchorage!"

"With respect, sir, these men helped find the treasure, dug it up, crated it, captured *La Perla*, loaded the treasure on board, and sailed the ship several hundred miles to here. They could have killed myself, the master, master's mate, Yorke and the Duke and his entourage at any point along the route and got away with it more easily than they could now."

"All right, don't be so blasted touchy. Why didn't you report this before now?"

"I have my reports here, sir." He waved the papers he was holding.

"Why didn't you deliver them when you first arrived?"

"I went at once to Admiral Goddard. I gave him the report on the loss of the *Triton*, sir, and was put under close arrest, before I had the chance to deliver the others, and was marched off with a Marine escort."

"You could have still delivered the report on the treasure."

"I could have done, sir," Ramage said flatly.

"But you were going to use the treasure to bargain with, eh?"

"Indeed not!" Ramage said angrily. "How could I bargain with it, sir, even if I'd wanted to?"

"Why didn't you put in the report, then?"

"Because without even reading my first report and without asking me one question, the Admiral told me he was bringing me to a trial under Articles ten, twelve and seventeen. That could only mean charges of cowardice, sir."

"Damnation!" Napier exclaimed. "Why am *I* appointed president of such a court! What have these gentlemen done" – he waved towards the other captains – "that they should be mixed up in all this?"

"With respect, sir," Ramage said, blinking rapidly, "what have *I* done to be accused of cowardice?"

Captain Robinson said: "Boy's got a point, Napier; nasty business, the whole thing. Wash our hands of it, I say; special report to Sir Pilcher. You prepare it; all the court sign it. Minutes of the trial so far can go with it. Ought to vote on it; damn silly of us to do anything else. That's my view."

"Mine, too," said Innes, and the others nodded in agreement.

"See here, young Ramage," Napier said suddenly, "you're not supposed to be hearing any of this. Go and give your escort a hail and take a turn on deck. Keep away from everyone else."

As Ramage walked to the door he heard an exasperated Napier growl: "Syme, you are the most bloody useless deputy judge advocate I've ever seen!"

Half an hour later the court was thrown open and Ramage and Goddard were called in. Syme was flushed and jumpy; Ramage guessed he had had an unpleasant time trying to provide precedents, laws, rules and regulations for the morning's events. The small pile of legal volumes that had been stacked in front of him were now an untidy heap, with many slips of paper marking various pages.

Napier looked up at Goddard.

"The court has decided that all the previous witness' evidence concerning finding the treasure shall be removed from the record."

Removed? Ramage felt the word had been spoken deliberately: "struck" or "deleted" would have been more usual. Removed *in toto*, to be sent to the Commander-in-Chief? It was all evidence given on oath…

"However, in view of the gravity of the charges," Napier went on, "the court has decided that the trial shall continue. Has the prosecution any more questions to put to the last witness?"

"No," Goddard said in a half whisper. The man seemed to be shrivelling; the usual haughty stance had given way to hunched shoulders; the broad chest and jutting belly had merged into a sagging paunch. His eyes were bloodshot and sunken. He looked like a guilty man on trial for his life, and maybe he was. Perhaps Goddard knew he had gambled with high stakes, and lost the gamble.

"Please call your next witness, then."

"I…the prosecution has no more witnesses to call."

"Very well, the defence will present its case."

Normally Ramage should have read out his defence against the charges, while Syme copied it down, then called his witnesses to prove the points of his defence. Instead he stood up.

"If it pleases the court, I wish to waive my right to state a defence…I'm prepared to rest my case on the evidence the court has already heard and what it will hear from the remaining witnesses."

"Very well," Napier said. "Note that in your minutes, Syme."

After Syme finished writing, Napier told Ramage: "You may call your first witness." Officially he was still on trial for his life and the minutes of the trial would be read in the Admiralty by men who knew none of the background.

"Call Edward Southwick."

The Master was sworn and Ramage questioned him so that the *Peacock*'s curious behaviour the night before the attack on the *Topaz* was described in detail and he was able to show why the written report on the episode was made to the Admiral and delivered on board the *Lion*.

Then, answering questions, Southwick described, simply but graphically, how the *Peacock* had been sighted in the darkness coming up the line of merchantmen, and how the *Triton* had been manoeuvred to save the *Topaz*.

Southwick's description of Ramage's handling of the *Triton* during and after the attack left no doubt in anyone's mind of his admiration for his captain.

Ramage's questions had touched only lightly on their stay on Snake Island, but the capture of *La Perla* and the voyage to Jamaica rounded off the evidence, except for a few last questions which Ramage could not resist, since it would make Southwick's name famous in the Navy.

"When *La Perla* left Snake Island, did she have a defect in her sailing qualities?"

"Yes, she was down by the head and griped a lot."

"Tell the court what orders you received concerning this."

"I was told to shift some cargo aft."

"How much did you shift, and what was it?"

"About two tons of gold and silver coins."

"I have no more questions to ask of this witness," Ramage said.

Napier turned to Goddard.

"Your witness."

"I have no questions."

Syme read the evidence aloud, and after Southwick signed it he was told to stand down.

"Your next witness?" Syme asked, as if at last deciding to take a more active part in the proceedings.

"Call the Duke of Brittany."

The Duke walked in and bowed deeply. Napier, uncertain what to do, stood up and bowed back.

"Your Grace," he said hesitantly, "I – er, is your Grace familiar with the English language?"

"Perfectly, thank you."

Napier went red. "You understand that I am duty bound to ask the question."

"Of course," the Duke said. "But I have no need of an interpreter."

"The oath," Napier said, motioning to Syme.

The Duke took the oath, using the Crucifix, and Napier said apologetically, "The deputy judge advocate has first to write down the question, and then your answer, so…"

"I understand perfectly," the Duke said.

"You travelled to Jamaica in a ship called the *Topaz*?" Ramage asked, hoping the Duke would realize the significance of the question.

"I travelled part of the way in the *Topaz*," he said, and before anyone could stop him, added, "I and my suite transferred to her from the *Lion* because of the behaviour of Admiral Goddard."

In the silence that followed Ramage heard his own heart thumping. Would Napier rule the answer out of order? Would Goddard protest? Quickly he asked the next question.

"What happened on the night of the eighteenth of July last?"

"The *Topaz* was attacked by a French privateer."

"Was the attack successful?"

"No, it was foiled completely because of the foresight and daring of the *Triton* brig."

"Did you make any complaints to the Admiral following the attack?"

"Yes, because he had been criminally negligent in allowing this privateer to sail in the convoy for several days."

Still no one challenged the legality of the reply and, hardly believing his good luck, Ramage plunged on, rubbing the scar on his forehead.

"Evidence has been given in this court that you sent the captain of the *Topaz* on board the *Lion* to accuse myself of cowardice in not coming to the defence of the *Topaz*. On what grounds did you make that accusation?"

"I made no such accusation," the Duke said quietly. "It is not for me to speculate about the motives of any man who makes such a claim."

Napier interrupted: "The court desires to know if the captain of the *Topaz* carried any message from you to the Admiral, and if so, the nature of the message."

"Mr Yorke certainly did carry a message. It was in writing. It praised Mr Ramage and said I was writing to His Britannic Majesty drawing his attention to Mr Ramage's bravery in ensuring my safety and allowing me to carry out the mission with which His Majesty had entrusted me."

"Thank you," Napier said.

"Have you any complaint of your treatment at my hands while on Snake Island, or on board *La Perla*?" Ramage asked.

"Yes," the Duke said gravely, his eyes hard, his face set and his lips squeezed tightly together. Goddard sat up and the members of the court leaned forward expectantly. Ramage looked dumbfounded.

"Would you please tell the court the nature of that complaint?" said Napier.

The Duke's face dissolved into a smile.

"Mr Ramage refused my request to sign on as one of his crew."

The members of the court bellowed with laughter and the noise they made drowned Ramage's own laugh, which had begun to sound slightly hysterical.

"Thank you, your Grace. I have no more questions to ask this witness."

Syme read back the evidence, and once again Napier turned to the Admiral.

"Have you any questions to ask this witness?"

Goddard shook his head, and Ramage said: "That was my last witness."

Napier picked up his watch. Ramage's sword was still lying across the table in front of him.

"The court will adjourn until eight-thirty tomorrow morning, when it will announce its verdict. The prisoner will, of course, remain in custody."

CHAPTER **TWENTY-ONE**

Next morning, as Ramage stepped from the *Arrogant* into *La Perla*'s dingy boat, with its peeling paint and heavy balanced oars, he was conscious only of smiling, welcoming faces. At the tiller stood Jackson, smartly dressed, freshly shaven, hair tied in a neat queue. In the stern sheets was Southwick, flowing white hair sticking out from under his hat, holding the scabbard of his sword close to his side. Next to him was Yorke, his grin no longer sardonic but exuberant, as though he had just won heavily while playing faro for high stakes. Beyond him was the Duke, whose face had the contented look of a man welcoming home a prodigal son.

Southwick reached out a hand.

"I'll take your sword, sir."

In this, his moment of triumph, shared by the friends who had helped bring it about, Ramage was close to tears. That one gesture by Southwick summed it up.

An officer brought before a court martial surrendered his sword – in effect his badge of office – to the provost marshal, who handed it to the court. Throughout the trial his sword had been lying on the green baize of the table in front of the captains. Round it was piled, almost symbolically, the paraphernalia needed for the administration of justice – the law books required for reference, ships' logs and muster books which had become numbered exhibits, and their entries, often made in a hurry, or later when memory could be at fault – capable of having an enormous significance in the legal re-creation of some long-past event.

Then, with all examination of witnesses over, the minutes of evidence read aloud for the last time, the seven captains having deliberated, the court had at last been ready to announce its verdict.

Ramage – "the prisoner" – had been summoned and the door into the great cabin was flung open in front of him. As he walked in, head erect, shoulders back, heart racing, he had tried to glimpse the sword on the table. But Syme and the three nearest captains obscured it. Knowing that everyone in the cabin was watching him, he went straight to his chair and stood in front of it, turning slightly to bow to the members of the court.

As he did so, he glimpsed the sword in its scabbard. It was lying on the table with its hilt towards him, indicating that the court's verdict was not guilty. Quite involuntarily, he had glanced at Goddard. The Admiral, too, was staring at the sword. By chance, as it was lying in its scabbard on the table, the blade was pointing towards the Admiral.

Napier had spoken the court's verdict and Ramage had accepted his sword from him. He had muttered his thanks to the court and stumbled from the cabin into the sunlight. He had gone to the bulwarks and stared over the side at the wavelets, and a swarm of small, minnow-like fish had leapt out of the water, frantically trying to escape from some hidden predator. Beyond, anchored at random, were the *Lion* and eleven merchantmen; the only survivors of the hurricane.

He had turned, and Jackson had been standing there alone, with the others waiting a few feet away.

"Your boat is ready, sir," the American had said, and spontaneously Ramage had shaken him by the hand and only realized he was trembling violently when he found he could put no pressure in his grip.

One by one, Stafford, Appleby, Southwick, Yorke and the Duke had shaken him by the hand, and the Duke had said:

"My wife and my daughter also thank you for all you've done, and all you've suffered for us."

As Ramage sat down on the thwart beside the Duke, Jackson gave the order to shove off. Stafford was rowing stroke, with Rossi behind him, then Maxton and another coloured man, who was a fraction of a second slower than the others. It was Roberto, the former Spanish slave and now rated a landsman in the Royal Navy.

Jackson was not steering towards *La Perla* and Ramage was just going to say something when he remembered that they would have to put the Duke and Yorke on shore.

Southwick leaned across and passed him a letter.

"Delivered this morning, sir."

It was addressed simply to "Lieutenant Ramage". Though the court had found him innocent and there was no risk of charges over the loss of the *Triton* – only a routine court of inquiry – he still had no ship. Sir Pilcher Skinner, having seen what Ramage had just done to his second-in-command, would not want to appoint him to command even a hired bumboat. That meant he'd have to return to England as a passenger, report his arrival to the Admiralty, and wait.

He'd go home to Cornwall, and his father and mother would be overjoyed to see him. For a few weeks he'd enjoy the atmosphere of Blazey Hall and he'd walk and ride over the Cornish moors. Gianna would probably be there too...And then he'd begin to feel unsettled, listless, unable to concentrate on what he was doing, unable to get pleasure from the things he had previously enjoyed. He'd long to get back to sea, but the Admiralty would never employ someone who had brought about the ruin of an admiral, however badly that admiral had behaved...

Rear-Admiral Goddard was now professionally ruined, although he was a wealthy man and could return to London society and perhaps be lionized. Certainly with his connections at court almost every door would be open to him. But Goddard, too, was a sailor, albeit – if that Marine corporal's comments and Croucher's behaviour at the trial had been anything to go by – a poor one in a hurricane, but he would never receive another appointment, and Ramage found that despite his recent hatred for the man he was beginning to feel sorry for him.

Southwick was watching him anxiously while he daydreamed. Perhaps the letter was important. He ripped it open, not noticing the seal until the wax was too shattered to recognize, and began reading.

It was from Sir Pilcher's secretary: Lieutenant Ramage was to call on the Commander-in-Chief at four o'clock that afternoon. He took out his watch. It was now just half past nine.

He held the letter out to Southwick but the Master shook his head.

"I took the liberty of questioning the lieutenant who delivered it," he said. "The lieutenant appointed to command *La Perla*," he added quietly.

Sir Pilcher had wasted no time.

"Your gear has been taken on shore, sir."

"The ship's company?" Ramage asked.

"The original Tritons are being temporarily transferred to the *Arrogant*, sir. The men from the *Topaz* are still on board. Mr Yorke's seeing about them."

"Oh, very well," Ramage said numbly. It had to come, but he was being parted from Southwick and the Tritons. Somehow each and every man had shared so much and now – as always in the naval service after a ship was lost – her company was going to be scattered like spindrift.

The Duke noticed his depression.

411

"A celebration lunch," he said. "We have taken the liberty of arranging one in your honour."

"Cheer up, Ramage," Yorke said. "Anyone would think the verdict went against you!"

"Where has your Grace chosen for the celebration?" Ramage asked politely, longing to know if Maxine would be there.

"It was not my choice," the Duke said. "In fact we are all guests: Mr Yorke, Mr Southwick, my family, the Count – who feels quite put out at not being called to give evidence: he has a sharp tongue and wished to unsheath it on your behalf – Mr Bowen and young Mr Appleby."

"Indeed?" Ramage said more cheerfully. "And to whom are we indebted for this invitation?"

"The Lieutenant Governor. We are on our way now to Government House."

"I'll be damned!" Ramage exclaimed. "Government House?"

"I have – er, how do you sailors say it: I've 'slung my hammock' there. The Governor has shown an interest in our recent – ah, excursion – and wishes to hear the details from you. After I had presented my credentials he was kind enough to express his pleasure that we were safe, and insisted we should be his guests. Indeed, I fear I kept him from his bed telling him of our adventures!"

"Your credentials?" Ramage asked, then realizing that he had been thinking aloud, waved his apology.

"I shall tell you later," the Duke said. "It will serve to explain the Admiral's discomfort when we left his ship for the *Topaz*. Alas, it was a move which brought about all your troubles."

"Your Grace!" Yorke exclaimed. "You are quite wrong. The privateer affair was only an evening's excitement; the hurricane would still have dismasted us even if you had been on board the *Lion*. My only regret is that the ladies have suffered so much."

"Suffered?" The Duke did not hide his surprise. "I assure you none of us would have missed a moment of it all. When you get to my age, you envy the exciting lives the young men lead. Now we've experienced it and, thank the good God, we live to tell a tale of almost everything the sea has to offer – a battle, a hurricane, shipwreck on a reef, hunting for treasure, a dangerous voyage in a tiny ship, and a naval court martial. Pray tell me, have I missed any of the other excitements the sea has to offer?"

Yorke pretended to ponder a few moments.

"I think not – do you agree, Ramage?"

"A hanging from the yardarm…flogging round the fleet…No, they're not offered by the sea, so I think His Grace can rest content," Ramage said, laughing.

"He does, I assure you," the Duke said, "and I'm grateful to you all for the experience. I have such a story that will out-bore every bore in every salon I shall ever visit!"

Jackson called: "Way enough!"

Ramage noticed, as they came alongside the jetty, that a carriage with four greys was standing close by, and men in livery were waiting.

"Ah," the Duke said, "how thoughtful of the Governor. And my ladies will be waiting for us, too."

As one of the Governor's carriages took him from Government House to Admiralty House for his appointment with the Commander-in-Chief, Ramage felt more than half drunk. For the whole of the morning and throughout the meal he had refused to drink anything except a single glass of champagne with which to answer the toasts.

413

The moment they arrived at Government House, Ramage and Yorke had sensed the Duke's importance to the British government, but had been startled when the Duke told them that the British government had planned to launch a heavy attack on Guadeloupe and Haiti, the last strongholds of Revolutionary France in the Caribbean. The Duke was to have been the figurehead, the man to whom all the Royalists still left in the islands would have rallied. In effect he would have been the Viceroy of a new French Caribbean empire, comprising Haiti, Guadeloupe and Martinique – an empire captured by the British and handed over to a French government in exile.

The object in sending the Duke out had been to remove the phrase "in exile" by establishing, on French soil in the Caribbean, the seeds of a new French nation.

But, as the future Viceroy told Ramage in his quiet, patient voice, many ships and many troops were needed, and the first news he had received when he met the Governor was that for the time being the attacks on Haiti and Guadeloupe had been postponed: a frigate sailing direct from England to Jamaica had brought a dispatch from Lord Grenville, the Foreign Secretary, to this effect. By chance the frigate had arrived only four days ago.

When Ramage and Yorke tried to express their regrets, the Duke had shrugged his shoulders expressively.

"I sometimes feel," he said, "we are trying to rebuild a new world in the shape of the old; and I have seen too much to ignore the old world's defects. But I am also too old to try and change it. Change is the enemy of age, my young friend, and we old people tend to fight it."

After that, Ramage had been led away to talk for half an hour to the island's Attorney-General, an amiable and breezy man who wanted to discuss the trial. The warnings he had then given, Ramage felt, had been as a direct result of the Governor's knowledge of the Duke's role in the case.

As the horses clattered towards Sir Pilcher's house, Ramage thought about his summons. It was silly to wonder why the Commander-in-Chief was interesting himself in a mere lieutenant; Goddard had seen to it that Ramage was no longer a "mere lieutenant". He now had all the notoriety of a queen's lover or a famous highwayman.

Ramage wiped the perspiration from his brow, straightened his hat, tucked his papers under his arm and grasped the scabbard of his sword: the coachman was reining in the horses in front of a large, four-square white house guarded by Marines.

Ten minutes later Ramage was being ushered into Sir Pilcher's office.

The Admiral was plump, shorter than Ramage and with a tendency to waddle. He had several chins and his cheeks were fat and sagging. He had the glistening pink complexion of a man who enjoyed good living.

"Ah, Mr Ramage?"

He gave Ramage a limp handshake.

"Come, let us sit comfortably."

He led the way to some armchairs set in the middle of the room round a small, low and highly polished table.

He sat in one chair and waved Ramage to one opposite him.

"A cool drink? No? Well now, I trust you are having an enjoyable stay with the Governor."

"Yes, sir, most enjoyable."

"Good, good, a delightful man, and so competent. And the Duke – in good health, I trust?"

"Yes, sir," Ramage said.

"I must congratulate you, Ramage, on bringing the Duke – and his entourage, of course – here safely."

Ramage nodded politely.

"The Duke has – er, explained his…"

"In great confidence, sir."

"Quite so, quite so. He told the Governor he wished you to know."

Sir Pilcher flicked imaginary dust from his lapels, obviously ill at ease.

"Er – I have just read your report to Admiral Goddard on the loss of the *Triton*…"

"I have the others here, sir."

"Oh, excellent; let me have them."

Ramage took the first one. "This takes up from the time we were wrecked on Snake Island, sir, until we arrived in sight of Jamaica in *La Perla*."

"Excellent, excellent."

"And this deals with the period we were on Snake Island."

"Ah – finding the treasure, eh?"

"Exactly, sir."

"Splendid business, Ramage, quite splendid. The Admiralty – indeed, the Government – will be delighted. We are having it unloaded now. I went down to look – boxes and boxes! My dear fellow, what a haul!"

"Yes, sir. I wonder who the pirate was?"

"Ah yes, the Attorney-General has been looking up some records. This place has a long history of piracy, as you know – Jamaica I mean. That fellow Morgan was after one particular man back in 1690. Seems they were shipmates at first – Brethren of the Coast – and then they fell out. The Attorney-General seems to think it was most likely his. There's some legend that he and his gang vanished, and after a quarrel with

Morgan he went to a lonely island and drank himself to death."

"A sad end," Ramage said, since the Admiral seemed to expect some comment.

"Ha, yes! All that gold and nothing to spend it on, what? Well, 'easy come, easy go' I suppose."

Ramage waited. The point of all this was bound to emerge soon.

Sir Pilcher stuck his finger inside his stock and gave it a tug, as if it was too tight.

"Sure you won't have a drink, Ramage?"

"Thank you, sir, no."

"I will, then: ring for a steward, there's a good fellow."

Ramage walked over to the long, richly embroidered bell pull, gave it a tug, and heard a distant, faint ringing. A few moments later a coloured steward glided in.

"Rum and lemon, Albert. The 'tenant's not drinking."

As soon as the steward left the room, Sir Pilcher said: "This court-martial business, Ramage…"

Ramage glanced up, his eyebrows raised, and waited.

"Deuced difficult, y'know."

"In what way, sir?"

"Doubtful if it was in legal form. Napier, the president, was in a damnably difficult position. The deputy judge advocate wasn't much use to him."

Ramage felt his skin go cold with fright. Had they celebrated too soon? He had forgotten that Sir Pilcher could declare his trial void and order a new one on some technicality. At a new trial, the cowardice charges could be forgotten and Sir Pilcher and Goddard, with the help of the best legal brains available, could draw up new charges…His talk with the Attorney-General took on a new meaning, and he tried to remember the past cases the man had cited so carefully. At the time they had seemed of little significance or relevance.

"In what way was it illegal, sir?"

"Well, not exactly illegal. Fact is, the charges were drawn up without the prosecution knowing all the facts – or about all the witnesses."

"But that's the prosecution's responsibility, sir," Ramage protested. "The witnesses arrived in time and the facts eventually emerged!"

"Oh, quite, quite; no one's disputing that. It's a question of how the evidence was introduced, an' all that sort of thing. You know what sticklers these lawyers are!"

"The court didn't express any doubts, sir."

"No, no, but as I was saying just now, that damned deputy judge advocate – what was his name? Syme? He didn't advise the president properly."

"What can be done now, sir?"

"Deuced difficult, Ramage; blessed if I know. I hate having to order a new trial, after all you've been through…there's still the court of inquiry on the loss of the *Triton*, of course."

Was this a veiled threat, Ramage wondered. Sir Pilcher was going to show what he could do to him if Ramage didn't agree with whatever the Commander-in-Chief had in mind. But what exactly had he in mind? His manner was still remarkably friendly.

"A similarity to the case of Captain Powlett, perhaps, sir?" Ramage asked innocently.

"Powlett? Powlett? That was way back in fifty-two," Sir Pilcher said, and Ramage knew that the Attorney-General's comments were based on solid ground. The case had been discussed in the past few hours: Sir Pilcher remembered the date too easily.

"The court sat for several days," Ramage persisted. "When they finally doubted if they could legally reach a verdict, they sent the minutes to the Admiralty for Their Lordships to decide."

"You sound like a sea lawyer, my boy," the Admiral said sharply.

"I've needed some sort of lawyer these last few hours," Ramage said bitterly. He spoke so rudely he waited for the explosion, but none came, and he decided to press the point the Attorney-General had given him.

"When Admiral Griffin said he would not proceed against Captain Powlett because witnesses were abroad, the court – "

"I know, I know," Sir Pilcher said testily, "I spent half the night reading the case!"

"Then I don't understand what the problem is, sir. Could you…"

"Damnation, Ramage," he exploded, "don't you see you've put Admiral Goddard in a deucedly tricky position?"

"My apologies, sir," Ramage said. "But the Admiral was trying to *hang* me." He wondered if Sir Pilcher yet realized that he was beaten even in his attempt to save his second-in-command from public disgrace. His next question should convince the man!

"Would you be kind enough, sir, to issue an order that I should be given an attested copy of the minutes of my trial?"

Sir Pilcher gulped the rest of his rum before asking: "What the devil d'you want them for?"

"Evidence, sir."

"You don't need them for the inquiry into the loss of the *Triton*."

"It's not for the inquiry, sir."

"What d'you want 'em for, then? A souvenir?" he asked.

"No, sir: I am advised I need them for my case against Admiral Goddard."

And that, Ramage thought to himself, is that; it either takes the trick or loses the game!

Sir Pilcher's eyes widened, and Ramage knew he was not sure he had heard correctly.

"The minutes of Admiral Goddard's case against you, eh? Yes, that's what I'm saying. You don't need them."

"I do, sir," Ramage said patiently, raising his voice slightly, "for the case in the King's Bench *against* Admiral Goddard."

"What the devil are you talking about? Are you threatening a senior officer?"

"Oh no, sir," Ramage said innocently.

"What case, then?" Sir Pilcher said suspiciously.

"For perjury, sir."

The Admiral's brow creased in concentration. "The King's Bench...for perjury..." he said softly. Abruptly he stopped. "My dear boy, surely you don't mean it!"

But the Admiral's jovial heartiness rang hollow.

"I'm advised the minutes prove perjury, sir, without the need to call more witnesses – although I shall be doing that."

"What, d'you mean to say you've been gossiping with attorneys already?"

It was the "already" that told Ramage his card had taken the trick. Keep up the pressure.

"Yes, sir." It was true, after a fashion.

"You think the charge can be proved?"

Sir Pilcher's manner had changed. Now he was matter of fact; his voice was crisper. He seemed more detached; more the Commander-in-Chief.

"Yes, sir; there are also the Bastia court-martial minutes."

"Yes, I haven't forgotten that," Sir Pilcher said slowly.

He was not a man who hid his thoughts, and Ramage could see the Admiral mentally holding a pair of scales: on one pan was Rear-Admiral Goddard, and on the other stood – what?

"Your witnesses," Sir Pilcher mused. "The Duke, the Count of Chambéry, the fellow that owns the merchantman…"

"And Lord St Vincent, and Commodore Nelson for the Bastia trial," Ramage added.

"Yes, yes, yes…an impressive list. It'd carry weight in Whitehall."

"It would indeed, sir," Ramage said, and added quietly, "if it was needed."

"A trial of that nature would finish you in the Service, my boy; you realize that, don't you? You'd never be employed again by the Navy, after you won it!"

"I'll never be employed again anyway, sir."

Sir Pilcher was thinking deeply, and Ramage guessed that Goddard had been weighed in the Admiral's scales, and found not to be heavy enough. Goddard's distant relationship to the King had been useful in the past, but now it would be wiser to forget that the man had ever been a friend.

"Your mind is made up, I suppose?"

"Not finally, sir: I just want to do the right thing."

Ramage sounded hypocritical to himself, but Sir Pilcher was busy preparing defences for Sir Pilcher…After all, Goddard was still his second-in-command.

"You want to get back to England?"

"Yes, sir."

"To bring Rear-Admiral Goddard to a trial?"

"If it proves necessary, sir." He made no attempt to keep the ambiguity from his voice: he and Sir Pilcher were now speaking the same language.

"You want to strike a bargain, eh?"

Ramage had not expected the Admiral to be so blunt so quickly, but he nodded.

"What do you want, then?"

Once again Ramage was taken by surprise, and for a moment all he could do was to remind himself to ask for the maximum. It ought not to be too difficult to persuade the man that what Ramage wanted was also best for the Commander-in-Chief.

"Very little sir. Justice, really."

He was surprised to hear himself speaking: it sounded so reasonable; almost naive.

"Of course, of course; you've every right to that! But," he said warily, "what do you regard as justice?"

"Well, sir, if there's a doubt over today's trial verdict, the Captain Powlett case should be treated as a precedent."

"Transmit the papers to the Admiralty, you mean, and let their Lordships rule on it?"

"Yes, sir."

"Very well, I was proposing to do that anyway. Anything else?"

Ramage gave him credit for the smooth way he had said it. Sir Pilcher had been proposing to do that for less than a minute: only since he had realized that Ramage was not going to help him to prevent a scandal.

"Only two things, sir, both quite routine."

He realized "routine" was an inspired word: like his earlier claim, it gave Sir Pilcher a way out. He had already decided to send the minutes to the Admiralty on the grounds of the Powlett precedent; now he could grant the rest as a matter of routine.

"Come on, man," the Admiral said impatiently.

"The inquiry into the loss of the *Triton*, sir. Could it be held in the next day or two?"

"I suppose so. Yes," he said hurriedly as though Ramage might otherwise insist on extra conditions. "The day after tomorrow. I'll issue the order this afternoon."

And that, Ramage knew, would make sure his witnesses could not be sent off on some pretext or other to ships about to sail.

"And what else?" demanded Sir Pilcher, as though justice was a mere word, a preliminary demand to some iniquitous request.

"Employment, sir: I'd like another ship, and to keep my crew together."

Sir Pilcher frowned and clasped his hands, staring at the polished table top with all the concentration of a fortune-teller looking into a crystal ball. Ramage was not surprised at the Admiral's preoccupation. Giving him a ship would advertise the fact that the Commander-in-Chief had disowned Goddard. Sir Pilcher had reached a critical stage: critical for all three of them. What he said or did now was a signpost to the future. Giving Ramage a ship told the Admiralty that Sir Pilcher approved of his activities; that he supported the Lieutenant against the Rear-Admiral.

Refusing him a ship meant that approval was withheld. That in turn meant that Sir Pilcher supported his second-in-command, even though the moment the court-martial minutes arrived at the Admiralty Goddard would be discredited, and some of the mud was bound to stick to his friend Sir Pilcher.

Yet, because of tradition and the fact that the Admiralty had to think in terms of the discipline of the whole Navy, discrediting Goddard did not mean automatic approval for the wretched lieutenant who, however unwittingly, had been the cause of the trouble.

Sir Pilcher unclasped his hands and looked directly at Ramage.

"Very well, I'll give you a ship."

Ramage had begun to thank him when the Admiral continued: "I've nothing available at the moment, but there'll be a vacancy in a few weeks. In the meantime, you deserve a month's leave. I'll have the Tritons transferred to the guardship and you can come back in a month's time. You'll be seeing the Governor again?"

"Yes, sir: he has been kind enough to let me sling my hammock at Government House for a few days."

"Excellent. Splendid, so you'll be seeing the Duke, too, eh?"

"Yes, sir," Ramage said, and added the words Sir Pilcher obviously wanted to hear. "They'll be glad to hear that various problems have been resolved."

"Capital. Very well, Ramage," he said, getting up, "I'm delighted with the way you handled the treasure business. The Attorney-General's looking up the book of words: no one's too sure whether it's treated as prize or what, because of the way it was found."

"I was hoping, sir," Ramage said, "that if it's not treated as prize, perhaps the Government would make some sort of *ex gratia* payment to the ship's company. They were very loyal: it must have been a temptation to make off with it – there were only three King's officers on board…"

"Quite, quite, I shall recommend it to the First Lord in my next dispatch – that's if they don't get a share automatically."

"Thank you, sir."

"Not at all, not at all. Have a good leave; I'll expect you back here in a month's time."

Back at Government House Ramage found Maxine in her room, dressed for dinner and with the maid combing her long, black hair. Without turning from the mirror, she said: "You've seen the Admiral?"

Her voice sounded muffled and Ramage, glancing at her reflection, saw that she had been crying again. She tried to smile but suddenly began sobbing, waving to the maid to leave the room as she buried her face in her hands.

Ramage stood helpless for a moment and then, as he heard the maid shut the door, put his hands gently on her shoulders.

"Oh Nicholas," she wailed, "I've been so worried!"

"Why, what happened?" he asked in surprise.

She dropped her hands and stared at his reflection in the mirror, her eyes wide. She looked so startled that Ramage gave a nervous laugh. In one movement she stood up, turned and threw her arms round him.

"It doesn't matter what I was worrying about," she murmured, burying her face in his shoulder. "Tell me what the Admiral said."

"Oh – well, everything's all right."

With that she pushed him away, holding him at arm's length, and smiled up at him.

" 'Everything's all right,' " she mimicked. "Nicholas – for days and weeks the St Brieuc family have been dreading the moment when you reported to the Admiral. My father has needed brandy to help him through this afternoon; my mother has taken to her bed. I myself lay on my bed and wept" – she waved at the rumpled counterpane – "and I've sat in that chair and wept. And finally" – she began sobbing again – "you march in as though there had never been anything to worry about and announce 'Everything's all right'!"

Before she started speaking Ramage had been dumbfounded to find her in tears and now he stood in front of the almost hysterical girl in total silence.

"Nicholas," she said quietly, "you are without doubt *le plus grand* bumpkin I've ever met. Why I should fall in love with you I don't know. But if 'Everything's all right,' then please kiss me!"

Fifteen minutes later, by which time she had bathed her eyes and powdered her face in an attempt to hide all traces of both tears and kisses, she called the maid back and Ramage left to find the Duke.

He was sitting in the large drawing-room playing chess with Yorke and watched by the Count de Chambéry. The moment they saw Ramage all three men stood up, looking at him questioningly.

Ramage grinned sheepishly. "I've just seen Maxine. I didn't realize that – "

When he broke off the Duke said: "Was your visit to the Admiral – ah, satisfactory?"

"Very. I get a new ship and I have a month's leave."

"I should think so," Yorke said. "Does that mean Sir Pilcher is abandoning his friend Goddard?"

Ramage nodded. "If I get the ship, it means that Goddard has been abandoned very publicly."

"A wise man, Sir Pilcher," the Duke commented. "So perhaps the vendetta is over now."

"I think so."

The Duke picked up the black knight from the board. "The knight's move, two ahead and one to the side...that sums up Goddard's way of life: he can do nothing directly. But, like the knight, he cannot change his moves."

Ramage suddenly remembered the convoy conference on board the *Lion* at Barbados: the canvas covering the cabin floor had been painted in black and white squares, chessboard fashion, and Goddard had reminded him of the knight and Croucher of the bishop.

"By the way," the Duke said, "one of the guests at dinner last night offered us the use of a big estate house up in the mountains: it belongs to his brother, who is away in England for a year. It is very beautiful up there, and cool."

Ramage's face fell. He wondered whether some of Maxine's tears had been shed at the thought of their early separation...

As though he had read Ramage's thoughts, the Duke said: "We were planning to leave tomorrow. The Admiral has given you a month's leave – will you spend it with us?"

A month in the mountains with Maxine. A few weeks ago he was fighting a hurricane; a few hours ago he was being court-martialled; a few minutes ago he was manoeuvring with the Commander-in-Chief. It was hard to take it all in...

"You'll have to put up with my company, too," Yorke said blithely. "I've been invited and assured that the shooting up there is splendid!"

Could they be interpreting Ramage's silence as reluctance to accept the invitation? He bowed to the Duke. "Thank you," he muttered.

"Good – my wife and daughter will be delighted," the Duke said. "We did not accept the offer at once because we wanted to be certain that your affairs at Admiralty House had been arranged to everyone's satisfaction."

The slight emphasis on the word "everyone" told Ramage that there had been pressure on Sir Pilcher from Government House. The Duke's influence, combined with a knowledge of all the facts, had been enough to mobilize the Lieutenant Governor and the Attorney-General.

"I'll leave you to finish your game of chess," Ramage said, and went back to his room to wash and change.

DUDLEY POPE

RAMAGE'S CHALLENGE

The Napoleonic Wars are raging and a group of eminent British citizens have been taken captive in the Mediterranean by French troops. The Admiralty traces their location and sends the valiant Lord Ramage to effect their release. As Ramage and his crew negotiate the hazardous waters off the Tuscan coast, they soon begin to doubt the accuracy of their instructions. Ramage comes to realize that in order for his mission to succeed he must embark upon a fearful and highly dangerous escapade where the stakes have never been higher.

Ramage's Challenge is another action-packed naval adventure from the masterful Dudley Pope.

RAMAGE AND THE GUILLOTINE

As France recovers from her bloody Revolution, Napoleon is amassing his armies for the Great Invasion. News in England is sketchy and the Navy must prepare to defend the land from foreign attack.

Lieutenant Ramage is chosen to travel to France and embark upon the perilous quest of spying on the great Napoleon. His mission is to determine the strength of the French troops – but his discovery will mean the guillotine!

'The first and still favourite rival to Hornblower'
– *Daily Mirror*

DUDLEY POPE

RAMAGE'S PRIZE

Lord Ramage returns for another highly-charged and thrilling adventure at sea. Instructed with the task of discovering why His Majesty's dispatches keep unaccountably disappearing, Ramage finds himself involved in a situation far beyond his expectations. Based on true events, *Ramage's Prize* is another gripping story from Dudley Pope.

'An author who really knows Nelson's Navy'
– *Observer*

RAMAGE'S SIGNAL

With Napoleon Bonaparte at the height of his powers, the Mediterranean can be safely considered exclusive French territory. So when Captain Ramage and his crew are sent alone into Mediterranean waters, they can expect to be outnumbered. But it is the French who discover they have an enemy they had not bargained for…

DUDLEY POPE

THE RAMAGE TOUCH

The Ramage Touch finds the ever-popular Lord Ramage in the Mediterranean with another daring mission to undertake. He soon makes a shocking discovery which dramatically transforms the nature of the task at hand. With the nearest English vessel a thousand miles away, Ramage must embark upon a truly perilous and life-threatening course of action. With everything stacked against him, he has only one chance to succeed…

RAMAGE AT TRAFALGAR

Lord Ramage returns to fight in the most famous of Britain's sea battles. Summoned by Admiral Nelson himself, Ramage is sent to join the British fleet off Cadiz where the largest battle in naval history is about to take place. Finding himself in the front line of battle, Lord Ramage must fight to save his own life as well as for his country. The result is a thrilling, hair-raising adventure from one of our best-loved naval writers.

'Expert knowledge of naval history'
– *Guardian*